RIDING VENGEANCE
with the
JAMES GANG

RIDING VENGEANCE
with the
JAMES GANG

Donald L. Gilmore

PELICAN PUBLISHING COMPANY

Gretna 2009

To Orlena M., Donald A., and Melissa N. Gilmore

Library of Congress Cataloging-in-Publication Data

Gilmore, Donald L.
  Riding vengeance with the James gang / Donald L. Gilmore.
    p. cm.
  ISBN 978-1-58980-626-9 (alk. paper)
  1. James, Jesse, 1847-1882—Fiction. 2. Outlaws—Fiction. I. Title.
  PS3607.I45245R53 2009
  813'.6—dc22

                                    2009005352

Printed in the United States of America

Published by Pelican Publishing Company, Inc.
1000 Burmaster Street, Gretna, Louisiana 70053

Here's a sigh to those who love me
And a smile for those who hate.
And whatever sky's above me,
Here's a heart for every fate.

—Lord George Gordon Byron*

*Southern leader William Clarke Quantrill employed the above stanza by Lord George Byron on February 26, 1865, to be included with some of his own poetry in an autograph book owned by Miss Nannie Dawson, who lived near Wakefield, Kentucky.

Preface

The writing of this novel was the natural culmination of my interest in two subjects, the Border War between Kansas and Missouri that took place from 1854 to 1865 and my interest in the lives of some of the guerrillas who took part in that war, specifically, the James and Younger brothers, who after the war became notorious outlaws.

At the outset of my interest in the conflict along the Missouri-Kansas border and the roles of the James and Younger families, I was determined to sort out the tragic events referred to as the Border War. As a way of accomplishing that task, I wrote an essay, "Revenge in Kansas, 1863," which was published in *History Today*, a British journal distributed worldwide. I followed up that article with an even more detailed essay on the Border War, "Total War on the Missouri Border." This essay appeared in *Journal of the West* in 1996 and was awarded its Best "About the West" Article for 1996. Later, the essay was used in the curriculum of the U.S. Army Command and General Staff College's history department, Combat Studies Institute, where I worked for seventeen years as senior editor. More recently, I published a comprehensive history of the Border War titled *Civil War on the Missouri-Kansas Border* (Gretna, LA: Pelican Publishing Co., 2005). I have also published historical articles about the James-Younger gang of outlaws: "Showdown at Northfield" (*Wild West*, 1996) and "When the James Gang Ruled the Rails" (*Wild West*, 2000).

Despite the fact that I had written four articles and a book on the Border War and its guerrillas, my treatment of the subject did not satisfy me. The methodology of history forced me to hold my subjects and personalities at arm's length. I could not immerse myself in my subjects and explore their psychological dimensions. For that reason, as a change of pace, I determined to write a novel on the subject. The conventions of the novel would allow me to transcend the bare facts, to create a vision of the lives of some of these ex-guerrillas that would capture their essential nature and reality, both in fact and in spirit. I wanted to write the book in relatively simple language, in an idiom that would reflect the subject—hopefully tough and coarse-woven.

So you might ask, how much of this novel is true? I have used historical facts extensively, until their possibilities ran out. Then, I gave my imagination full reign so that I might imbue my characters with complete and complex personalities. Those who wish to investigate my story's authenticity are welcome to do so, in which case, they, like historians who search through historical novels for historical correspondences, will find a considerable number of them, far more than usual. In fact, this book, because it draws upon data from Minnesota newspaper accounts from a four-month period, from the robbery of the Northfield bank to the incarceration of the Younger brothers, has one of the most informative accounts of the Northfield robbery and pursuit found anywhere. In this book, the essential information concerning the James gang's robberies of banks and railroads is scrupulously adhered to. I hope my characters ring true.

If my vision of life in Missouri at the time of the Civil War seems bleak to readers, the actual events experienced by those living during that period were every bit as hopeless as I picture them. Between the years 1861 and 1865, ordinary law and order disappeared from the border counties of Missouri as invaders from Kansas turned the area into a chaotic, treacherous zone akin to twentieth-century Bosnia. As William V. "Bill" Powell, the former mayor of Belton, Missouri, in Cass County, related, his grandfather told him, "The only time you traveled about the country was at night."

And the fear was not of Quantrill's guerrillas, but of roving Federal and militia patrols. In response to the invasion of the area, young, mostly teen-aged men (you could not easily describe them as "boys" although some of them, like Clell Miller, were as young as fourteen) banded together, led first by Andrew Walker, the son of a large slaveholder, and then by William Clarke Quantrill, a renegade Kansan. They took to the bush, fighting a bitter and bloody guerrilla war against the occupying Union forces and marauding Kansas Jayhawkers led by Col. Charles Jennison and Gen. Jim Lane. The guerrillas also fought Red Legs, hired, quasi-military thugs that included William "Buffalo Bill" Cody and "Wild Bill" Hickok, men whose reputations have been sugared over in more recent historical accounts. They fought these invaders constantly until 1865, by which time most of the guerrillas' principal leaders had been slain. When the war ended, many of the guerrillas attempted to surrender. Some of them succeeded; others were assassinated or driven permanently into the "bush." Cole Younger was among these men.

Postwar conditions in Missouri were miserable, and many of the guerrillas returned to their homes feeling rootless. Their homes were destroyed and their livestock stolen. The entire agrarian infrastructure of western Missouri had been mangled, almost beyond repair. Some of the guerrillas failed in their attempts to adjust to ordinary farm life. Out of the war's adversity, a gang of outlaws appeared unlike any seen before in America. These young guerrillas, now bandits, possessed war-learned skills and training that suited them perfectly for lives of crime. They were brave fighters, superb horsemen, excellent judges of horseflesh, crack shots, geniuses at eluding pursuit, and masters of deception. Now bandits, they would pose an extreme threat and challenge to law enforcement officers in

Missouri and elsewhere. They were called the "James gang."

Few bandits or thieves have had any great intelligence. The leaders of the James-Younger gang, in contrast, were bright, practical, and resourceful. They were not your ordinary lower-class criminals; they came from good families and carried with them an inherited intelligence and shrewdness. For that reason, among others, it took more than sixteen years for lawmen to destroy the gang, and then their destruction had to be accomplished in unorthodox ways. It took the combined resources of a national detective agency, the Pinkertons; sheriffs from various states; detectives and policemen from major cities; politicians in Missouri from governor down; and the citizens of Minnesota and Missouri to destroy the gang. Ultimately, the gang's enemies had to finish them off through clandestine, extralegal means.

Acknowledgments

Most of the people who helped me with this book did so indirectly, often merely by encouraging me, sometimes without half knowing it. Among these people is Michael Yates, my English instructor many years ago at the University of Missouri-Kansas City (UMKC), who took me under his wing momentarily. I also owe a debt to the late Llewelyn Williams, another English composition teacher; Dr. Jonas Spatz; Dr. William Ryan; Dr. David Wineglass; Dr. Jeremiah Cameron; Dr. S. J. Lewis; Mrs. Frances Vaughn; Jim Beckner; Tim Apgar; Carolyn Bartels; Dr. Robin Higham; Carol Williams; author Dennis Giangreco, one of my most-trusted mentors; author Kathryn Moore; Dr. Richard M. Swain; John Seals; Bruce Gregory; Mike Marlow; Annette Gregory; Jack Chance; David Chuber; Gary G. Ayres; author David Reif, my superb advocate; Dr. Milburn Calhoun; Nina Kooij; John Scheyd; Scott Campbell; Katie Szadziewicz; Betty Ann Woody; Harold Dellinger; Mike Calvert; John Martin; Thomas Rose; Terry Ramsey; Stafford Agee; Jerry Blain; Larry Yeatman; and Melissa Tune.

I wish to thank especially Col. Jerry Morelock, Ph.D., former director, Combat Studies Institute (CSI), the history department at the Command and General Staff College (CGSC), where I worked as the senior editor of CSI and the CGSC Press. Dr. Morelock is the editor in chief of *Armchair General* magazine. Colonel Morelock, an open-minded scholar, encouraged my interest in the Border War and allowed me to lead staff rides to Lawrence, Kansas; the James farm in Kearney; and the Jesse James home in St. Joseph. He has been immensely helpful to me in every conceivable way and has generously acted as my mentor. I cannot thank him enough.

Thanks are also due to Carl Breihan, an old correspondent and friend no longer with us; Col. Jim Speicher; Kathleen Calhoun Nettleton; Ray McBerry, Dixie Broadcasting; John Mark Lambertson, National Frontier Trails Museum, Independence, Missouri; Melanie Glotfelty; Phil Roberts; Barnett Ellis; Howard and Margaret Hersh; Robert Capps; John Allen, director, UMKC Public Relations; Nancy Cervetti; Jack Lindberg; Lt. Col. Ed Kennedy; Arba and Carole Gilmore; Allen and Mary Gilmore; Roberta Dumais; Dr. Jerold E. Brown, my friend and adviser; Dr. Paul Perme; Anthony Arthur; Dr. John Michael Moore; Barney Klaus; Dr. George Gawrych and Joan Gawrych; Roger Ramirez; Jack Mason; Frank Medina; Cathy Devlin; Richard Bussell; Jay Longley; George Mordica; Carolyn Conway; Sharon Torres; Robin Kern; John and Danna Garabedian; Ed Carr; Alfred "Al" T. and Sylvia Dulin; Bryce Benedict; Don Pile and Ray Williams; Buddy and Betty Farmer; Alinda M. Miller; Leslie Terrill; Jack and Peggy Dryden; Dodie Maurer; author Patrick Brophy, for his favors and brilliant, insightful support; Carole Garrison; Paul Clum; Debbie Lake; Christie Kennard; Jan Reding; Martin Northway; Brian Grace; author Paul Petersen; Jackie and Jay Roberts; Patrick Marquis; Rick Mack; Emory Cantey; Carole Bohl; Lori Vermillion; Jesse Estes; Connie Asero; and Dr. John M. McCoin.

Further thanks go to Maj. Gen. Andrew B. Davis, commander, Marine Mobilization Command (MMC); Lt. Col. Bart Pester (MMC); Alisha M. Cole; Neil Block; Nancy Malcolm; Dr. Gary Bjorge; Don Carlson; Scott Porter; Chuck Rabas; Diane Christensen; Vicky Spencer; Dr. Lawrence A. Yates; Vanessa and Robbie Smith; Bob and Nadine Markle; Betsy Beier; John Dreiling; E. R. Snoke; Andrea Rotondo; Kevin Ulrich;

Carl Driskill; Susan Douthit; Morgan Carlyle; Valencia and Gary Francis; John Marvin Henderson; Judi Gidicum; Lynn Kamplain; Dorothy Lane; Dick Nelson; Julie Paliter; Irvin Ward; John R. Helt; Bob Clutter; Verne and Betty Herrick; Claiborne Scholl Nappier; Leslie Terrill. I want to especially thank my painstaking and meticulous editor, Lindsey Reynolds, for her great mastery in editing this book. Her efforts were superb.

All of these people I thank for their help. Books are not written by authors alone, but by authors with the help of their supporting friends and associates. I am no exception. Nonetheless, what I have written is purely the product of my own knowledge, perceptions, and imagination, and I, alone, am responsible for any failures in its content.

RIDING VENGEANCE

with the

JAMES GANG

1

November 9, 1861

The cavalry plodded along a rough Missouri trail, a great cloud of dust billowing behind it. At the head of the column rode Col. Charles Jennison, commander of the Kansas Seventh Volunteer Cavalry, a unit popularly known as the "Jayhawkers." Behind Jennison, a soldier carried a fluttering red, white, and blue American flag. The soldiers were at ease, believing that few rebel troops or guerrillas were in the area.

Lots of prizes waited for them today, William Addington, one of the cavalrymen, reflected as he rode near the end of the column—a few chickens here, a purse of gold there. From his position, Bill could see a small log cabin several hundred yards ahead, at the edge of a wood.

The soldiers rode between tall, neat rows of partly shucked, sun-burnished corn. Addington admired the dry, yellow ears bulging from the stalks. He wished he had corn like that back in Kansas—a blasted desert there! They hadn't had rain in months, and his corn had shriveled up and died. His ground was poor besides. The soil here was deep, rich loam.

As the column traveled around a curve in the road, he saw a woman fleeing from the log cabin. She was pulling two small children by their hands, and a third, larger child ran frantically behind her, trying to keep up. The wind upset the woman's hair, and she stumbled several times, tripping over her long dress.

Then Addington heard the crash of rifle butts striking the windows of the cabin and saw the sparkle of spraying glass. The cornfield to his right was aflame, and he saw some of his comrades leading off the farmer's horses and cattle to the end of the formation. The log cabin was ablaze, and white smoke roiled from its roof into the faint blue sky above.

Addington felt jubilant. He knew they were destroying this butternut. But then, he figured, the fellow deserved it, curse him! Didn't these Missouri pukes deal in human chattel? What did they expect? It hardly occurred to Addington that this poor farmer couldn't afford slaves. In fact, Bill hadn't seen a slave all day. But the farmer was likely doing the bidding of the slave power. That's what Jennison had told the soldiers anyhow.

That's nice corn going up in flames, Bill reflected. The pungent odor of the stalks had reached him as a cloud of smoke. He was glad there was more in the farmer's granary for him and the boys. They'd need some this winter to tide them over. As for these Missouri scoundrels, they could eat grasshoppers for all he cared. Or maybe they could find some nice juicy grubs next spring. Bill giggled at his silly thought.

Thirty minutes later, the troopers approached another house. Addington could see an old man standing on the front porch of the house, a mansion, peering at them as they approached. Old coot! Addington remarked to himself. What's the fool hanging around for? Brazen, that's what he was!

The call rang out to halt, and the advance guard pulled up in front of the house and dismounted. The rest of the men slid off their horses and hitched them to a nearby fence. Bill followed suit; he wanted to see what Jennison had planned for the old man. The eyes of the men sparkled. It was like attending a darned cockfight, Addington thought. As he approached the house, he could hear Jennison haranguing the old man. Addington laughed. He and the men liked the way Jennison put the spurs to these butternuts.

"You old jackass!" Jennison screeched loudly at the old man in his high-pitched, nasal voice. "We've got you now, you old wretch. We've been wantin' to get hold of you for a long time, Johnson. I guess you know you've lost your niggers. Why don't you count your gold eagles now? They'll be missin', you know, come nightfall.

Then Jennison's voice slowed and took on an even more ominous tone: "But you won't have to worry about gold and niggers no longer."

The farmer was stunned. He'd been told horrible stories about the Kansans, but he hadn't believed them. They'd seemed exaggerated. Now he knew things were worse than he'd expected. And he feared for his life.

Jennison, all five feet two inches of him, paced back and forth in front of the old farmer. Because of his tall, conical bearskin hat, Jennison seemed taller than his height. The hat towered above his small, bearded head. He was dressed in a fringed leather coat and coarse trousers. On his feet were dusty boots that seemed huge in comparison to the rest of him. Some people, behind his back, said he seemed to peep over the top of his boots. Yes, Jennison appeared bizarre, all right, and relatively harmless on the surface. But when you looked into his eyes, the darker message radiated from him. Although he was a colonel in the U.S. Army, Jennison was dressed like a man on the hunt. And, yes, he was hunting today.

As Jennison berated the old man, his small tongue flicked nervously across his lips. Meanwhile, the smirking soldiers formed a ring around Jennison and his quarry. This was the only fun they'd had all day. The farmer's wife stood close to her husband and tried to pull him toward the house. But it was useless; Jennison and his men had him all right. The man was a goner, Bill figured.

"Rope!" Jennison screamed, and one of his lieutenants rushed back into the ranks and returned with a strand of hemp cord.

"Ready him," Jennison ordered two of his men. "We're gonna make a good Missourian out of this varmint."

The men grabbed the old man by his arms, and one of Jennison's lieutenants quickly coiled the rope into a crude hangman's noose, draped it over the farmer's head, and tightened it. Without waiting for further orders, the soldiers led the old man onto the farmhouse porch; they were well practiced. The soldier with the rope threw the loose end over one of the porch joists, and several of the men grabbed the end of the rope and hoisted the old fellow off the ground.

At first, he struggled to speak, frothing at the mouth and making crude, gasping sounds, but as he rose farther off the ground, he writhed and twisted silently at the end of the rope, his face reddening. The man's wife attempted frantically to force her way through the soldiers to aid her husband, but the soldiers formed a tight, impenetrable circle around the Missourian, preventing her passage.

The old lady began sobbing. "Colonel, he's just an old man," she cried out. "Help him."

"Help him? Help the old man?" Jennison muttered softly with feigned concern. "Yep, let's help this ol' fella, boys!" He turned to two of his men and whispered into their ears, pointing at the man's feet. The soldiers walked over to the old farmer and fell on his legs with their full weight. The old man stopped shaking.

August 4, 1862

> First couple out with a right hand star,
> It's a right hand round and there you are!
> Now a left hand back and don't be slack,
> Around you go on the same ol' track!

The caller shouted out his instructions rhythmically, and the dancers tripped feverishly around the ballroom of Col. Cuthbert Mockbee's mansion at the east end of Harrisonville,

Missouri. Capt. James "Irvin" Walley, a Union soldier of the
Fifth Missouri Militia Cavalry, looked on indifferently. His dark
brown eyes, sharp and shifting, darted around the room. He
then peered aggressively at the dancers through squinting lids.
All of these farm folks swirling around in circles bored him out
of his head. What's more, he didn't trust them; they were all
traitorous secesh scum to his mind. He was interested in the
young women, though, with their bright skirts and pretty faces.
They were smart and pert, he thought. He could detect enticing
hips bulging from beneath their full skirts. But cold, that's what
they were!

But he reckoned he'd have a good old time this evening
or know the reason why. That little Younger girl, the pretty
blonde, looked right nice to him. He thought he'd ask her to
dance. She'd better say yes, too, or he'd make it hot for her
Reb daddy and brothers. Her old man, Harry, thought he was
some kind of potentate in this neck of the woods with his livery
stable, stores, and niggers. But the boys in blue were running
things now, and Irv Walley would teach 'em that!

Walley felt superior to these hayseeds; after all, he was a
soldier, and they were just clodhoppers. As the mandolin and
violin players strummed and fiddled their musical magic,
Walley walked over to Sally Younger. He knew he cut quite a
figure in his blue uniform, shiny brass buttons, and polished
black boots. Sally seemed occupied in a conversation with one
of her girl friends, but Walley knew she was watching him out
of the corner of her eye. They were bright, pretty blue eyes,
he'd noticed.

"Say, young lady, how about a dance," he said as he
approached her. "You look a mite too rested."

Sally turned toward Walley but averted her eyes. "Not
interested," she replied curtly.

Walley's face reddened and he exploded: "Us Yankees not
good enough for you Rebs?"

"Maybe," Sally answered, refusing to look at him.

Meanwhile, Sally's brother, Thomas Coleman Younger—
"Cole" they called him—had been talking to his cousin John
McCorkle. When he heard Walley's loud voice, he looked over
at Sally with a concerned and irritated expression. Impudent
Yankee, he thought to himself. If he's botherin' Sally, I'll thrash
him good. Cole, a large, muscular seventeen year old with
blondish hair and red sideburns, dropped his conversation and
walked over to his sister, unconsciously jostling some of the
dancers as he proceeded.

Walking up to Walley, he squared his shoulders: "Say, soldier
man, you got some sort of problem with my sister? If you
do, let me hear about it. I'll take care of the matter to your
satisfaction. Meanwhile, stop botherin' our ladies."

"Listen, boy," Walley replied brusquely, "this don't concern
you. I just asked your sister to dance, that's all. Stay out of it!"

"Sally," Cole said, turning to his sister, "are you tired of this
fella? If so, I'll take care of ol' Blue Pants." At this special expression
of antagonism, Walley stepped into Cole's face and glared.

"What's that you called me?" he demanded.

Not taken aback, Younger shoved Walley, pushing him onto
the dance floor. The officer tripped and reeled under a swirl of
skirts and dancers and fell on his back. Walley jumped to his feet
and drew his .44-caliber Army Colt and charged Cole, but some
of the male dancers grabbed the two men and separated them.

"Listen, Reb, and you hear me out!" Walley finally
sputtered, his face a bright scarlet. "If you put your hands
on a U.S. soldier again, I'll have you rottin' in a jail cell. Do
you hear me? This ain't over yet, puppy. You'll be payin' for
your insolence!" Walley took his sword from a nearby rack,
strapped it on, and clanked out the front door, his sullen
friends following behind him.

When Cole informed his father, Harry, of the incident
that night, the old man gave him five hundred dollars and
ordered him to leave the area until Walley cooled off. Harry
was concerned that the Union officer, an experienced soldier,

would be too much of a match for his son or that he would use skullduggery to do the boy harm. But though he was a boy, Cole was game, his father knew.

September 1, 1862

Henry Washington "Harry" Younger snapped the reins, and his buggy shot down the dirt road out of Westport, Missouri. Harry was tired from his train trip to Washington, but he'd gotten some important concessions from the U.S. government, money mostly. Harry owned the mail distribution rights in western Missouri, but when Jennison's Jayhawkers had ridden over from Kansas recently, they had stolen thirty of his livery horses, all of his wagons, and burned his stable and two of his stores. They'd ruined Harry's business. He hadn't been sure if the government would make good on the damages or not. Finally, though, they had compensated him for part of the loss, reimbursing him for his stable, horses, and wagons. But the government said they had no obligation in regard to the retail buildings and their contents.

Harry had warned the officials in Washington that something must be done about Jennison, but they turned a deaf ear to his complaint. "Out of our jurisdiction," they had told him. Harry was convinced that Jennison and his henchman, Dan Anthony, a brother of Susan B. Anthony, the suffragette, were ruining Missourians along the border. While Younger was for the continuation of the Union, he believed that if the Kansans didn't stop their raiding, western Missouri would explode into downright anarchy and guerrilla warfare. Despite all of these problems, Harry remained optimistic that things would come out all right in the end.

It is a beautiful day, he thought to himself. When he got home, he'd have a glass of bourbon and square things with the world. As he rounded a corner in the road, he brought his horses to a halt. Blocking the road ahead was a small detachment of Union soldiers. Harry wondered what kind of trouble this was. Then he saw Captain Walley at the front of the squad and became apprehensive. *What does that devil want?* he thought to himself. He edged his horses forward until Walley was directly in front of his buggy.

"What's the meanin' of this?" Younger challenged.

"Well, if it ain't old Younger," Walley replied sarcastically. "Fancy meetin' you. We're just checkin' things out, lookin' for some of them ornery bushwhackers runnin' loose in these parts. It appears we've found one." Walley grinned aggressively at Younger.

"What do you mean?" Younger snapped back.

"Old man, I think you're a bushwhacker at heart, that's what I think. The only thing lackin' is a cocky plume juttin' from a Reb hat and some big Colts on your hips!"

"You're outrageous," Younger complained. "Get out of my path. You can't intimidate me. I have influence in this country, and I won't stand for this harassment. The regional military authorities will hear about this."

"Now, what makes you think you're so high and mighty, you old Copperhead?" Walley retorted. "Just 'cause you got money, I reckon. Money ain't no good if you're a Reb, is it Joe?" Walley said, turning to one of the grinning soldiers standing nearby. "Hey, Joe, Mr. Younger here is makin' out like he's one of them rich Johnny Rebs. Why don't we just pull him off that buggy of his and inspect him to see how rich he really is. Maybe he's takin' on airs to impress us poor boys."

"This is absurd," Harry argued, becoming angrier. "You're actin' like white trash!" Walley reddened at this last remark and raised his pistol to arm's length, pointing it at Younger.

"Get off that buggy!" he screamed, then paused for a moment, seemingly to consider his situation. "But . . . hey, I don't have to ask you for anything." Walley cocked his Army Colt, pointed it at Younger, and shot him in the chest. The old man recoiled, then plunged forward off his buggy into the dirt. As Younger struck the ground, Walley's men leaped from their horses and rushed to rifle the old man's pockets. They pulled his wallet from his coat pocket and turned his pants pockets inside out looking for change. In his wallet was six thousand dollars in greenbacks. A much larger amount of money, recently given to Harry by the Federal government, remained undetected in a secret belt around his waist.

"Gimme that money!" Walley yelled at one of the men. "I got to keep it for the U.S. Army, know what I mean? Haw! Haw! We got to do everything by the book." Walley grabbed the money and greedily stuffed it into his saddle pack.

October 15, 1862

Cole Younger, curled in a fetal position, squirmed from time to time on the grass beneath him. The ground wasn't all that comfortable, but at least a bed of grass was softer than the rough, baked ground, he thought, and the chiggers seemed nearly through for the season. He and Ike Berry were camped in a patch of woods north and west of Harrisonville, Missouri. The sun had risen but Cole found it difficult to rise. His butt was still sore from a day in the saddle. He felt like he'd barely slept, and he twisted his face away from the sunlight. He could hear Ike, his friend, rustling up breakfast. He hoped his fire wasn't making a lot of smoke. They didn't need a pack of Yankees jumping on them. He knew they were out there. They were always out there, searching for them, all of the time, ready to slip up on them any moment.

The tantalizing aroma of coffee wafted toward him. At least they had one amenity. It would taste good this morning, even full of grounds. He was almost ready to rise, but he knew that Ike would shake him when things were ready, so he relaxed for a bit longer. Then Cole fell fast asleep.

Suddenly, out of the void, he heard horses snorting and jostling. He raised himself on one elbow. Adrenaline flowed instantly through his body, and he leaped to his feet. He ran to the edge of the woods and stared through the trees. In the distance, he saw a long, disjointed rank of blue mounted soldiers. They were formed in a large, irregular U shape and were closing in on the two guerrillas from the south. One of the guerrillas' horses made sweeping motions with its head, and its eyes gleamed white as it pulled at its reins. The horse smelled trouble, smelled Yankees. Then Cole saw Ike. He was peering at the soldiers too from behind a nearby tree.

"They're on us," Ike muttered in a low voice. "We'd best get out of here."

The two men stuffed their .36-caliber Colt revolvers, four each, into their belts, grabbed the reins of their horses, and led them along a winding, woodland path. Cole reached into the large bullet pockets of his guerrilla shirt and felt for the extra cylinders he kept there; they were there all right.

Cole knew their escape plan. He and Ike had talked about it over the fire the night before. They always had an escape plan. That's why they were still alive. The guerrillas led their horses to the edge of the woods and to the open prairie where they would make a break for it. They knew they had better horses than the Yankees—if they could get into the open. There, they could elude them. They were better riders too, they thought, if it came to a dash or a tumble through the woods. Cole pulled his large, muscular body up into the saddle and secured his reins.

"If we get through this, meet me at Atkins' place," Cole said to his partner.

"Okay," Ike replied, then he said defiantly, "Let's show them blue bellies some Missouri ridin'!" With that, the two men plunged their spurs into their horses and started forward in unison. Galloping southeastward along the main trail, they raced toward the right flank of the arrayed Federal troops to gain some riding room. Woods lay to the guerrillas' left.

As the guerrillas approached within three hundred yards of the Federal line, the soldiers dismounted and scrambled quickly into a line of battle. Responding, the guerrillas angled off the trail and slanted their course to the left, parallel with the woods. As they did so, the soldiers fired a quick volley. The bullets tore into the ground around the guerrillas, kicking up dirt. The Federals mounted their horses and took up the pursuit, trailing the guerrillas doggedly. Gradually, the guerrillas pulled out of range, and Cole turned toward his friend. He saw blood running down Ike's pant leg and upon the side of his horse.

"They hit you," Cole cried. "Are you all right?"

"I'm fine," Ike yelled back over the noise of their furiously galloping horses.

"Let's split up or they'll get us," Cole shouted. He believed it would be harder for their pursuers to catch them if they separated.

Soon, the trail entered woods. After a few hundred yards, Cole saw what looked like a bridle path on his left and steered his horse down the narrow lane. Branches slapped him in the face while his horse leaned forward and charged recklessly. When the trail opened up, Cole spurred his horse into a hard gallop, stirring up a cloud of dust. Ike had proceeded along the main trail.

Behind him, in the distance, Cole heard muffled shots. The Feds must be on Ike's trail, he figured. A half-mile down the lane, Cole dismounted and led his horse into the bush. Reaching a small stream, he entered it and followed its course for several hundred yards to erase his trail. Then he walked his horse out of the water and into a thick growth of persimmon trees and stopped to listen. He could hear only the twittering birds. Cole tethered his horse, sat down, and leaned up against a tree. Moments later, he heard several reports in the far distance. Then everything was silent. Cole decided to hole up for the night.

The next morning, Cole retraced the path to his old camp. As he crossed the prairie, a meadowlark sang its lively song. He reckoned the soldiers were miles away by now. In fact, it was difficult now to imagine that they had ever been on this rolling plain. Except for some trampled grass where horses had passed, there was little evidence of their presence. Cole was getting hungry, so he decided to ride to Harrisonville to look for Ike and Adkins. He trotted his horse across the field and parallel to the main road, where he would leave few traces of his passing.

As he proceeded, he noticed buzzards circling to his south.

Cole approached the hovering birds and saw the carcass of a large animal. As he approached the dark mound of flesh, the birds rose clumsily into the air and soared in wide arcs. Cole wondered if that's how he would end up some day—buzzard bait. Now he saw what had drawn the birds, a dead horse.

"Confound it!" he exclaimed. It was Ike Berry's roan. Several hundred yards away, another object protruded from the grass. Cole rode up to it and dismounted.

It was Ike. "Dead as Christ," he muttered aloud as he approached the body. He recognized his friend's clothing. The soldiers must have shot Ike's horse then rode him down, Cole realized.

He reached out and touched his friend's arm. It was like rock, and his head was covered with black, dried blood. The sight sickened Cole, and something hardened in him.

"Curse their souls!" he cried aloud, and tears formed in his eyes.

February 19, 1863

At her home twelve miles north of Harrisonville, Bursheeba Younger, Cole's mother, worked diligently at her spinning wheel, slowly twisting wool into yarn under the faint light of a kerosene lamp. Nearby, Cole sat in a chair, squinting as he read the *Farmer's Almanac*. Cole hoped to learn what the weather might bring. Anything was better than the blizzard they'd been getting. He had just gotten home from a stint in the field with his squad of guerrillas. They had been living in a dugout, and he had finally succumbed to the lure of a warm farmhouse and bed and had left his friends for a short but risky visit to the old homestead.

"Aunty" Suze, the Younger's former house slave, busied herself cleaning the evening dishes. She was glad to have Cole back. She had practically raised that boy since he was a child. Suze loved him, and he was attentive to her, almost like a son. The family had been inside all day while the snow piled up outside. In some places, the drifts were up to three feet deep. Now the weather was clear but cold, and the moon shone brightly on the white blanket of snow. The wind howled fiercely, and the family's sheep, cattle, and poultry clustered in the barns and lean-tos for protection. Because of the bitter cold, most of the chores, except for feeding the livestock, had been skipped that day.

Suddenly, the dogs howled. The Youngers' first thought was that it was a coyote edging up to the barn to prey on their chickens and geese, but the din seemed louder than normal. Cole rose from his chair, ran to the window, and peeped nervously through a crack in the curtains. To his surprise, he saw the dark silhouette of a cavalry detachment against the snow.

The troops rode up to the Youngers' dooryard while the family's dogs barked at them, nipping at the horses' flanks. When one of the dogs leaped at a cavalryman's legs, the soldier reached down and struck it on the head with his sword. It yelped loudly and stumbled off into the darkness, leaving a trail of blood in the snow. The other dogs shrank from the horsemen but continued to growl and bark at them nervously.

A soldier dismounted in front of the Youngers' front gate and drew his sword. One of the bolder dogs dashed at him, and the soldier swiped at him with his saber. The dog shied away deftly while the others formed a ring around the cavalrymen and continued howling and harassing them from a short distance away. One of the soldiers fired his revolver, striking a dog. It writhed in the snow, rolling in its own blood. Again the dogs pulled back apprehensively.

With the dogs now at a safe distance, a captain and two of his men dismounted and advanced through the front gate. One of the soldiers pounded on the front door with the butt of his musket, and a small glass pane at eye level shattered, scattering shards of glass onto the snowy porch.

"Open up!" Capt. Si Davidson of the Missouri State Militia yelled.

"Open up, or we'll break down your door!"

Inside the house, the kerosene lamps still burned, but their wicks were turned low. Suze, the Youngers' black servant, believing that she was the only one who could safely answer the door, threw a large blanket over her shoulders. As she bravely walked to the front, she grabbed Cole by his hand and pulled him along with her. Approaching the door, she raised the back of her blanket and motioned Cole to get underneath. Then she threw the door open wide.

"What you all mean makin' such a ruckus!" she said loudly to the soldiers. "Don't shoot me! I'se just a poor ol' nigger goin' to her cabin.

"If you got trouble with the white folks, well, let me plumb outa heah!" she continued and bumped into the soldiers blocking the doorway. The soldiers opened up a path for her. After walking several feet, Suze lunged to the right and Cole darted out from under her blanket.

"Run, son! Run for yo' life!" she screamed at him and dove into the snow.

The soldiers saw the guerrilla and fired at him. Cole leaped headlong over a rail fence surrounding the yard, rolled, and rose to his feet and began running. He was scrambling for his life. The soldiers saw his dark figure silhouetted against the snow and fired at him again but missed. When Cole reached the nearby woods and cover, he continued to run. He was soon out of breath, but he continued at a fast walk, stuffing his hands inside his coat and shirt and nestling them against his warm skin to thaw his fingers, which tingled with pain. He'd try to reach the Wigginton place, he reckoned. They'd help him, he knew. Back at the farmhouse, the soldiers confronted Bursheba.

"That son of yours has gotten away for now," Davidson said sharply. "I suppose you think you're goin' to walk away from this situation too. Well, you ain't, I promise you that! Your harborin' that boy has cost you your home. We aim to burn this place to the ground and everything in it!"

"Get me a torch," the captain yelled to one of the soldiers.

"But what about the children?" Bursheba protested.

"You all just skedaddle; I said, all of you! That goes for your niggers too!" A soldier approached with a lighted timber. "Now, start burnin'!" The captain commanded Bursheba, handing her the lighted torch.

At first Bursheba ignored Davidson and held the torch limply in her hand. But she realized she must obey him. She grabbed the burning ember and placed it under the edge of her front porch and watched the wood ignite. She stepped back and stared as her house burned. She ached inside. Her life was over, she believed. This was the home where she had made love to Harry and raised their children. Part of her soul was inside that burning house. If it weren't for her children, she would lie down and die.

Minutes later, the troop of cavalry left in search of Cole, and the fire burned and crackled, creating a lurid glare on the snow. Nearby, the slave quarters burned brightly also. Soon, parts of the Younger house collapsed. Bursheba and her children— little Bobby, Johnny, Martha, and Mary—watched their home disappear in flames and smoke. Bursheba knew that when the fire died down, they would have to find shelter. The nearest neighbor was over a mile away through the blowing snow and bitter wind. Fortunately, before the fire gained full force, Suze had run back into the house and gathered winter clothing for the children.

The Younger party formed a ragged column and headed single file across the snowy fields toward the Wigginton farm.

They could see a light from that farm twinkling faintly in the distance. The wind whistled through the trees and blew sharply in their faces. Bursheba was glad that the day's snows had given way to a clear night; at least, they would be able to find their way, she hoped. The larger children plodded quietly through the deep drifts of snow, stumbling though the darkness, sometimes falling, and then raising themselves, their clothing and bodies becoming wetter and icier with every step. The group's only chance was to keep moving and reach the Wiggintons' place as quickly as possible.

When the children tired, some of the slaves lifted them to their shoulders. Young Bobby grabbed Prince, one of the male slaves, tightly around the neck. As she walked, Bursheba coughed uncontrollably. She had contracted tuberculosis a few years earlier, and the cold air aggravated her lungs. After this awful night, she would never be the same again.

2

May 18, 1863

Jesse Woodson James, a tall, slim sixteen year old with black hair and angular features, held the handles of the family plow as it dug into the deep loess soil of Clay County. He liked the rank smell of the earth as it rolled over in furrows before his plow. Every so often he directed his horse along a straighter course. He wondered, as he walked along, how the corn crop was going to do this year. The weather had been mighty good; they had been getting rains. In fact, they'd had fine crops the last couple of years. Before that, he'd been too young to care. But now he was getting nigh to adulthood, and he began to see the reason for a lot of things that were transpiring on the little farm. Of course, the Samuels didn't have as much land, animals, or slaves as they once had, folks had told him. When his father, the Reverend Bob James was alive, they said, the Jameses had one of the best farms in Clay County. But his stepfather, Dr. Reuben Samuel, was doing all right with the old farm. The sweat ran down Jesse's forehead into his eyes, and he brushed the drops away with the back of his hand. Dang it, he thought, that just made the salt sting more. It was a hot June day, but it was a perfect beauty.

Moments later, Jesse heard the dogs making a row back at the Samuels' log cabin, and he gazed in that direction. A cloud of dust rose from the small dirt road leading to the farm. He wondered who was visiting. It could be Frank, he thought. He had been off with Charley Quantrill's guerrillas. They hadn't heard a peep from him in weeks. He hoped his brother had managed to bag some Yankees. Who did they think they were—Jennison's Jayhawkers, Jim Lane, and those Iowa and Illinois farm boys—invading Missouri? But he figured Frank and the guerrillas would put a stop to that. He wished Quantrill would let him join up. He was as good a shot as any soldier. All he wanted was a chance to prove it. Quantrill said he was too young, just sixteen. But age didn't make a man.

Jesse's eyes began to squint, and his eyes twitched. He was becoming concerned with the amount of dust stirring at the end of the road. It signaled more than one man. There seemed to be a number of men coming. Then he caught a glimpse of dark blue at the curve in the road and his heart leaped. "Dang Yankees! Jayhawkers!" he screamed aloud. Jesse dropped his reins and dashed toward the house to get his rifle. One of the family dogs raced after him. The soldiers were already at the front door. He loved and respected his stepfather, Reuben; they'd better not touch a hair on his head, he thought.

Then, four armed horsemen headed in his direction. He was unarmed, so he reversed his path and fled down a furrow toward a copse of oaks. Just before he reached the trees, a horseman charged into him with his mount, knocking him to the ground. Jesse's left shoulder ached from the impact, but he raised himself quickly. Another soldier jumped from his horse and grappled with him. A third dismounted and grabbed him from behind and pulled his arms tightly behind his back. While he was struggling to get loose, a soldier struck him in the face and stomach with his fists.

"Get out of the way; I'll handle this whelp," another soldier cried out. When Jesse's arms were released, the soldier struck him in the face and across the shoulders with a riding crop, leaving bloody welts. Jesse dashed at the soldier headlong and threw him to the ground, but the other soldiers quickly grabbed him again and began beating him with the barrels of their revolvers until he lost consciousness.

Back at the farmhouse, two soldiers held Reuben Samuel while another pointed a pistol at him. Jesse's mother, Zerelda, heavy with child, railed at the soldiers.

"What do you think you're doin'?" she screamed. "He's a doctor. What do you mean comin' out here and assaultin' us? Get off our farm!" She grabbed at one of the soldiers and clubbed at him with her fists. Zerelda was a large, powerful woman.

The soldier giggled sheepishly. Despite himself, this woman's aggressive blows intimidated him. She almost made you "skeered," the soldier thought to himself. Another soldier grabbed Zerelda from behind and struggled to hold her.

Maj. James Cook, who stood nearby, looked at the middle-aged woman with disdain.

"Mrs. Samuel, we are looking for your boy Frank," he said finally. "We know he's runnin' with the guerrilla Quantrill," the officer continued. "You can either cooperate with us or suffer the consequences."

"Cooperate? We're not cooperatin' with the likes of you!" Zerelda screamed. "You're saloon scum, attackin' a woman and her family. Get off our farm. You've no right to be here!"

"Don't preach to us, you infernal Rebs," the major replied, irritated by her outburst. "You've been askin' for trouble for a long time; well, now you got a heap of it!

"Okay, Samuel," the major said, turning to Reuben. "Where's that boy of yours? Out with it. You won't be hurt as long as you tell us his whereabouts. It's up to you. Otherwise, you'll ride the end of a rope."

Dr. Reuben Samuel looked straight ahead, his teeth clenched. They could kill him, but he wasn't going to talk.

Almost in answer to Reuben's thoughts, one of the soldiers formed a noose and placed it over his neck. Several of the soldiers dragged him to the coffee bean tree near the Samuels' cabin. Within seconds, Reuben's arms were tied behind his back, and he was hoisted into the air. He gagged and twisted and his face turned red. After he was left to swing awhile, the soldiers dropped him back to earth and loosened the noose.

"All right, Samuel, talk! Where's that boy of yours?" Cook shouted at him. Samuel, half-dazed, remained silent.

After raising Samuel off the ground several more times, the soldiers realized that he was unconscious and left him dangling from the rope. Major Cook formed his men into a column of twos and rode up the road, leaving a cloud of dust in their wake. At their departure, Zerelda rushed to the tree and attempted to lift her husband and relieve the pressure from the noose around his neck. He was too heavy for her.

"Help!" she screamed out to one of the family's slaves, "help me!" While the two women held Samuel aloft, Zerelda pulled at the coils around his neck with her spare hand until she relaxed the rope a little. Finally she loosened the noose completely and pulled it over her husband's head. Then, overcome by exertion, the two women let Reuben fall to the ground. He lay motionless, either unconscious or dead. Within minutes, however, he began breathing fitfully, then normally.

When Jesse was later found and revived, he vowed revenge. Days later, he left the family farm to join Quantrill.

Early August, 1863

The Anderson girls, Josephine, Mary Ellen, and Janie—sixteen, fourteen, and ten years old, respectively—worked busily in the kitchen preparing the noonday meal for their brothers and their friends. Josie snapped green beans and threw them in a boiling pot. Mary Ellen stood at the stove frying bacon in a skillet, and the wonderful aroma of corn pone circulated from a pot in the fire. Little Janie tended it from time to time to see that it didn't burn. They'd have plenty of food for the boys when they came in.

"Say, Josie," Mary Ellen chided. "Wasn't that the Privin boy you were makin' eyes at in church Sunday?"

"What?" Josie replied. "I saw you lookin' at him too. He ain't that bad a lookin' boy, is he? I think he's got his mind set on Martha Pence, though, appears to me," and she giggled.

"Who says she's got her number on him?" Mary Ellen countered tartly. "Oh, well, there's lots of fish in the sea. I noticed that Plunk Murray is sweet also."

"Oh, Plunk Murray! Plunk Murray! That's all you talk about. What's that boy got?"

"Oh, you're just jealous. He's got plenty. That's what," replied Mary Ellen. "Besides that, he's old enough to marry. That boy you keep lookin' at, little Bud Storey, ain't nothin' but a pup!"

"Oh, Mary Ellen, you're ornery!" Josie retorted, pretending anger.

Across the hollow and proceeding down a steep ravine, a small column of soldiers in blue rode along the dirt trail leading to the Anderson farm.

"Their house is around the next bend," a man in coarse farm clothes said.

"You sure?" a soldier with silver bars on his shoulders questioned.

"Sure, I been down there lots a times," the farmer replied. "I used to live not more'n a mile from here. I could take you to the Anderson's place blindfolded. I'm only takin' you 'cause I want to see somethin' bad happen to the family. They're Rebs, all of 'em, and mean too. If I weren't with you fellas, I'd be afeared to get within a country mile of 'em. But they burned me out a year ago, and I ain't forgettin'."

"Okay, Smith," Lt. Johnny Pearson answered in a bored tone.

As the troop of soldiers rounded a curve in the road, they saw a small log cabin at the end of the trail. Family washing was hanging nearby, and a curl of smoke rose lazily from a large fireplace at one end of the house. The cabin, a two-part affair, had a breezeway between its two sections, and the soldiers could see three women doing their chores in the walkway.

The girls noticed the soldiers too. The column of fourteen men halted, and Pearson ordered three of his soldiers to dismount and accompany him to the cabin. He motioned for Smith, the civilian, to follow them. Lt. Chad Brookes, another officer, unfastened the snap on his holster and pulled out his revolver. Spurs jangling, the five men proceeded to the walkway.

"Howdy! Howdy!" Pearson greeted the girls.

"Afternoon," Josephine replied coolly.

"All right, Smith, are these the girls we're lookin' for?" Pearson asked his guide.

"It's them all right! I'd know 'em anywheres. They's the Andersons; I've seen 'em in church lots a times."

"Ladies," the lieutenant said in a firm voice, "you're under arrest for aiding and harboring guerrillas. You're comin' with us."

The girls looked dumbfounded. "You've got to be kiddin'," she said to the lieutenant in a puzzled tone. "I've never heard of women being arrested for that kind of thing."

"You have now. And where you're a goin', there's goin' to be a whole lot of women just like you. You're off to jail."

As the lieutenant was speaking, some of the soldiers had gone to the barn and saddled up horses for the two older sisters to ride. They now returned to the cabin with them. The Anderson girls felt trapped. They knew their brothers Bill and Jim and their band were somewhere close by, but they were out of hearing range. Little Janie, watching as her sisters were arrested, began wailing loudly.

Pearson became apprehensive. "Shut your mouth, kid," he cautioned her. "Sergeant Wilson," he said, turning to one of his men, "get the girls on the horses. Let's get outa here. Anderson and his men may be nearby. We don't want to stir up a hornet's nest."

Wilson and another soldier helped Mary Ellen and Josie onto their horses as little Janie continued to scream at the height of her voice. One of the soldiers walked over and slapped her hard in the face. That only made her cry louder as the soldiers rode away with her sisters.

At a nearby stream, Bill and Jim Anderson and the rest of the guerrillas relaxed at the edge of a small pond. Their fishing lines dangled in the water, but they weren't intent on catching anything. Fishing was just a diversion for them, and they used the time to spin endless yarns to each other. Bill Anderson leaned against a tree, his long legs extending toward the water's edge. The toes of his large dusty cavalry boots pointed heavenward. He was stylishly dressed in a beige-colored frock coat, and underneath the garment was a black shirt embroidered in rich floral designs. Between his shirt and coat, he wore a smart loden-green vest. On the ground beside him lay his favorite tools—shiny, well-oiled .36-caliber Navy revolvers—and a gray felt hat decorated with a jaunty red plume. The hat's wide brim was curled up rakishly on one side and fastened in place with a shiny silver star. Bill's hair hung in oily dark ringlets to his shoulders, and his high cheekbones gave his face a sharp, angular appearance. He was a handsome man all right, with a thin mustache and a somewhat stringy beard that came to a ragged point.

Bill was a specimen of manhood, over six feet high. Although he had yet to earn his sobriquet, "Bloody Bill," he had already won a reputation with the Yankees as a dangerous man with a murderous temper. His father had been killed just a few years earlier by Kansas abolitionists, and Bill had thrown himself in with the Missouri guerrillas to even the score. Once, Bill had been considered easygoing and affable, but that was years and grievances ago. All he knew now was that Jayhawkers and abolitionists were invading Missouri and Kansas, and he meant to kill as many of them as he could lay his hands on. He hated the Yankees and their blue uniforms, but increasingly he and his men donned blue to disguise their presence while in Yankee-infested areas. He and his men liked to ride up to unwary Federal patrols and open up a murderous fire on them before they could discern the true identities of their attackers. When the Yankees fled, he dispatched them one by one, until he had killed every last man among them.

Suddenly, one of Bill's guards, Bud Parkinson, rushed out of the woods. "Bill, somethin's up! I heard Janie cryin'!"

Bill leaped to his feet and the men ran for their horses, mounted, and raced in the direction of the cabin. As they approached the house, they could see Mary Ellen and Josie being led on horseback by soldiers. Anderson and his men drew their revolvers and rode to within a hundred yards of the Federal detachment and formed into battle order. Their horses shuffled nervously.

In response to the armed men confronting his troops, Lieutenant Pearson ordered the Federals to dismount and take up firing positions with their muskets. Anderson knew he had the drop on the outnumbered Federals. If the blue bellies opened fire with their rifles, a few guerrillas might go down, but the guerrillas would get every Yankee in sight, he believed. The guerrillas' pistols gave them superior, rapid firepower at close range, and they easily could fire six rounds to every musket shot fired at them.

Once the men were formed, Anderson rode forward to parley with the Yankees, leaving his men with the order to attack instantly if anyone fired on him. He stopped within twenty-five yards of the Union cavalry.

"What are you doin' with my sisters?" Anderson demanded.

"We didn't expect you, Anderson," Lieutenant Pearson replied, riding forward to meet the guerrilla chief.

"I know you didn't, you devils!" Anderson cried out. "Now, let the girls go or I'll kill you all. Every one of you."

The soldiers looked nervously at each other and toward their commander. They were clearly frightened. Then, by a predetermined signal, two of the troopers pointed their pistols at Josie and Mary Ellen.

"All right, Anderson," Lieutenant Pearson said nervously. "We have the upper hand on you now. If you shoot any of my men, the girls will die."

Anderson's face turned white with anger, and his eyes rolled wildly. "Let my sisters go or we fire!"

Pearson turned to his men and said loudly, "At the first shots, kill the girls." He was calling Anderson's bluff. He had no choice. If the guerrillas opened fire at this range, his patrol was doomed. But if he gave up the girls, his and his men's lives were worthless.

Anderson remained motionless, his face a rigid mask. His men looked toward him, waiting for their orders. After a minute, Anderson motioned his men with a slow, backward wave of his arm, and the guerrillas backtracked to a position off the main trail. From this vantage point, the guerrillas watched the Federals as they filed past on the way to Kansas City. Anderson was enraged. He had been beaten. He followed the Union patrol for a mile or so, and then he veered off the trail. There was nothing else he could do.

August 14, 1863

In a dilapidated brick building between Fourteenth and Fifteenth and Grand Avenue in Kansas City, a small border town, the Anderson girls lay on their bunks on the second floor of an improvised jail. Guerrilla John McCorkle's sister sat nearby, and on the other side of the room was Cole Younger's cousin Nannie Kerr. Nine women and two children were held prisoner in the building, one of them little Janie Anderson, who had joined her big sisters when she could find no one else she liked to care for her. From the floor below them, the young girls heard the vulgar giggles, shrieks, and profanity of the prostitutes who resided in that part of the building. The guerrilla girls, all from good families, were appalled at their situation. When they had carried food and ammunition to their brothers and spied for them, they had never dreamed it would come to this, that they would end up prisoners of war.

The young women were also apprehensive about the building they were kept in. It creaked loudly at night and occasionally quivered and shook dangerously. The building seemed unsafe to them. When they complained about the situation to their guard, he merely shrugged his shoulders. Gen. Thomas Ewing, commander of Union troops on the border, had specifically appropriated the building they were in because it was owned by one of his enemies, George Caleb Bingham, a prominent artist and Unionist. Bingham found Ewing's policy toward the rebel Missourians deplorable and attacked him politically and socially at every opportunity. For that reason, when Bingham recently left town on a trip east, Ewing appropriated his building for use as an impromptu jail. He knew this would infuriate Bingham, and it did when he discovered the act upon his return.

This afternoon, the girls complained again to their guard about the safety of the building, but the jailer replied that they were lucky to be alive. Toward nightfall, the building began to shake again and the floor sagged. The situation was unnerving the girls.

"Josie, I think this building's goin' to fall in if it shakes any more," Mary Ellen said. She ran to the stairway and yelled a loud complaint to the guard, who stood at the foot of the staircase. Finally, the guard walked to the top of the stairs.

"You ladies okay?" the guard asked. He seemed somewhat nervous himself. Then a loud noise issued from the first floor, and the building began to shudder more vigorously. The guard rushed down the stairs and leaped out the back door of the building. Behind him, the building collapsed in an enormous heap of bricks and shattered timbers. A billowing cloud of dust and soot rose into the air. The women had screamed loudly when the ceiling over their head collapsed, but now there was complete silence. From beneath the debris, a few of the young women began moaning.

Josephine Anderson and three of the other guerrilla girls were crushed and killed. Many of the other young women were seriously injured. Mary Ellen Anderson was horribly disfigured and remained a cripple the rest of her life, always walking with an awkward gait. Both of little Janie Anderson's legs were broken. Any sense of compromise or mercy in Bill Anderson died in this avalanche of brick and broken timbers.

3

September 24, 1864

Frank James and his fellow guerrillas were stirring up quite a plume of dust as they ambled along a winding Missouri road. They had been flanking the Missouri River all day, and so far they had avoided contact with Federal troops. Virtually all of the guerrilla bands, including Frank's, were heading toward Centralia to link up with Bill Anderson and George Todd. Frank and his boys would eventually have to cross to the north side of the river to reach that town. He had been asking passersby if any strangers had passed through, in case any of them happened to be Anderson's or Todd's men.

They called Bill Anderson "Bloody Bill" these days, a product of the newspapers to some extent, but Frank knew that Bill was a violent fellow, even by guerrilla standards. But was it any wonder? The Federals had destroyed everything precious to the man, killed his father and sister, and maimed another sister. Now Bill was obsessed with revenging himself on the Federals. Anderson seemed to have no fear of the Yankees, which boded ill for any that came within his grasp.

Barker Lane, a handsome, heavyset young guerrilla with black, wavy hair, rode next to Frank. The other nine men rode several hundred yards to the rear. Frank and Barker were acting as pickets, positioning themselves to spot any Federals. Frank, a tall, long-faced, serious young man with sandy hair, was running things in this little pack until they linked up with Anderson. Of course, in the ordinary sense of the word, no one "ran" the guerrilla units. He and the boys were a committee of nine. When the guerrillas united for a big operation, like the one that was coming up, they became a committee of three hundred.

Because they were in the advance guard, Frank and Barker wore Union uniforms to make themselves less conspicuous. You never knew when one of those infernal Federal patrols would descend on you, emerging out of some woods or thicket where they were hidden. The Feds didn't exchange calling cards, just attacked you on sight—if they recognized you as rebels. Frank and his boys followed the same practice when they met small Union patrols. The guerrillas dressed in their captured Union uniforms just rode up to them like they were buddies then fired a volley into them before the boys in blue figured it out. Frank always wondered at their surprised faces.

If Frank and the boys ran into any large Yankee patrols as they proceeded east, they intended to split up, operate individually for a while, then rejoin the main force at Centralia. That was their general rule of engagement when they were confronted with a superior force at close quarters. But when they got to Centralia, the blue bellies had best beware: the guerrillas would have the biggest show in town. There'd be no more cut and run. It always bothered Frank to run; he'd rather fight. But if the individual bands tried to fight every rotten Yankee in these parts, they'd all be dead in the sight of a week. The guerrillas had to fight smart, pick their fights, and play the odds to stay alive.

Frank hoped the Feds would run some steamboats up the river; he and the boys needed a little target practice. They'd send the boats packing for St. Louis for sure. It fit their orders too. The guerrillas had been told to attack the Federals' logistics train, whether it was composed of river traffic, the railroad, or wagon trains. That way fewer Union troops and supplies would be available in western Missouri to fight Confederate general Sterling

Price, "Ol' Pap," when he started his campaign along the Missouri River in a few weeks. It was thought that he would be entering the area from the south, around Pilot Knob, then he would head toward St. Louis, and finally turn west toward Kansas City.

This guerrilla business was dangerous work, Frank thought, but it had gotten more treacherous when they'd reached central Missouri, a place sometimes infested with Yankees. In western Missouri, nearly everyone was their friend or kin. Here, in central Missouri, along the river, there were a lot of good Southerners, but the place was lousy with "Dutch" also—kraut-eating Germans barely dry behind their ears after crossing the "big pond." The Dutch spoke a sort of pidgin English. They were tough, he knew, smart and gutsy, and they handled guns well. Many of them had been soldiers in Germany in the revolution there in 1848. The guerrillas respected them for their skills—but for little else. Frank and the others knew that the Dutch would shoot a Southern fella in the back if they got a chance. The Southern men who fought at the Battle of Wilson's Creek in 1861 complained that the whole Federal army seemed to be a sea of Dutchmen, except for old Lyon and a few officers. The Southerners almost felt like they were fighting Germany. When you captured a Dutch, you could hardly understand their gibberish. This was a sad state of affairs, Frank thought, the country overrun with "furriners." And they were killing good Missouri men on their own land.

Up ahead, Frank saw a log cabin nestled against the hillside, smoke curling from its chimney. Well, it was about eating time, he thought. Maybe they could find food there.

"Hey, Barker, signal the boys to catch up," Frank said. "Over yon looks like a good place to eat and hole up tonight."

Barker rode several yards to the rear, raised an arm over his head, and then extended it directly in front of him, fingers down, signaling the guerrillas to move forward as a group. The men quickly assembled and the squad rode up to the cabin amid a chorus of yelping and growling hounds. The farmer's wife peeped from behind the front door, and Frank tipped his hat to her. "Howdy, ma'am," Frank saluted her. The lady of the house stared at him sullenly. The farmer and his young boy soon emerged from behind the woman and met the guerrillas at the door.

"Howdy, mister," Frank greeted the farmer. "How's it goin'? Don't suppose you could feed and water a few men and horses?"

"Vee dun't relly haf dat much here, boyss," the German farmer responded. "Sorry, dere's too many of you and . . ."

"Listen," Frank interrupted him, "we really don't need a whole lot." Then he said ominously, "Do as I say and you won't get hurt."

"Oh, vell, vee fix you up, huh?" the German replied uneasily.

"That's better. We don't want no blasted trouble with you while we're here, understand me?"

"Yah, yah, I understood," the German answered, now seeming to fully digest their presence. Frank looked into the German's eyes and imagined devious thoughts spinning through his dark wooly head. He didn't trust him. He didn't trust any of the Dutch. Frank motioned the other men forward, and they dismounted and followed Frank into the cabin. It was very crowded.

"Say," said Dolph Carrol, one of Frank's men, "what kind of food you folks got today? I wouldn't mind hav'n some of them Dutch sausages you folks are always braggin' about."

"Oh, vee got some of dem," the farmer replied, seeming to warm somewhat to his visitors for the first time. But Frank guessed his chumminess was a front.

It seemed that the farmer had been about ready to eat when they arrived, so their timing was good, Frank reflected. But the German's wife would have to cook up a whole lot more food for this hungry bunch. Meanwhile, Frank sent Dock Rupe down the road to act as a sentinel. He'd have to miss lunch for a while, but they had to take precautions in this country. Dock could take his grub later, when they spelled him.

After grumbling a bit, the guerrilla rode up the road several hundred yards, dismounted, and tied his horse behind some trees. He sat down and leaned up against a tree that faced the road.

Frank felt a little ill at ease taking the German's food without paying him for it, but the guerrillas didn't get salaries. They had to make do any way they could. When the Union army moved through the country, they told the newspaper boys they were living off the land. Whose land? Frank thought to himself. It wasn't theirs. Well, that's what he and the boys were doing too, just livin' off the land, that's all. The Federal press referred to the guerrillas as "bandits," but Frank guessed that was because they were just small potatoes when it came to stealing. They didn't own printing presses like their enemies, who made dawn out of night and demons out of good men.

Frank and a few of the guerrillas pulled up some chairs so they could eat at the German's table. They wanted to watch the farmer in case he had any ideas about escaping or springing an alarm. The rest of the guerrillas waited outside for their meal and leaned up against the house or some trees in the front yard.

The German's wife soon brought the steaming sausages and kraut she had cooked for them to the table. Frank, always suspicious, had the woman taste the food first to ensure it wasn't poisoned. As he turned to his food, he felt something tug at his pants leg. Hanging to his pants by its tiny claws was a small tabby kitten that was attempting to climb up his leg. Frank reached down and lifted the creature onto his lap. He hadn't seen a cat in months. He'd always liked cats, liked their spirit. Any one of them was braver than ten men, he thought, if the odds were right. He missed the half a dozen mousers they had back home at the Samuels' farm. He stroked the kitten between its ears with his index finger, then laid it down on the floor gently.

After dinner, Barker Lane queried the German: "Hey, Dutch, you got any fire water?"

"Fire vasser? Vas is dat?" the German replied.

"Red-eye . . . booze! You know. You got some?"

"Oh, yah, I tink vee got dat," the German answered and walked over to a cupboard and opened it. He drew out a china jug inscribed with ornate German writing and pulled out its stopper.

"Here, boyss, help you selfs," he said, reaching the bottle toward Barker.

"No! You first," Barker said, eying the German. The little man raised the bottle to his lips and took a small taste.

Barker took the bottle out of the German's hands and placed it to his own lips. "What's your name, little man?"

"I be Jakob Quell," the German replied.

"We noticed that you're Dutch. What you doin' in this country?"

"Oh, vee just decided dis good place to live, dat's all."

"Oh, yeh?" Barker snapped, turning red. "Well, what if I was to tell you to get your hides out of this country? What'd you say to that, huh?"

"Oh, vell, maybe vee do dat some day," the German answered.

Frank heard a gunshot. Dock Rupe must have stirred up some Yankees, he thought. The guerrillas in the house jumped to their feet, while the guerrillas outside dashed through the front door and took up firing positions in the windows. As Barker Lane closed the front door, a volley of bullets tore through the door and riddled his body. He slumped to the floor, blood pouring from his side and out of the corner of his mouth. Frank dragged him over to the wall. Then he threw the door wide open and fired at the blue-clad horsemen circling the front yard. The guerrillas fired at them rapidly from the windows and door. The house filled with acrid gun smoke, and the guerrillas could scarcely see one another, but they could see outside.

The Feds must have sneaked up on Dock and killed him, Frank reckoned, or he would have warned them. Someone must have alerted them to the guerrillas' presence. Now, they had to shoot their way out. He wondered if it was their little

German "friend" who had been the snitch. Maybe he'd sent his young son for help, and he'd ridden to warn a Union patrol nearby. Frank couldn't be positive about the man's role, and he wasn't for shootin' a man based on suspicion alone.

The German was cowering in a corner. As the men continued their firing, Frank strode over to the German, grabbed a fistful of his black hair, and slapped him solidly across the side of his face with the barrel of his pistol, creating a large, bleeding welt. Then he let go of his hair and cracked him sharply across the top of his head, knocking him unconscious. "You little scoundrel, I ought to kill you," he mumbled to himself. But Frank was bent first on escaping.

"Jamison, Dolph—the rest of you. Get in Indian file. We've got to get out of here. When I say 'Now' keep movin' and firin' and throwin' lots of lead at them. Go for the woods and our horses. Keep up a hot fire!"

Once the men were in position, Frank screamed, "Now!" and the men hurtled through the front door, shooting in every direction. Even as he ran, Frank saw some of the men falling around him, but there wasn't time to stop. The guerrillas ran for the woods and scrambled into the heavy brush, spitting lead behind them.

They had hidden their horses in the woods to the west of the house, and they rushed to the spot, untethered their horses, and leaped into their saddles. They rode through the woods, weaving their way until they reached an opening onto the prairie. Then, they spurred their horses sharply.

Frank was confident they could escape. As he looked around, he was startled to find only five of his men still with him. They galloped over the rolling hills, spurring their horses to the limit. The Yankees hadn't figured on them exiting through the woods onto the open prairie, so they had the jump on them.

The guerrillas raced toward the Missouri River, several miles to the north. When they reached the river flood plain, they rode along it looking for cabins. They needed a boat. Frank saw a cabin ahead and signaled the men in that direction. They raced to the dock north of the cabin and found a boat moored. They were in luck. The guerrillas dismounted and tied their horses next to the dock. Frank looked the boat over quickly. It would do. It was chained and padlocked to a post, so he drew his revolver and shot the rusty chain in two.

"Get in, boys," he shouted. "When you're settled, I'll hand you our horses' reins." Frank led the horses, one by one, to the stern of the boat and handed the reins to the men.

"Now push off, Dolph, and start rowin'," Frank called. Dolph pushed hard with his oar against the dock, edging the boat into the current. He began rowing briskly. Meanwhile, Frank grabbed a small fishing pole lying nearby and forced the horses into the river. As soon as one of the horses plunged into the river, the rest followed.

Frank dove into the cold, muddy water after them then rose to the surface and splashed his way toward the boat. It was hard swimming with his boots on, and the cold water nearly paralyzed him, but he grappled his way onto the boat with the help of one of the men.

"We've made it, boys," Frank stated as he pulled himself aboard. "They'll have a hard row to hoe to catch us now."

The guerrillas were none too soon. On the horizon, Frank could see a cloud of dust. The Yankees had seen them and were galloping toward the river, but they were too late to stop them. The river's fast current carried the boat and horses swiftly downstream while Dolph and Sim rowed briskly. The men were floating diagonally toward the opposite bank, some several hundred yards away.

On September 26, two of Bill Anderson's scouts found the bodies of some of Frank's men south of the river. They had been scalped, and wild animals had chewed on their remains. Upon hearing this news, Anderson flew into a rage.

September 27, 1864

A column of eighty men abreast in rows of four trotted toward Centralia, Missouri. In the advance guard rode four horsemen in blue. As the soldiers approached the town, a few townsmen noticed them and stared at them curiously. Accelerating to a gallop, the advance guard began uttering a strange, yipping wail, the famous rebel yell. The main troop followed them, mimicking the cry in a wild, discordant roar. The men, their reins held tightly between their teeth, galloped boldly into town, firing their Navy revolvers from both hands. Holding their weapons at chest height, they fired them instinctively to the left and right, directing their fire at the hotel, stores, houses, and anyone loitering in the streets or sticking their heads out of windows. The bullets shattered windows, splintered doors, and riddled the sides of buildings. The town dogs, excited by the commotion, ran with their tails between their legs. Two old-timers who had been sitting on a bench along the main street crouched low and scurried between brick buildings. Meanwhile, the town marshal, experiencing an epiphany, dashed from his office, mounted a horse, and galloped out of town in search of what he considered more important business: saving his life. Rising smoke and dust clouded the air as the horsemen twisted and milled around in circles in the middle of the main street, firing loud blasts from their revolvers. Bill Anderson had come calling.

The guerrillas dismounted and tethered their horses then raced into the stores, stealing anything that attracted their attention. One guerrilla dashed out of a haberdashery with a long bolt of red cloth, mounted his horse, and trailed it behind him like a blanket down the full length of the main street, whooping as he rode. Other guerrillas broke into a full keg of whiskey stored at the railroad depot. Men cupped their hands while their friends poured the liquor. The guerrillas drank their fill, the whiskey running down their chins and spilling onto their vests. Soon the partisans were staggering through the streets like so many drunken sailors. One of the guerrillas knocked down an unwary citizen, placed one of his feet atop his chest, and yanked off the man's boots. Then he reached down and plucked the man's wallet from his back pocket. Back at the depot, the guerrillas broke into cases of boots packaged to be mailed and wrestled them into the street. Finding their correct sizes, they tied them onto their saddles, cursing and laughing as they did so. One guerrilla dunked one of his new boots into the open keg of whiskey, filled it, then offered the other guerrillas a drink.

When a stagecoach pulled into town from Columbia, Missouri, it was surrounded instantly. Its occupants were forced into the street, and as some of the men exited the coach, they began complaining. A Union congressman, James S. Rollins, and a local sheriff were asked who they were. Using their powers of duplicity, they fabricated names and histories, posing as Southern men to fit the occasion. Congressman Rollins even ranted at the guerrillas indignantly: "I am the Reverend Johnson, minister of the Methodist Church, South. We are Southern men and Confederate sympathizers, and you ought not to rob us!" A guerrilla ignored this outburst and snatched Rollins' wallet from his pants, at the same time pruning his gold watch and chain.

"Say, I see the church business has been pretty good to you lately!" the guerrilla exclaimed, examining the fancy, solid-gold watch in his hand.

At 10:00 A.M., a whistle sounded in the distance and the muffled chugging of a locomotive could be heard. Bill Anderson beamed with surprise and yelled, "Men! Grab those loose ties and pile 'em on the tracks."

Guerrillas came running from every direction and jointly grabbed and stacked stray railroad ties across the rails. Other partisans pulled a wagon onto the tracks. Two guerrillas rolled a wooden stock-watering tank atop the rails and turned it over loudly.

Steaming closer, the locomotive belched smoke and fiery embers from its stack in a large unfurling spiral. As the train entered the outskirts of the town, the engineer, Jim Clark, became suspicious of the strange-looking men milling around the tracks and motioned the fireman to throw on more wood. Clark believed they were running into an ambush, and since it was too late to put the engine in reverse, he hoped to race through the town unimpeded. The train picked up speed and thundered under a full throttle.

When the train barreled within firing range, the guerrillas shot their pistols and rifles at it, the bullets pinging against the train's surface and singing across its dark steel surface in whining ricochets. Just before the cowcatcher plunged into the ties and debris blocking the train's path, the guerrillas heard the high squeal of the train's brakes. Frightened by the gunfire, the brakeman had lost his nerve and applied the brakes. When the train ran into the debris, it slowed and—after a few final, frantic lurches—came to a dead stop, a pile of timbers and debris scattered in front of it. One of the guerrillas mounted the locomotive and placed a pistol to Clark's ear.

"Take those flags down," he demanded, pointing at the two star-spangled banners attached to the locomotive's headlamps. Clark scrambled atop the engine and unseated the flags, unceremoniously throwing them to the ground.

The guerrillas immediately charged the baggage car and broke into the express safe. Frank James seized a leather suitcase, split it open with his bowie knife, and three thousand dollars in greenbacks tumbled out. Alexander Franklin James, one day to become America's premier outlaw, had discovered his first cache.

Anderson's lieutenants ordered everyone off the train, and a large group of passengers, military and civilian alike, filed out. Anderson ordered the civilians separated from the soldiers. Soon, twenty-five Union soldiers, some of them wounded from battle but most of them on furlough after Sherman's March to the Sea, were lined up on the west side of the platform. The civilians were formed on the east. One well-dressed civilian was ordered to give up his money but produced only a couple of bills. Anderson ordered him to produce the rest instantly. When he pulled more money out of his boot, one of the guerrillas placed the muzzle of his pistol against the man's head and blew a gaping hole in his skull.

The soldiers were then ordered to strip off their clothes: the guerrillas needed new outfits. Soon, a long line of forlorn men dressed only in their long underwear lined the western side of the station platform. They looked back and forth at each other apprehensively. Most of them were terrified.

Archie Clement, a five-foot-tall guerrilla who functioned as Anderson's right-hand man, paraded back and forth in front of the men, strutting and posturing. Clement turned to Anderson with a smile and pointed at the soldiers.

"Bill, whatcha want me to do with these fellas?" he said in a loud, serious tone.

Anderson looked at Clement soberly and said, "Parole 'em, Arch. Parole 'em."

"I thought so. Haw! Haw!" Clement cackled. He walked over to the guerrillas and whispered a few words.

The guerrillas took up a position about ten paces from the Union troops who faced them in a long rank. Clement looked toward Anderson. Bill gazed indifferently at the horizon and slowly raised his right arm. When Anderson's arm was raised over his head, Clement screamed, "Fire!" and a loud report rang out. Gun smoke swirled along the station platform in a gray-white cloud.

A number of men fell at the first fire, but the shooting continued sporadically. Some of the surviving Union soldiers fell to their knees and begged for their lives. A few placed their arms over their faces. Others merely stared at the guerrillas soberly until felled by bullets. A few of the soldiers ran, making themselves special targets. One large soldier, falling to his knees, rolled over the edge of the station platform and scrambled under its surface for safety. The guerrillas promptly lit the platform and station house afire. Within minutes, the man, Valentine Peters, rushed from the inferno with a timber in his hand and began knocking down guerrillas. He was stopped by an explosion of pistol rounds that almost blew him apart.

Meanwhile, the baggage and passenger cars had been set ablaze. After ordering the tracks cleared, Anderson commanded the engineer to start the locomotive and to accelerate it in a westerly direction. He directed the engineer to tie down the whistle cord and when the engine was well away to jump off.

The flaming train puffed out of the station and went screaming westward. After the train had proceeded several hundred yards, the engineer leaped off, and the train sped away, trailing a roll of white smoke. Only one soldier, a Sergeant Goodman, remained alive in Centralia. He would be used as a hostage in bartering for one of Anderson's men who had been captured recently and was to be executed soon, the universal treatment for captured guerrillas. While a deal was unlikely to be struck, the hostage would give Anderson an opportunity for a dramatic reprisal when an agreement failed.

Thirty minutes after Anderson left town headed southward, a column of 147 Union militiamen—Companies A, G, and H of the Thirty-ninth Missouri Infantry—plodded toward Centralia, to their west. As they approached the town, their commander, Maj. A. V. E. "Ave" Johnston, noticed smoke rising from the buildings and ordered his troops to a gallop. When the soldiers entered the town, they found mayhem: dead bodies stripped of their clothing lay sprawled in the streets, some scalped, some still bleeding. The town leaders rushed out of their hiding places and sought out the Union commander and complained to him about the raid. Interrupting them, Johnston asked how many guerrillas had taken part in the raid. One of the townsmen guessed maybe a hundred, but another supposed that there was a larger force of some four hundred guerrillas south of town. Emboldened on hearing the smaller number mentioned, and ignoring the larger number as improbable, Johnston informed the townsmen that he was going to pursue the guerrillas immediately and destroy them, whatever their number. The thought of the soldiers departing, however, made the leaders of the town uneasy.

"You ain't goin' to leave us, are you, major?" the mayor asked desperately. "The guerrillas might come back. We've got to have protection! Besides, it's folly to fight them; they're well-trained and desperate men."

Johnston finally relented: "I'll leave thirty-five men here—but no more. I'll need the rest. While the guerrillas may have me outnumbered, I will have the advantage of them in arms. With our Enfields, we will kill them from a distance."

"Listen, Johnston," one of the townsmen interrupted. "Do you know Anderson? He's a devil. You'd best stay here in Centralia until you get some reinforcements."

"We'll take care of Anderson," Johnston cut him off. "You look out for the townsmen; I'll take care of the fighting."

With that, Johnston ordered his men into a column of fours and followed the guerrillas' trail south of town on the Columbia Road. Just minutes later, his scouts reported a small troop of riders ahead, perhaps ten men, wearing Union uniforms. After they were sighted, the guerrilla band fled to the southeast. Johnston was sure that they were Anderson's men and ordered his troops to a trot. He wanted to hit Anderson quickly, before he was adequately warned and prepared. From the attic window of his home, Dr. A. F. Sneed watched Johnston's force move south of town. He also saw the small troop of blue-clad guerrillas fleeing in the distance.

Ten minutes later, Dave Poole and his squad of guerrilla decoys rode into Anderson's camp two miles southeast of Centralia. They had been the scouts seen by Johnston. Anderson was ecstatic over Poole's report.

"So, they want a fight," he said. "We'll give 'em what they want. How many of 'em are there?"

"Looks like maybe a hundred or so," Poole answered.

"Good!" Anderson replied. "One of you ride over to Todd and the other chiefs and have 'em get over here. Poole, go back to the Feds and lure them here. We'll be waitin' for 'em."

George and Tom Todd, John Thrailkill, and Si Gordon, the guerrilla chieftains, were dismounted nearby with their men. They had missed out on the Centralia raid and were champing at their bits. With these newcomers, the guerrillas had a combined strength of over three hundred men. A few short minutes later, Anderson arrived to consult with the chiefs about how they would attack the Federals once they arrived.

In Anderson's camp, Frank James, always reflective but drunk from his visit to Centralia, turned to his brother Jesse: "What do you think, Jess. Are you ready to fight? We been pussyfootin' around so far, I grant you. But you're goin' to see some real fightin' today. If the Feds think this is goin' to be a dance, they've got some new steps to learn."

"I've been waitin' a long time for this," Jesse replied soberly. "Whoever is leadin' 'em, I want that man." A small stain of fresh blood oozed from a chest wound Jesse had received on the Ray-Carroll County line on August 12. The flow of adrenaline was prodding him into the proper fighting mettle.

"Hah! What makes you think you'll get close enough to try?" Frank chided his brother. Jesse remained silent.

While they waited, Frank carefully polished and oiled his revolvers, placing caps on the cylinders, and whirling them to try them. He was a bit nervous, but no more so than usual during the preparation for a fight. Of course, there'd be more Yankees than usual today, but that would make it interesting, he thought. The Federals were crazy to tangle with the guerrillas. Maybe they didn't realize how many of them there were. They likely thought they were just after Anderson and his band, but they were taking on the better part of the rebel force.

Frank expected the Feds to fight dismounted; he thought that was stupid, but it's what they usually did. What egotistical know-it-alls! Their leaders liked to call themselves "professional soldiers" and boast of their prowess. They ought to save that palaver for their wives and girlfriends; they'd likely lap it up. Well, he'd better saddle up and stop fighting with his mouth like some worthless Yankee.

Only two miles away, Johnston's column rode toward the guerrilla encampment at a trot. A small band of guerrillas led by Dave Poole was in front of him, fleeing across the open prairie, luring him on, and occasionally firing a random shot at Johnston's scouts. Johnston was positive they were Anderson's men and would lead him to the prize. He had no fear of Anderson. The guerrillas were just callow farm boys, he thought, without formal military training; he was a professional officer. Oh, he'd heard about Baxter Springs and Lawrence, but the guerrillas had just been lucky and caught the Yanks off guard in those surprise attacks. Besides, the guerrillas were no longer fighting under Quantrill, who was reputedly their most skilled commander. The guerrilla leaders had had a falling out among themselves recently, Johnston had been told, and Quantrill was off sulking somewhere. Of course, Johnston's own men were pretty inexperienced, he had to agree, but he'd been working with them. In his view, all ordinary soldiers were interchangeable, except for the officers. He was confident his men would do their duty. His men and their weapons would give these guerrillas the shock of their lives. But were his men sufficiently brave for this encounter? He was confident that they were. While they were untested, he believed they would weather this baptismal.

A mile ahead, Johnston's scouts reached the top of a rise and halted. Johnston noticed them stop and wondered why. From his position at the front of the main force, he motioned the scouts back, and a rider galloped toward him.

"Sir, they're ahead, at the bottom of a large prairie. Looks like a bunch of 'em."

"Bunch? What does that mean?" demanded Johnston.

"Maybe a hundred, sir," the soldier answered.

"Okay, sergeant, go to the rear and fall in with your unit." Johnston sent for his lieutenants and they soon rode up.

"Let's look the situation over," he said to them. "We'll be forming into a line of battle."

When the officers reached a vantage point, Johnston saw the guerrillas forming into battle formation, just to the east, at the far end of a prairie at the edge of a wood. In a fringe of woods nearby, to his left and right, Johnston saw a few guerrillas milling around on horseback. Johnston was pleased; the guerrilla force was not as large as he had expected.

He turned to his lieutenants: "Get back to your units and have them dismount and form into two ranks. Every fourth man will hold the horses in the rear. Advance on my signal, and be quick. We don't want them attacking us in disarray."

Johnston's men quickly fell into formation and spread out in two long ranks. Johnston signaled them to advance east, down the open plain. After they had marched several hundred feet, he ordered the men to halt. Meanwhile, 28 of Johnston's men had been left on the backside of the formation to hold the horses. Lacking the 35 men he had left in Centralia, that meant that Johnston had only 80 of his 147 men to do the actual fighting. The officer pointed his binoculars down the hill again and was startled. He could see scores of horsemen coming out of the woods along draws on both sides of the prairie in front of him. There were more guerrilla fighters than he had thought. Unknown to Johnston, the force on his right flank was led by John Thrailkill and Thomas Todd, the one on his left by George Todd and Si Gordon. The main force at the bottom of the hill was commanded by "Bloody Bill" Anderson. The guerrilla force stretched across the bottom of the prairie and a throng of men on horseback now massed on both sides of the valley. It was clear that Johnston faced a superior force, but he had no recourse but to fight. If he retreated now, the guerrillas would chase his men down like deer.

He must fight and win; he knew that. He ordered his men to advance in two ranks, one behind the other. After they had moved one hundred yards, he screamed to them to form into line of battle. The two ranks closed up, with the first line taking aim while those in the second rank placed their muskets over the shoulders of the men in front to steady their own weapons. The soldiers were ready to fire a volley at Johnston's order. In the meantime, the guerrillas had dismounted from their horses.

Johnston turned to the lieutenant standing next to him. "Will they fight on foot? What does this mean?" But then he noticed that the guerrillas had only dismounted to tighten their saddle cinches and check their weapons. The guerrillas stuffed their blue Union shirts—the need for disguise was now over—into their packs and remounted their horses.

Jesse James positioned himself at the center of the rebel line. He hoped that the Union commander was directly across from him on the other end of the field, at the center of his force. Noticing that his brother Frank was several horsemen away, Jesse squinted toward the top of the hill, searching for his target.

Frank was excited but he was an old hand at this sort of thing. He had fought at Wilson's Creek with the regular Confederate army in a set-piece battle. But this was the way he liked to fight, with his friends, on horseback, with pistols in both hands. He gave the soldiers at the other end of the field little chance. He'd seen infantry fight in situations like this. At Baxter Springs, he thought, they were a sorry lot.

John Koger, two horsemen down from Frank, looked down the line toward the elder James brother and cried, "Frank! The fools are goin' to fight us on foot, just like drunken doughboys, God help 'em."

Finally, Johnston became impatient and called across the valley to the guerrillas: "We are ready! Come on!"

Anderson, atop his black mount and garbed in black, rode deliberately to a position in front of the left flank of the main force of guerrillas. He raised his black hat in a wide, swinging circle over his head, and hundreds of pistols cocked. Then Anderson raised his hat over his head three times, its red plume swirling in the breeze, lowering it each time slowly, a signal for the guerrillas to advance. Anderson began walking his horse slowly in the direction of the Federals. The entire force followed suit. Anderson, human scalps dangling visibly from his bridle, picked up the pace, and the guerrillas advanced up the hill, accelerating as they went.

Then Anderson cried, "Charge!" and the guerrillas plunged their spurs into the flanks of their mounts and rode forward at a breakneck gallop. "Left flank," Anderson screamed. "Break their line and go for their horses. I want the hides of those Yankees—*every one of 'em!*"

The horses accelerated into a dead run, and the guerrillas began yipping and shrieking their strange cadence, their voices carrying eerily across the plain in a discordant, rising roar. When the guerrillas got to within three hundred yards of the top of the gently sloping prairie, they could make out individual Yankees. Hugging the necks of their horses to present a more difficult target, the guerrillas rapidly rode to within firing range of the Federals.

From his position at the center of his men, Johnston screamed, "Fire!" A great volley erupted from the Federal line, and a cloud of smoke billowed forward. Minié balls ripped up the sod around the guerrillas, but most of the bullets whizzed harmlessly over their heads. Not all of them, however. Frank Shepherd, riding adjacent to Frank James, fell from his horse, his brains splattering on his friend's trousers. On the guerrilla's right, Jim Kinney, another friend, yelled, "I'm shot!" and slid awkwardly from his mount. Nevertheless, as he looked down the line, Frank saw surprisingly few other empty saddles. The soldiers had overshot them.

Now the Federal troops were frantic. They had fired their initial volley and it had failed to repulse the guerrillas. As the bluecoats stood amid clouds of smoke, they gaped at the advancing guerrillas, who were almost upon them. Many of the soldiers had too little time to reload their weapons and turned desperately to their bayonets. Others remained calm and bit into their powder bags, hurriedly pouring the silvery dust into their guns in hopes of driving another bullet into place in time to fire another volley. But most of the troops seemed paralyzed. As Frank James dashed toward them, he thought they looked hypnotized.

Then the guerrillas opened fire, and the roar filled the valley, seeming to reach the very sun. Unlike the Federals' single explosion, the guerrilla fire continued in a torrent of booming, unending, exploding pistol fire. Men in blue fell everywhere, and the Federal soldiers began panicking, then running in every direction.

In the midst of the chaos, Jesse James spotted a sprig of gold on the shoulder of one of the men still fighting in the ranks. Here was the officer he had been looking for. He had found his quarry, the force's commander in chief. Jesse rode toward the officer at a gallop, and when he approached to within a hundred feet of him, he began pouring a rapid fire. Jesse watched triumphantly as Johnston collapsed to the ground, the front of his blue uniform drenched in blood.

With the death of their commander, many of the Union soldiers raced for their horses only to discover that Anderson's men had driven them off. In fact, some of the men guarding the horses had been the first to panic and had ridden wildly from the scene, leaving the horses to wander off. A few of Anderson's men rode after these fleeing soldiers, following them closely and firing at them continuously, watching as they fell, one by one, until finally only one mortally injured man escaped the field.

Back on the battlefield, order had dissolved and mercy was nonexistent. One of the Union soldiers pleaded with a guerrilla to save his life and told him that he was a Mason. The guerrilla blew his brains out.

In Centralia, Dr. A. F. Sneed looked out the second story window of the Eldorado House hotel with his field glasses. He was watching a small cloud of dust approaching from the south. Finally he identified a single blue-clad soldier galloping toward the town, and the doctor ran into the street to meet him. The horseman raced by Sneed, however, screaming, "Get out of here! Get out of here! Everyone will be killed!"

For the Federals remaining on the battlefield, the soldier's warning was true. The guerrillas continued firing until every soldier had fallen. When the firing ceased, guerrilla chieftain Dave Poole began walking on the dead bodies, using them as an improvised boardwalk. Occasionally, he lowered his gun and dispatched a soldier who appeared to be breathing.

Thomas Todd, a preacher, objected: "Poole, cut that out; it's inhuman!"

"Ain't most of 'em dead?" Poole replied sheepishly. "And if they're dead, I can't hurt 'em, can I? "Besides, I can't count 'em good without steppin' on 'em," he added defensively.

Several of the drunken guerrillas pulled out their bowie knives and began scalping soldiers, roughly incising their foreheads and ripping away their scalps in bloody swatches. Anderson's reins were already decorated with the scalps of Union soldiers, and the men wanted to emulate their chief. Some of the guerrillas slit the throats of the dead Yankees and severed their heads from their bodies. Then, in a macabre game, they leaned a few of the bodies up against nearby trees and purposely matched the bodies to the wrong heads. The guerrillas had waited a long time to revenge themselves on the Yankees, and no one was going to stop them. Their hands and clothes were covered with blood, and even in their drunken state, they felt guilty about what they were doing. But what they were doing seemed, at the same time, strangely necessary. The war had consumed them and turned them into wild men.

Polk Helms, a guerrilla, stood and looked upon the scene of carnage. He was repulsed. What had they become? Now they were like their Yankee tormentors. Usually, he was unbothered by the sight of blood, but this was different. Nauseated, he walked into the nearby woods and vomited.

Helms was tired of the war, but he couldn't go home; he had no home. When the Federals instituted Orders No. 11 in 1863, expelling Missourians from their homes along the state's border with Kansas, they had shot his father, driven his family off their land, burned their house, and seized their cattle and livestock. He didn't know where the rest of his family was. He was rootless, lost, without a moral compass. To him, there was no God anymore, no country, no right or wrong—nothing—just kill or be killed. He was no longer even positive he was fighting on the right side. He didn't know if there was a right side. It all seemed like a ghastly nightmare.

October 26, 1864

In a small farmhouse in Clay County, forty miles northwest of Kansas City, Bill Anderson preened before a mirror. He combed his long curly locks and washed his hands and handsome face in a basin filled with cold well water. He looked intently at his image and bowed.

"Good morning, Captain Anderson," he said aloud.

"How's it goin'?" the face in the mirror replied sardonically.

"Right well, thank you," he chimed back.

Ten miles away, Indian scout and tracker Maj. Samuel P. Cox forged his way across Ray County with a 150-man mounted infantry battalion. Cox had received word of Anderson's location from a Federal spy in the area, and his unit had been selected to attack Anderson's guerrillas and destroy them.

Ten minutes later, as his force neared Anderson's camp, Cox sent out a screen of cavalry to his front to make contact with the guerrillas. As this squad of scouts trotted through Albany, Missouri, they met Anderson's pickets and drove them back. Cox dismounted his main force and ordered them into a fighting formation. Meanwhile, he sent word to his scouts to move forward again, this time to flush out the main guerrilla force and decoy them back to his own position along the Missouri River, if they could. He was using Anderson's own Indian tactics against him.

When Anderson heard of the Union contact with his scouts, he immediately set out with his entire force, galloping down a narrow roadway toward the Federal pickets. Anderson had taken the bait, and he had failed to send his scouts out ahead of him to learn the size of the enemy force. As Anderson's men approached, the Federal scouts gave way and retreated rapidly toward Cox's ambush position. Anderson, riding forty yards in front of his men, galloped after the Federals, his long hair streaming behind him. Upon seeing the Federal infantry in line of battle, Anderson, with another guerrilla at his side, raced toward the blue-clad troopers without hesitation, in a moment of madness.

"After 'em!" Anderson screamed, galloping toward the long blue line, ignoring its danger. Then a volley rang out, and scores of bullets whizzed by him.

Clelland Miller, fourteen years old but large for his age, rode in the troop immediately behind Anderson. He had been with the guerrillas for only three days. When most of Anderson's men fell back in response to the deadly Federal volley, Clell also retreated. He'd never heard such firing in his life, and the bullets whistling around his head frightened him. Slugs struck the dirt road around him, sending up bursts of dust. Some of the guerrillas fell to the ground wounded or dead. For the first time in his life, Clell Miller was terrified.

Anderson, enraged at the ambush, refused to turn back and rode directly through the Federals, firing to his left and right as he passed through the line. As he exited the rear of the Federal formation, some of the troops who had held their fire and were armed with revolvers directed their blasts at him, and two bullets ripped through the back of his head. Anderson threw up his arms involuntarily and plummeted backward off his saddle onto the ground dead. Anderson's men rallied and attempted to retrieve his body, but they were forced back by the horrendous fire. Nonetheless, one of Anderson's men, John Pringle, a huge redheaded guerrilla, galloped up to Anderson, dismounted, and flung a lariat around his waist. Pringle hoped to pull his leader from the battlefield but was cut down by a dozen musket rounds and collapsed in a pool of blood.

After the battle, the soldiers searched Anderson's body and equipment and found six revolvers, several military orders from Confederate general Sterling Price, six hundred dollars in gold and greenbacks, and a small Confederate flag. They also discovered a tintype image of his wife, a lock of her hair, and several letters from her to Anderson.

Anderson's body was loaded onto a wagon and taken to Richmond, Missouri, where he was placed on display in front of the courthouse as a trophy of war. Later, Anderson was decapitated and his head placed atop a telegraph pole, a grisly warning to the guerrillas in the area. After the Union soldiers finished with his body, he was buried in the local cemetery in an unmarked grave.

In Richmond, captured guerrillas, one of them the young Clell Miller, were being questioned before being executed. "Say, soldier," one of the Union officers asked Clell, "how old are you? You're big, ain't you, but you got no beard. You sure you ain't just a big boy?"

Clell Miller rose to his full height of six foot one and answered defiantly: "You don't have to be an old geezer like you to fight."

"So how old are you?" the soldier continued.

"I'm fourteen years old," Clell answered defiantly.

"Why, you pup! We don't kill babies. But we *are* goin' to put your big carcass in jail, so don't think you're gettin' away with anything. I hope you rot there."

"By the way, who's your pappy?" the soldier added.

"None of your business," Clell replied.

"You're Moses' boy, ain't you? Well, he's a no-account, just like you."

That evening, the guerrillas who had escaped the ambush rested in camp. They quietly mourned Anderson while fighting off feelings of guilt because they had not been able to help him. Few of them had been brave enough to ride into the Federal onslaught; it had seemed like suicide to them. With their leader lost, most of the men felt the war was over for them, and their hearts were empty.

4

December 15, 1864

> The blue skies are our cover
> The green sward our bed
> We'll drink from the river
> And root for our bread . . .

Thirty-five soldiers in blue rode singing down the winding road to Tuscumbia, a small hamlet in Miller County in central Missouri. The town, built on a narrow ribbon of flood plain, was situated along the Osage River and held a small garrison of Union troops. As the horsemen approached the village, they proceeded down a steep incline bordered by oak, hickory, and ash trees. The lane led to the main street and opened onto a vista of broad, surging river beyond.

When the horsemen reached the bottom of the hill, an armed picket charged into the middle of the road.

"Who goes there?"

The troop halted and its commander replied loudly: "Capt. James Clarke, Fourth Missouri Cavalry."

"Advance to be recognized!" the guard answered.

Clarke, silver bars shining on his shoulders, rode up to the young private and leaned down.

"It's all right, private. We're headed for Nashville to link up later with Sherman. I want to talk to your commander."

"Yes, sir," the private replied crisply. "Foller me, sir. He's at yon hotel." The troop of blue-clad men followed the young guard down the dusty main street.

"Here's headquarters, sir," the private said as they reached the building where the officers were billeted. "I'll tell Major Benson you're here."

The captain and two of his men dismounted, hitched their horses, and followed the private into the hotel lobby. A Federal officer seated in a chair near the door looked up curiously and then returned to reading his newspaper. Two lieutenants seated nearby were hotly engaged in a game of cards. The private soon returned and motioned the visiting captain and his two fellows to follow him.

"Major Benson's upstairs," the private said.

When the men reached the top of the stairs, they walked through a large doorway and confronted a middle-aged officer ensconced behind an impressive desk.

Walking up to the desk, his spurs jangling, the captain saluted the older officer crisply and announced himself.

"Sir, Capt. James Clarke, Fourth Missouri Cavalry."

"Maj. Tom Benson," the major replied. "Pleased to meet you."

The older officer looked Clarke over carefully. He was impressed. The younger man was tall and good looking with a dashing imperial mustache, light blue eyes, and blondish hair. The only thing unusual about him was his eyes, which had a somewhat oriental look to them. But all in all, he was quite a fine-looking chap, the major thought.

"Good to see you," Benson continued. "We have few visitors in this godforsaken place. What brings you to Tuscumbia?"

"Sir, we are headed south to support Sherman. We've a long way to go and need your help."

"Of course," said Benson. "How may I help you?"

"Sir, if you don't mind, before we begin . . . ," Clarke started, "may I smoke? We've come a long way, and I sure could use a

cigar right now. I've a couple fine 'long nines' here in my coat."
With that, the captain drew two cigars from his coat pocket and
extended one to the major.
"Fine idea! Capital!" Benson exclaimed and drew a match from
his desk drawer, struck it, and extended it to the captain. The
captain bent over, lit his cigar, and drew heavily on it. Then Benson
held the match under the tip of his own cigar, and both men sucked
luxuriously, blowing rich, aromatic smoke into the air.
    "Well, sir, to begin with," said the captain, finally continuing,
"our intention is to ride to Memphis. We're interested in learning
the best routes. We'd also like to know about the army camps
along the way; we have horses to forage. The grass is through
for the year, and we've had trouble findin' hay and oats."
    "This ain't exactly the best time to travel," replied Benson, "but
if you boys are bent on it, the best way is through Waynesville.
It's south of here a piece, near the Wire Road. There's plenty of
forage there. Then, if I were you, I'd pass through Salem and Van
Buren. When you get to Caruthersville, I'd head south till you
get to the ferry that crosses the Mississippi. It's a few miles north
of Memphis. The first army post you're likely to come across,
though, is Waynesville. After that, there's slim pickings."
    "Well, sir, you've been a great help," the captain replied. "To
show my gratitude, I have something else for you." Benson
looked up at the captain in anticipation. In a flash, William
Clarke Quantrill, commander of guerrillas in western Missouri,
drew his Colt revolver from his holster and pointed it directly
in Benson's face.
    "You're under arrest," Quantrill declared.
    "Well, I'll be cursed," uttered the startled Benson.
    Flanking Quantrill on his left and right were Frank James and
Babe Hudspeth. They had drawn their revolvers too, almost as
fast as Quantrill. Frank marveled at the way Charley had deceived
the Union officer. Charley—that's what the guerrillas called
Quantrill—was slick, a smooth talker. In fact, Frank thought,
Charley was the smartest man he'd ever known. And he was a

consummate liar and actor to boot, as Frank had just witnessed. The guerrillas had made him their leader even though he was from Canal Dover, Ohio, which was hardly a part of the South. Quantrill was also a cool man under fire and a crack shot. Frank smiled at the way he had elicited the reconnaissance information from Benson. He was sure it would get them to Memphis.

But Quantrill had come upon bad times. Anderson and Todd had relieved him of almost his entire command in 1864. They thought he was weak and wishy-washy, not tough enough or violent enough for their tastes. That might be true, but Frank had learned that he had topped them in cunning. Anderson and Todd had wanted to meet the Yankees head-on. They had done so and now both were dead, as well as a whole lot of the guerrillas who had fought with them. Frank liked the way Quantrill finessed the Yankees. Of course, that wasn't as exciting as Anderson's and Todd's charges. And the boys liked charges—like at Centralia and Baxter Springs. Three years ago, Frank had been one of Todd's boys. He liked the fearless way George had taken the battle to the Yankees, but he'd learned the hard way that Quantrill had been right all along. The guerrillas had to fight smart against the blue bellies or they'd all be killed.

The guerrillas now traveling with Quantrill had joined up with him on the Sni-A-Bar Creek and were following him to Kentucky. They intended to continue the war there. The war on the border was over. Frank understood that; so did the rest of the guerrillas. So many Feds infested Missouri now that if you stayed there, it was only a matter of time until they killed you. That was why he and Jesse had hooked up with Quantrill. They still had some fight left in them, but they weren't for suicide. Quantrill also had made it clear to them that if they were forced to surrender—and the war seemed lost at this point—it was safer to give up outside Missouri. If they gave up in Missouri, they were sure to be shot.

Quantrill held his pistol to Benson's back. "Major, muster your troops on the main street in front of the hotel. Tell them that you want to talk to them. Order them to report without their weapons. I'll be right behind you, and if you fluff it, I'll blow your head off."

With that, Quantrill, urging Benson into the lead and followed by James and Hudspeth, moved down the flight of stairs. At the bottom of the stairs, Benson called to his adjutant.

"Phillips, muster the men. Tell 'em to form here in front of the hotel. Tell 'em to leave their weapons behind. I have an important announcement for them."

Phillips immediately left for the camp at the end of the main street where the enlisted men were billeted. A few minutes later, the men were in formation. When the soldiers had found their positions, Benson walked to their front, his body stiff and erect. Quantrill and his men clustered along the town's boardwalk.

"Men," Benson began, "I regret to inform you that we are prisoners."

The men tittered. Some of them laughed out loud. It was a good joke, they thought, and continued to giggle. But when Benson maintained his sober demeanor, some of the men became apprehensive and began shuffling. A few cleared their throats. Quantrill and his men drew their revolvers, and the soldiers became deathly silent. For the next hour, Quantrill systematically paroled the entire company of men and ordered their muskets thrown into the Osage River.

December 20, 1864

One rocky hill after another. It seemed to Jesse James that the hills rolled endlessly south of Waynesville, spanning to the horizon. Snow beat on his back, and his horse puffed steaming clouds of vapor. The guerrilla column looked like a steam engine, with smoke issuing from men and animals. But the cold! Jesse thought. He could barely feel his hands. He kept wriggling his numb toes to keep up the circulation. He wondered how the horses stood the cold. He guessed their movement kept them warm. But Jesse was used to pain; he'd been in some kind of pain now for over two years. He'd come to almost expect it. At least his wounds had finally healed, and he didn't have to worry about them becoming infected with gangrene.

He wondered how he'd ever gotten into this war. And the shame of it was that they were losing. Maybe Quantrill and Frank hadn't accepted it, but he had. Why fight on? They'd been driven out of western Missouri. That was home; that's what he'd been fighting for all along. He'd heard some of the boys grousing about going to Tennessee and Kentucky. He agreed with them: it wasn't their country, but it might be their last resting place.

They didn't know those lands well enough, the trails and bridle paths and such. He felt they would be at a big disadvantage. Of course, there were plenty of Southern sympathizers there, but there were also plenty of Yankees and their spies. Babe Hudspeth and Oliver "Ol" Shepherd talked of separating from Quantrill once they got into Arkansas. They planned to head for Texas for the winter like the guerrillas had in past years, returning to Missouri in the spring if the war was still going on. Hudspeth and Shepherd weren't sold on fighting on Kentucky soil; neither was Jesse. As far as he was concerned, he'd fight in Missouri or nowhere.

Jesse knew the war had coarsened him, had made a wild animal of him. When he joined Quantrill, his speech had been untainted. Now he often cursed like a sailor. Once, he had hurt his hand while loading his revolver and had shouted, "By dingus!" instead of cussing. The boys laughed and began calling him "Dingus"; they had found humor in his innocent state. But he wasn't innocent anymore. He could shoot Yankees now like he'd shot rats in his father's corncrib. In fact, he'd learned to savor bringing down bluecoats, grown to love the excitement of the chase. Killing Yankees was like shooting deer or squirrels to him. It gave him a strange, intense exhilaration. When he killed a Yankee, he felt a dark energy soar in him, and he liked that feeling, even though part of him seemed to loathe it. He was like Bill Anderson, he guessed; he craved the opportunity to strike his enemies. When his anger rose against his enemies, he felt empowered, beyond any restraint on earth. When he felt that way, he didn't believe in good or bad anymore; it didn't exist for him.

Of course, he believed in God, but what did that have to do with fighting and killing? In this war, it was simply kill or be killed. The guerrillas had become gods in their own right, with the power of life and death over their opponents. And they intended to use that power, just as their enemies used it against them.

John Koger, Ol Shepherd, and Rufus and Babe Hudspeth separated from Quantrill at Pocahontas, Arkansas, and headed for Texas for the winter. Jesse accompanied them. Quantrill headed south and east until he arrived at Devil's Elbow, on the Mississippi River. There he commandeered a yawl and crossed the river north of Memphis. With the addition of twenty-one men who had joined him along the way, Quantrill now had forty-six men. With a force that size, he thought, they ought to be able to do the Yankees some mischief.

Once they arrived in Kentucky, Quantrill's men quickly acquired new horses to replace their exhausted ones. While raiding for horses near Houstonville, guerrilla Allen Parmer was accosted by a Kentucky militiamen while exiting a barn with the soldier's prize mare. The soldier rushed up to Parmer and grabbed the horse by its halter.

"If this horse leaves here, it will be over my dead body!" the militiaman screamed.

"That's easy," Parmer shouted in reply, shooting the man in the head. Parmer then galloped down the road to join the rest of the guerrillas.

About this time, Quantrill's own horse, Charley, bolted while being shoed at a local blacksmith. The animal severed a tendon and had to be shot. This demoralized Quantrill; he loved the horse and its death caused him to become morose and fatalistic.

Compounding this grief, Jim Little, Quantrill's best friend, had been badly wounded and died of his injuries. Quantrill felt like he was losing his balance. He had been a cornerstone for his men, but the pain of his wounds, the deprivation, and the years of being pursued like a wild animal had stolen some of his edge, his spirit, and his élan. Like Jim Little, in some ways, his horse, who had saved his life a dozen times, had been a friend, a fellow creature he could count on. Now, he felt like his legs had been cut out from under him.

He knew that the war was winding down, and the surrender or capture of his force had become inevitable. He told one of his men: "My career is run!" Already, the newspapers had made him the symbol of the guerrillas' violence, and he was convinced that he would become a scapegoat when captured. He was likely to be hanged, even if his fellow guerrillas survived. As a Confederate commander, he willingly accepted that fate.

Despite their leader's dwindling spirits, the guerrillas found Tennessee and Kentucky a fertile ground for warfare, with Southern sympathizers everywhere to provide them with aid and comfort. In the beginning, Quantrill was able to forage his horses at Union camps, pretending to be a Union officer. But as the guerrillas' operations intensified, the Union commanders became more cautious and wily and pursued them energetically whenever they were discovered. Within weeks, the situation became even more chaotic than it had been in Missouri.

At the end of January, the guerrillas plundered Danville, Kentucky, pillaging the local boot store, robbing the citizens, and destroying the telegraph office. Afterwards, they fled toward Harrodsburg and stopped for the night. Unknown to them, J. H. Bridgewater of the Kentucky militia was leading a rapid pursuit. He surrounded a house occupied by twelve of them, and his force killed John Barker, Henry Noland, Foss Ney, and Chad Renick. Jim Younger, Andy McGuire, Bill Gaugh, Tom Evans,

Vess Akers, and others were captured. This was a disaster for Quantrill; overnight a third of his force had been captured and was imprisoned in a Lexington jail.

February 5, 1865

Cole Younger's brother Jim Younger, a quiet young man of gentlemanly appearance and manners, had been stirring in his bed all night, unable to sleep. Rolling in a hard bunk in a Kentucky jail was not his idea of rich living. He guessed the guards would rouse them soon for breakfast, but he couldn't get excited about it. They were being fed slop unfit for hogs. What rankled him most was being a prisoner of the Yankees and being treated like a thief rather than a soldier. The Yankees were threatening to hang the guerrillas. He had expected that treatment in Missouri but not in Kentucky. Was the whole world mad?

Jim was glad the guerrillas were kept in a common area of the prison so that they could talk to each other. Even though they had been in prison only three days, they had already hatched a plan to escape. It couldn't happen soon enough for him. For the last two days, their jailers had marched them into a courtyard and lined them up like they were to be shot. Jim didn't know whether they were serious about killing them or not, but he was apprehensive about their safety. Jim turned in his bed and noticed that Vess Akers was awake in the next bunk.

"What's the matter, Vess, couldn't you sleep either?" Jim asked.

"No," Vess replied. "Who could sleep in this hellhole, especially when you're thinkin' you might get hung or shot any time."

"Well, cheer up. Dyin' can't be much worse than what we've been through lately." Then the two men heard the jangling of keys at the door.

"All right, men. Fall out," yelled a guard. "We want to look at your pretty faces."

The guerrillas shuffled out the cell doors and into a large courtyard used by the prison warden to exercise the prisoners. When they got outside, they noticed a long rank of soldiers lined up on the far side of the compound, muskets at the ready. It looked ominous to Jim.

"All right, Rebs, get into a rank, double quick! Up against that north wall, all of you!" one of the guards ordered. After the guerrillas formed into a line facing the assembled soldiers, a lieutenant shouted, "Ready!" and the soldiers placed their muskets against their shoulders, raising them into firing positions.

"Aim!" the lieutenant proceeded.

Then the lieutenant faltered. He seemed confused. Jim had seen enough. "Go ahead, you rascals," he screamed. "Shoot us! Shoot us all!" The other prisoners also began taunting the soldiers.

"Hooray for Jeff Davis and Bobbie Lee!" whooped Andy McGuire, adding his touch to the affair.

"Gutless wonders, you stinkin blue bellies!" screeched Chad Renick. "You ain't got the nerve to shoot us."

"You think we're afraid of you," bellowed Kit Chiles. "Throw down your guns and find out!"

The guerrillas continued to jeer at the soldiers for several minutes while the Yankee soldiers appeared bewildered. Their officer remained unsure what to do. The guerrillas were so much like the rest of them—even spoke like ordinary hill folk—that they didn't feel right shooting them. What is more, the Yankee soldiers sort of admired their pluck. They were unarmed; shooting them seemed cowardly, like murder.

Finally, the lieutenant regained his composure, took on a firm demeanor, and ordered the prisoners back to their cells. Later, he talked over the problem with his commander at Louisville. They decided to march the guerrillas there. Several weeks later, with the help of Southern collaborators, Jim Younger and most of the other guerrillas escaped.

May 1865

Maj. Gen. John Palmer, the Union commander in Kentucky, finally became so exasperated by Quantrill's raiding that he commissioned a young Kentucky guerrilla and Southern turncoat, Edwin Terrill, to pursue Quantrill and his men. He was on their trail when, on the morning of May 10, Quantrill and his guerrillas put up at the barn of James Wakefield, a Confederate collaborator near Taylorsville. They rested there while waiting out a drizzling rain. Unknown to the guerrillas, spies had informed Terrill about their whereabouts.

In the barn, some of the guerrillas amused themselves by tossing corncobs at each other. Quantrill and one of his lieutenants climbed up into the hayloft to sleep.

"Here, catch this on your fat noggin," Dick Glasscock teased and tossed a red cob at the head of Nat Tigue. His target then grabbed several cobs and sent them spiraling wildly back at Glasscock.

"How do you like that? Just like cannister, huh?" Tigue chided him. Their game was interrupted when Clark Hockensmith ran into the barn out of breath.

"Bluecoats!" he screamed. "We got to get out of here!"

The guerrillas dropped their fun and rushed to mount their horses. Quantrill tumbled out of the hayloft and ran for his horse. In the excitement and noise, his new mount became unmanageable and ran excitedly in circles around the inside of the barn, refusing to be mounted. Finally the horse streaked out the barn door and into the adjoining woods. Quantrill was in a fix.

"Wait up, men!" he called. "I'm unmounted!"

Clark Hockensmith and Dick Glasscock, who had just saddled up and were riding off, reined in their horses and waited for their leader amid the violent gunfire. Quantrill raced to Glasscock's mount. As he reached up to mount behind his fellow guerrilla, the horse was struck by a bullet. Wild with fright, the animal pulled away from Quantrill. The man then rushed over to Hockensmith's steed and attempted to pull himself up into the saddle. At that instant, a bullet tore into Quantrill's spine, and he plunged headlong into the mud. As he fell, another bullet tore off his trigger finger. Quantrill was paralyzed. Seconds later, Glasscock and Hockensmith fell dead in a torrent of gunfire.

After pursuing and killing as many of the guerrillas as they could, Terrill's men returned to where Quantrill lay. One of them took the guerrilla chief's revolvers. Another grabbed Quantrill's boots and pulled them off. Paralyzed below the waist, Quantrill lay in the driving rain, his face partly mired in manure. He was covered with blood. Finally, Terrill approached Quantrill, noticed that he was still alive, and rolled him over onto his back.

"Say, partner, who might you be?" he asked.

Quantrill answered weakly, "Captain Clarke of the Fourth Missouri."

"Yeah, sure you are," Terrill replied skeptically.

Terrill rolled Quantrill up in a blanket and had him carried to the nearby Wakefield house. Their load delivered, the men began ransacking. James Wakefield followed after the soldiers in an attempt to stop them as they lay waste to his home.

"Stop that! What do you think you're doin'?" he shouted at one of them. Wakefield realized that something must be done about the pillaging or they would destroy his house and steal everything in it. He motioned to Terrill, and the Union guerrilla chief walked over to him.

"Here," Wakefield said, handing Terrill a handful of gold eagles. "I've got more where that came from and some good whiskey. How about you and I have a drink? I'd like you to call off your men," Terrill agreed and ordered his men out of the house.

That night, several of the guerrillas, including Frank James, returned to Wakefield's home to learn about Quantrill's condition. The local doctor told Frank that Quantrill was dying.

Snakes filled the boat, white snakes, opaque and slimy. Quantrill lay helplessly in the stern while the snakes slipped in and out of the craft, slithering across his arms and legs. Some of the snakes were six feet long, and the river heaved with the masses of them rippling from shore to shore. As the boat carried him downstream, Quantrill struggled to his feet and grappled with the snakes, throwing a number of them overboard. But more of them slipped into the boat and wrapped themselves around his body, their long tongues tasting his flesh and their fangs bared to delivered their horrid stings.

Then Quantrill jerked and he opened his eyes. A nun at the prison hospital in Louisville, Kentucky, looked down on him and wiped the sweat from his brow.

"Where am I?" he managed.

"Brother, you are in the military hospital at Louisville, Kentucky. One of your men is here to talk with you. Do you want to see him?"

Quantrill nodded weakly.

Frank James heard Quantrill's voice through the open door leading to his room, but his voice was so faint that he had made out little of what was said. Frank knew that this would be his last chance to talk to Quantrill. Charley's life was finished. The nun had told him that Quantrill had received the last rites only a few minutes earlier and was experiencing his last minutes on earth. Apparently he had made himself one of the Pope's boys. But anything that made Quantrill's last moments bearable was acceptable to Frank.

Frank himself had given up religion since the war began. He couldn't imagine a God that would tolerate the injustices he had seen, the war and all its violence. The world was filled with men and their awful venality, but that was all there was to it. There was no great overseer; men were alone in the universe with all their individual passions and greed. Men clashed, exerted their power over other men, and killed others for selfish advantage. And the powerful would always prevail, whether they were wrong or right. That was what was happening in this war, Frank thought, and it must have been true since the world began. He was a farm boy and he saw animals kill and be killed, live and die. Men were no different, except in one way, he reasoned: men understood the enormity of their crimes.

Frank walked slowly into Quantrill's room and approached his bed.

"Charley, can you hear me?" Frank said gently. Quantrill nodded.

"Charley, this is Frank James—one of the boys." He leaned closer to Quantrill.

"The prison folks don't know I'm a guerrilla. I managed to get in. I just want you to know that we're all pullin' for you, prayin' for you. Don't worry. We'll get you out of this."

Frank didn't believe any of this nonsense, of course. He just wanted to relieve Quantrill in any way he could, to soften death's blow as life ebbed away. Frank had seldom cried in his life, but tears welled in his eyes and ran down his cheeks as he saw his brave leader dying. He had been a great commander. Frank had marveled at his mind and spirit. But it was all lost now, taken away by a single bullet. To Frank and the other guerrillas, Quantrill had been a great patriot to the South.

Frank guessed the war was lost now, and the North had the field to itself. They would paint the losers in the darkest pitch, and there was nothing Frank or anyone else could do about it. The newspapers had already pictured Quantrill and the guerrillas as the worst sort of demons after their raid on Lawrence, but Frank knew that the abolitionists in Lawrence had gotten exactly what they deserved. He knew that histories would gloss over the Northern atrocities in Missouri and in the Deep South as well. That was life; the victors got the spoils, in this case, his beloved South, and they'd paint the war to their liking, blackening the names of great men and their suffering. Well, there was nothing Frank could do about it. He placed his hand on top of Quantrill's.

"Charley, we'll always remember what you did for us." With that said, Frank turned and walked dejectedly out of the room.

Quantrill heard Frank, but he was unable to respond. He was

slipping away. He was in the boat again, propped up against the stern, looking down a now-calm river. The boat faced into the sun, and he moved slowly downstream, drawn inexorably toward the warm rays. Then, the sun, the river—everything— suddenly melted into one, bright, all-suffusing light and Quantrill was dead.

5

June 4, 1865

Eight guerrillas trotted down the road to Lexington, Missouri. The war was over. One of the guerrillas carried a tattered white flag suspended by a hickory stick and fluttering lamely in the breeze. Jesse James, riding with the main pack, was disconsolate. He never thought the war would end like this, in dismal defeat. It was embarrassing, humiliating even, and he wasn't sure how he would make the transition back to normal life. The guerrillas had made so many enemies during the war. Would people forgive and forget? He doubted it.

The small troop rode over a hill and into a large tract of corn stubble. In the distance, they saw a Union patrol and reined in their horses. Ordinarily, such a sight would have excited them to attack, but the war was over. Instead, this meeting presented them with a good opportunity to surrender. The guerrillas nodded to their lead man, and he waved his white flag back and forth in long, sweeping motions. The soldiers apparently saw the signal, for they changed their path and rode in the direction of the partisans. When the soldiers approached to within several hundred yards of Jesse and the others, they halted and dismounted. Jesse and the others expected a parley and rode toward them.

As he rode toward the soldiers, Jesse's eyes twitched

nervously. He scanned the blue ranks instinctively. Something didn't seem right. As the men drew closer, he saw that the soldiers were forming into a line of battle.

"Let's get outa here! They're attackin'!" screamed Ki Harrison, who rode just behind Jesse and noticed the same threat.

The guerrillas turned their horses and spurred them to a gallop. A volley rang out and Jesse's body rocked from the shock of a bullet. He tumbled headfirst onto the ground and somersaulted onto his back. He was seriously wounded, and he choked for breath. Looking down at his chest, he saw dark blood oozing from his shirt, and he coughed up a red froth. Some of the soldiers, now remounted, raced toward Jesse. The guerrilla's eyes searched for cover. The woods were less than thirty yards away, so he staggered to his feet and stumbled toward them. He was stunned and weak, but he felt surprisingly little pain. Two horsemen galloped toward him, and Jesse drew his revolvers and fired at them. One of the cavalrymen fell from his horse, but his leg caught and he dangled from a stirrup. The soldier's horse raced across the stubble, dragging the soldier with it. The second soldier, fifty yards behind the first, fired at Jesse, and a bullet whistled over the guerrilla's head. Jesse fired at the second trooper, and the knees of the soldier's horse buckled, throwing its rider onto the ground where he remained motionless.

Jesse clawed his way into the brush, stumbling through the tangle of woods as far as his strength would carry him. As he scrambled through the undergrowth, he pressed his hand tightly over his chest to staunch the bleeding. The blood, nonetheless, flowed in dark rivulets through his fingers. He thought he was a goner, but he was determined to fight for his life. Huddling in the bush, he could hear firing in the distance. He listened for approaching pursuers, but all he could hear were the birds twittering and singing, oblivious to the shooting and killing. He felt weak, like his life's energy was escaping him. He became sick and retched, then he fell on his face unconscious.

Jesse didn't know how long he had been unconscious. He guessed a long time, for the sun was down and the birds were quiet. He felt his head, and it was steaming hot. He raised himself to his feet but collapsed. They had hit him good all right, flush in the chest and through his lung, he figured. He thought he was going to die.

He had only the roughest idea of where he was and no idea where help might be. And it was getting dark. His fever raged, and he felt like he was burning up. He thought he heard a stream bubbling so he dragged himself in the direction of the sound. In the dim light, he reached for the branches of small trees and bushes, pulling himself forward, crawling and twisting toward the sound of the water. Now the faint noise seemed closer. He turned around and noticed that he was leaving a trail of blood behind him. Ahead of him, a small stream came into view. It looked several inches deep. He made his way toward it and rolled over into the water with a splash. He let the stream circulate around his body and again he lost consciousness.

When Jesse woke up, he thought it was morning, and he winced at the pain. He attempted to rise to his knees but fell backwards. He had to get out of the water. If he stayed where he was, he would die like an animal. Slowly and painfully, he slid onto his stomach and lifted himself up onto the bank of the stream. He pulled himself in the direction of the light that issued into the woods. Each movement was excruciating. Finally, fifteen minutes later, he reached the edge of the woods and dragged himself onto the field of corn stubble. He crawled across the rough ground, wincing continuously from the pain, until his strength failed him. Then he collapsed into sleep.

It seemed to Jesse that he had died. Strange dreams filled with outrageous events floated through his head. In one dream, he was back on the old farm attempting to plow, but his horse refused to move. When he slapped it on its flanks with the flat of his hand, the horse only turned and looked at him. Other dreams were about fighting, frantic shooting, and chaos. Then out of this gray, twisted world, he felt someone tugging at his shirt.

"Hey, youngster. What's the matter?"

Jesse opened his eyes slowly and focused them on an elderly farmer who leaned over him.

"Who are you, brother?" the man asked.

"Mister," he said slowly. "I'm . . . " Jesse had to think hard. Who was he? He couldn't remember who he was. He strained to recall his name.

He finally remembered. "I'm . . . Jesse James of Clay County," he finally blurted out.

"How'd you get here, boy?" the old man asked him.

"Soldiers shot me," he answered weakly.

"Well, my boy, how can I help you?" the farmer asked.

"My father's Dr. Samuel," Jesse replied. "If you, uh, well, could get me back to my friends, I'd be obliged."

The farmer, a Southern sympathizer, asked no further questions and went for a wagon. He carried Jesse back to his nearby homestead.

July 9, 1865

A horse-drawn wagon had carried Jesse across rough, dusty roads to the small town of Rulo, Nebraska. That's where Jesse had discovered the Samuels now were living. The trip had taken several days, and the wagon continuously jostled and shook him, causing him extreme pain and making his wound bleed. He had gritted his teeth with each jolt of the wagon and prayed to God to save his life.

Once at the Samuels' home in Rulo, Jesse was placed on a feather bed. That helped ease some of his pain. But it embarrassed him to have his mother wait on him. She was wonderful and never complained; in fact, she seemed energized by her ministrations. Nevertheless, Jesse felt like a child, and his condition galled him. He could hardly raise himself in bed, he was unable to gain his feet, and every time he tried, he failed. He even had to be helped onto and off a chamber pot. He was an invalid in every sense of the word. He had been wounded in 1864 and made a miraculous recovery. This time, it was different. He thought he might never get well. One day, he asked his mother for a mirror, and when he saw himself, he was astonished; he looked like a walking corpse. His cheeks were pallid, his eyes sunken and lifeless. He was forever coughing up blood, and his life seemed futile to him. He seriously considered shooting himself and ending it all.

The idea of dying in Nebraska, though, was especially galling to him. If he had to die, he wanted it to be in Missouri, his homeland, where he had experienced most of his short life. From the time he arrived in Rulo, Jesse campaigned for his mother to return him to Missouri. Although in early 1865, the Samuels had been banished by the army from their old home in Clay County, Jesse had relatives in Missouri. Some of them might take care of him when he got better and could be moved. Missouri became a sort of sanctuary in his mind, something to focus his attention on, and he thought ceaselessly about returning there. If he were there, things would be all right.

September 3, 1865

Jesse had been at the Mimms' home north of Kansas City for all of three days. The move south by boat had been tolerable, but the wagon trip to the Mimms' place had set his teeth to grinding again. He had hoped that it would be better here than in Nebraska, and it was. Uncle John Mimms, his mother's brother, and the family had made him feel at home. He was kin, and they made that clear to him. To the Jameses, kinship was everything. To the Mimms, he was more than kin; he was a hero because of his war experiences. But Jesse didn't feel like he was anything but a bother. He was largely helpless. He'd gotten so he could get out of bed with difficulty, but when he did, it was painful and it winded him. At least he finally could take care of his bodily functions without embarrassment. That was a small consolation.

His cousin Zerelda—he called her Zee—brought him his meals, and she was good company, though he felt a little uneasy about his relationship with her. She was his cousin, but she was such a pretty thing with her fine, fair skin, shiny brown hair, and long dark lashes. And she had a beautiful, sparkling smile. But what really attracted him to Zee was her good heart, her sincerity, and, yes, her charm! He couldn't help but be drawn to her. She was such a comfort to him. If he needed something, she was at his side instantly. Most importantly to Jesse was that she had given him back his life.

When he was in the bush, he had been simply a man among men; there hadn't been any boys there. The only boyish thing about the guerrillas was their ages. Jesse had been a man in every sense of the word when seventeen years old. Anything of the child in him had died years earlier. But Zee had taught him to laugh again, and naturally. He had laughed sometimes during the war, but it had been a cruel, cynical laughter. Now he could see humor in simple, wholesome things, and he owed it to Zee. She was always pulling at his hair and chiding him about his serious expression. She even played small pranks on him, like hiding his fork when she brought him his food. Then she would look innocently down on him, pretending nothing was wrong. She would finally giggle at his discomfort and produce the utensil happily.

Zee was always asking him what the war was like. But he changed the subject. She wouldn't want to know. It was better she didn't know. She had already seen enough of the war as it was; the terrible parts he would keep from her, he decided.

What he most avoided talking about to Zee was what was really eating at his heart. In his current situation, where he had all the time in the world to dwell on it, he had become conscious that he was a killer. Zee didn't suspect it, but it was the truth. He could kill a man as simply as he could smash a grasshopper or a roach between his thumb and forefinger—

and with as little regret. In fact, it had given him pleasure to kill Yankees. He had learned also how easy it was to take the property of others, leaving them nothing and not caring, even being happy about it. In the bush, he had considered these practices needful for survival. He knew that the Yankees stole from his people, and as far as he was concerned, that gave him perfect license to do the same to them. That's what the war had done to him: hardened him and made him mean by ordinary standards. But he wasn't sorry; he'd do it all over again. The Yankees had destroyed his life, his family's security, the family's farm—everything had been destroyed. He'd learned to cut a Yankee's throat like he would that of a chicken. He would never forgive the Yankees for what they had done to Missouri, to his people, and to himself. The wrongs he had suffered ate at him.

Zee crept quietly into Jesse's room. The curtains were drawn and the light in the room was dim. The sun was just peeping over the horizon. She knew that Jesse liked an early breakfast, so she had fixed him everything she knew he liked: ham and eggs, sliced fried potatoes, and a large glass of milk. She hoped it would please him. He appeared to be asleep, so she lay his breakfast down on a small table at the side of his bed. Then she carefully took out his knife and fork from her apron pocket and placed them neatly next to his plate. She looked down at Jesse. He looked so pitifully pale and weak that her heart went out to him. He had felt so much pain. God must have a plan for Jesse, she believed, but she wasn't sure what it was. Zee bent over and kissed him on the forehead.

Jesse was awake as Zee kissed him. He opened his eyes, looked up at her, and smiled calmly. He knew then that he loved her. She was something special. She seemed so natural and full of life, and he was barely alive. He eagerly awaited her visits to his room, and he drew great pleasure from her chatter. He had forgotten the delight of small-talk the last two years. While there had been a closeness between the guerrillas, there was something reserved about their relationships. They were like lions in the same pride, brothers maybe, but always violent competitors, and there was a distance. Maybe this was because the guerrillas never knew when their friends might be killed, and they simply didn't want to get that close to them. Being friends just made the loss harder. Jesse was starved for human companionship and especially for women and their gentle charms. He loved talking with Zee. He felt like he was the luckiest man in the world to have her care for him at this terrible time in his life. He would never forget what she was doing for him. Yes, he was going to marry that girl!

"Well, lazy bones, you're still asleep," Zee finally chided him.

"I reckon I'll just stay in bed today," Jesse answered imperiously. "I've been wantin' to think upon some deep business matters," he added pompously.

Zee giggled. "You goin' to buy one of them local banks or somethin'?"

"Well, I'm thinkin' on it. It may take me a while, to raise the money, I mean, but who knows?"

"Where you goin' to find that kind of money?" Zee replied, still keeping up the banter.

"Oh, I guess that's why I'm goin' to stay in bed today," Jesse chuckled. "I've got a whole lot of serious thinkin' to do."

Zee laughed again. Jesse was learning to take his affliction better, and that's why she kept up this sort of talk. She wanted Jesse to become more lighthearted, like he had been when she knew him before the war. Of course, she had been just a young girl then, and he hadn't paid her much mind. But she felt that he was learning to like her company, and that pleased her. In fact, she was beginning to have great affection for Jesse. She might even set her cap for that boy! It pleased her that he was beginning to show his old sense of humor. He was such a smart talker, a bright young man. Only she worried about his health; he looked so haggard and skinny.

That winter, it was finally legal for Jesse's family to move back to the farm near Kearney, and Jesse joined them. Before he left the Mimms, Jesse and Zee were betrothed. Jesse was still unable to stand on his feet much.

December 13, 1866

Archie Clement, Bill Anderson's second in command, and twenty-six armed guerrillas rode down the dusty road to Lexington, Missouri, an important river town sixty miles east of Kansas City. Since the Civil War ended, the town had been occupied by a 180-man Federal garrison. Even though the war was over, animosities remained high. When the guerrillas turned onto the main street, they adjusted their revolvers, spun the cylinders, and looked cautiously out of the corners of their eyes at the buildings they passed to detect possible trouble.

Seven months earlier, guerrilla chief Dave Poole had ridden into town and surrendered 85 of his men. Since that time, Poole had negotiated the surrender of 115 other guerrillas. Archie Clement, however, had been deliberately tardy in surrendering his men. He wasn't sure the Federals weren't still laying for him and the boys. He and his men wanted to return peacefully to Missouri society, but Archie wasn't certain they would be allowed to do so as the Feds still seemed to have a grudge against Bill Anderson's men. Recently, Archie had learned from Dave Poole that even though Clement's men had not surrendered, they were still required by law to register for the Missouri State Militia or be considered outlaws. Poole advised Clement to come to Lexington, surrender, and register. After thinking over the proposal, Clement had agreed—he knew the guerrillas couldn't just ride around the country without some sort of status—but he and his men were apprehensive and before entering town had taken the precaution to arm themselves.

When they arrived in town, Clement rode up to the army headquarters and sent one of his men, Bill Gaw, in to ask the local commander, Major Montgomery, about their registering for the militia. Gaw was to invoke Dave Poole's name to speed up the process. Gaw talked with Montgomery's adjutant, who carried Clement's message to his chief. Montgomery was familiar with Clement's reputation and, after thinking the matter over for a few minutes, decided that Clement and his ex-guerrillas were a menace. He told his adjutant to order them out of town. When Clement received Montgomery's word, he told his men to ride out. But little Archie and one of his men, Hop Wood, remained at the hotel bar drinking.

"Whatcha goin' to do, Archie?" Clement's sidekick asked him. "They told us to get out of town, didn't they?"

"Oh, I reckon I'll go when I get the notion," Clement replied. He had experienced too much violence over the years to become frightened by a pantywaist Federal commander's rebuff. Moreover, he wanted to settle the matter now rather than continue to be intimidated by the Federal authorities. He and his men needed to establish themselves in postwar Missouri, and if it took a firm, aggressive hand on his part, then he was ready to assert himself.

"Dontcha think they'll come after us, Archie?" Hop queried him again, working at his drink nervously.

"I don't know as I care," Clement said, affecting indifference but quietly adjusting the six-shooters stuck in his belt.

If they want to come, let them come, he thought. He'd never been afraid of blue bellies before, and he didn't intend to run from any of them now. He knew if Bill Anderson were still with them, he wouldn't have given them a thought.

"Hey, bartender, another whiskey," Clement bellowed.

The bartender walked slowly over to Clement, curled his fingers around the guerrilla's glass, and poured it full to the brim from his bar bottle. Clement raised the glass to his lips and sipped the whiskey slowly, savoring its bite. It never occurred to him that he ought to get out of town before trouble started. All he knew was that he wasn't going to be pushed around. He reasoned that if the war was over, then it was over.

The authorities were just going to have to come to some sort of agreement with former guerrillas, and he was ready to be accommodated now.

As Clement emptied his glass, he glanced at the mirror behind the bar and saw the reflection of several armed soldiers entering the open door behind him. Without thinking, he leaped off his stool, dropped to one knee, and fired repeatedly toward the doorway, fracturing one of the door jams leading into the saloon. Some of his stray shots blew out the plate glass window at the front of the building, and it clattered noisily onto the barroom floor and the sidewalk outside. Meanwhile, Hop Wood opened up a second barrage. Amid the roar of guns and crashing glass, the soldiers fled for cover. Using this lull in the action, Clement and Hop sprinted out the side door of the bar and mounted their horses.

As Clement trotted down the main street, the muzzles of muskets crept over the sills of the upstairs windowsills of the buildings along the street. Archie spurred his horse to a gallop. An officer in one of the buildings screamed, "Fire!" and a barrage of bullets ripped through Clement's body. The little guerrilla tumbled headlong over the neck of his horse onto the ground. Blood poured from his mouth and thick rivulets coagulated in the dust. Meanwhile, Clement's horse slowed to a walk, stopped, and gazed back at its young master.

The war was over for twenty-one-year-old Archie Clement.

6

November 6, 1866

Cole Younger stepped over the stone foundation of his old home and walked gingerly across the burnt wreckage. The timbers crumbled under his size thirteen boots. Standing where the family kitchen had once stood, he pressed the toe of his boot on a black joist leaning against the fireplace and it collapsed under his weight. Aunty Suze, the family's black servant, had once hovered over many a meal at that hearth, Cole thought, but that was several years and a war away.

Cole had been away from home for a long time. He had heard that the house had been destroyed, but now he could see the extent of the destruction. He had a lot of mending to do, he reckoned. But what would he do for money? It would take a fortune to fix the old place, rebuild the house, outbuildings, and barns.

On his return to the farm, every turn in the road had brought back memories to him. He remembered haying in that field, plowing in another, a horse foaling in the pasture beyond the house. It made him sad, those memories of a bygone life. He recalled his father and tears came to his eyes. He would always reverence the old man's memory. His loss had been a hard burden to bear.

At first, Cole had been reluctant to visit the farm. He feared it would remind him of another world, a distant one now, where he and his family had amounted to something. Before the war, his father had been wealthy and important in the community. Now, he and his brothers and sisters were virtually penniless vagabonds. While they still had land, its value was diminished severely. The entire countryside was desolate. The Yankees had burned their home, destroyed and dismantled their outbuildings, and driven off their livestock.

Even though the war had ended, their enemies still plotted against them. All of the political offices in Cass County were filled now with swaggering Jayhawkers or old Yankee militiamen formerly under Neugent, a Civil War commander who had been stationed in Harrisonville, a base he used to pursue the guerrillas and harass their families during the war. Ex-Confederates were barred from office and could not even vote. Because Cole had been one of Quantrill's officers and a prominent member of the resistance, he doubted that he would be able to live on the old farm in safety. But he was going to try! Meanwhile, he'd have to fix up the old place. He'd noticed that all the rail fencing had either rotted away or been stolen.

Once, this place had been one of the dearest spots on earth to him. But the Yankees had destroyed it. The Youngers were not the only ones dispossessed, Cole reflected. When General Ewing instituted Orders Number 11 in 1863, the Yankees had burned nearly all the homes remaining in the four counties along the Kansas border and driven most of the Missourians' herds into Kansas for the use of their enemies. So the Youngers were no worse off than their neighbors. That's one thing he could say for the Yankees: they were efficient. They'd stolen every hog, sheep, cow, chicken, and goose the Youngers owned—leaving them absolutely nothing. As he walked around the place, he ran across small clusters of faded feathers. He guessed a few Shanghai roosters and hens had eluded the Yankees. The coyotes had picked these off, likely one by one.

As he walked by some bushes, however, a hen running through

the brush startled him. It flew a few yards and then darted into some tall horseweed. Cole smiled. It pleased him to think that there was some chance of escape in this world. Maybe the Youngers would find a way out of their troubles too. The hopes of his early years crowded into his mind, and he wondered how he might regain the Youngers' old position in the community. It would be difficult. The authorities considered him a hardened guerrilla, a criminal even, and there was a warrant out for his arrest for crimes the Yankees claimed he'd committed during the war. He knew that the Yankees had committed their share of crimes during the war. Oh, hadn't they! But apparently, their atrocities didn't count.

If he and the guerrillas had become criminals, he thought, it was something thrust on them, not a natural tendency. They were not inherently wicked. Before the war, people had trusted his family and the families of the other guerrillas. Cole was proud of his family's history. They were descended from "Light Horse Harry" Lee, the father of Gen. Bobby Lee. He was also descended from Chief Justice John Marshall, a signer of the Constitution. How had the Youngers been brought to such a low estate? he wondered helplessly.

Cole had heard that Bill Hulse, one of his guerrilla comrades, had been shot down recently while he was harvesting corn—likely by their old enemies. Someone had killed Tuck Hill. That didn't make a man feel secure. He'd also heard that George Maddox and Bill Reynolds had been arrested recently, put in a Lawrence, Kansas, jail and refused bail. What's more, some of his old enemies had captured his brother John and hanged him by his neck, trying to find out where he and Jim were. John had resisted their torture, though; he was as tough as any of the Youngers. It made Cole wonder if the war was really over.

Cole's mother was staying in Pleasant Hill with his brother-in-law, Lycurgus Jones. His heart bled for his dear mother. He hoped to build a new home for her on the farm, to bring her back where she would be comfortable. He knew that his mother's health was frail. Tuberculosis had taken a toll on her, and when the Yankees had burned their home and driven her out into the terrible cold, it had damaged her plenty.

Cole mounted his horse. He'd go for his brothers; they'd help him. He would put the bitterness behind him. The job on the farm was going to be a big one. Everything was ruined, and the banks were tight as ticks with greenbacks now. He wasn't sure if he could borrow seed money. And he'd heard that the railroads charged so blasted much to haul a crop to market that there was precious little left after a season of hard work except grimy sweat on a man's collar and empty gunnies. But money! How would he get started? The problem puzzled and perplexed him. But he wasn't going to whimper; the Youngers would prevail.

November 21, 1866

Frank James rode down the main street of Liberty, Missouri, mounted on his favorite chestnut. Reaching the square, he dismounted and hitched his horse. Frank cut a rather coarse figure in his wide-brimmed slouch hat, coarse-woven pants, and dusty boots. He brushed the dust from his worn blue jacket and clothes and walked over to a bench where he sat down to observe the traffic. Being idle didn't particularly appeal to him, but he was at loose ends. He pulled out a sheaf of cigarette papers, drew one, and cupped a single paper in his left hand. Grabbing a pouch from his pocket, he sprinkled a narrow row of tobacco in the paper trough, licked the edge of the paper, and then grabbed the pouch in his teeth while he rolled the cigarette. He returned the pouch to his pocket and tucked the cigarette into his mouth. Pulling out a match, he drew it across his pant leg and lit it. Soon, an aromatic cloud swirled around his head.

Frank watched as farmers drove their wagons around the

courthouse square and parked them. He noticed that many of them wore ragged clothes much like his own. Obviously, they had endured the same hardships as his family since the war ended. He also observed that some of the people traveling around the square seemed relatively untouched by the war and quite prosperous. He wondered if they were Yankee collaborators. Something about the situation rubbed him wrong.

Frank thought of stopping at the hotel restaurant for breakfast, but the only money he had on him was a twenty-dollar bill, and it needed cashing. He wasn't sure that the restaurant could cash such a big bill. Then Frank noticed the Clay County Savings Association on the corner. They would have change. He felt a bit pretentious, cashing a twenty-dollar bill, but he needed the change if he was going to conduct business around town. He walked up to the bank, opened the door, and strode up to the cashier, Greenup Bird.

"Sir, how about cashin' a twenty-dollar greenback?" he asked.

Bird looked up from his accounts and cautiously surveyed the long-faced, handsome young man. He looked somewhat familiar to him. Satisfied by Frank's looks, Bird reached into his cash drawer for the correct change. But finding that he lacked it, he walked to the vault and flung open the door. He walked inside and pulled the door nearly closed behind him.

Frank, almost unconsciously, squinted through the crack. His eyes bulged at the large stacks of greenbacks and swollen sacks of gold in the vault. Bird grabbed a handful of bills, entered the teller's cage, and closed the door behind him.

"Fives and ones okay, young man?" Bird asked.

"Uh . . . yes," Frank answered, glancing around. It was a small bank, like most small-town banks, but Frank noticed something special about this institution: it carried lots of money. He scanned the teller's cage, the height of the window through which Bird made his transaction, and the location of the nearby vault.

"Thanks, partner," Frank said and moved toward the door. "You've been a great help to me."

As Frank walked into the street, he looked over Liberty Square in a new light. His guerrilla instincts resonated. He quickly identified the best routes onto the square, the key places where pickets should be placed to guard the area during a robbery, and he calculated how many men would be needed to overpower the town. He'd seen with his own eyes that the bank held a horde of gold and greenbacks.

As he walked around town, Frank's mind explored a wild scenario: How many men would it take to rob the bank? Where would they ride in the getaway? How long would it take a posse to form and pursue them? How many men were apt to ride with such a posse? How would the bandits elude the law? Where would they hide and who would hide them? His mind teemed with a grand plot. He turned over the details in his mind, sifting them for the right combination to make the robbery work.

Who would perform the robbery? That was no problem, he thought. He knew dozens of men who could and would do it. These were tough times. But he needed trusted men, men who would hold their tongues. That would be the rub. He'd have to pick his men carefully, and a few of them would have to be brought into the planning. The robbery couldn't be done casually. Cole Younger, his old friend from the war, might be a good man—if he could persuade him to join up. He was a good shot and had steel nerves and a practical head. And Younger had brothers! There were also Payne Jones, Tom Little, Andy McGuire, and Jim Devers. The list grew wildly in his head: Bud and Donny Pence, Ol Shepherd, James Wilkerson, Frank Gregg, Joab Perry, Ben Cooper, Red Monkus, and Jesse, his own brother, a man to be reckoned with. By God, they would cash in their six-shooters!

Frank's mind reeled with the thought of pulling off such a daring robbery. He walked into the hotel and ordered three eggs, sausages, potatoes, and coffee. He would celebrate. As he sipped his coffee, he reflected that it would be like old times, during the war, with Quantrill and the boys. He felt elated and the adrenaline surged in him. He couldn't wait to tell Jesse about his plan. He knew Jesse was becoming impatient with the soft life. They were all bored with it; all of Quantrill's old boys were tugging at their bits. They needed excitement, craved it. Accustomed to high-tempo lives, this desultory life of farm work was killing their spirits. Their lives were hopeless. Oh, yes, they could be somebody's wretched hired hand, but they were made of better stuff. And times were hard, and the economy in the area had been virtually destroyed so even those who could stand the life were finding it hard to make a living.

He was sure his old friends were wild for adventure. Besides, he was fed up with these people who had all of the money, had enriched themselves while he and his Southern friends had bled for the South. The situation incensed him. If these people lost their money, curse 'em! It was time they shared some of the grief the rest had suffered.

This would be an enterprise of brave men. The war was over, but the fighting wasn't. But could he persuade the boys to join up? It was stealing, he knew. But they'd done plenty of that in the service of the South, or so the Yankees had claimed. At the moment, the fine points of distinction escaped him completely. He thought his friends would join him. Most of them liked him, called him "Buck." They'd go along—yes!

"More coffee, sir?" the young waitress asked. But Frank was immersed in thought. Had he looked up, he might have noticed a pretty young girl. But he looked straight ahead, absorbed in thought.

"Would you like some more coffee?" the waitress repeated.

"Uh … yes, thank you, ma'am," Frank replied absentmindedly, and he continued to shape his plot. Frank walked out of the hotel so preoccupied that he hardly realized that he was walking toward his horse and saddling up. As he rode out of town, his life took on new purpose.

December 3, 1866

> When our weeping's over,
> He will bid us welcome,
> We shall come rejoicing,
> Bringing in the sheaves.

Jesse James sang the lines of one of his favorite hymns with gusto, if a little out of tune. He'd always liked to sing hymns with the congregation; it made him feel like he was a part of the community. The Baptist church was a sort of sanctuary to him after his recent, turbulent life in the war.

The church was filled with people, and as they sang, small wisps of vapor issued from their mouths and noses. It was cold in the church, but everyone had on heavy coats, so they were quite snug. The wood stove in the corner of the church took off some of the cold's sharp edge.

Jesse liked the solemness of the church and its high ideals. He was planning on being baptized soon. That's why it was hard for him to reconcile what he was about to do. He had agreed to help Frank rob the Liberty bank! The thought, in many respects, shocked him. But he'd agreed to participate anyhow.

He was dissatisfied with his current life. Sure, they were now safe, unless some Yankee knave called them out into the street to fight or a lynch mob nabbed them. But that sort of threat didn't really bother Jesse; if it happened, he'd just shoot him some fine-feathered Yankee scum! But it was Jesse's personal life that was in disarray. The economy of western Missouri had been destroyed by the war. Most people's homes in the area south of Clay County were burned and the livestock depleted. Things weren't much better north of the river. Conditions were tough. Meanwhile, the banks refused to loan a body some money, fearing they'd never get repaid. And maybe they were right.

Because Jesse was a young man, things were even worse. He didn't own a stick or stone. He wanted to marry his cousin

Zee, but how could a fella do that when he was poorer and more pitiful than a field mouse? The robbery seemed the only way out for him. But could they pull it off successfully? He wasn't sure. He knew it would set the law into a frenzy, and he reveled at the thought. He felt like the police and sheriffs were just another arm of the Union government that they had been fighting only months before. Soldiers in blue, lawmen in blue: what was the difference? Some of the officers, when they left the Yankee army, had just changed one pair of blue pants for another; they all stood for the same corrupt and oppressive system in his view. He would as well shoot one Yankee snake as another.

He prayed for guidance, but he remained unsure about the path he had charted for himself. He knew that Frank was not as beleaguered by doubt. Frank didn't believe in God. He'd told Jesse that if there were a God, he would have killed the accursed Yankees during the war because they were evil thieves and fanatics and deserved to be destroyed. When evil men triumphed, Frank believed, you had a right to defend yourself anyway you could. If Satan existed, as far as Frank was concerned, the banks, the railroads, the whole corrupt Northern establishment and its police and army were in league with him. For Jesse, though, it was hard to reconcile the robbery they were planning with his religious beliefs.

He intended to take part in the robbery anyway, whatever the result. It was the only way out for him. He had still not recovered from his war wounds, and he felt weak. He was in no condition to do much ordinary work. He wasn't sure if he ever would be. But he could mount a horse and point a gun. And he needed the money. That was the point.

February 13, 1866

The sun rose on a crisp dawn, and snow flitted from the

clouds, spreading a thin white veil over the river bottoms. Payne Jones walked over and threw more limbs on the bonfire, and flames shot in the air. He recalled that the old-timers used to say that an Indian built a small fire, got up close, and got warm but that a white man built a big fire, stood far away, and froze to death. He figured those injuns had been right. But he threw on more wood just the same. Old white man's habit, Payne reckoned.

It was around noon and ten horsemen had arrived at the rendezvous along the Missouri River. Another two were expected soon. It was a good place to meet, along the river, Payne thought. It wasn't on anybody's land, so the locals would largely ignore them. He looked at the river, a quarter mile away. It had been frozen just the month before, but now it flowed powerfully eastward through a margin of sycamores and Willows. The thick, young sycamores lining the riverbanks reminded Payne of white arms reaching toward heaven. Across the river, a dense fog shrouded the white hills.

Payne reckoned that since they all wore blue Union army overcoats (taken from the bodies of dead soldiers in the recent war) people would think they were a local army detachment. But they were simply the only decent coats they had, and they made good disguises. Since the Union soldiers in the area had earned such a bad reputation during the war, Payne knew that ordinary people would avoid their band of blue.

The men huddled close to the fire, and a number of them drew flasks of whiskey from their coats and sent the biting liquid down their throats in long, studied swallows. Some of the men had brought chunks of ham and sausages with them, and they carved on the links and small butts of meat with their Bowie knives, gnawed on the meat, and washed it down with hard liquor. They hoped it would tide them over until their next meal, whenever that might be. Meanwhile, Frank and Jesse James talked to Cole Younger, fine-tuning the afternoon's plan.

Payne knew most of the plan. Two of the men, Jim Wilkerson

and Joab Perry, were commandeering a nearby ferry for the gang's getaway across the Missouri River. They had eaten earlier and gone to capture the ferryman. The rest of the gang would enter Liberty, fifteen miles to the north, from various roads, riding in clutches of twos and threes, entering the town a few minutes apart. Once in town, Donny Pence and Clell Miller would stake out near the sheriff's office. If shots were fired, they would intercept and disarm the sheriff—shoot him, if need be. The rest of the men would form at the corners of the square and stop anyone attempting to enter the downtown during the robbery. Payne was satisfied the robbery would be pulled off without a hitch. But if there were a hitch, by heaven, they would seize the money and shoot their way out!

Within fifteen minutes, everyone had arrived. Payne smiled to himself; everyone wanted a payday, he figured. He wasn't surprised. They were all pretty desperate. None of them had any money, nor saw any chance of getting any in the ordinary way. If they pulled off the robbery, they would be fixed for a time. If Frank James was correct, the bank was spilling over with green.

Jesse and Frank James and Cole Younger rode their horses up to the hitching post in front of the Clay County Savings Association, dismounted, and tied their horses. Frank looked across the street and nodded to Pence and Miller, who were standing near the sheriff's office. Then Frank looked down the line of brick buildings to his left and right. Some of the men were milling around at the corner of the square. He tipped his hat to them. Everything was going as planned. The men pulled their wide-brimmed hats low and turned up their collars to obscure their faces.

Cole Younger, his spurs jangling with each stride, took up a position outside the door of the bank. He was there to spoil any attempt to interfere with the robbery. Meanwhile, Frank and Jesse walked casually into the bank. Frank sauntered up to the cashier's window. Jesse strode over to a wood stove and turned his back to it, pretending to warm himself. Greenup Bird and his son William were diligently at work on the bank's books. William, noticing the arrival of customers, rose to his feet and walked to the teller's window.

"Say, fella," Frank said, laying a bill on the counter, "how about cashin' a fifty-dollar greenback for me?" When Bird approached the window, Frank drew his revolver and pointed it at the cashier's head. Without uttering another word, he grabbed the side of the teller's window with his left hand and hurdled through the opening, landing on the wooden floor on the other side with a loud thump.

"Back up and raise your hands, or I'll blow your infernal brains out!" Frank yelled. William Bird was flabbergasted. Jesse followed Frank through the same opening, and the two bandits faced the cashiers. Jesse held an empty two-bushel grain sack in his left hand and a pistol in the other.

"Don't make any noise or I'll kill you," Frank warned. Jesse walked over to William Bird, grabbed him by his shoulder, and whirled him around. Then he stuck the muzzle of his revolver sharply into the young man's ribs and pushed him into the vault.

"Get in there and start fillin' this bag with money. Gold, bonds—everything!" Jesse demanded.

Frank turned to Greenup Bird.

"Where's the rest of the money?" Bird opened up a large tin box near the teller's counter, and Frank reached in and grabbed a large stack of gray-green currency. Meanwhile, William Bird had nearly filled Jesse's cotton sack with bags of gold, silver, and greenbacks. Frank had been right, Jesse reflected, the bank was loaded. Jesse dragged the sack out through the door of the teller's cage, leaving William Bird in the vault. Frank dropped his deposit into Jesse's bag and pulled the elder Bird into the vault by his shirtsleeve.

"Say," complained Bird, "You're not goin' to . . . "

Frank gave Bird a shove and closed the door on the bankers. Unnoticed by Frank, the vault's latch failed to lock securely.

Frank and Jesse leaped through the front door of the bank.

Cole, who was guarding the door, met them, and the three men ran for their horses. Meanwhile, the Birds ran from the vault and rushed to the door screaming, "Robbers! Robbers!" George "Jolly" Wymore, who had been walking down the street, heard Bird and ran from the square repeating the teller's screams of, "Robbery! Robbery!" One of the bandits shot Wymore, and he tumbled onto his face dead. Another man, S. H. Holmes, also ran from the square screaming an alarm, but he luckily escaped.

Frank grabbed the sack of loot from his brother and ran to his horse. Pulling a small length of rope from his pocket, he formed a loop knot around the top of the sack and tightened it. Then he hoisted the weighty bag to his saddle and tied the loose end of the rope around his saddle horn. The bandits mounted their horses and spurred them into a canter down the main street. A low shriek issued from the bandits' throats, rising to a yipping crescendo: it was their old rebel yell. The sound echoed down the street, and the outlaws converged into a pack and galloped out of town, firing their weapons wildly. The ex-guerrillas, now bandits, had struck a bonanza.

The sheriff heard the firing and ran from his office. When he saw the armed robbers, he dashed behind the side of a building. Minutes later, he walked cautiously into the street and stared in astonishment after the outlaws. It would be half an hour before he formed a posse to pursue the bandits. Meanwhile, the men galloped southward toward the river, churning up a cloud of dust in their wake. It was snowing, and large flakes soon covered their tracks.

As Frank rode toward the river, he marveled at how easy the operation had been. Only a few random shots were fired, and no one had pursued them. It had been a lot easier than he had expected. It was a Sunday school picnic of a raid compared to what he and the boys had been accustomed to during the war, when bullets whistled around them like bees and men were bloodied and killed. And the take! Frank bet there was fifty thousand dollars in his sack. He was excited and jubilant. He knew that a man had been shot and likely died on the square, but he had asked for it, hadn't he?

Turning to his right, Frank yelled to Jesse: "How 'bout that, Dingus?" A smile covered Jesse's face. Cole Younger, riding to the right of Jesse, looked straight ahead, satisfied as a cow in clover.

"Yippeeee!" Frank exclaimed jubilantly.

It was too soon for Frank to reflect on the law's reaction to the first daylight bank robbery in U.S. history. That response would come, and it would be fierce. Within days, a $10,000 reward was posted (equivalent to $140,000 in today's money) for the capture of the bandits and the return of the stolen money.

Once across the river, the gang met at a prearranged spot to divide their spoils. Frank James offered the men their choice of cash or bonds as their share of the take, with those taking bonds receiving the lion's share of the money. Most of the men chose greenbacks, believing that the bonds would be hard to cash. Frank, Jesse, and Cole, however, took most of their money in bonds, sure that they could eventually be exchanged for cash. Thus, the leaders came away with the larger share of the loot, although it would take some time for them to realize their fortune.

7

March 25, 1866

Jesse James rode up to the Mimms' place in Harlem, north of Kansas City, dismounted, and hitched his horse to a post. It had been several weeks since Jesse had visited Zee, and he was excited about the opportunity to talk with her. He was flat bored with farming, and he had been looking forward to this visit. He had so many things he wanted to talk to Zee about.

He wore his new blue trousers, gray frock coat, and black tie. And he'd bought a new saddle, halter, and reins for his horse. He thought he cut quite a figure. He liked nice clothes, but you sure couldn't wear them when you were plowing and pitching hay. He probably should have been a minister or a lawyer, he reflected, but that seemed out of the question now. Former guerrillas and prominent ex-Southerners were barred from the professions. But that was okay. He had his own profession now. The authorities might not like it, but a man had a right to make his way in the world, and he intended to. The Mimms' dogs had eyed Jesse as soon as he rode up. One of them wailed at him and then ran up to him with its tail and rear wagging and tongue licking.

"Get down, Pooch, you rowdy rascal," Jesse protested, swatting at the dog. "Tip, get your muddy feet off me," he fussed at the Mimms' other dog. Before Jesse had time to pound on the familiar iron knocker, John Mimms came to the door and opened it.

"Pooch! Tip! Get down!" Mimms called sternly. "Jesse, where you been keepin' yourself? We been expectin' you for weeks."

"Been right busy, Uncle John," Jesse replied. "Gettin' ready for the plowin'. Been cleanin' and sharpenin' shares—nasty work, you know."

"Right," his uncle replied. "Zee's in there fittin' to be tied. You better get in there before she busts down the door and knocks over the hounds."

"Daddy!" Zee exclaimed from inside the door. "It ain't true. But I'm sure glad to see you, Jesse. Boy, where you been hidin'?" she said as she peeked around the corner. "I been thinkin' I might have to ride all the way over to Kearney to check on your activities."

Jesse laughed. "Hey, I'd just hitch you up next to my ol' mare Betty and start plowin'. It wouldn't be long before you'd be headin' back here to Harlem, I suspect."

Zee laughed. "You'd probably use me for a horse, all right. You're good at horsin' around. But who knows, I might make a good horse. I got the sense for it."

"Well," Jesse teased, "there's only one way to find out!"

"Yes, you would, wouldn't you," she giggled.

After shoving the dogs out of the way, the three closed the front door and entered the Mimms' parlor. Once pleasantries had been exchanged, John Mimms excused himself.

"You kids keep up the chatter," he said, "I've got chores to do out to the barn."

"We'll do our best, Uncle John," Jesse said as Mimms walked out the front door.

When Mimms closed the door, Jesse walked up to Zee and placed his arm around her narrow waist and kissed her hard on the mouth. She responded timidly at first and then warmed to him.

"Well, young man," she scolded him, pulling away for a moment. "Aren't you takin' liberties?"

"I'm sure tryin'," Jesse replied jokingly.

"Well, now, it's taken you an awful long time to come visit me. We thought you'd forgotten us," she reproached him lightly.

"That's one thing you never need to bother about," Jesse said, his voice taking on a serious tone. "I'll always be at your side when you need me. I had things to do."

"Such as?" she asked, teasing Jesse.

"Well, there's all that farmin' for starters."

"Say, dear one," Zee continued, finally noticing Jesse's new clothes, "where'd you get those spiffy duds you're wearin'? I didn't know I had such a flashy beau."

"I been savin' my money. I get tired of wearin' overalls all the time."

"Well, you look wonderful, darlin'."

"Say, how long is it going to take you to tell me about it?" Zee continued.

"What do you mean?" Jesse replied. "Tell you about what?"

"You know what! The robbery, of course! You don't have one of those every day in Liberty, do you? I never heard of such carryin' on. What do you know about it?"

Jesse hesitated for a moment. "Oh . . . that. Not much. Why? What do you hear about it around here?" he asked, trying not to sound too inquisitive.

"We only know what we read in the papers," Zee answered. "Appears someone did some robbin' up in your neck o' the woods. I wonder who it was."

"Oh," Jesse answered, "probably some of them darned Jayhawkers; they got pretty practiced at it during the war."

"I don't know," Zee wavered. "The word's goin' around that some of Quantrill's old boys are on the prowl. Who would they be?"

"Oh, I hardly think the boys would be up to somethin' like that. That's just Yankee newspaper talk. In fact, I heard someone say that the bandits were wearin' blue coats. They had to be Jayhawkers, I reckon. Hey, let's talk about somethin' else besides robbin' and killin'."

"Okay, you have the floor," Zee replied.

April 2, 1866

Clell Miller lifted a tumbler of whiskey to his lips, took a long swallow, and savored the sting. He sat at a round walnut table surrounded by three gamblers, and he was down to his last twenty dollars. Of course, he had more money at home, but he had dropped plenty in the poker game tonight, much more than he ought to have, he realized. It seemed to him like gambling was getting into his blood and he was losing his senses.

He looked across the room. Some fellows dressed in butternut and red-colored shirts and broad-brimmed hats leaned against the bar. One of them wore a bowie knife in a scabbard on his hip. They all carried pistols in their waistbands. One fellow drank his whiskey straight from the bottle. The others drank their poison from small shot glasses like his own, he noticed.

A lurid light gleamed down on the players from the red-shaded lamp overhead. On Clell's right, an old farmer peered at his cards sharply. Clell supposed the old geezer was hoping to win some seed money or the price of a steer if he was lucky. On Clell's left, a miner fresh from Denver was out to better himself. He was a mangy, devious-looking specimen, with grimy hair and a nasty, drooping mustache.

But the main attraction was the professional gambler directly across the table from him. He was a tall, gaunt fellow who wore a fine frock coat, striped pants, a garish tie, and a shiny stickpin. He had been lucky all night, lucky beyond reason, Clell thought. But Clell hadn't caught him cheating—yet anyhow. In contrast to his flashy clothes, the gambler had dark, bloodshot eyes, a sallow complexion, and tobacco-stained teeth that smiled darkly from under a sagging black mustache. The gambler sat smugly

behind a large stack of gold half eagles. He was a dapper knave all
right, with his shiny pumps. A regular jaded dandy, Clell thought.
His shrewd black eyes flitted back and forth from hand to
hand like a wolf looking for prey, as if he could see through
the other players' cards and detect the hidden diamonds and
clubs. He was sure cunning, probably knew every deuced card
in the deck, when one had been played and another was likely to
occur. But even then, the rascal was just too lucky, Clell decided.
He was doing something fishy. But what? It puzzled Clell. He'd
been losing all night, and the farmer next to him was a big loser
too. Only the shark and the roughneck miner were winning, and
they were winning big. Clell wished he hadn't drunk so much; it
was hard for him to follow the game's movements. The gambler's
hands moved as fast as a snake's tongue, and the cards whirled
by, little diamonds, hearts, and spades fluttering by in a blur.
Watching it made Clell's head swim.

"I think I'll pass for a couple hands," Clell finally said and
pushed back from the table.

"What? Losin' your nerve?" the gambler chided him
sarcastically.

"Nah, just want to clear my head a spell. Then I'll whip your
carcass or go to tarnation for the effort," Clell replied. The
gambler and the miner chuckled cynically.

As the game proceeded, Clell pretended to stare around the
room idly, but what he was really doing was focusing on the
gambler's movements rather than the course of the game. A few
minutes later, from his position pushed back from the table, he
saw the miner nudge the gambler's foot. It was an obvious signal,
Clell was convinced. The two men were working together as a
team. Clell continued to watch the gambler as he dealt out the
hands and picked up cards from the table. He noticed that the
gambler seemed to deliberately pick up certain cards last. After
watching him awhile, Clell was sure he detected him placing
those cards on the bottom of the deck. It was hard to detect,
hardly noticeable at all. But the crook was protecting cards on

the bottom of the deck and then drawing them when he needed them; that's what the wretch was doing. And he was using the cards to hit hands when the betting was right. He was a slick dude, all right!

As the game progressed, the old farmer seemed to have hit into a full house. In response, the old man placed a handsome bet. Meanwhile, the professional gambler dropped out. Then Clell noticed the miner casually drum on the top of his cards with his fingers. Clell guessed it was a signal too. Seconds later, in what seemed a response, the gambler casually rubbed his chin with his thumb. While the miner only showed one ace and the rest worthless cards, he raised the bet. The farmer, emboldened by his own good hand, raised the miner again. The gambler now hit the farmer with a card. Clell supposed that it did him neither good nor ill; the old fellow likely had his house already. Then the gambler hit his confederate, and it was from the bottom of the deck—no question about it. So preoccupied was he with the betting, the farmer failed to notice the move. When the two men turned over their cards, the miner had won with four aces.

"Outrageous!" the farmer screamed, rising to his feet. "I've never seen anything like it. I don't believe it! Somethin's wrong with this game!"

The gambler stood up menacingly and reached for a derringer he kept in his coat pocket. Pulling out the small weapon, he said, "Sir, are you accusin' this good man or any other players present of cheatin'? I assure you, as a fellow player, I saw nothin' improper—nothin' whatever! Are you not a sportin' man? This man defeated me. Why are you such a disgustin' loser?" The farmer, sensing that he was outnumbered and also intimidated by the aggressive posture of the gambler, got up in disgust and walked out of the saloon.

Clell raised himself to his feet. "Fellas, I think I've had about enough of this play for the evenin' myself."

"This game too much for you poor farm boys?" the gambler remarked slyly.

"Reckon it is," Clell replied and walked slowly out the front door of the saloon into the dark street. Once he got his bearings and adjusted his eyes to the darkness, he examined the gambling hall. A number of horses were tethered behind the place; he could see them by the light of a partial moon. Very likely the gambler's horse was one of them. He walked around to the back of the hall and leaned up against the building near the back door. He'd wait awhile for his lanky friend to come out, he decided.

After smoking several cigarettes, Clell heard the noise of someone opening the back door, and he squeezed himself up against the building and pulled his revolver from his belt. The door opened wide and one of the men who had been drinking at the bar walked out. He stood outside the door a moment, then saw Clell. "Hey! What ya doin' fella?" the drunk slurred.

"None of your business. Get out of here," Clell answered instantly, and the drunk stumbled off toward his horse.

A few minutes later, the door opened again, and the gambler walked into the darkness. Clell pulled his revolver and lunged toward him, striking the gambler on the head with the barrel of his gun. The gambler fell like a bag of oats. The gambler hadn't known what hit him, but Clell had to be careful; someone else might come out of the saloon. He grabbed the gambler under his arms and pulled him behind some bushes. He lifted his wallet and probed his waist for a money vest. Yes, he had one. Clell had struck pay dirt. He untied it from his waist and yanked it free.

"You won't be needin' this, chum," Clell muttered to himself. He stuck the gambler's wallet into his pocket and plucked the greenbacks and gold from the money belt and stuffed them into his pockets. He left the gambler's gun where it lay. "Popgun anyway," he whispered to himself, disgusted at the small, to him totally worthless, derringer. Clell threw down the money belt and ran to his horse and mounted it.

As he trotted down a dirt lane away from the Kansas City saloon, he contemplated the last month. It had been a sad affair. Through his gambling, he had lost a considerable portion of his share of the gold from the Liberty robbery. If he kept up this wayward behavior, he reflected, he'd be poor again before long. And he wouldn't always be able to rescue himself like he had tonight. Luckily, the miner had stayed for a nightcap and left his accomplice to fend for himself. He'd like to get the miner too, but he'd leave that for another day.

May 22, 1867

From various directions, horsemen converged on Richmond, Missouri's town square and began firing. Clell Miller reined in his horse at the edge of the square and poured a heavy fire into the windows and doors of the business buildings and at the men milling in the street. The townsmen fled indoors. Meanwhile, four bandits entered the Hughes and Wasson Bank, their guns drawn.

A fifteen-year-old boy, Frank Griffin, ran out of the local jail with a cavalry rifle, crouched behind a tree, and blasted at the bandits circling around the square. Several of the bandits noticed the boy and fired at him. He fell dead with a bullet in his head. The mayor of Richmond, John B. Shaw, dashed out of a building and ran toward the bank, hoping to stop the robbery. Several bullets struck him also, and he tumbled to the ground, blood running from his chest and mouth. The jailer, B. G. Griffin, the father of the dead boy, now ran out of a haberdasher's shop, his pistol drawn. He dashed toward the bank. A bandit standing next to the door pointed his revolver at Shaw's head and sent him to his Maker.

Some of the other outlaws raced into the jail and unlocked the cells where several former guerrillas were kept. The prisoners rushed from the jail, excitedly mounted some of the horses tethered around the square, and galloped out of town. Finally, the four bandits raced out of the bank with a grain sack filled with four thousand dollars in gold, silver, and greenbacks.

One of the men tied the bag to his saddle horn and climbed onto his horse. Amid shrill cries, the men raced out of town, their guns spitting fire.

A hundred-man posse formed immediately and chased after the bandits, catching up with them a number of miles outside of town. But the posse came only close enough to fire a few harmless shots, and the outlaws vanished into heavy woods by dusk. Back in Richmond, a number of the townspeople came forward to identify many of the men who had participated in the robbery. Within days, warrants were issued for the arrests of Jim and John White, Payne Jones, Dick Burns, Ike Flannery, Andy McGuire, and Allen Parmer. There were rumors that the Youngers were involved in the robbery too, but no one identified them specifically and no charges were filed against them. No one saw the James boys at the robbery either. But they were there.

May 26, 1867

A posse of eighteen men led by Marshal P. J. Mizery of Kansas City rode through a driving rainstorm toward the Jones farm, two miles west of Independence. Dr. Jim Noland's little girl, Sally, who knew where the Jones family lived, acted as their guide. As Mizery rode through the storm, he looped his reins around his saddle horn for a moment and pulled up his collar. Reaching up with one hand, he formed a sharp crease in the brim of his wide-brimmed hat to funnel off the pelting rain.

The marshal and his men rode up to the Jones home, dismounted, and tethered their horses. Mizery was convinced that Payne Jones was inside, so he had his men circle the house. When everyone was in position, the marshal whistled sharply, signaling his men to advance on the house. Mizery walked up to Jones' front door and pounded loudly.

"All right, Payne Jones, come out with your hands up!"

Mizery yelled. "This is Sheriff Mizery; you're surrounded. Come out and you'll be well treated. If you don't, we're comin' in to get you!"

As Mizery waited for a response, a loud blast sounded from the side of the house. Jones had leaped out a window of the house and discharged both barrels of his shotgun at the law officers waiting there, one of whom was Deputy B. H. Wilson. Wilson fell dead from the gunshot. Jones threw down his empty shotgun, drew his revolvers, and raced through the rain and darkness, firing behind him as he ran. Little Sally Noland was wounded critically by a stray bullet, either from one of Jones' weapons or from one fired by the posse. As rifles and pistols boomed behind him, Jones ran to where he had hidden his horse, mounted it, and galloped away in the darkness.

As Jones made his dash for freedom, Dick Burns, another of the Richmond robbers, fled out another window of the house, disarmed one of the posse members, and escaped.

Several days later, on exiting the front door of a friend's home, Jones was cut down in a hail of gunfire by unknown assailants. A day later, Burns was chased down and shot by a posse. Not long thereafter, detectives in St. Louis arrested Andy McGuire, another of the Richmond bandits. He had been posing under the alias James Cloud. He was taken to Richmond and placed in jail. Several days later, he was dragged from his cell by a mob and hung from a nearby Catalpa tree.

June 3, 1867

It was little more than a week since he'd participated in the Richmon robbery, and Tom Little was relaxing in a barber chair in Warrensburg. He'd needed a haircut and shave for some time, and he had decided he could wait no longer. Now, his long brown curls lay strewn on the floor. Little thought he needed a new look.

"Hey, John," he kidded the barber, "are you skinnin' me? Nobody's likely to recognize me if you keep on a shearin'. What are my many girlfriends gonna say?"

"Say, pardner, all that thatch has been weightin' you down, pressin' on your measly brains, causin' you to talk silly. Besides, you asked for a close cut. Maybe the girls won't know who you are anymore, and that'll be a plus. But I'm doin' you a favor, makin' you look right smart."

McGuire looked up quickly and noticed someone staring at him through the window of the shop, and his attention was riveted. The man looked familiar and seemed to know him.

"Hey, John, finish up," Little said nervously. "I gotta get outa here. Right now! Right now, you hear me?" he said, his speech quickening.

"Just a moment, boy," the barber said, continuing to putter with his scissors.

"Now, I said! Right now!" commanded Little, raising himself in the chair.

As he rose, three burly men rushed through the front doorway of the barbershop and leaped on top of him, pinning his arms down. Little struggled, but with the barber's apron circling his chest and waist, he was unable to resist, couldn't reach his guns. He was yanked into the street and surrounded by a mob. His arms were held fast behind him, and several men struck him in the head and face with their fists. Another man kicked him in the groin. Little tasted blood and spit out several teeth.

"All right, you schemin' trash!" one of the men screamed.

"Get a good hold of him, Joe!" another man yelled. "Let's see this villain ride a rope!"

Blood ran from Little's nose, and his face and jaw were numb. The faces of the men in front of him were flushed and their eyes dilated. Little's revolver had been stripped from him. If the barber's apron hadn't hogtied him, Little thought, he might have had a chance. As it was, he was helpless, completely at the mercy of these men. Well, he wouldn't give them the satisfaction of showing fear. He wasn't afraid of them; he'd seen plenty of violence in his life, and this was just more of the same. But Little knew his time was up.

The mob grabbed Little by his arms and legs and carried him roughly down the dusty street. Little realized they were looking for a tree. He was carried headfirst and upside down, and he twisted his head forward to see where they were taking him. Everything looked topsy-turvy, and things spun in a blur of colors. Still, he could see a large tree looming ahead. Through the din of the crowd, he heard the high-pitched voice of a woman pleading for his life, but the woman was pushed aside brusquely, and the proceedings continued.

Someone tied Little's wrists behind his back, and another tied his ankles. After he was trussed, the man behind him released his arms and let him stand under his own power. He was surrounded on all sides. He would have liked to spit in the faces of these people, but his mouth was as dry as powder. Someone in the mob had fetched a hemp rope and another tied it into a noose and flung it over Little's head. The outlaw was powerless as it was tightened around his neck.

"Hey whippersnapper, you want justice?" one of the men screamed. "Who votes we hang this boy like a hog?" The mob began chanting, "Hang him! Hang him!"

Someone hurled the loose end of the rope over a large tree branch, and several men pulled on it, raising Little off the ground. As he rose from the ground in jerking motions, the rope bit into his neck, and he began choking. Then, he blacked out—forever.

July 8, 1867

Frank James sat at the foot of a coffee bean tree near the Samuels' home, a cabin erected before the Civil War. The tree had luxuriant, spreading branches that created a pleasant shade.

It was a hot day and the shade of the tree refreshed Frank after his hours in the hot field. His shirt was drenched with sweat. He figured it must be 105 degrees, at least. And it was only lunchtime, he thought. He'd been out with his scythe haying when his mother rang a large iron bell signaling him and Jesse for lunch. But it would be awhile before the meal was ready.

No matter, it gave him a chance to think about pressing matters. Frank was concerned about the recent shootings and lynchings in the area. Someone had spilled the beans about the Richmond robbery, all right; how much he didn't know, but critical information and people's names had leaked out. He wondered if he and Jesse were on the short list, and if they would be the next targets. He and Jesse were on their guard. Things were getting hot, sure enough.

Jesse had been working in the north forty acres repairing fences, and he trudged by Frank carrying a large water bottle under his arm. He had wrapped it earlier in wet gunny cloth to keep the water cool, but the burlap had dried out long ago.

"Hotter 'n blazes, ain't it?" Jesse noted to Frank as he passed. "Think I'll visit the well. I got a bottle needs fillin'."

"Don't drink too much of that ugly stuff," Frank shouted after him. "It'll poison you, make hair grow on your teeth."

"I'll take my chances," Jesse replied over his shoulder.

Inside the house, Zerelda Samuel poked at the fire in the fireplace. She and her black servant were watching two pullets as they sputtered juicily on a spit over the fire. The women gave the chickens a turn every few minutes, and they were nearly done. The rich aroma of corn pone wafted from a Dutch oven immersed in the red coals of the fireplace. Zerelda opened the lid and saw that the crust was beginning to brown, almost done. Meanwhile, Zerelda's servant, a former slave of the family, pulled on a handle and swiveled a simmering pot of navy beans away from the fire to let it cool. Zerelda carried a plate of pickled cucumbers and sliced tomatoes to the table and laid it down. Things were about ready.

"Hey, boys!" she cried. "Get yourselves in here; we're fixin' to eat! You, too, Reuben," she added, calling to her husband, who sat in a nearby rocking chair reading a newspaper. Reuben folded the paper carefully, laid it down, and walked over to the table and pulled up a chair. The family seated itself around a circular oak table in the center of the main room of the Samuels' home.

Frank, hearing his mother's voice, rose to his feet. He had hoped to have a few words with Jesse before lunch. He'd have to catch him later, he guessed. They had a lot to talk about, he and Jess. He was concerned about the lynchings. You never knew what these Yankees and their pet lawmen were up to, and if you waited for them to act, they might get you in a bind. Frank believed it was time for him and Jesse to leave Missouri and pronto.

Frank eased down into his chair. After listening to Reuben's blessing, he began piling food onto his plate. When he had finished with one serving, he passed the dish around the table clockwise; Jesse, on the other side of the table, did likewise.

"Get those fences fixed yet, Jesse?" he asked, starting the table talk.

"Yep, 'bout got 'em. How's the hay goin'?"

"Most of it's cut," Frank replied. "I reckon we'll have to get the wagon hitched and do some pitchin' this afternoon. This bunch goes in the barn."

After the meal was over and the women had begun clearing off the table, Frank walked over to Jesse's side of the table and leaned over.

"We need to talk. I'm thinkin' we need to take a trip south." Jesse looked at Frank quizzically. He wondered what was bothering him. The two young men went outside and walked over to the well at the side of the house.

"I been hearin' lots of talk in town about the robbery," Frank began. "Our names have been mentioned. I'm thinkin' we ought to get scarce, go down to Uncle John's farm in Kentucky or thereabouts for awhile till things cool off. 'Out of sight, out of mind,' the old man said. What do you think? I don't like surprises."

"I'm not sure how Zee'll take this," Jesse said hesitantly. "She's been keepin' pretty close tabs on me lately." "Hey, maybe the law boys have too!" Frank replied. "We need space between us and them before they make their next move. We can fight 'em, sure enough, but that ain't the point; there'll be more where they came from. We need to get out of harm's way." "I'll think on it," Jesse replied. "You do that," Frank said and walked off toward the hay field.

July 15, 1867

Jesse's horse fidgeted nervously, shifting from one foot to the other. Zee looked up at Jesse and tears ran down her face. Jesse tried to comfort her.

"Dear one, don't take it so badly. I'm not goin' away forever," Jesse said.

"Yes, darlin', but you can never tell. Remember Aunt Sall and your cousin Riley? They went off to St. Louis one year, and the next thing we knew, they were both gone forever. Cholera got 'em. I'll miss you so much. Are you sure you've got to go?"

"Honey, we've talked it over. If we're ever goin' to get married, I've got to look to my best chances. I think there's opportunity in Kentucky; that's what Uncle John tells us. And I won't be there for long anyhow."

Zee began crying aloud. "I can't stand bein' without you," she whimpered.

"It'll only be for a couple months, I promise you," Jesse answered, hoping to quiet her. "I'm fixin' to do some horse racin' down there, too. That's a quick way to make money."

"But you can lose too, can't you?" Zee asked apprehensively.

"Not if you've got a good horse under you like my ol' Bob. But Frank and I will be doin' serious work mostly. The racin' will be for fun. Goodbye, darlin'." Jesse leaned down from his horse and planted a kiss on Zee's mouth. That done, he jerked on his reins and urged his horse to a trot, heading south toward the ferry crossing the Missouri River so that he could link up with Frank.

As Jesse rode out of sight, Zee continued to cry. She knew that she loved Jesse, but there was something wild stirring in him. She had noticed it when he returned from the war. He was different, and she didn't understand him anymore. He had suffered plenty in the war, and it had changed him from the happy, carefree person she once knew. She watched the plume of dust left in Jesse's wake until it disappeared from the horizon.

8

March 18, 1868

Cole Younger tethered his horse, dusted off his brown denim jacket, and adjusted his broad-brimmed hat. Then he strode through the entrance of the Nimrod Long Banking Company in Russellville, Kentucky, and walked up to the teller's cage.

"Sirs," he said, addressing the balding man behind the counter and the clerks nearby, "I have some business."

Nimrod Long, who had been examining his accounts, looked up. A tall, sturdily built young man stood before him. Long had never seen him before, but he looked decent enough. He was well dressed, perhaps a cattle speculator or well-to-do farmer, Long figured, and his carriage seemed to suggest breeding. Long somehow sensed something was wrong about him though, but the cashier was always suspicious of strangers.

"What do you want?" Long replied rather gruffly, continuing to scrutinize the young man before him. Younger, not taken aback by Long's coolness, looked him straight in the eye.

"Sir, I have a fifty-dollar note to change," Cole said and pulled a bill from his wallet and passed it to the banker.

Long grabbed the bill firmly between his fingers and stretched it lengthwise. He examined the bill carefully, allowing his eyes to move slowly across it. He'd seen lots of fifties, and he knew just what to look for in a counterfeit one.

He looked the bill over cautiously since a stranger wielded it. "Yes, it's all right," he finally answered grudgingly. "What brings you to these parts? I don't believe I know you," Long said. Never trusting of strangers, the cashier thought he'd pump the young man for more information. "I'm a cattle buyer," Cole replied. "Colburn's the name. Lookin' for someone in the market to sell?" Long stiffened a little. "Ranchin' is not my business. There are men along the square that might help you." Then he turned to his money tray. "What kind of bills do you want?" Cole looked at Long, unblinking: "Tens, fives, and ones."

Long focused on his cash tray and carefully lifted out three tens, three fives, and five ones and reached them to Younger, placing the bills, one by one, into his outstretched hand, counting them as he did so.

"Much obliged, my friend," Younger said as he tucked the notes neatly away in his wallet. While Long had been plucking the bills from his tray, Cole's eyes had been darting furtively around the bank, noting how many clerks were present and where the vault was. He had glanced sidelong at Long's money tray too and noticed the general layout of the room, the height and width of the teller's cage openings, the location of the doors and windows. Jesse, who had looked the bank over earlier, had been right, Cole reflected; it was perfect for a stickup. It was a bit crowded in the streets, he granted, but some random gunfire would clear away the gandies and loafers.

As he walked toward the door, Cole shouted over his shoulder, "Gentlemen, despite the wonderful weather we've been having, I predict snow." No one replied.

March 20, 1868

At the Regal Hotel in Chaplin, Kentucky, Frank James leaned back in his chair, totally engrossed by his volume of Shakespeare.

He loved the writer's work. He had brought a copy of *Macbeth* with him all the way from Missouri, and now he was glad he'd tossed it in his pack. Frank loved the language, so well written. He marveled at how a man could write so well. But the story was what entranced him. The scheming and killing in the story, which on the surface of things seemed incredible, were really all too true, like life, he thought. Shakespeare was describing real men and women and their greed and passions. Men were always striving to obtain power and money. That's what the recent war had been all about. But Shakespeare's play was more personal: one man's pursuit of power. He could understand that. He wanted a little power himself. He guessed maybe he had got some now. Sure, he had obtained it at the end of a gun, but wasn't that the source of all power—money and guns? Kings had their retainers and their weapons; Frank had his friends and, yes, their guns. Somehow, it seemed all the same to him.

Might made right in *Macbeth,* just like it had for the Yankees in the late war. According to the press, the men in blue were the fine-feathered fellows now, the knights in shining armor. If the South had won, though, the Northerners would have been so many villains. Sherman would surely have been hung for his crimes. What the public considered good and bad was just so much opinion; Frank knew that with certitude. Napoleon had been right about history: it was just a lie agreed upon. The real state of affairs in this world was simply every man for himself, just a naked grab for power and money. He was convinced that the politicians who ran the country were venal, crooked, conniving, lawyerly, lying scoundrels from start to finish. How could anyone believe in these knaves after witnessing their disgraceful antics? They would steal from their own mothers given the opportunity. And the businessmen? They too were nothing short of a gang of thieves. They called him and the boys "robbers." Ridiculous! They were small potatoes, compared to the Union government.

Then Frank's mind turned to Cole's report on the Russellville bank. That had been good news. Jesse had been right. They had found a bank ripe for the taking—and right in their own backyard. He had let Cole do the close checking; he was astute and reliable. But it was not all that hard to recognize a bank that needed a sizable "withdrawal."

While Frank assessed the situation, Jesse sat in a nearby rocking chair whittling on a wooden gimcrack, letting the chips fly in disarray at his feet.

"What do you think about tomorrow, Jesse?" Frank asked, turning to his brother. Frank respected Jesse's counsel. "Younger agrees it's primed and ready," he continued without waiting for Jesse to reply. "It may get a bit sticky for us though, gettin' back here. But we should be able to pull it off, don't you think?"

"I told you earlier; it's perfect. Younger was just wastin' his time ridin' over to Russellville and latherin' up his horse. He should have saved his nag for tomorrow."

"Well," Frank continued, "we can't be too cautious. One mistake on our part, and a world of trouble will descend on us. There's always a chance that somethin' will go wrong, somethin' unexpected. If bank robberies were so easy, men would be standin' in line to do 'em. I've had the boys lookin' the roads over in this neck of the woods."

"We know this place well enough," Jesse replied crankily. "All we have to do is lose the posses and get back here—take any pursuers for a jaunt first, that's all."

While Jesse argued with Frank sometimes and exhibited a certain bravado, he still appreciated his brother's caution. Frank was slick. Of course, Jesse thought his reading habits were a bit pretentious. But Jesse never doubted that Frank's spring ran deep.

That afternoon, the gang loitered in the street outside the Russellville bank chatting to each other casually while they waited for the bank clerks to leave for lunch. Soon a clerk left the bank from a side door. That left only Long and one clerk behind, Cole figured. He touched the bill of his hat, and the four men near him acknowledged his signal with knowing glances. Ol Shepherd, one of the outlaws, now took up a position on the right side of the front door of the bank. His brother George walked around the corner and stood at the bank's side door. Meanwhile, Arthur McCoy and John Jarrette led their horses to strategic positions along the square and held them by their reins.

Cole, Frank, and Jesse walked through the front entrance of the bank, Cole leading the way. As Cole walked up to the teller's window, Jesse and Frank milled about inside the door, pretending to chat as they waited their turn in line. Cole stood before Nimrod Long's window.

Long looked up and saw a familiar face. Oh, yes, it was the fellow who had come into the bank only the day before, the stranger, he remembered. Long knew faces, especially new ones in town.

"I have a bond to cash," Younger said, pushing a scrap of paper toward Long. The banker took a long look at it and looked up suspiciously. The young man seemed to be cashing a lot of paper lately, he thought to himself. After a few moments, he handed it back to Cole and shook his head dubiously.

"Sir, you don't like my money?" Younger questioned, feigning anger. "You don't think it's genuine?"

"I will not cash it," replied Long in a blunt, unfriendly voice. He looked for the first time beyond Younger, at the tall, slim men who stood behind him. He noticed that one of the men's eyes twitched. He got the notion that the three men were all of the same party, and he became apprehensive.

"My bill not good enough for you?" Cole continued, half smiling. "Then, take a gander at this! It's real," he said, pulling a concealed pistol from his duster.

"Back up! Get out of my way!" With this warning, Younger hurdled through the teller's window in a tangle of legs and shoved Long roughly to the floor. Frank and Jesse followed, scrambling through the window behind Cole.

Sprawled on the floor, Long quickly jumped to his feet and dashed for the back door of the bank as George Shepherd burst into the bank by a side door. He grappled with Long, but the cashier struggled from his grasp and ran wildly through the door. Shepherd fired at him and a bullet creased Long's head. With blood coursing down his face, Long continued running, and Shepherd fired at him again. This time, a bullet hit him in the upper arm, nearly knocking him to the ground. Regaining his balance, the cashier dashed headlong up the block searching for cover.

Gunfire erupted in the street as Ol Shepherd began firing at the townsmen gawking from the doors and windows of the businesses along the square. Citizens began firing back, and Ol began mumbling to himself: "Time, time, time, *time!*" Then, he screamed aloud to the men in the bank: "*It's time!*"

Meanwhile, Jesse and Frank had forced the clerk to open the vault and had entered the safe and filled their grain sack with fourteen thousand dollars in gold and currency (close to two hundred thousand dollars in today's money). Their sack filled, the bandits rushed through the front door of the bank and into the street. Some of them began firing up the street to clear the way. After tying the loot to his saddle, Frank James mounted his horse.

"Let's get out of here!" he screamed.

The bandits shrieked rebel yells and galloped out of town in a flurry of dust. The citizens of the town gathered in the middle of the street and fired after them. Some of the townsmen stuffed their waistbands with revolvers and mounted their horses to take up the chase. They spurred their horses to a quick gallop and thundered down the road after the outlaws, passing through the dense cloud of dust left by the robbers. The James-Younger gang had managed to get a small lead on them. Soon the bandits began to pace their horses for the long haul, and the posse began to slowly gain ground on them and to commence firing.

As Jesse turned to look behind him, bullets whistled by his head. The posse was getting close. Jesse decided to dust them off, and he raised his pistol, aimed, and fired. One of the pursuers fell from his horse onto the ground, and some of the posse stopped to help the fallen rider. The others merely dodged the fallen man and kept up the chase. Jesse felt a sharp pain in his leg. Somebody had pinged him, he guessed. He turned to Frank. "We'd better split up! It's gettin' hot!"

Frank turned to the other riders. "Break up, boys! Cut off the main trail!" he ordered.

After six hundred yards, Frank darted to his right down a narrow bridle path at a full gallop. Several of the posse followed him. Frank had received a shoulder wound, and the blood stained his shirt. He'd make a race of it though, he reckoned, and he spurred his horse sharply. A half-mile farther along the main road, Jesse and Cole pulled to the right and descended a tree-lined trail. Soon, they came to a ravine, jumped their horses across it, and scrambled up the other side.

Several hundred yards ahead, the two men walked their horses over several large trees straddling the path. Within minutes, they had lost their pursuers and proceeded at a more comfortable gait. The Shepherd brothers, Arthur McCoy, and John Jarrette, chased by the remaining posse, fled down the main road a mile farther, then took detours themselves. Traveling down some of the wilder local paths, they soon lost their own pursuers. The posse had been forced to split up into small units, and the outlaws' main chance was to keep moving and outdistance their pursuers before reinforcements arrived.

Frank was glad he had picked a room at a hotel with a back stairway and entrance. He and Jesse had been in no shape to walk through the lobby when they returned from Russellville. Both men were splattered with blood and covered with dust. Jesse had gotten to the hotel first and cleaned up some by the time Frank arrived. Jesse had already bandaged his leg by tearing up one of his bed sheets and dressing his wound with it. When Frank arrived, he was still bleeding from a painful flesh wound to his shoulder.

Under the circumstances, the brothers had gotten off lucky, Frank thought. He had been right; you could never be certain about what might happen when a posse took up the chase. This posse had been mounted on pretty good horses, and they'd made a close race of it. In the end, they had lacked sufficient riding skills, and their horses lacked endurance. But they'd gotten close enough to riddle them. Despite them, Frank and the boys had gotten away with a big haul. They'd been prepared to take the risks, and now they had their plunder. But the robbery could have gone a whole lot better, he admitted to himself.

After Frank arrived, Jesse hobbled to the well at the back of the hotel and dropped a wooden bucket into the water, giving the rope a twist so that the pail struck the water at an angle and filled. After raising the bucket, he used the water and a broom to clean the blood from the wood steps leading to their room. They'd have to hole up at the hotel until the posses gave up the pursuit, and they didn't want to leave any telltale signs.

Back in their room, the brothers reloaded their revolvers and oiled and checked them. Once Jesse had bandaged Frank's wound, he moved the horses to the nearby woods in case they had to make a quick getaway. They were probably safe since the posses were likely to think they had headed for another county or state. If that were the case, the hotel made a good temporary refuge.

Before he lay down in bed, Jesse reached for a bottle of whiskey lying on a nearby table and took a long drink. Then he poured some of the liquor onto the bandage covering his wound. The wound was becoming painful, but he'd handled worse. The bullet had missed the bone; that was the main thing. Frank appeared to be asleep, but Jesse figured he was wide awake too.

"Frank?" Jesse said softly.

"Yep," Frank replied.

"Try some of this," Jesse said, handing the bottle of bourbon over to his brother.

While the brothers lay in bed, they listened unconsciously for strange sounds. Their revolvers were stuffed in their belts, and they could spring into action instantly. Meanwhile, their pain kept them from sleeping soundly. Every so often during the night, the building creaked, and the brothers reached for their pistols.

April 4, 1868

Delos "Yankee" Bligh stood before the proprietor of the Regal Hotel. Bligh was a short, barrel-chested man with small round spectacles. A large .44-caliber revolver protruded from the front of his coat. He viewed the owner of the Regal suspiciously, peering into his eyes as if he were looking into the soul of Jack Turpin or some other famous highwayman. Bligh, like most detectives, treated the objects of his attention like they were Public Enemy Number One, never less than number two.

As he began speaking, Bligh pulled a Louisville Police Department detective badge from his pocket and stuck it obtrusively into the hotel owner's face.

"Think hard now! I want to know if you have had any lodgers lately who fit the bill as the bandits who robbed the Long Bank in Russellville a couple weeks ago."

"Say, what makes you think I keep that sort of people in my hotel?" the hotel manager replied defensively.

Not taken aback, Bligh replied firmly, "I'm not here to judge your hotel; I'm here to track down outlaws. Have any strangers visited your hotel recently, maybe twenty or thirty years old, big men, with no visible means of support?"

"Well, I reckon I've had quite a few folks fittin' that bill," the hotel operator replied. "But come to think of it, I did have a couple of fellas recently, looked like brothers. They stayed with me several weeks ago. Had fine horses. Hey, they looked like racers! Kinda smart-talkin' fellas."

Bligh's eyes brightened. This was his best lead yet on the robbery. Fine horses, he thought to himself. Most people didn't have fine horses. His robbers did though.

"What sort of horses?" Bligh questioned.

"Well, one had a bay, the other a roan," the hotelkeeper answered.

"How did these fellows sign your register?" Bligh continued, showing keen interest.

The hotel operator rubbed his head and reached for the register. "Let me see . . . I forget now." He turned through the pages slowly and then stopped. "Yep, here they are. One of 'em signed himself Ben J. Woodson, the other John Howard."

"Do you think those were their real names?" Bligh replied. "Did you hear them use any other names?" he asked insistently.

The hotel operator thought for a moment. "Well, I did hear one of 'em say Dingum or Dingas or somethin' funny soundin', referrin' to the other fella. It might have been a nickname though."

Bligh reached into his pocket, pulled out a pencil stub, and jotted the name and other particulars in a small notebook he kept in his pocket.

"Did you notice anything strange or extraordinary about these men?"

"Well," the hotel operator continued, "they didn't come out of their rooms much the last few days. And when they did, the dark-haired one had a limp; he was the one who wore silver spurs. Actually, he was havin' a real hard time gettin' around. He was the one mounted on the bay horse. He used a Morgan saddle if I remember right. And . . . oh, yes, he also had somethin' wrong with his eyes, always blinkin'. The other fella was, uh, well, ordinary. Say, they stole one of my sheets!"

Bligh's eyes squinted for a moment; he was lost in thought. "You've been right helpful to me," he finally replied.

May 20, 1868

Ol Shepherd had lathered his face and was carefully shaving. He steered his razor neatly around his drooping mustache and cleanly shaved his chin, cheeks, and neck. As he ran the razor down his neck, he heard the dogs wail.

"Confound it!" he cried out. Shepherd had nicked himself, and a stream of blood trickled through the white lather on his face and ran down his bare chest in red rivulets. He stopped shaving and washed his neck with a washrag. He held the wet cloth over the cut to stanch the flow. He would have to run around holding a cloth against his neck until it stopped bleeding. He was losing his patience. Shepherd walked into the kitchen.

"What's the matter with the dogs? Why they raisin' such a ruckus?" he said to his father.

The old man looked up from his breakfast. "What's botherin' you, boy? Probably just a bitch in heat. You know dogs."

Ol ignored his father and looked through the kitchen window. He saw nothing unusual, just a thick morning fog. Holding the cloth against his neck, he walked around the house, looking out the various windows as he strode. Then he grabbed a shirt and put it on, buttoning it quickly while he balanced the washrag against his cheek to stop the bleeding. His mother noticed his agitated behavior.

"What's your problem, son?" she asked. "Why're you so jumpy?"

"Nothin', Mom," he answered and continued walking around the house, checking the windows. When he got to the east side of the house, he peered out the window and his head jerked. Several men were huddled among the fog-shrouded trees at the edge of the yard.

Shepherd grabbed two revolvers, stuck them in his belt, dropped the washrag, and looked out another window facing toward the barn where his horse was corralled. He had to get out of there.

Without saying anything to his parents, he ran out the back door and dashed for the barn. A number of rifles boomed, and he was hit in the shoulder and chest. Shepherd fell to the ground dead. The firing continued, with more bullets ramming into him, and his body jerked with each impact. Once the firing stopped, one of Shepherd's hounds ran from the barn and scampered over to him. He sniffed at the blood, shook his ears, and bolted for cover.

Within weeks, George Shepherd, Oliver's brother, was arrested, tried, convicted, and imprisoned for three years in the Kentucky Penitentiary.

May 25, 1868

To the sound of clucking hens, Zee Mimms entered the family chicken house. She grabbed the eggs nestled under one of the setting hens and placed them in her basket. When she reached under another hen, it pecked at her.

"Now, listen here, lady," Zee scolded the bird, "that's not polite."

As she exited the chicken house with her basket of eggs, Zee looked unconsciously toward the road leading from Kansas City and her eyes brightened. She saw a faint trace of dust on the horizon and her heart raced. There weren't that many people who traveled down the Mimms' road, she thought. Was it Jesse? She wished it were. She picked up her pace and ran back to the house.

"Mother," she cried. "I think Jesse's a comin'!" Zee's mother was preparing lunch, and she looked up from her work.

"Goodness, child, is every traveler comin' down the road Mr. Jesse Woodson James? Get hold of yourself, young lady."

"But, Mother, you know he promised he'd be back from Kentucky sometime this month."

"Yes, darlin', but the month's still with us. Now, calm yourself down and get back to your chores."

Zee walked out into the Mimms' front yard and continued looking in the direction of the dust. She was positive it was Jesse. It had to be. She went to the granary with a basket to get some feed to throw to the chickens. After scattering it, she walked back toward the house. Now, she could see a rider approaching. She recognized the horse's smart gait. It was Jesse's horse, all right! She ran as fast as she could to the Mimms' house, arriving just as Jesse rode up. When Jesse saw Zee, he dismounted and ran to her. As he raced toward her, Zee noticed that he was favoring one of his legs, as if he had hurt it recently.

Jesse grabbed Zee around the waist and swung her in a wide circle.

"Zee, I'll bet you reckoned I'd never return," he said, pausing to kiss her warmly on the mouth. Zee responded enthusiastically. She was happier than she had been in months. As Jesse held her in his arms, Zee questioned him. "Darlin', I notice that you're favorin' one of your legs. What happened? Did you hurt yourself?"

"Oh," Jesse replied, "darned horse got excited while I was brushin' her one mornin,' gave me a kick. It's nothin', just a love tap. She's a spirited girl, that horse."

"Are you sure?" Zee continued. "Are you sure you don't need a doctor?"

"Positive, darlin'," Jesse replied. "Don't worry about it; it's nearly healed, and it's just a bruise. Don't fret about it." Then the two, arm in arm, went into the Mimms' home to greet Zee's mother and father.

9

December 7, 1868

The James brothers rode up to the hitching post in front of the Daviess County Savings Bank in Gallatin, Missouri, dismounted, and tethered their horses. Frank was a little apprehensive about this robbery. It would be only him and Jesse this time. They were undermanned, but they were out of money and needed some quick. He had a good man to help him, his brother—if he could restrain him, hold him in check. Jesse could be hotheaded at times. He hoped he would remain cool today because the robbery had to be executed perfectly and a clean getaway made. Frank entered the bank and walked up to the cashier while Jesse stood outside the door.

"I've a hundred-dollar note to change," Frank said casually, laying the bill on the counter in front of the cashier.

"Let's see it," the cashier replied, picking it up. Nearby, another clerk ruffled through his accounts.

The cashier, Capt. John W. Sheets, a former Union army officer, looked the bill over and walked to the vault for change. As he did so, Jesse entered the bank and called after Sheets: "We'd like a receipt for that too!" Sheets, amenable to the request, halted his trip to the vault and walked back to his desk, sat down, and began writing out a receipt.

Frank was disturbed. Why had Jesse changed their plan?

They didn't need any special formalities. But Jesse had wanted a better look at Sheets, thought he recognized him. While the cashier was writing the receipt, Jesse looked him over carefully and his face reddened. The cashier looked like S. J. Cox, the man responsible for Bill Anderson's death during the war. Jesse knew that Cox lived in Gallatin. He walked over to Frank and whispered, "It's him. It's Cox, ain't it?"

Frank looked the banker over closely. "Well . . . he kind of looks like Cox." Jesse's face turned an ashen hue.

"It's him, Frank. I know it's him!" Jesse was talking so loudly now that Sheets looked up and stared at the two men in surprise. Jesse turned toward Sheets.

"You pig!" Jesse screamed. He pulled his revolver out from under his coat and fired a bullet into the cashier's head at point-blank range. The bullet struck Sheets in the eye and issued out the back of his head. Blood splattered on Jesse's coat. As Cox slid to the floor, Jesse fired a second bullet into his chest.

The clerk, William A. McDowell, who had been watching the scene from a few steps away, was astonished. Who were these men? What was happening? Jesse turned toward McDowell, regaining some of his composure.

"That's the man who killed my brother, Bill Anderson," he said. "We've given him exactly what he deserved. Now, open up that blasted vault!" The teller was almost paralyzed. He didn't know the combination. What is more, he was convinced that these men wouldn't believe that he didn't. As the Jameses emptied the bank's money tray, the teller dashed through the front door. The outlaws ran after him firing, and a bullet tore through McDowell's shoulder. He hardly felt it. In fact, he hardly knew that his feet were moving; he seemed to fly through the air, running faster than he had ever believed he could run.

"Sheets is dead! Sheets is dead! Robbers!" he screamed as he ran.

Men poured out of the local businesses, drew their weapons, and began firing at the brothers. Jesse fired back at the men, holding them off, while Frank stuffed the money they had collected from the cash tray into a pouch attached to his saddle and mounted his horse. His brother in the saddle, Jesse grabbed his own horse's reins and attempted to mount. But his steed, excited by the gunfire, wheeled from his grasp. While Jesse attempted to get his foot in the stirrup and mount her, the horse shied and swiveled some more. Before he could fully seat himself, the horse gave a nervous jerk and spun Jesse backwards onto the ground and began running, with Jesse dangling by one leg from the stirrup. The horse dragged Jesse down the street for forty feet while the townsmen fired at him excitedly. Finally, he untangled himself from the stirrup and wrenched free. Frank, recognizing Jesse's predicament, rode up to him. Jesse vaulted onto the rump of Frank's horse and clutched the back of his brother's coat with his fists. With bullets whistling around them, the two brothers galloped out of town, stirring up a great cloud of dust.

Some miles outside of Gallatin, the brothers stole a saddle-less horse and continued southward. Several miles down the trail, they pulled into some woods and covered their tracks as best they could, holing up until after nightfall.

That evening, traveling in the bright moonlight, they rode their horses into Kidder, a nearby town. There, they forced the Reverend Helm to act as their guide, ordering him to lead them to the tracks of the St. Joseph and Hannibal Railroad. When they reached the railroad tracks, they held Helm captive. Thirty minutes later, the brothers heard a locomotive approaching, and Frank slapped his horse on its rump, driving it into the woods. He ordered Helm to return home on foot.

The brothers pulled the little money they had stolen out of their saddlebag and stuffed it into their pockets. Soon, the noise from the train grew louder, and a bright light beamed around a curve in the track. When the locomotive passed, the brothers chased after the cars, grabbed the ladder rungs at the front of two separate cars, and pulled themselves aboard. When they reached Kearney, they jumped off the train and headed for home.

The next day, a witness at Gallatin told lawmen that he recognized the horse left behind by one of the robbers. He said a J. James of Kearney, Missouri, owned it.

December 20, 1868

"HOOOEEE! PIGEE, PIGEE, PIGEE!" Sammy hollered in a high falsetto. Hogs, their heads held low and their feet stirring up dust, ran from the remote ravines and gullies of the Samuels' farm toward the black boy. Sammy had placed shelled corn in the hog troughs and had just finished pumping a wooden tank full of water. He watched as the pigs raced to the trough and scuffled for a place, grunting and squealing loudly. Finally, the hogs sorted out who would eat where, just like humans usually do, and began munching noisily on the corn.

As they ate, Sammy looked around the farm. It was cold, he thought. But he'd seen it a lot colder this time of year. The sun shone brightly and that made it feel warmer, he reckoned. The ground was free of snow.

He was glad Frank and Jesse were back from Kentucky. They often helped him with the chores. His mother was glad to see the boys too. She had helped raise them, just like she'd raised Sammy. Now that he was thirteen Sammy was expected to work in the fields like everyone else. He was a free black now. But when he thought about it, he couldn't see much difference in his condition from what it had been earlier when he was just a slave. Of course, he and his ma and pa could go anywhere they wanted to now. But what would they do when they got there? How would they buy things? They didn't have much money. The Samuels didn't have a whole lot either, but they had more than his folks. What had the Civil War been all about, he wondered curiously, all those white folks killing other white folks, blowing their guts and brains out? It was puzzling as all get out to him. But then he wasn't sure the problem even related to him. He thought you just lived out your life and kept your nose clean. He was free. That was good enough for him.

He liked it when Frank and Jesse were home though. When they were at the Samuels' place during the winter they slept in the loft with the black children, like they had when they had come home during the war. The boys kept up a loud banter at night before they went to sleep, and Sammy and his brothers and sisters liked to listen to them chatter and tell stories. They told some interesting stories too, he thought, and he believed most of them—no, all of them.

Sammy was on the lookout today for strangers. Mrs. Samuel had told him to watch out for visitors. She said that if he saw anyone, especially a group of men, he was to warn her and the boys immediately. She didn't say whom these men might be or why they would be coming, but the family seemed concerned and apprehensive about them, so Sammy was too.

As he watched the hogs, he noticed a small pig being shoved out of the way. He walked over and poked one of the big hogs with a stick to make room for the little one. The big hog snorted at him and nipped at the stick but moved down the trough.

Sammy looked up suddenly. Something had caught his attention. Across the farm, he saw a cloud of dust in the distance. Not many people came down that road, and he was startled at first. Then he understood the cloud, and he ran as hard as his legs would carry him to the Samuels' house, falling down twice. Finally reaching the house, he opened the back door and scrambled into the main room where Jesse and Frank were warming themselves in front of the fireplace.

"Someone's a comin'! Someone's a comin'! Bunch of 'em, I reckon," Sammy screamed. Mrs. Samuel, who stood a few feet away from the fire, became excited.

"Get out of here, boys," she said, grabbing Frank and Jesse by their shirts. "Come on!" she urged. Frank and Jesse rushed for their heavy coats. As they came back into the room, Sammy noticed that they had revolvers stuck in their belts.

Frank said something to Mrs. Samuel, sort of private, that Sammy couldn't make out—something about the barn where the horses were kept. Meanwhile, a half-mile up the road, two law officers from Gallatin and Deputy Sheriff John D. Thomason and his son Oscar from Liberty, Missouri, rode toward the Samuels' farm at a trot.

"The Samuels' place is just over that next rise," the elder Thomason yelled to the other lawmen. "When we reach the top of the hill, let's talk the situation over. We'll need a plan," Thomason added. As the sheriff crested the hill, he reined in his horse and dismounted; the others followed suit.

"That's the Samuels' homestead ahead," Thomason said, pointing down the hill in the direction of a log cabin.

"Now, do as I say. These are mean fellas—killers! What I want you two to do," he said, speaking to the two men from Gallatin, "is to ride around to the back of the place and set up in the woods with your rifles. Oscar and I will go to the front door and flush 'em out. If the boys run out the back door, shoot 'em. If they make trouble at the front door, that's my call. But when trouble starts, you two come runnin'. Got it? We'll support you too if it comes to that. We'll give you five minutes; then Oscar and I will start down the hill." The two men from Gallatin nodded and rode in a circular route toward the back of the Samuels' homestead.

After five minutes, Thomason nudged his horse lightly, and he and his boy proceeded over the hill to the Samuels' place. When they arrived at the fence that encircled the house, the two men reined up, dismounted, and tethered their horses. They advanced through a gate and went to the front door of the cabin. The Samuels' dogs roared but didn't attack. The elder Thomason was in the lead. He rapped on the front door with his fist and waited for an answer.

Mrs. Samuel, who stood silently inside the door, motioned to Sammy and whispered in his ear. When he heard her message, his eyes widened in surprise. He was a little frightened, but he would run into hellfire if Mrs. Samuel told him to do so. Zerelda Samuel opened the door wide, and Thomason stared at her intently. "Where's those two boys of yours?" he demanded brusquely. As Thomason questioned Mrs. Samuel, Sammy ran for the barn as fast as his small legs could take him. When he reached the barn, situated at the rear of the house, he grabbed one of the two heavy barn doors and dragged it open. Thomason, seeing the child's flight and now somewhat confused, walked quickly to the side of the house to see where the black boy had gone. As Thomason looked on, Sammy pulled the other door open, and Frank and Jesse James burst out of the barn on horseback bristling with revolvers.

The brothers spurred their horses and sped across the yard in a wide arc, leaping over a rail fence. Thomason fired at the brothers then rushed for his horse, mounted it, and raced for the fence, clearing it easily. By this time, the lawmen from Gallatin had arrived, but lacking the skill to vault fences, they dismounted and laboriously moved the timbers aside. Oscar helped them. By the time they were remounted, Thomason and the Jameses were out of sight.

Thomason, well mounted, had spurred his horse sharply through a stand of oak and locust trees and sped after the James boys at a gallop. He was in no way intimidated by the brothers and meant to bring them in. Within two miles, he realized that he was gaining on them and roused his horse to a greater effort. Jesse, glancing over his shoulder, saw that Thomason was overtaking them. He screamed to Frank, "Let's finish him."

The two men turned their horses around in the road and halted. The brothers leveled their pistols and fired. Frank's bullet went wild, but Jesse's penetrated the front leg of Thomason's horse, and it tumbled forward, throwing the sheriff to the ground. Thomason rose slowly to his feet, then drew his revolver, and fired a wild shot at the Jameses as they rode out of sight.

Soon, rewards were printed offering three thousand dollars (forty-five thousand dollars in today's money) for the killer of Sheets and the robbers of the Gallatin bank. Meanwhile, Gov. Joseph W. McClurg wired sheriffs in the counties adjoining the Jameses' own Clay County to organize militia units to capture or kill the bandits. The James boys, for the first time since the war, were sought formally as outlaws.

To offset the "bad publicity" caused by the Gallatin robbery, Jesse James wrote a letter to the *Kansas City Times:*

> I will never surrender to be mobbed by a set of bloodthirsty poltroons. It is true that during the war I was a Confederate soldier, and that I fought under the black flag, but since that time I have lived as a peaceable citizen and obeyed the law of the United States to the best of my ability.
>
> —J. James

At the *Times,* John Newman Edwards, former Confederate general Jo Shelby's adjutant during the late war, read Jesse's letter and smiled.

"Williamson!" he called to his subordinate editor. "Here's somethin' for page one." Then Edwards lit up a cigar and blew a perfect ring into the air. So the Yankees thought the war was over, Edwards mused.

June 3, 1871

As the seven gang members entered the town of Corydon, they marveled at the people. Surely thirty thousand people crowded around the main square. Corydon was the county seat, but the crowd assembled must have come from all over Iowa. They were gathered to hear old Henry Clay Dean speak. They said Dean was another Daniel Webster, Clell Miller recalled, as he rode along with the other bandits. What is more, he was a rock-ribbed, fire-eating Democrat in a black Republican bastion. Clell sure would like to hear the old fellow give them Republicans hell. But the gang had work at hand, around the corner at the Ocobock Brothers' Bank. Business first, Clell thought. It was a rich town, so Clell and the rest of the gang expected fine pickin's.

Frank James rode alongside Miller. He smiled too when he saw the crowd. It was just as he had expected, a grand throng. What a wonderful opportunity for a holdup, he thought. The people of the town would be distracted at the speaking, and he and the boys could just walk into the bank and clean it out. Jesse, who rode a few yards behind Clell and Frank, was disappointed that they would not be able to hear old Dean; he'd always wanted to hear the fellow, see if he lived up to his billing. Everyone said he was a spellbinder. But the bank was a golden opportunity for the gang. They had a couple of new men along for the robbery, Jim White and Jim Koughman, but Jesse thought they'd work out all right. The gang didn't expect any problems. Everyone would be too preoccupied with the festivities.

The men rode around the corner of the square, pulled up in front of the bank, and dismounted. Jesse, Frank, and Cole Younger went inside. Only one banker was present. The bandits drew their weapons, took the key to the safe from the acting cashier, and opened up the vault. Within seconds, they had plopped forty thousand dollars into their wheat sack and bound and gagged the bank clerk. Then, at Jesse's suggestion, the gang decided to have a little fun before they left town. Jesse wanted to bandy words with the famous orator, the Honorable Henry Clay Dean. The rest of the bandits were not averse to the proposal.

As the gang rode up to the square, Jesse angled his horse toward the speaker's platform. When he approached the platform, the eyes of the throng turned toward him. The other men rode several yards behind Jesse. Frank, riding directly behind his brother, balanced a bulging grain sack on the saddle in front of him. No one guessed what was in it.

Jesse reined in his horse directly in front of the famous orator. Dean had been speaking in a heated manner, but when he saw Jesse approach, he halted in midsentence, waiting to hear what the young man on horseback had to say.

"Mr. Dean, I rise to a point of order," Jesse said loudly.

Dean answered him in mellifluous tones: "What is it, my friend and fellow citizen? What prompts you to interrupt this proceeding at such an infelicitous moment? Nonetheless, I yield to the gentleman on horseback and importune him to express himself with alacrity."

"Well, sir, I reckon it's important enough. You see, the fact is, Mr. Dean, while you've been enlightenin' this mass of people, some fellas have been over at the bank robbin' its safe of every blamed dollar. And they tied up the cashier too. If you and the folks aren't too busy talkin', you might want to go over and untie the poor fella. I've got to be goin'."

With that, Jesse let out a whoop, and the seven riders lifted their hats over their heads and galloped down the road leading south of town. Dean, aggravated by the disturbance, turned to his audience.

"Ladies and gentlemen, I apologize for this interruption. There are people who feel they must impose themselves upon the consideration of others while, at the same time, shedding but little light on the important matters of this world!"

Half an hour later, the townsmen found that their bank had been robbed and formed a posse in pursuit of the outlaws. Again, the trail led to Clay and Jackson Counties in Missouri. Two months later, Clell Miller was arrested by Kansas City, Missouri, detectives and extradited to stand trial in Iowa for the robbery. He was found not guilty of the crime on the grounds that no one could state positively that he had ever been in Iowa, and his friends testified that he had been in Missouri during the robbery.

July 2, 1871

William A. Pinkerton—his friends called him "Billy"—sat behind a large walnut desk in his Chicago office. A look of supreme confidence radiated from his countenance. His father, Allan, had led General McClellan's secret police during the late war and commanded Lincoln's bodyguard when the president was inaugurated. Now, the old man had entrusted Billy and his brother Robert to manage the operations of the Pinkerton National Detective Agency, renowned for its wily and dogged pursuit of criminals. The Pinkertons were America's Scotland Yard, but without a governmental connection. Whenever any person, any company, any institution wanted a topnotch policeman to settle a difficulty, they called on Billy and Robert. And they had plenty of men at their service, men of nerve and spirit. After the Civil War, the company had hired a number of crack policemen and ex-military officers, all of whom needed the work and were willing to do the Pinkertons' bidding. They were rugged men, and like all good policemen, would kill for a price. And Pinkerton paid his men well.

Billy sat proudly at his polished desk. He had a large bulldog face with carefully trimmed walrus whiskers extending down the sides of his mouth. He seemed more of an elemental force than a man. While he was generally congenial with his men, they all feared him. Billy expected the ultimate sacrifice from them if it was necessary, and they knew that. When the company specified enemies to be exterminated, Billy demanded that his men carry out their orders thoroughly, meticulously, and successfully—whatever the risk to their personal safety.

That's why Billy had ordered this meeting. He had just identified several new criminals for his company to eradicate. He was confident that his men would eliminate them without much trouble. When his four men entered the room, Billy ordered the door closed and cleared his throat.

"Ahem! Men, I've asked you to meet with me about a problem

that's come up. It has to do with Iowa. Recently, a number of men robbed the Ocobock Bank at Corydon. The governor of that state has asked me to enter the case and capture these criminals. I am assigning you to do that. I don't think this will pose a great problem for you. I want you to pursue these criminals aggressively until you capture or kill them."

Losing his composure, he screamed, "I want them! Do you understand me? I want these men dead!" Billy looked around the room at the assembled men. He thought he had made his point. Then, he continued.

"We think we know who the robbers are. What we need is enough evidence on them so that the prosecutors in Iowa can bring them to trial and convict them if they are brought in alive. But we are not required to bring them in alive. They are wanted men. If they resist—if they resist you in any way—I want you to kill them. They are dangerous men, no better than common rats. Show them no mercy."

Louis Lull, an ex-officer in the Union army, listened intently to the boss. He was used to Billy's impassioned exhortations. The men expected it of him. But Billy and his brother Robert usually got their man. It was their intensity, their doggedness that got them. Billy was like a wolf trailing a stag: he would get his animal or drop dead trying. But Lull knew, of course, that it was he and the men who would do the killing and dying.

Near Lull stood John Whicher, a cocky, tow-headed young man barely twenty-three years old. Old Billy bored John. All talk, all talk, he thought to himself. When it came to catching outlaws, it would be he and the other detectives who did it, not this squat, fair-haired son of the company's founder. It would be the guns of Pinkerton detectives, their courage, and their blood that did it. Whicher looked at Billy; he thought that he was a fat blow-hard. But he wasn't about to tell Billy that. He knew Billy brooked no resistance. Whicher knew his place.

Pinkerton continued to harangue the men. "The men we will

be capturing are primarily from two families, the Youngers and Jameses of Missouri. But they have numerous confederates that operate with them from time to time. They are guerrillas from the past war and know how to use guns. The James brothers— Jesse Woodson and Alexander Franklin are their names— fought with Bill Anderson during the war. You know Anderson, the one they called 'Bloody Bill.' If you know anything about Anderson's men, you know they are brutal killers. I want you to be careful, but I want you to get them. I want no excuses.

"Remember, they are ignorant butternuts, unsophisticated country boys," Billy went on. "They have little intelligence, courage, or tenacity, but they are wily. In addition, they have potent political allies. The Missourians may not cooperate with you. They are mostly treasonous Rebs, so even when you're talking to local lawmen, you cannot be certain they are your friends. Remember that. They may be informers for the gang.

"The reason I'm assigning the four of you is that it is a big job. I want you to circulate around western Missouri and find out where these outlaws are and capture or kill them—without arousing the attention of the local authorities. We will have the governors of Missouri, Iowa, and Kansas behind us if we need them. But for political reasons, they must keep a low profile. Our real problems will be with the county sheriffs. When you leave the city, trust no one. These buckwheats are all traitors, ruthless swine, who will sell your life for a crumb. Don't forget that. Have you any questions?"

"Sir," said John Boyle, one of the detectives, "you said these fellows might be killers. What if . . ."

"You idiot!" Pinkerton broke in, red-faced and outraged. "Of course they're killers. I want you to kill *them! You* will be the killers! That's what I want you to do, *kill them!* That's what I'm paying you to do. Now go out and do it and stop talking about it. How you kill them is of no consequence to me."

The men filed silently out of Pinkerton's office.

September 26, 1872

It was Big Thursday at the Kansas City Exposition, and more than thirty thousand people had paid their admission and were viewing the fair exhibits, races, and demonstrations. This year the fair featured a race between the famous trotter Ethan Allen and a contender, Smith's Hope. A couple of hours earlier, the horses had gone through their paces. Now, the fairground flourished with exhibits of fruits, vegetables, handiworks of all varieties, and general novelties and gimcracks. Hucksters and vendors screamed at the top of their voices: "Popped corn! Ice treats!"

At the main gate, in a small booth, John Hall, the secretary and treasurer of the fair association, counted the returns. After tallying the money, he placed it carefully in a tin box to be taken to the First National Bank. Arrangements had been made for the bank to receive the money after normal banking hours. After writing down the amount of the returns in a notebook, Hall handed the box, filled with ten thousand dollars in cash, to his young assistant, James Ross.

"Here it is, Jimmy. Watch it carefully. Get to the bank quickly, and don't stop and talk to anyone, do you hear me?"

"Don't worry, Mr. Hall, you can trust me," replied Jimmy. "I'll get it there directly." Then Jimmy Ross walked in the direction of the bank at a fast gait, holding the handle of the cash box in a strong grip.

Before the young man had walked fifty feet from the main gate, however, three horsemen raced toward him. One of the horsemen, Jesse James, reined in and dismounted. He ran directly up to Ross and wrenched the tin box from his grasp violently, shoving the messenger to the ground. Frank rode by on his horse, and Jesse reached the box up to him. Then Jesse remounted his horse and rode off with Bob Younger, Cole Younger's brother, who was operating in his first robbery. As the outlaws rode off, they fired their weapons in the air to intimidate possible pursuers. The crowd at the gates panicked at the gunshots, scurried in every direction, and clogged the entrance to the fair, preventing anyone from chasing after the gang. Adding to the pandemonium, a small girl ran in front of one of the bandits' horses as he raced from the scene and was trampled. A cluster of people immediately huddled around the child, further congesting the area.

"Police! Police!" the crowd screamed as the outlaws rode off at a gallop, but no one rode in pursuit.

10

June 14, 1873

Frank James stretched his long legs and yawned. He sat at a large, circular walnut table at the Junction Saloon near the railroad yards in Omaha, Nebraska. He had been mingling all day with the retired railroad workers and clerks, gray-haired old men with sunken cheeks and smelly breath, who congregated there. The joint reeked of rancid beer and whiskey, and cigarette and foul pipe smoke hung in the air. Around Frank's table splotches of slimy tobacco juice stained the wood floor where the railroaders had missed the spittoons. Frank lifted a tumbler of whiskey to his lips and pretended to drink heartily. Periodically, however, he slyly emptied some of the contents of his small glass into a spittoon he'd carefully positioned near his leg.

Frank needed to stay sober for the game he was playing. He had boozed it up enough during the day just pretending to drink the stuff while he talked to some elderly former railroad men. He'd told them that he was an agent for a Wyoming mining company searching for a railroad on which to ship the company's gold. Frank knew that railroad men frequented the Junction, so it was the logical place to do his undercover work. That afternoon, a retired railroad man, a fellow named Jack, plied by Frank's liquor, had mentioned a Tom Feagins, a shipping clerk for the Chicago, Rock Island, and Pacific Railroad, as someone who might help him. Now that the regular railroad men had gotten off work and were trickling into the saloon, Frank intended to have Jack direct him to Feagins.

"Jack," Frank said to the old-timer sitting across from him, "remember that Feagins fella you mentioned to me earlier? Where is he? I'd like to talk business with him."

"Hey, he's right over there," Jack said, pointing toward the front of the saloon. "See that fella with the black mustache and pile of hair sittin' by the window? That's him. Let me introduce you."

Jack led Frank to Feagins' table, and Frank extended his muscular hand to the shipping clerk.

"Feagins, this here's Ben Woodson, a friend of mine," Jack said. "He works for a minin' company near Cheyenne, Wyomin'. He's got some business that might interest you." Then, Jack left the two men and went back to his own table. Frank proposed that he and Feagins have a glass of whisky together, and Feagins was agreeable.

"Say, partner," Frank finally said to Feagins after they had downed most of a glass of bourbon, "my company, Parmalee Mining Company, has got a big shipment of gold that we want to send east by rail sometime next month. Jack told me that you are the man to see about it. Do you know a road that can handle the job?"

Before Feagins had a chance to reply, Frank added, "I thought maybe . . . well, some of the boys around here thought that the Union Pacific might be the best road to use. What do you think?" Frank intentionally mentioned the rival railroad, knowing that it would stir up Feagins and hopefully loosen his tongue.

Feagins reddened at the mention of the Union Pacific. "Who told you that?" Feagins asked hotly. "The UP's too expensive. Besides, they'd probably misroute your shipment or some fool thing! Why, they're a bunch of bungling idiots!"

"Well, I don't know," Frank continued. "This is goin' to be a good-sized transaction. I'm not sure that just any railroad has got the . . . you know what I mean . . . the savvy, to ship gold.

Of course, I don't know much about the Rock Island."

"Are you listenin' to me?" The railroad clerk replied heatedly. "The Rock Island's got the best system of gold freightin' in the country, don't you know?"

Frank smiled to himself. He'd been waiting, talking, cajoling, and entreating men for days trying to find a railroad man who knew something about gold shipments through Omaha. He'd hit pay dirt.

"Hey, boys," Frank said loudly over his shoulder to the men in the saloon. "I think it's time for another round of whiskey. Bartender! This one's on me!"

Frank turned again to the railroad clerk. "Well, now, I've been lookin' for an informed man like you. Say . . . uh. Can I call you Tom? Well, I guess I'm pretty ignorant about the Rock Island, Tom. Maybe your company is just what we're lookin' for after all. But we need to send this shipment to Chicago real soon, and it's got to be perfectly safe."

"Chicago?" Feagins said. "That's one of our main shippin' points. When're you sendin' it?"

"Soon, my friend," Frank replied. "You fellas got security?"

"You bet we do," the clerk answered without hesitation. "Wells Fargo will carry the gold to the car. And we'll have a couple of men waitin' there to guard it—good men. Gold shipments are our specialty."

"Now, say I was to ship that gold in three weeks," Frank continued, "give or take a couple of days, of course. Are you sure that your boys can handle it?"

"Call it done," Feagins replied. "We've got a big shipment goin' through here on the eighth of April from San Francisco. We can just add your shipment to it. It'd be cheaper that way, save on guards."

"Yes, certainly, certainly," Frank agreed, suppressing his delight at obtaining the unexpected, inside information. "But what time will the shipment arrive in Chicago? We want to have some good men ready to transport it when it gets there. We'll be shippin' a *half-ton* of the stuff, you know," Frank said, boasting.

The clerk laughed out loud. "Hah! That ain't a lot of gold. We're carryin' a shipment on that train makes yours look puny. But we've more room!"

Frank feigned anger. "You say our shipment is puny? I doubt that," he said testily. "You're just braggin', I betcha. What do you call a *big* shipment?"

The railroad clerk, somewhat intoxicated, caught himself: "Oh . . . it's big enough, I grant you."

"Well," said Frank, "when does this train of yours arrive in Chicago?"

"Around 5 o'clock in the mornin', unless it's runnin' late."

"Perfect," Frank replied. "Listen, I've hired a fella, Ed Noland from Omaha, to oversee the unloading in Chicago. What time should he be ready to board the train?"

"Tell him to ticket on the 519 for Chicago and be ready to board by 7 P.M.," Feagins replied.

"Fine!" Frank said with a broad smile. "I'll be talkin' with you further on this." Frank raised his glass slowly to his lips and took a genuine drink.

July 21, 1873

The James-Younger gang had been surveying the area southeast of Council Bluffs, Iowa, for two days. The night before, Clell Miller had broken into a section house and stolen a hammer and spike bar that the gang needed for its operation. While they were looking over the area, Clell made himself useful again and visited some of the local farmhouses to purchase pies and foodstuffs for the outlaws to eat. He'd paid liberally for the food, but the people he visited, while curious about visitors, seemed undisturbed by the strangers' presence in the area. At first, Clell had rankled at his role of errand boy, but he finally decided that his share in the robbery would more than take care of that indignity.

The sun was still above the horizon when the men assembled at the site of the prospective robbery, a rolling and wooded prairie southeast of Council Bluffs. The gang had selected a stretch of track just beyond a blind curve for the robbery. That way the engineer would be unable to see the gang until it was too late to halt the train or reverse its direction. The gang unfastened the fishplate between two rails. Then they used their spike bar to pull out the spikes that held down one end of the rail. With the end of the rail free, Frank James tied a thick rope around it. When the train approached, he and the other men planned to pull the track inward and out of alignment and secure the rope to a tree. One of the trainmen in Omaha, coaxed with hard liquor, had informed Frank that that was the surest way to derail a train. He'd told Frank that if the rail was pulled outward, the train might skip over the break, land farther down the rail, and continue down the track unharmed.

After preparing the rail, the outlaws relaxed for a while on the south side of the railroad tracks. The sun rested on the horizon like a boiling red ball. It was around 8:30 P.M., and they expected the train soon. They were ready for it, and several of the men had large packs to carry off the loot. Once the train was derailed, Frank and some of the men planned to keep the passengers buttoned up while Cole and Jesse robbed the express car. When they were finished, the bandits would board the train and rob the passengers.

Finally, the outlaws heard the chugging of a train in the distance and donned their masks, white cloth ones with holes for the mouth and eyes.

"She's a comin'! I can see her smoke!" John Younger yelled. John, Cole's brother, was stationed around the curve in the line and was hidden from the train by the tall weeds and bushes alongside the tracks.

The sound from the locomotive became louder, and Frank and the other outlaws pulled hard on the end of the long rope they had attached to the track, yanked the rail inward, and tied it. When the locomotive arrived, they expected it to run off the track, sink into deep gravel, and founder. As the train drew nearer, the ground trembled under the men's feet. The locomotive appeared around the curve, its front light blazing. Aboard the Rock Island, the engineer, John Rafferty, braked as he approached a blind curve, ensuring that his train would make a safe passage through this stretch of line. Just as his locomotive sped around the curve, he blinked in amazement. The track ahead had moved. He turned off the steam and applied the brakes. Fireman Dennis Foley saw the track move, too, and became excited.

Suddenly pistol fire erupted, and a bullet struck Rafferty in the thigh. The brakes failed to stop the engine, and the locomotive lurched sharply to its right, teetered, and toppled over with a huge crash. Rafferty was thrown into the metal parts of the engine, his neck breaking at the impact. As the locomotive rolled over, the fireman was scalded by the hot steam issuing from the boiler and thrown clear of the engine like a rag doll, falling unconscious in the rank weeds along the railroad's right of way. A towering cloud of dark smoke and steam spewed from the wreckage, and a loud scream blared from the engine's pierced boiler. Behind the overturned locomotive, the train folded into a zigzag of wreckage, and the shrieks of the women and bellowing voices of the men onboard rose above the din.

Sporadic firing continued as Jesse and the Younger boys broke into the express car. Once inside the car, the bandits bullied the express messenger, Jack Burgess, and the registered letter clerk, O. P. Killingsworth, into a corner and took nearly two thousand dollars in cash from their express satchels. Stacked in beige-colored sacks were large bars of gold and silver, three and a half tons of bullion. Lifting one of the bags, Cole Younger estimated their weight at around eighty pounds each. When he saw his brother wrestling with one of the bags, he grabbed him by the arm.

"Where are you going with that? Lay it down. It's too heavy for us! If we carry it, the posse will be on us instantly." John laid down the bag without argument. This was one treasure they would have to pass up. Then the outlaws from the express car joined the rest of the bandits, and the band entered the passenger cars. When the train foundered, the passengers had crawled under their seats to shield themselves from flying bullets. They were still there when the bandits boarded the train. Some of the passengers had blood running down their faces; a few had broken arms and legs and one a smashed nose. A number of the women, their faces shielded in their hands, cried loudly. The outlaws yanked the passengers to their feet and collected their wallets, purses, gold watches, and rings. Before the outlaws entered the cars, however, some of the passengers had stuffed gold and silver coins into cracks in the seats and stashed their valuables in hiding places, hoping to save them. But the outlaws searched the cars carefully. In the baggage car, valises and boxes were broken into. Clell pulled out a plumed lady's hat and put it on his head as a lark.

"Hey, Dingus, what do you think of this? Pretty, huh?" he yelled to Jesse, who was rummaging through nearby boxes.

Soon, the bandits had satisfied themselves with their pillaging and mounted their horses. Raising their voices in a parting roar, they rode off over the prairie.

Hours later, the railroad sent a posse of detectives and lawmen on a southbound train, depositing them at several locations in the area southeast of Council Bluffs. The manhunt was on. As the posses rode southward in pursuit, it became apparent to them that the robbers were traveling in the direction of Clay and Jackson Counties in Missouri, in short, toward James and Younger country. But they were unable to intercept the bandits. The descriptions of the outlaws provided by people in the area closely fit those of Jesse and Frank James. In fact, Jesse James was identified as the leader of the bandits. Meanwhile, an eleven-thousand-dollar reward for the capture of the outlaws was offered. The U.S. Express Company promised an additional reward of five hundred dollars (seven thousand dollars in today's money) for the capture of any of the gang. Four months later, Jesse James wrote a letter from Deer Lodge, Montana, to the *St. Louis Dispatch* complaining about his name being associated with the robbery. Jesse denied the James brothers' complicity in the crime. Moreover, he claimed, if Governor Woodson "will guarantee me a fair trial, and Frank also, and protect us from a mob, or from a requisition from the Governor of Iowa, which is the same thing, we will come to Jefferson City, or any other place in Missouri, except GALLATIN, surrender ourselves, and take our trial for everything we have been charged with." Cole Younger, not to be outdone, sent a letter through a relative, Lycurgus Jones, to the *Pleasant Hill Review* saying, "As to the Iowa train robbery—I have forgotten the day—I was also in St. Clair County, Mo., at that time, and had the pleasure of attending preaching the evening previous to the robbery at Monegaw Springs." Then Cole listed a number of St. Clair County residents who could vouch for his and John Younger's innocence (without mentioning, for the reader's convenience, the day the robbery had been committed).

August 9, 1873

Cole and John Younger made themselves comfortable in a dry sandstone cave south of the town of Monegaw, Missouri. The room-sized cave, only a rock's throw from the little village, was secluded enough that it provided the brothers with an excellent summer hideout. The brothers had several blankets with them and they were content with their temporary quarters. The cave's open mouth, moreover, gave them a magnificent view of the Osage River and the country south. If they walked to the top of the bluff above the cave, which they did periodically, they could see for miles and identify large parties of men entering the country. They'd been holed up in the cave for several weeks now, but they'd still found time to go to the Monegaw Springs Hotel in the evenings to attend the lively dances. And when they were hungry, all they had to do was ride over to John and "Aunt" Hannah McFerrin's place for fried chicken dinners. Hannah was the sister of Aunty Suze, their one-time slave, and one of Hannah's boys, Speedy, acted as their cook while they were at the cave. Sometimes the McFerrins allowed the Youngers to sleep at their log cabin. So, all in all, the Youngers were doing quite well, despite the fact that lawmen were scouring the state searching for them.

January 31, 1874

John Younger and his confederates rode along a rutted trail, with Cole leading the way. The outlaws wore Federal army overcoats to ward off the cold. For the last few days they had been camping in heavy woods along the Iron Mountain and Cairo Railroad in Wayne County, a sparsely inhabited area a hundred miles south of St. Louis. Now, they moved toward the tiny hamlet of Gads Hill, named, oddly enough, after Charles Dickens' homeplace. The Little Rock Express was expected to pass through the town shortly, and that was their target.

As John rode through the dense pinewoods, he reflected on his brother Cole. He'd been in the war and had become a sort of folk hero in western Missouri. John himself had missed the war and had been forced to stay home to take care of his mother. That rankled him. But he had proved himself to his older brother recently by shooting Deputy Sheriff S. W. Nichols, a former Confederate army officer, near Dallas, Texas, during a wild fracas. It had all happened by accident when John had wagered drinks that he could shoot the pipe out of the mouth of the town drunk, "Old Blue." Accidentally, he had nipped off the old fellow's nose. When Nichols had attempted to make a big issue out of it, John had killed him. Cole, if he had ever doubted John's courage, knew now that his brother was tough

enough to hold his own. But John still strove to prove himself
to his brother and the rest of the world. John knew in his heart
that he was as bold as Cole. He only needed a chance to prove
it. Nonetheless, he always deferred to his brother and Frank
James when it came to the robbery business; they were the
cunning hands in the band, no question about that.

The bandits had been snooping around the Gads Hill area for
several days now, casing it out. It didn't seem to John that they
had to worry about being detected. It was a great wilderness of
rolling hills and beautiful forests fragrant with the smell of pine,
and the whole county appeared empty of people. One morning,
John had walked to Gads Hill. He'd found it dinky. A saloon and
blacksmith shop were about all there was to the town, except
for a few crude shacks. There wasn't even a railway station,
just a platform where the locals placed their outgoing mail or
picked up new mail. Once in a blue moon, a stray passenger
might stop the train to go to St. Louis or return from there. But
there must be precious few passengers coming to or going from
this godforsaken place, he thought. Well, that made their work
that much easier. There wouldn't be a posse bristling with guns
plaguing their getaway.

As they approached Gads Hill, Frank rode to the front of the
riders and joined Cole. Frank held up his hand and reined in
his horse. He motioned the other riders to come forward.

"Okay, boys, we're here," Frank said. "The station platform
is dead ahead with the addition of a few houses and a general
store. Just ride in natural. When I draw my pistol, do the same.
Then do as I say. But be watchful; I don't want anybody hurt.
Put your masks on now and keep 'em on."

Frank pulled a white mask over his head. His eyes peered
eerily through the large peepholes. The whole group took on
a macabre appearance as they slipped into their identical
disguises. Frank slapped his reins and directed his horse
toward the tiny village; the rest of the bandits followed him
at a walk. Riding up to a small saloon, Frank dismounted and

tied his reins to a hitching post with the others following suit. "John, Clell," Frank snapped, "Fetch the townsmen. Tell 'em to line up on yon platform. Tell 'em we'll shoot 'em if they cause any trouble. The rest of us are goin' to drop in on our local saloon keeper."

Frank walked into the town's only businesses and approached its proprietor, Ives McMiller. "Raise your hands," Frank demanded, pointing his revolver at the man.

McMiller, astonished at the presence of masked and armed men, raised his arms and remained silent.

"Take your coat off. Make it quick," Frank ordered. "Get his wallet," Frank said to his brother.

Jesse pulled McMiller's wallet roughly out of the inside pocket of his coat and handed the coat to Cole. Cole patted the coat carefully. A broad smile brightened his face. He tugged at the lining of the coat with his large fingers, and the material ripped wide open. Green notes cascaded onto the floor.

"I believe this gentleman has left us a further contribution," Cole said and scooped up the notes greedily. "Good man! Good man!" he said to the shopkeeper. "Generous!"

Jesse emptied McMiller's wallet and handed the contents to Cole, who dumped all the loot into a sack. Then they led McMiller outside.

By this time, John Younger and Clell Miller had assembled the townspeople—men, women, and children—on the station platform. The occupants of the town fidgeted in the raw wind. While it was not bitterly cold, it was not comfortable either.

Frank pulled out his gold pocket watch and flipped open the case. "The train should be here any time," he remarked. "Remember what I told you earlier. A Pinkerton may be aboard. That's what our man in St. Louis told me. Be ready for him. If he makes a false move, shoot him and ask fine questions later."

After half an hour, the gang heard the rumble of a locomotive in the distance. It was 5 P.M., and the outlaws were seated on the edge of the station platform. They sprang to their feet. Cole took a long bar, stuck it into a slot, and pulled hard. This would force the incoming train onto a siding if it proceeded beyond the station platform.

The train, a puffing locomotive with two coaches and a sleeping car, loomed into view. John Younger walked up the track waving a red flag to get the engineer's attention. The engineer saw the flag, threw on his brakes, and the train screeched to a halt in front of the station platform.

The conductor, C. A. Alford, descended from one of the cars with a confused expression on his face. Cole ran up to Alford, drew his gun, and grabbed the conductor by the arm. He pointed a pistol at his head. When the conductor squirmed, Younger cautioned him, "Stand still, you fool, or I'll blow your head off." Then Cole deftly removed Alford's gold watch and chain from his vest, dropping them neatly into his own side pocket.

The passengers, meanwhile, had raised the fogged-up windows of the coaches and now gawked at the masked men on the platform. Cole, somewhat concerned that one of them might be carrying a gun, yelled at them: "If a shot is fired out of the car, I will shoot the conductor. Get your heads in, and don't move from the cars," he added.

John Younger, armed with a double-barreled shotgun, captured the engineer and firemen and brought them to the platform.

"If you want to stay alive, don't budge," John warned them.

With his gun still fixed on the conductor, Cole pulled another lever, trapping the train in place. Cole was learning how to be a regular railroad man.

Jesse, Frank, and John entered the express car. The agent, William Wilson, drew his revolver, but when he saw John's double-barreled shotgun aimed at him, he threw his gun down.

"Open up the safe or I'll kill you," Jesse yelled at the agent.

Wilson opened the safe, and Jesse grabbed the cash and registered letters and tossed them into the gang's wheat sack.

Noticing Wilson's record book and pen lying on the counter of the car, Jesse smiled broadly and opened the book to a blank page. He scribbled, "Robbed at Gads Hill."

Rejoining the rest of the gang already in the passenger cars, the James brothers and John boarded the coaches. Clell Miller and the others had begun robbing men and women of their valuables. One man resisted Clell, and the outlaw punched him in the face, knocking him to the floor.

Jesse moved among the passengers with a purpose. "Are you Mr. Pinkerton? Ho! Where is Mr. Pinkerton?" he cried out.

Frank suspected that one of the passengers at his end of the car was a Pinkerton man or the man himself, and he motioned to Jesse. The brothers took the man into a private car and forced him to undress so that they could examine his clothing for identification. As the man stood before them in his long underwear, the brothers questioned him hotly but discovered he was just a passenger.

"Let's see your palms," Clell ordered one of the passengers. "We don't want to rob workmen with callused hands. Workmen are exempt. We want plug-hat gentlemen only," he said, referring to the tall stovepipe hats the wealthier men wore. "You're the only ones who've got any money anyhow."

John got testy with the passengers. "Give me your pistol," he demanded of one. Moving to the next man, he yelled, "You've got more money than that. Out with it!"

After forty minutes, the train had been thoroughly robbed and ransacked, and the men sauntered to their horses. Their take: ten thousand dollars. Before Jesse remounted his horse, he walked over to Conductor Alford and handed him a small sheet of paper.

"Here, give this to the newspaper boys," Jesse said. "Maybe they'll get the story right this time."

Alford looked at the paper. At the top of the sheet was written, "A True Account of This Present Affair." Later, when Alford had the opportunity to read it, it said:

The most daring on record—the southbound train on the Iron Mountain Railroad was stopped here this evening by five heavily armed men and robbed of ———dollars. The robbers arrived at the station a few minutes before the arrival of the train and arrested the station agent and put him under guard, then threw the train on the switch. The robbers were all large men, none of them under six feet tall. They were all masked, and started in a southerly direction after they had robbed the train. They were all mounted on fine-blooded horses. There is a hell of an excitement in this part of the country.

—Ira A. Merrill

As fine snow fell, the splendidly mounted bandits rode south out of the little village, then turned northwest in their intended direction. Later, a twenty-five-man posse from Ironton and Piedmont pursued them but were unable to overtake the outlaws. The governor of Missouri offered a two-thousand-dollar reward "for the bodies of each of the robbers."

John Newman Edwards, the famous Kansas City journalist and former Confederate officer who had been so pleased earlier by the James gang's rebelliousness, was now the editor of the *St. Louis Dispatch.* During the robbery, Edwards was on assignment in Jefferson City. While he was away from his desk, the newspaper's city editor, Walter B. Stevens, wrote up the story of the robbery in the *Dispatch,* saying that the Gads Hill robbers were Jesse and Frank James and Budd and Cal Younger, identifying the Younger brothers erroneously. When Edwards read the article, he shook with anger. After swallowing a double shot of whiskey, he telegraphed Stevens: "PUT NOTHING MORE IN ABOUT GADS HILL. STOP. THE REPORT OF YESTERDAY WAS REMARKABLE FOR TWO THINGS UTTER STUPIDITY AND TOTAL UNTRUTH."

11

March 3, 1874

From the third-story window of his Chicago office building, Billy Pinkerton watched the snow drift down to collect on the street. As he puffed on his cigar, he surveyed the large workhorses below pulling their heavy delivery wagons. He wondered how his operations were going in western Missouri. For the last three years, he had stationed detectives there to capture the James and Younger brothers. Their failure had exasperated and infuriated him. But now he was through with the eternal scrabbling after the gang in the conventional way, working through sheriffs and posses. He wanted them destroyed.

To achieve his goal, he had recently ordered some of his best detectives to Missouri to confront the gang, man on man, wherever they found them and to kill them. He had chosen John Whicher to extinguish the James brothers. While Whicher was a young man, only twenty-six years of age, he was bold and audacious, a man of pluck and cunning, just the man to exterminate the outlaws, Billy thought. Of course, Whicher's mission was dangerous. But he was being paid to face peril; it was part of his job, by heaven! Nonetheless, Billy had been impressed with Whicher's enthusiasm for the project. He had been pleased with the assignment, even eager.

Pinkerton thought that a cool man operating alone like

Whicher would find it easier to get close to the outlaws than a group of detectives. That's why he had ordered Whicher to go to Liberty, Missouri, to track them down. That shouldn't be difficult, Billy reflected. The outlaws' family lived nearby, east of Kearney, and his spies had informed him that the brothers had been frequenting the family farm of late. Apparently, they were living on the Samuels' place, untouched and unmolested by the local lawmen, who either were being paid off by the brothers or were too cowardly to challenge them.

Pinkerton was becoming concerned about the bravery of his agents too. The petty excuses they had given him for their failure to capture or kill the outlaws had enraged him. He'd told them to get off their butts and kill the outlaws, or he'd get men who would. These same procrastinators had harped and whined about needing reinforcements, large posses to accomplish their mission. But Pinkerton had tried posses, and they had failed. They had only alerted the gang that they were being hunted, and they had simply fled the area. What he needed were brave, resolute men, agents who would follow the James and Younger brothers aggressively into their lairs. And now he thought he had them.

Pinkerton was aware that the choice of a solo agent to exterminate the Jameses made the operation appear to be an assassination rather than a criminal apprehension. But at this point, he didn't care. What the newspapers or anyone else said or wrote about his activities was unimportant. He still had a number of highly placed Missouri politicians and businessmen in his camp. If need be, through their influence, he would have the Missouri newspapers carry his own line of propaganda for the consumption of the backwater bumpkins. The James-Younger gang was making a laughingstock out of his national detective empire and that had to stop. The cost of getting rid of them was no longer an issue. They must be killed.

But Pinkerton was not just after the Jameses. He wanted the Youngers' hides too. At the same time he had sent Whicher north of the Missouri River, he had ordered two of his crack agents, Louis Lull and John Boyle, south of the river to St. Clair County to round up or kill the Youngers. Pinkerton had warned his men to operate under aliases. He wanted to conceal his men from the outlaws and their spies until they were ready to strike. This also protected his detectives from the surveillance of some of the local law officials, whom Pinkerton distrusted.

March 10, 1874

John Whicher stepped down from the St. Joseph stagecoach onto the dusty streets of Liberty, Missouri. He was dressed in a gray twill suit and conservative dark blue tie. He walked around the square with assurance. Some people might have viewed him as cocky, and maybe he was.

Whicher had dressed well today to make a good impression on the people he was meeting. He thought that a detective's appearance should befit his status. As he walked around the square, he looked for the Commercial Bank. The boss had told him to seek out D. J. Adkins, the president of the bank. Adkins was to provide Whicher with information about the Jameses and the Kearney area. Apparently, Adkins was trusted by the boss, so Whicher trusted him too.

But Whicher didn't need any advice on capturing the outlaws. His plan was simple and well established in his mind. All he needed were directions to the Samuels' farm. His plan was to disguise himself as an itinerant laborer and obtain work at the farm. For that purpose, he had already purchased work clothes from a used-clothing store in Chicago. They were in his suitcase. He had taken great care so that he would look the part of a laborer. People were always looking for cheap labor to do the chores on a farm. He thought that was the best way to get close to the James brothers. He'd visit the Samuels' farm and offer his service cheap. Once he got close to the brothers—and he felt they would eventually appear—he'd capture or kill them. Which resolution was immaterial to him. Yes, he might kill the brothers, he considered; it would make him a star at the Pinkerton agency—and a public hero to boot.

The boss had been confident that Whicher would succeed in the mission—so was Whicher, for that matter—but it had occurred to Pinkerton that there was a chance the young detective might die in carrying out his directive. That thought hardly occurred to Whicher. Like most young men, he felt invincible. He'd never been wounded during his years as a detective. He had recently married and he hoped to finish this little operation quickly and get back to his wife in Chicago. These outlaws should pose little difficulty for him. After all, he was a professional lawman, wily, and an excellent shot. The boss had been frustrated at the failure of his other detectives. People, especially the press, were laughing up their sleeves at the Pinkertons. That had exasperated Pinkerton, but it had incensed Whicher and the other detectives too. Whicher hoped to provide a quick remedy for the adverse publicity. Turning the corner, Whicher saw the Commercial Bank ahead and walked up to its entrance, opened the door, and stepped directly up to the cashier.

"Sir, would you direct me to Mr. Adkins, the president of the bank?" Whicher requested. "Tell him George Phillips is here." Whicher knew that Adkins was expecting him and was aware of his alias.

"I'll tell Mr. Adkins you're here, Mr. Phillips," the cashier replied and walked from the cashier's counter to a small room adjacent to the teller's cage. In a few moments, he returned.

"Mr. Adkins will see you," the cashier said and went to the door of the teller's cage and unlocked it for the detective. The cashier then led Whicher to Adkins' private office and closed the door behind him.

"Whicher!" Adkins greeted the detective, shaking his hand vigorously. "I'm pleased to see you. Been expectin' you, of course. But, say, if you're not too pressed for time, do you mind if I summon a good friend of mine, Mr. O. P. Moss. He's a former sheriff. I think he'll be of considerable help to you."

"Not at all," Whicher replied, not caring one way or another about Adkins' request. One person was as good as another when it came to the information he needed, which wasn't much anyhow.

As they waited for Moss, Adkins offered Whicher a cigar, and the two men filled the room with the luxuriant smell of Havanas. To while away the time, they chatted about the weather and national politics. Within a few minutes, Moss appeared. He was an elderly man with a large gray mustache and doddering appearance.

"Whicher, good to meet you," Moss exclaimed, extending his hand. "Adkins here has been tellin' me all about you."

Whicher shook hands with the sheriff, but this statement visibly shook him. How did Moss know his name? What had Adkins been telling Moss? His identity was supposed to be secret. Pinkerton had promised him that his name would be confidential. He hoped that Moss's conversation with Adkins had been held in private. He didn't need some old nitwit blowing his cover.

"Good to see you," Whicher replied, recovering his composure. "To get down to business, if you gentlemen don't mind, I'd like to ask you a few questions about the James brothers."

"Sure, shoot," Moss replied.

"Well, Sheriff," Whicher continued, "I'd like to know how long you've known the Jameses. That is, do you know them personally? And what do you know about them that might be useful to me?"

"Brother," Moss answered, "it's been awhile since I was sheriff of Clay County, and I only know the boys casually, I admit. But I do know their reputations—and from good sources, I promise you. Everyone who knows them says they're dangerous fellas. In fact, if I was you, I'd get a bunch of Pinkertons to go with you to confront them, especially on their own land." Moss paused for a moment, then added, "Now, my friend, I hate to say this, but you ain't exactly goin' about this in a smart way, if you want my honest opinion. These boys are gunnies, I'm tellin' you.

And they're not your average criminals either; they're smart.
When you go out there, you ain't goin' to be foolin' nobody."
Whicher suppressed a smile. He'd heard about such tough,
smart men before, but when he had backed some of them into
a corner, he found them little more than ignorant bullies.

"Well, time will tell on that," Whicher responded stiffly. "I
think the best way to put these fellows out of business—and
so does Mr. Pinkerton—is to confront them, head-on, and
kill them. So far, everyone's been running from them. That's
going to stop. It has only emboldened them to commit more
robberies. To put it simply, the Pinkerton National Detective
Agency has selected me to rub 'em out."

Adkins now broke in, "Well, uh . . . sir, maybe you ought to
listen to Moss. He's been a lawman in this area for years. He knows
an awful lot about these boys. He might be right, you know. The
Jameses just might kill you if you were to go off half-cocked. Are
you sure your company has thought this out thoroughly?"

"We know exactly what we're doing," countered Whicher.
"We're professional detectives, the best in the country."

"Yeh?" Moss answered, "Well—and I don't mean to offend
you—but in my opinion, if you was to go out to the Samuels'
farm, if the boys don't kill you, old lady Samuel will."

Whicher had heard enough. He was getting nowhere with
these crotchety old squirrels.

"Listen, I appreciate your help," he continued, "but all I need
from you gentlemen is the way to the Samuels' farm. What's the
easiest way to get there?"

"Mr. Whicher, if you're bent on goin' there," Moss replied
hesitantly, "the best way is to latch onto a freight train goin'
south and hop off right before you get to the Platte River. Then
head south down the road skirtin' the river until it heads east—
that's left. Go east on that road and it'll take you right past the
Samuels' place; it's a small cabin along a dry creek. You'll know
when you're there; they got some of the finest horses you'll ever
see outside of a Kentucky racetrack. But don't plan on bein'

inconspicuous. And you'd better be extremely careful, I'm a tellin' you."

"Well," replied Whicher rather coolly, "I think all I need now from you men is a place to change clothes. I'll be dressed as a farmhand when I go to the Samuels' place. I've got the clothes in my suitcase."

Adkins offered, "If you don't mind a short walk, my home is right off the square. You're more than welcome to stay there before you set out for the Samuels' place. In fact, there's a Hannibal and St. Jo freight goin' through Liberty this afternoon about five. You can just jump aboard. Despite our reservations, Moss and I wish you the best."

Whicher thanked the two men and left with Adkins. He had decided, as an afterthought, to accompany him to his home.

As the freight train approached the Platte River, Whicher lowered himself from the ladder at the front of the car. When he felt sure of his balance, he leaped and hit the ground running. Still, the speed he was traveling at nearly propelled him onto his face. After stumbling for a few steps, he fell to one knee but regained his balance and began walking down a nearby road leading south. Within minutes, he reached a dirt road leading left and east and turned down it. It was becoming twilight, so he picked up his pace. He was wearing a slouch hat and a long, faded, somewhat frayed blue denim coat that concealed the large .45-caliber Colt revolver stuck in his belt. Another smaller revolver was stuffed in a pocket specially sewn inside his denim jacket. The Samuels' farm was some three miles away, so he began walking faster in hopes of reaching it before nightfall.

After almost three miles, he noticed a herd of cattle to his right and a few horses grazing in the distance. The sheriff had been right, he thought; the Jameses did have good horses, fine ones. Minutes later, at dusk, Whicher saw a small log house in the distance. A dry, meandering stream ran to its right. It must be the Samuels' place, he figured. Then he heard the wailing of hounds; they had picked up his scent. Although he tried to remain cool, Whicher felt a surge of adrenaline running through him. He wasn't frightened, but he was tense. When he came to within several hundred yards of the cabin, he looked for a stick to fend off the dogs he saw approaching him. Walking to the side of the road, he yanked a dead limb from a tree. As he neared the Samuels' home, the dogs barked louder, and a brown and white hound approached him and attempted to nip him. Whicher fended the dog off with the limb, and it retired to a safe distance. The hounds continued to wail.

Frank and Jesse heard the dogs howling and knew they had a visitor. And they knew exactly who he was. Banker Adkins' son had arrived a couple of hours earlier with the news that a Pinkerton agent named John Whicher was on his way to the Samuels' farm. On learning this, the brothers had sent Sammy to fetch Clell Miller and Jim Anderson, dead Bill Anderson's brother. They had arrived earlier and tethered their horses behind the house and out of sight.

Frank smiled at the thought of Whicher's arrival. It had been a good idea to make friends with old Adkins, he thought. Adkins had been only too glad to help. An old Confederate sympathizer, he had no love for Yankees and Easterners anyhow. And Frank had made it clear to him for some time that he had no interest in robbing the Commercial Bank of Liberty. But Adkins was never quite sure about the James brothers' intentions. So he had become Frank's close friend, and the association had become an alliance. Frank's other spies in Liberty had also reported the arrival of a stranger in town. But Adkins had the complete story on Whicher, which was useful to the James boys.

So, Frank thought, the Pinkertons wanted to kill the James brothers. He would see about that! He'd been thinking about the situation. They could just ride off and let this cocky fool harass his family. But that would let Whicher off too lightly, allow the simple-minded jackass to avoid the hook. What did Pinkerton think he was doing sending out a lone henchman?

Simple worlds for simple minds, Frank reckoned. He and Jesse
were used to fighting companies of infantry and sheriff's posses,
and Pinkerton was sending this buffoon to confront them on
their home ground? Whicher must be arrogant, incredibly
naive too, Frank thought. But while the brothers had the
jump on Whicher, Frank realized that the detective was quite
dangerous, a killer, in fact.

For that reason, Frank had decided not to confront Whicher
inside the Samuels' home. He didn't want his family caught
in possible crossfire; it might complicate things. But Frank
would give Whicher little chance. The detective would not be
given the luxury of a gunfight with the brothers—unless he
was lucky. Frank had learned during the war that there were
just too many enemies out there to give any of them a break.
When possible, the odds must remain in your favor. Duels
and challenges? Those were for gentlemen, not the likes of
slinking thugs and Yankee scum like Whicher. So how would he
exterminate this cutthroat? That question occupied less than a
minute of Frank's time.

"C'mon, boys," Frank said, gesturing to Jesse and the other
men, "I guess we ought to offer our greetin's to ol' Whicher." As
he opened the door of the cabin, a cool breeze rushed in. The
four men left their coats behind and walked out into the crisp
March air.

"Okay, brother," Frank addressed Jesse, "you're the fastest.
When we're ready, take him, and we'll support you. We want
him alive, if possible. When I touch my chin, grab him. We'll
cover you."

Near the front gate was a large lilac bush. Clell Miller and
Jim Anderson walked behind it and blended into the shadows.
In the distance, Frank and Jesse saw a lone figure walking up
the road, and their eyes hardened. Both men were calm. As
Whicher approached them, Frank saluted him.

"Howdy, partner! What brings you out this evenin'?"

Whicher stared hard through the dim twilight. He saw two

tall men facing him. They looked like a couple of typical young farmers to him, but larger than most. As he approached the men, though, the expression in their eyes made him wary and uncomfortable. They must be the James brothers, he realized. But they didn't look all that dangerous to him. When he got closer, he noticed that one of the men's eyes seemed to twitch nervously, and both men had revolvers stuck in their belts.

"Why, hello, good friends," Whicher replied cheerfully. "I'm just a poor fella lookin' for some farm work. Do you need any help? I'm reasonable."

"Well, now," Frank answered, "it all depends on how good a hand you are. You've done lots of farmin'?" As Frank said this, he and Jesse moved closer to Whicher, almost to within arm's length. Whicher, made nervous by their closeness, slowly backed up a step.

"Yeh, but it's been a while," Whicher continued. "I've been out of work lately. Sure do need to get back to it. I'm a hard worker."

"That's most interestin'," Frank continued. "Yes, it must have been some time since you did any farmin'. Even in this light, your face looks white as the belly of a catfish." Again, he and Jesse moved closer to Whicher. This time, the detective stood his ground.

"But you see," Frank went on, "you're lucky. We've been plannin' on takin' a new man. I think you're him!" Frank reached up and scratched his chin.

At this signal, Jesse leaped catlike on Whicher, throwing both of his arms around the man's chest and pinning his arms to his sides. As Whicher squirmed to get at his revolver, Clell leaped from behind a lilac bush and struck him on the side of the head with the barrel of his revolver, stunning him. Frank and Jesse wrestled the half-conscious detective to the ground, then pulled his arms behind him and searched him. Frank reached into his own back pocket, pulled out some cord, and tied Whicher's hands behind his back. Jesse had already grabbed Whicher's revolvers.

"Well, Whicher, it's real fine knowin' you," Frank said, puffing from his exertion. "Yes, we been needin' a man like you, a good Pinkerton man, to do some of the grunt work around here. Jesse, go into the house and get me some heavier rope; this bull's got to be well tethered." Whicher, half-stunned, was astonished at his predicament. As he regained his senses, he wondered how these men could have been waiting for him. How had they known who he was? He realized he was in a fix; his situation was desperate, in fact.

Jesse returned and handed his brother some rope, and Frank tied the detective securely, placing the new, larger rope over the first rope. As he did so, he noticed that Whicher had the letters J.W.W. tatooed on his wrist. Then Frank tied Whicher's ankles together tightly.

"How do you like these restrainers?" Frank asked Whicher. "Now tell me, detective man, what made you think you could just come out here and capture us bad boys all by yourself?"

Whicher, much sobered, replied, "Who put you wise?"

Frank replied, "Now, detective man, don't be so nosy. We were born wise. But I'll ask the questions. I'm tellin' you right now, you're in a heap of trouble." Frank turned to Jesse and Jim Anderson.

"I think we need to send a message to Billy Pinkerton that will sober up that ol' boy!" Whicher now realized that it would do him no good to talk, and he turned sullen and quiet.

Five men rode in the moonlight to the home of Buster Parr, the Blue Mills Ferry operator, on the Missouri River south of Liberty. One of the men, Whicher, was gagged, his hands tied behind his back. His feet were trussed together under his horse's belly so that he could lean sideways but not wrench free of the animal. When the group reached Parr's, Frank dismounted and walked up to the ferryman's door and knocked loudly. It was 3:00 A.M. Parr eventually answered the door, somewhat surprised by his late-night callers.

"We want your ferry this evenin'," Frank said to Parr. "We've captured a horse thief and are in hot pursuit of another. That villain has escaped across the river, so we must cross too—and now."

"Well, I shut down some hours ago," answered Parr. "I'm tryin' to get some sleep."

"We're sorry to bother you, friend," continued Frank, his voice taking on a sharper edge, "but it's important. Are you goin' to take us, or are we goin' to take you?"

"Well, I hadn't been plannin' to run more people over tonight," the ferry operator whined, "at least this time of night." The operator, however, recognized the earnestness of his visitors and added, "But if you're positive you gotta go, well, I'll be with you in a minute. Got to get my coat."

"Much obliged," Frank replied. "We regret troublin' you, but these bandits don't allow us to live by a proper schedule."

"That's right," chimed in Jesse. "We been chasin' these scoundrels all day and now we're nigh sick and tired."

The ferry operator went inside, grabbed his coat and hat, and returned quickly. He saw that the outlaws had dismounted and were leading their horses to the boat dock. It didn't take long to ferry the group across the river to Independence Landing. Once on the south side of the river, the outlaws said goodbye to Parr and rode to a stand of woods near Independence. There they dismounted. They untied Whicher's feet and led him through the bright moonlight to a large oak and tied him to it.

"Say, Whicher, you've been awful quiet for the last couple hours," Jesse taunted the detective. "You want to talk to us?" Jesse removed the gag from the detective's mouth, and the detective gasped for air.

Whicher cried out, "Do you think you're going to get away with this? The Pinkertons have lots of men. They'll be after you, I promise you. Especially if anything happens to me."

"Now, Whicher . . . What do they call you? John?" Jesse said and laughed. "Now, John, don't get so riled up, young man. Who said anything was goin' to happen to you? Why on earth would we do anything to *you*? You just came out here to Missouri, all the way from the East, to have a friendly chat with us, make a cordial visit to our family farm, and help us with chores. We want to continue things that way, in a friendly spirit. We just want to ask you a few questions, that's all. We aren't goin' to hurt you. Why, mercy, why would we want to hurt you? We're humane fellows, God-fearin' ones and all that. You've been readin' too many of them dime novels about us, don't you know."

"You'd better turn me loose, right now," Whicher screamed, "before you get yourselves in more trouble!"

"Are you accusin' us of things we ain't done?" Jesse asked. "My, my, young man, what a fierce detective you are."

"I'm through talking," Whicher said with finality.

"I don't know about that, Whicher," Frank replied. "You ain't even begun to talk. We need to know what you Pinkerton boys are plannin', what sort of party you've been cookin' up for us. How many of you are operatin' north and south of the river, for instance. And we want to hear agents' names, boy. You best start talkin'."

Whicher remained silent. He had no intention of telling these thieves anything. He'd been a fool to listen to Adkins. And Pinkerton had led him astray too. He'd needed help, all right! But he should have trusted his instincts from the start. He should have known when Adkins brought Moss into the affair that his mission had been compromised. Now, it was too late; he was a goner and knew it. They were going to kill him. But he'd go out like a man, he vowed.

"I thought you'd make it easy for us," Frank continued. "But if you want to be difficult, you leave us no choice. We want the names of your friends and what their plans are, and we aim to hear it all."

"Clell, run and get a piece of strong rope," Frank called. "I think Whicher wants to raise himself in the world." Miller went over to his horse, unfastened a lariat, and brought it to Frank.

James made a loop at the end of the rope and wound the coils into a noose.

"All right, Whicher, you've been refusin' to cooperate, so we'll just have to do a little old-time encouragin'." Frank threw the end of the rope over a large limb and placed the noose over Whicher's head and tightened it. The outlaws pulled on the loose end of the rope until Whicher rose slowly, in jerking motions, off the ground. The detective's face reddened and saliva ran from the corners of his mouth.

"Okay, Whicher, sing!" Frank taunted him. "Sing us a song!" The men lifted the detective higher off the ground. "You came out here to Missouri to shoot us like rats, didn't you? How does it feel now, Whicher? How do you like it?"

After a while, Frank said, "Let him down, boys," and Whicher's feet fell to the ground. Jesse loosened the rope around the detective's neck.

"Okay, let's hear it," Frank demanded, but the half-conscious detective remained silent. The men raised Whicher off the ground several more times. Finally, Frank motioned the men to stop. Whicher was lowered to the ground and tied fast to the tree.

"Clell," Frank prompted, "why don't you wake him up, make him talk to us." Frank touched the sheath of Miller's bowie knife, which hung from the outlaw's belt. Clell approached Whicher and unsheathed the blade.

"Whicher," Clell said in his deep voice, "tell us where your boys are hangin' out and their names." He grabbed the detective by the collar of his blue-checked flannel shirt and tore it open. Then Clell stuck the point of his knife into Whicher's bare stomach and began pressing steadily into the detective's flesh until a small spurt of blood ran along the tip of the blade and coursed darkly down the detective's belly and trousers.

"I can't hear you, Whicher. Speak up, boy!" Clell taunted him. After piercing Whicher several times, Clell wiped his knife on the gray grass at his feet and stuck it back into its sheath. Then he grabbed Whicher and encircled his neck with his powerful arms and pulled down heavily until he heard the cartilage pop. The detective gagged and grunted but remained impassive. They could kill him, Whicher thought, but he would tell them nothing.

It had become obvious to the outlaws that they would get little out of Whicher without more painful torture. Torture was not a sport that appealed to them. They even had a peculiar admiration for Whicher's spunk. As guerrillas in the war, their boys had been tortured, and torture seemed unmanly to them. Frank and Jesse consulted for a few moments. Then, Frank approached Whicher, drew his revolver, and shot him in the head. The detective slumped forward. The outlaws carried his body to the middle of the nearby road and dumped it unceremoniously in a heap, the rope still dangling from his neck. Frank turned to Jesse. "I hope they tell Billy Pinkerton about this."

Then the men split up. As Frank rode toward a friend's farm to spend the rest of the night, he pondered Whicher's fate. It seemed to him that the poor fool had been destroyed by his own arrogance and lack of vision. He had been woefully misguided by wishful thinking and fatal misconceptions. Frank had long known that life was complex and had hidden dimensions that a man of the world needed to recognize. The man on the street, of course, believed simply in lofty concepts of democracy and the rule of law. That suited ordinary workin' folks, he reckoned; it described the world that history books talked about. But there was a harder reality, a parallel world, difficult to fathom, ruled by influential families, big money, businesses, politicians, their armies, and an elaborate network of hangers-on like Pinkerton. It was a cruel, manipulative world, its intentions largely obscured from most people, shrouded in propaganda, lies, deception, intrigue, scheming over money, and sometimes murder, when it was expedient. And that world had roots that extended all the way to Clay County, Missouri. Frank understood that world, even though he was largely outside it. Adkins had tapped into that world for a spell and to his advantage. Whicher—a simple-minded man with tunnel vision—had been naive about that world. Frank reckoned these two worlds had existed always and everywhere, from Julius Caesar to President Grant. Whicher's lack of insight into the interplay between these worlds had cost him his life. He had walked into their trap like a simpleton.

March 16, 1874

After finishing their breakfast, Pinkerton agents Louis J. Lull, posing as J. W. Allen, and John Boyle, alias James Wright, walked out of the Roscoe House hotel. A sometime deputy sheriff of St. Clair County, Edwin B. Daniels, whom they had solicited as a guide and expected to aid them in any gunplay, accompanied them. Daniels was known for his courage. The detectives were on the trail of the Youngers, any they could find, with the orders to arrest or kill them. None of the detectives was averse to collecting the large rewards offered for their lifeless bodies.

The detectives had been questioning the locals in Roscoe and had determined that the Youngers were residing somewhere in the area north of town, either with the McFerrin family, former Younger slaves, or with Theodrick Snuffer, a Younger family friend and farmer in the area. On leaving the hotel, the three lawmen mounted their horses and directed them north, down the Chalk Level Road. As a ruse to obtain information, they intended to ask the locals for the location of the Widow Sims' farm, where they would claim they intended to buy cattle. They had learned that the farm was adjacent to the Snuffer and McFerrin places. As they rode toward the Sims' farm, their queries would give them an excuse to snoop around.

Just before reaching the cemetery along the Chalk Level Road, the detectives turned right, down a dirt lane. After traveling a few hundred yards east, they passed a schoolhouse where children played in the yard. A few of the tow-headed youngsters

noticed them go by and gaped nosily at the strangers. Past the
schoolhouse, the lawmen turned left and north again, down
another small lane. The Snuffer place was just ahead. In fact,
they could hear the farmer's hounds baying. As they approached
Snuffer's house, Lull motioned Boyle to fall back and wait for
him and Daniels so that the size of their party would draw
less attention. Lull and the local lawman proceeded down the
lane together until they were in front of Snuffer's yard. As they
reached a point parallel to Snuffers' log home, the farmer peered
out the front door of his cabin to discover why his dogs were
barking. Lull and Daniels reined in their horses, and Snuffer
walked toward them, at the same time calling off his hounds.

"Come here, Nell! You too, Ben, cuss you!" As he walked
toward the strangers, Snuffer looked them over carefully.

"Howdy!" Snuffer said as he walked up to the fence and
shook Lull's hand. "How can I help you boys?"

"Sir," Lull replied, "we're looking for the Widow Sims' place.
We'd like to talk to her about buying some cattle. Could you tell
us where she lives?"

"Sure," Snuffer replied, still looking the men over. "She lives
up the road a piece." Snuffer pointed north up the trail. "See
yon gate? Her place is just beyond it."

"Yes," Lull answered, "I think I can see it. Much obliged."
After exchanging a few pleasantries, Lull and Daniels prodded
their horses and started up the road in a northerly direction.
Snuffer watched them for a minute or two and noticed that a
couple of hundred yards ahead, the two men veered northwest,
up the old timber road toward the McFerrin place, rather than
toward the Sims' farm. This aroused Snuffer's suspicions. He
also noticed how closely the men had looked over his house and
yard while they were talking to him, as if they were looking for
something or someone. And one of them talked like a Yankee,
he thought.

Jim and John Younger had been eating breakfast when they

heard the hounds baying. They got up and peeped through the holes in the chinking of Snuffer's log cabin to get a view of the road. Both men were wary of the two strangers they saw talking to Snuffer, especially of their large, expensive-looking revolvers. What is more, they recognized Daniels as a local lawman, although the fellow who accompanied Daniels was a stranger to them. As Snuffer returned to the house, the two brothers saw another stranger race past to catch up with his two associates. He was well armed too, the brothers noted. John Younger had seen enough.

"Dad blame it," said John. "They're lawmen, sure as wolves got teeth. Let's go after 'em!"

"Wait a minute; let's think it over first," Jim replied, always the more cautious of the two brothers.

"To blazes with talk! They're lawmen; I can smell 'em. Let's give 'em a lesson."

"I think you're right," Jim finally relented after reviewing the matter quickly. "No use hidin' from 'em. If they want a fight, we'll give 'em one." Both of the brothers grabbed their revolvers and stuffed them in their belts. John grabbed a double-barreled shotgun for good measure. The two men rushed out the front door of the cabin and ran for their horses, tied behind the cabin in a clump of trees. They mounted and spurred them to a gallop, racing up the old timber road toward the junction of Chalk Level Road and the lane to Monegaw Springs, a site called the "Forks." John cocked his shotgun as he rode. After almost a mile, the Youngers saw the three detectives ahead and approached them.

"Hold up there!" Jim yelled as they approached the lawmen.

Instead of reining in his horse, however, Boyle drove his spurs into his horse's sides and galloped away frantically. Jim fired at him, and Boyle's hat flew off his head. The detective continued wildly up the Chalk Level Road, leaving a cloud of dust behind him. The other two lawmen reined in their horses and turned around slowly in the middle of the junction.

"Throw down your guns," ordered Jim, "and make no funny moves."

Daniels threw a single revolver in the road, and Lull followed with two pistols that sent plumes of red dust rising in the air. One of Lull's pistols was an expensive, high-caliber Tranter, of British manufacture.

"Jim, go after that other fellow," John urged. "I'll take care of them."

"I'm stayin' right here," Jim replied, apprehensive about leaving John by himself.

Then Jim turned his attention to the revolvers lying in the road. "Those are fine pistols you have there," he said. "We must make a present of them. Where are you fellas from?"

"Osceola," Lull answered.

"That's odd. I'm thinkin' you're some kind of Yankee, a detective maybe," Jim replied. "What are you boys doin' in this part of the country?" he questioned.

"Oh, just rambling around," Lull said evasively.

"You were in the area yesterday askin' questions about us," Jim challenged him.

"No, I don't know you," responded Lull.

"I know your friend here; he's a lawman. I think you're one too," Jim replied.

"Why are you ridin' around here with all them pistols?" John chimed in.

"What?" Lull replied heatedly. "Is not every man wearing them that is traveling, and have I not as much a right to wear them as anyone else?"

"Hold on, young man," John Younger cried out. "We don't want any of that." He leveled his shotgun at Lull.

Lull believed that the Youngers intended to kill him. He had thrown down his two guns, but he still had a small No. 2 Smith & Wesson revolver in his hip pocket. He must use it or die, he thought.

While John covered Lull with a shotgun, Jim dismounted to

pick up the lawmen's weapons. As Jim bent down to retrieve the revolvers, Lull saw his chance and leaped into action. Drawing his pistol from his rear pocket, he fired at John, striking him in the neck. John fired one barrel of his shotgun at Lull, and the detective's right arm fell uselessly to his side. The loud noise panicked Lull's horse, which dashed down the road heading east. Lull had lost his grip on the reins, so the horse ran unchecked. As Lull looked behind him, he saw John Younger in hot pursuit. Younger had dropped his shotgun and drawn one of his revolvers. He pulled alongside Lull and fired twice, one of the shots hitting the detective in the left side. Lull clung desperately to his horse, but it bolted sharply left, dashing through some persimmon trees. A low-lying limb knocked the detective from his saddle, and he tumbled onto the ground. He got up with great difficulty, staggered into the nearby road, and tumbled forward on his face, unconscious.

John now turned his horse westward and rode back to his brother's aid. After only a few yards, his vision darkened and he tumbled dead from his saddle onto the ground. Back at the Forks, Jim Younger had shot Daniels in the neck, the bullet crushing his spine and killing him.

After collecting John's watch and revolvers, a grieving Jim handed one of the pistols to G. W. McDonald, a bystander who had run to the scene upon hearing the gunshots. Jim asked McDonald to tell Snuffer what had happened and to have the old man bury John.

Meanwhile, the McFerrins, who lived in a cabin across the road from where Lull fell, carried the wounded detective to their home. When law officers came later that afternoon from Osceola, they placed Lull, still alive, onto a wagon and transferred him to the hotel at Roscoe. Daniels' body was taken to Osceola for burial. Lull remained at the Roscoe House for a couple of weeks, fighting for his life, but he finally succumbed to his injuries. Within scarcely a week, three Pinkerton operatives had been killed and another nearly frightened to death by the James gang.

After getting his wits together, Jim Younger began the long trek to Hot Springs, Arkansas, hoping to find his brothers Cole and Bob. As he rode along, he thought about his situation. Depressed, he didn't know how he'd gotten involved in this lawlessness. Being an outlaw disgusted him, but it was too late to back out now. He was a hunted man. He might just as well get used to these bloody encounters. Once you were on the wrong side of the law, they would hunt you down until they captured or killed you. Now he'd lost his treasured brother, John.

The Younger brothers, and the Jameses, too, for that matter, had fallen into this wild life so easily and naturally after the war, Jim thought. They had accepted this life routinely, recognized its immediate advantages, and ignored the enormity of their actions. Now, they were hunted criminals, pursued and stalked like they had been during the war. Jim could see no resolution in sight. Jim had a woman picked out, Clara, whom he'd like to marry, but who would marry an outlaw? And, even if she would have him, how could he involve her in his sordid world? His life had become dreamlike, a bizarre world filled with brutal encounters and death. His was a life, strangely mechanical, over which he had little control. He was like a cog in some complicated cosmic machinery that carried him, despite his resistance, into what was essentially repellent to him and likely to end in his early death. He was ambivalent about this life. In a way, he liked the wild pursuits, the violent confrontations— craved the excitement. But he felt like a moth, fluttering helplessly toward an all-consuming fire. Seeing no way out of his predicament, he felt hopeless.

In the meantime, Gov. Silas Woodson, the governor of Missouri, asked the state legislature to supply him with money so that he could hire agents to capture or kill members of the James-Younger gang. The measure passed in both houses. However, a bill to pay for militia to hunt down the outlaws did not.

April 24, 1874

Jesse James, twenty-six years old, stood proudly in the living room of the Boling home near Kearney, Missouri. He wore a black broadcloth suit and stylish tie. Zee stood next to him and held his hand tightly. She was happier than she had ever been in her life. She had been waiting nine years for this day, and now that wonderful day had arrived. She had always known that Jesse would marry her; there was never any doubt about that. But they had finally decided that it must happen now. She hoped that somehow she could protect Jesse from the law, from himself. He was in constant danger, she knew, and it was everywhere. She refused to trust even his friends. There were huge rewards out for his capture and anyone might be tempted to reveal his whereabouts and cause him to be killed. Despite the danger and uncertainty, she still intended to marry him.

Even Jesse's family had railed against the marriage. The Reverend William James, Jesse's uncle, had argued strenuously with Jesse against marrying. He said Jesse was not likely to live long and that he would leave Zee a widow with uncared-for children, a disaster. Nonetheless, Jesse and Zee had decided they would go through with the marriage.

Zee looked up at Jesse. She thought he was the handsomest and finest man she had ever known. He was so strong of will and purpose. She found him irresistible. When he was a boy during the war, he had been her white knight. She realized now that most people considered him a black knight. That was okay; he was her knight anyhow, black or white—now and forever. She would never leave him, and she knew that he would never leave her. She never doubted his loyalty. He would always be true to her; she knew that. As Reverend James pronounced the wedding ceremony, tears rolled down Zee's cheeks. They were not tears of sorrow; she was elated, joyful beyond measure. When it came time for her to express her affirmation, she quietly said, "I do" and continued to cry. She looked up at Jesse and smiled. He grinned back at her; he was ecstatic too.

June 1874

Annie Ralston sat at a desk in her bedroom at her parents' farm. She placed her pen in the ink well in front of her, shook it lightly, and wrote:

> Dear Mother:
> I am married and going west.
>
> *Annie*

She laid down the pen, folded the sheet, and placed it on her pillow. Then she grabbed her suitcase and valise and descended the staircase into the Ralston parlor.

"Goodbye, mama, I'll see you soon," she said to her mother as she walked through the parlor. Annie had told her mother that she was going by train to visit her aunt in Kansas City.

Once aboard the train to Kansas City, Annie looked for her seat, 14B. It was about midway down the car. She had the porter throw her suitcase and valise into a metal basket overhead. Then she took her seat next to the window. As she looked around, out of the back of the car, a tall, slim young man about six feet tall with a long face and tawny hair walked to her seat and sat down beside her.

"Annie, I'm here," he said and held her hands in his.

"Darlin', it's about time. We should have done this long ago," she replied.

Annie was eloping with Frank James, America's premier outlaw. When her father found out about it, he disowned her. But Annie had found her man.

12

November 1874

Bud McDaniels had been working for some while as a part-time switchman for the Kansas Pacific Railroad when Frank James, an old acquaintance, invited him for a drink at Flanagan's, a local Kansas City saloon. During the meeting, Frank invited Bud to become one of his spies. McDaniels was flattered by the famous outlaw's attention. Frank was a former guerrilla like himself and part of the brotherhood, so Bud agreed to the proposition. Besides, he could use some extra money—lots of it.

Frank told Bud that he was interested in gold shipments. Rumor had it they were being carried by the Kansas Pacific Railroad. He wanted McDaniels, who knew some of the shipping agents for that railroad, to act as his spy and go-between. Naturally, the intention was to rob the K&P. As an added incentive, and at Bud's insistence, Frank agreed to let McDaniels take part in the robbery. This pleased Bud immensely. He had always had fantasies about becoming a desperado like Frank and Jesse James.

Since that meeting, in an attempt to obtain information, McDaniels had spent several evenings buttering up Tom Maxwell, one of the K&P's shipping agents. He cozied up to Maxwell by buying him free drinks then deliberately leaving the stray dollars and change on the table when he walked out of the saloon, seed money to help loosen his informant's tongue. Meanwhile, McDaniels had told Maxwell—confidentially, of course—that information on the Kansas Pacific's gold shipments might be worth as much as five hundred dollars (worth seven thousand dollars today), two hundred dollars up front, another three hundred dollars afterward, if the robbery were successful. This sounded good to Maxwell, who earned $1.54 a day. He hadn't expected to pocket that much money in a lifetime. Besides, Tom had been gambling a lot lately, mostly on credit, and some of the local card sharks were threatening him with violence unless he paid up. McDaniels' offer was a godsend. After sifting through railroad schedules and invoices and questioning his fellow shipping clerks, Maxwell discovered that a large shipment of gold dust was due from Denver, Colorado. It would pass through Muncie, Kansas, four miles east of Kansas City. Hours later, Maxwell sent a mutual friend to Bud McDaniels to set up a meeting between the two men at a local saloon. Maxwell intended to pass on the information at that time—if the promised money was forthcoming.

When Maxwell entered the Flycatcher, a small bar at Fifth and Main in Kansas City, he saw McDaniels sitting at a table in the corner and approached him.

"What's up?" Bud greeted as Maxwell approached him. "What have you heard?"

"That depends on what you've got for me," Maxwell answered.

"I've got twenty double eagles for you if you've got what I want," Bud promised.

"I've got it, all right," Maxwell continued. "The train arrives at Muncie at 5 o'clock on December the eighth. She'll be loaded—I mean *loaded*."

McDaniels reached into his pocket purse and stealthily handed Maxwell ten twenty-dollar gold pieces. The shipping agent pocketed the coins with a grin and ordered a beer. After finishing his brew and saying goodbye to Bud, Maxwell walked out of the saloon humming happily. It felt to him like his pants cuffs dragged the ground from the weight in his pockets. He laughed at the thought and strolled down Grand Avenue singing an Irish tune at the height of his voice. After walking a block, he reached his right hand into his pocket and fingered the sharp, knurled rims of the gold pieces. They were beautifully rough to his touch. He couldn't believe his good fortune; he thought he'd try his hand at poker and buy his baby a toy.

December 8, 1874

Six masked and well-mounted horsemen trotted up to the railway depot at Muncie, Kansas, five miles west of Wyandotte, and dismounted. After tethering their horses, they strode up to the depot almost like they were conducting official business. Once inside the building, the outlaws drew their weapons and commandeered the railroad employees. They ordered the male employees outside to pile railroad ties on the tracks. When the captured men had finished their chore, the bandits locked them in a nearby shed while the gang waited for the expected train to arrive. After fifteen minutes, Clell Miller became impatient and sank to his knees, holding his ear to the rail. He could hear a faint humming.

"She's a comin'!" he cried to the others. Several minutes later, a locomotive puffed its way into the rail yard. On sighting it, Clell walked up the tracks waving a red scarf. The engineer, noticing him, pulled the train up to the depot and stopped. Only then did the bandits draw their pistols and begin firing into the air. Bob Younger and Bud McDaniels raced up to the locomotive and captured the engineer and firemen. Meanwhile, Jesse and Frank, Cole, and Clell attacked the express and baggage cars.

"Raise your hands, boys!" Clell ordered the two messengers as he leaped up into the express car and raised himself to his feet.

"Say! What you doin'? Get off this car!" one of the messengers cried out. Miller rapped the man across the top of his head with the barrel of his pistol, and he tumbled onto the floor unconscious.

"Open the safes," Clell shouted to the other messenger. "No more small talk."

Back at the locomotive, Bob Younger had ordered the engineer to uncouple the passenger cars and bring the express and baggage cars forward so they could be unloaded near the outlaws' horses. The gang preferred the quickest means of loading up. When the cars were brought forward, the outlaws began carrying heavy sacks filled with gold dust from the cars to their horses and wagons. McDaniels carried a wheat sack filled with bank notes and other loot. Before he tied the sack to his saddle, he opened it up and looked inside. Jewelry glittered among the bundles of bank notes. None of the other outlaws were watching him, so McDaniels grabbed a handful of jewelry and stuffed it in his pocket. He knew someone who'd like the baubles.

When the robbery was complete, the outlaws mounted their horses and trotted eastward. Later that evening, their trail was picked up by posses and followed as far as the Blue River wilds east of Kansas City. There, the trail was lost. Lawmen, nonetheless, kept up a constant vigil for any signs of the bandits. Police informants reported that the James boys had been recognized in Kansas City during the past week, and the James gang became the prime suspects in the crime.

December 12, 1874

Bud McDaniels stood before a mirror admiring his finely chiseled face. He took out his comb and ran it carefully through his bushy mustache, smoothing out the little kinks until he looked just right. Reaching atop his head, he tugged his comb through the coarse brown curls until they, too, untangled under his hand. Then he twisted his head back and forth, tilted his chin up and down, peering at himself carefully and approvingly. Finally, reaching for a bottle of cologne, he poured a liberal amount into his hands and patted himself lightly on the face. Had he forgotten anything? Yes, he thought to himself, the jewelry! He walked over to a chest, pulled out the top drawer, and grabbed a glittering bracelet that he had taken at Muncie and slid it into his coat pocket.

Then he walked down the stairs of his rooming house into the street where his rented horse and buggy were tethered. Mounting the buggy, he shook the reins lightly, and his horse trotted proudly down the street. McDaniels headed for 406 Olive, the home of his girlfriend, Sally. He knew she would be waiting, and he had a big surprise for her.

McDaniels pulled up in front of the girl's home, stepped down from his buggy, and tied up the rig. He walked briskly to the door and knocked loudly. When a middle-aged woman answered the door, Bud said in a low, soft voice, "Would you tell Sally that Bud's here?"

"Why, brother, she ain't here," the lady at the door replied hesitantly. "Why? Was she expectin' you?"

"Ma'am," Bud answered, "we had an engagement. Where is she?" he questioned indignantly.

"Well," the lady replied, "she left with a young man more'n an hour ago. You sure you ain't mistaken about the time and day?"

"I ain't mistaken," Bud answered bitterly, and he turned on his heel in a huff. Within seconds, he was driving on Grand Avenue through downtown Kansas City headed for the first saloon he met. It happened to be the Arrow. When he was settled there, he ordered a glass of Tennessee whiskey and downed it in a gulp. For the rest of the evening, he caroused from saloon to saloon until he was roaring drunk.

At 3:00 A.M., McDaniels left the Home Place saloon and boarded his buggy, lashing out at his horse. "Giddap! Yah, mule!" he bellowed. "Darned contraption!" he roared at the buggy, kicking at it. "Slower'n walkin!" The buggy sped through the middle of Kansas City, nearly out of control. Bud beat his horse until its mouth foamed, and he fairly flew down the street.

A patrolling Kansas City police sergeant, Sandy McCarthy, saw the buggy speed past a warehouse on Sixth and Walnut and galloped after it in hot pursuit. Spurring his own mount, the policeman raced alongside Bud's horse, grabbed the halter in one hand, and forced the animal to slow to a trot. McCarthy eased the buggy to a complete halt. Dismounting from his horse, the policeman walked up to McDaniels.

"Say, cowboy, where yah think you're goin'?"

Bud, his hair in wild disarray and his eyes bloodshot and bleary, replied, "Hey, whads goin' on? Da hoss wudn' stap. Whads goin' on?"

"Let go of them reins, boy," the policeman said sternly. "I'm takin' you in for reckless drivin' and for bein' drunk in public." The policeman grabbed McDaniels' reins and pulled hard on them, jerking them from his grasp. Bud lost his balance and leaned awkwardly over the edge of the buggy, almost falling to the ground. The officer pushed him back into the buggy and led his horse to the side of the street, tethering it to the first hitching post. Then he reached up into the buggy and grabbed Bud by the arm and yanked him roughly. McDaniels tumbled from the buggy onto the ground, his knees and new pants covered with dust. Slowly, he raised himself onto one knee and looked up at his captor quizzically as another patrolman rode up to help the sergeant.

"What you got there, Sandy?"

"Not much, Riley," McCarthy replied, "just an ignorant drunk."

The two men dragged Bud to a nearby police station and placed him under arrest for the night. Before they led him to his cell, Patrolman Riley emptied his pockets.

"Hey, McCarthy!" Riley cried out. "Look what I found on this boy." He handed a heavy sheepskin bag to the officer. The sergeant untied its string closure and looked inside. The light of a kerosene lamp revealed the glitter of gold dust.

"Pardner," McCarthy replied, "looks like we done struck a gold mine." Reaching into another of McDaniels' pockets, McCarthy pulled out a diamond bracelet and several rings.

"Hey, Riley, this cowboy appears to have been up to considerable mischief. Ain't nobody carries this much gold, exceptin' a miner. And I ain't seen nobody carry ice like this, period. By the looks of this cute boy's soft hands, he ain't no miner. I'll put this stuff in the safe and tell the chief about it come mornin'."

Bud, noticing them examining the jewelry, shouted loudly. "Take it! Take it all! I got no use for such trash!"

By late morning, Bud had become a major suspect in the Muncie affair. And within a day, the jewelry had been identified as loot from the recent train robbery. McDaniels was in big trouble. Because the train robbery had occurred in Kansas and the stolen jewelry was from a Lawrence wholesale house, he was taken to a Lawrence, Kansas, jail. A cell was ready for him when he arrived. After two hours of intensive interrogation, however, he revealed nothing useful to the Lawrence city marshal or Detective Con O'Hara of the Kansas City police. But they had more than enough evidence on him to indict him.

Several weeks later, Bud was taken out of his cell and walked to the courtroom to be arraigned. On the way, he overpowered his guard and escaped. Days later, a citizens' posse saw him skulking along the Kaw River, recognized him as the escaped bank robber, and ordered him to surrender. When McDaniels attempted to escape, a posse member named Baumann raised his rifle and fired. Another James-Younger gang member was eliminated from the gang's dwindling roll call.

Meanwhile, the express company offered a five-thousand-dollar reward for the recovery of the money lost in the robbery and one thousand dollars for the capture or killing of any of the bandits. The governor of Kansas responded by offering a twenty-five-hundred-dollar reward, and the Kansas Pacific Railroad promised five thousand. For its own good, the James-Younger gang retired to its hideouts in Texas and Kentucky.

December 25, 1874

Jack Ladd sang fervently at the Christmas service of the First Baptist Church in Kearney. Ladd wore a frayed suit with a small patch on one elbow and a crumpled and badly faded maroon-colored tie around his neck. As he looked down the pew, he saw Zerelda Samuel pouring her heart out in the same hymn. "Rock of Ages, cleft for me/Let me hide myself in thee." The church seemed to ring with the stirring melody as the singers captured the spirit of the song. Ladd added his own enthusiasm. Ladd was a rather awkward, homely fellow from southern Missouri, but he fit in around the Kearney area. They were tolerant of hill people, whatever their fortunes. Most of the locals knew Ladd, even though he had lived in the area only a short time; he was what the locals called a "mixer." Mrs. Samuel, for instance, always said hello to Ladd when he passed her at church. Old Dan Askew, his employer, had told his neighbors the Samuels that Ladd was a good hand.

When the churchgoers exited the service, Ladd hung around the door chatting with people he knew. When Mrs. Samuel passed him, he took off his hat.

"Mornin', Miz Samuel. Good to see yah!"

"Why, hello, Mr. Ladd," she replied politely. "How's things goin' over at the Askews'?"

"Jes fine, Miz Samuel. Course they got me humpin', they do; they's always lots to do at the ol' place. Say, I passed Frank on the road t'other day. He's jes as ornery as a bear. Ha! Ha!"

"Frank's doin' fine," Mrs. Samuel replied and followed her husband out to their buggy. Zerelda had enjoyed the service, but she was anxious to get home to start the family dinner.

January 25, 1875

Jack Ladd, hunched over, slowly worked his way to the top of a ravine. Just before he reached the top of the hill, he dropped onto his stomach. Using his knees and arms to propel himself forward, he edged toward the crest. When he reached the top, he rested on his elbows and cautiously looked through a parting in the prairie grass. He reached into his coat pocket and pulled out a telescope and extended it, poking it through a gap in the grass. He focused it on the Samuels' cabin. He'd been up that same ravine a number of times in the last two weeks and had seen Frank James in the yard once and Jesse twice. But he hadn't seen them recently. Yesterday, Billy Pinkerton had left a telegram for Ladd at Liberty ordering him to check the house daily from now on to determine if the boys were at home. If they were, Ladd was to wire Pinkerton immediately and wait for instructions. In light of that order, Ladd was prepared to stay the rest of the day. He had dressed warmly, donning long wool underwear, two shirts, a heavy coat, and thick wool socks. There was no telling how long he might have to lie there, he reckoned. But the money was right, he told himself; he had no quarrel with it.

Around 12:30 P.M., he saw the front door of the cabin open, and two men ventured into the cold. Both were tall. They pulled out tobacco pouches and appeared to be rolling cigarettes. Ladd refocused his telescope. Yes, it was them, all right—the James boys! That would interest Billy and Bob Pinkerton. They had some sort of operation planned, he knew. He'd be let in on the details eventually, he guessed. In fact, he suspected he was already playing a major part in the enterprise. He turned around in the gully and started down the hill toward the Askew place. He'd make a quick ride to Liberty.

A messenger boy from Western Union had just delivered a telegram from Jack Ladd to Billy Pinkerton at the Pinkerton's Kansas City office. The detective examined it carefully. Yes, it was as he had hoped: the James boys were at the Samuels' farm. Billy grabbed a pen and began writing telegrams. First, he would inform Robert and his father at the Pinkerton's Chicago headquarters. Grabbing a sheet of paper, he scrawled a telegram message:

FLXOD GPBMEJT STOP TFMM PNWS STOP EBVPWM 9B4

STOP MEGSOQA RP WCZ STOP JVWW PLSRWQ 3K9VV
QVYPN STOP JVWW UMBB OLVWTY

ZD

Then, Billy composed two uncoded telegrams, one to Gov. Charles H. Hardin of Missouri and a third telegram to Millard Foster, president of the Chicago, Rock Island & Pacific Railroad. He would need the unscheduled use of the Rock Island railroad tonight, and he wanted no police interference.

That evening, at the Chicago, Rock Island & Pacific Railroad yard, Archie Smoot read the latest telegraph message from Chicago and squinted his eyes. He must be seeing things. He turned to Tom Sorrels, the other clerk.

"Tom, what's goin' on? I just got a wire sayin' that the trains scheduled from Chicago this evenin' have been canceled. I know for certain that they were booked to roll. What's happenin'?"

"Beats me, Arch," replied Sorrels. "I'll check with the station agent." Sorrels walked to the back of the station and entered agent Polk Helms' private office. After talking to Helms a few minutes, he returned.

"It's okay, Arch," Sorrels reassured the other clerk. "The trains have been canceled."

"Oh yeah?" Arch replied. "How come?"

"I asked Helms why," Sorrels continued, "and he said it wasn't any of my business. He said when I needed to know, he would tell me. I guess we're just goin' to have a quiet time this evenin'."

Thirty minutes later, a large Irishman, Pat O'Donnell, one of the yardmen, rushed in the front door of the station with a frustrated expression on his face.

"What's happenin' around this place tonight? It's bedlam out there," O'Donnell complained. "There's a bunch of railroad dicks and coppers runnin' around like they was ownin' the place. What's goin' on?"

"Don't ask us," Smoot replied. "We don't know what's happenin' either, and the stationmaster told us to keep our snoots out of it."

O'Donnell, disgusted, exited the station and walked back into the railroad yard. In the main yard, detectives were swarming everywhere. O'Donnell stopped to watch them. With the help of some of the railroad hands, the detectives had erected a cleated ramp leading up into one of the cattle cars. Several men were leading horses into the car. Once the last horse was aboard, the men loaded the ramp materials and closed the car's side door. Then a ladder was leaned up against the next car, and a number of men ascended it and disappeared into the car, dragging the ladder behind them.

My word! O'Donnell thought to himself. Looks like a dad-binged army going off to war. And they're armed like one too, by gum! O'Donnell noticed that the door of the car filled with detectives was left partially open to allow air to circulate. The cattle car was naturally ventilated with openings between the slats. The last man to enter the unvented car was a burly fellow with a large, walrus-like mustache and a cigar stuffed in his mouth. Once aboard, he leaned out the door of the car.

"All right, get this fool thing rolling!" he yelled to the engineer. "Pour the cobs to her!" Billy Pinkerton was taking personal control of the operation. Standing next to him were conductor William Westfall and eight Pinkerton agents.

The engineer whistled a warning, and the engine chugged slowly through the yard. As the train picked up speed, the engineer yanked on a cord and released a long screaming whistle. Black and white smoke and a shower of sparks erupted from the locomotive's stack as the engine puffed and rattled its way out of the yard into open country. There, the engineer accelerated. The train was composed of an engine, a tender full of wood, and two boxcars. It sped at top speed across the countryside in a northerly direction, a long trail of smoke streaming behind it in the moonlight.

Once the train reached a point south of Kearney, one of the detectives ordered the engineer to bring the train to a halt near a curve in the line. When the train screeched to a stop, the agents jumped from the boxcar. One of the detectives ran to the cattle car and slid the door open. The agents pulled out a wood ramp and leaned it against the car to unload the horses. The horses were led down the ramp, fully saddled and ready to mount.

One of the Samuels' longtime black servants opened her eyes. Something had startled her from her sleep. From her little cot next to the wall, she looked across the room at the fireplace. The fire smoldered and the hot ashes from the banked logs emitted an eerie light. Tobacco rods, long sticks with hands of tobacco hanging from them, leaned against the fireplace. She wondered if she had just imagined it. She often woke up in the night thinking she'd heard noises. They usually amounted to nothing more than the house creaking. She didn't hear anything now, but the sound had seemed real enough. Then she heard it again. A rattling, as if someone was opening the shutters. Then she heard the rasping sound of a window being raised.

"Help! Help!" she screamed in a high-pitched shriek. Someone was breaking into the cabin. She jumped from her bed.

"Miz Samuel! Miz Samuel!" she yelled loudly. Zerelda and Reuben Samuel rose up in their bed nearby and looked around the room.

"What's the matter?" Zerelda asked in a concerned voice. Reuben slid out of bed.

A large burning ball had been rolled through their upraised window and was bounding across the wooden floor of the Samuels' cabin. It fizzed and sputtered fire as it wobbled erratically. Reuben ran to the fireplace and grabbed one of the tobacco sticks. Fearing that the floor would ignite and the whole house would go up in flames, Reuben pushed the heavy ball toward the fireplace hearth with the stick. As he guided the ball, it seemed to roll in every direction but the right one. Finally, he wrestled the fiery ball in front of the open hearth and shoved it into the coals with his foot. Then, another ball tumbled through the window, this one nearly eight inches in diameter, and rolled across the floor. It fizzed loudly and blazed. The object was too heavy to move with his stick, so Reuben grabbed a shovel leaning against the wall and pushed the fiery bundle into the fireplace. When the object reached the flames, it exploded with a roar. Samuel was blown off his feet and thrown almost to the ceiling. He fell to the floor, wounded on the right side of his head and bruised and dazed. The Samuels' children and a grandson of their servant began crying loudly. Zerelda moaned. Her arm had been broken above her wrist and her arm splintered by shrapnel from the bomb. Her hand dangled uselessly at her side. Their black servant was struck in the head by shrapnel but not seriously hurt.

Outside the cabin came cheers from the Pinkerton detectives—and then loud reports. Firing had broken out. Jesse and Frank had been sleeping in the Samuels' barn and had sprung into action. At the first noise, they had run into the woods. Now, they were firing down on the Pinkertons from a wooded knoll above the cabin, their revolvers spitting fire in small flashes. The Pinkertons returned the fire, but the brothers moved continuously from position to position, preventing the Pinkertons from accurately locating them. In contrast, the fire silhouetted the detectives and made them vulnerable targets to these former guerrillas who were waging their kind of fight.

"Let's get out of here!" yelled Billy Pinkerton as bullets whistled around the men. "Run for the horses! They have the advantage on us!" The detectives continued a heavy fire as they fled. The James brothers recognized the awkward gait of Jack Ladd, and he fell in a fusillade of fire. His pistol, engraved P.G.G. for Pinkerton Government Guard, fell from his hand. Two of the agents grabbed the dead Ladd under the arms and dragged him toward the horses tethered nearby. They wanted no evidence left at the scene. The Pinkertons had expected to surround and surprise the James boys, but the situation had been reversed. Billy had had enough. There was no point in losing any more men, and they were not likely to capture the criminals in the darkness.

When the firing stopped, the Samuels' servant ran for a kerosene lantern and lit it while Reuben smothered the few remaining flames on the floor of the cabin with a pitcher of water. The servant went after another pitcher of water to wash Mrs. Samuel's wound. She eventually stanched the blood flowing from Zerelda's arm by winding long strips of clean rags around it. While their mother was being cared for, Zerelda's children— Fannie, Sallie Quantrell, and John Samuel—hovered around her skirt, hiding their faces and clutching at her dress. Zerelda stood with a blank stare on her face, stunned and in shock. Her servant looked around for young Archie. Where was Zerelda's eight-year-old son? she wondered.

"Archie! Archie!" the black woman yelled. She heard a moan coming from a dark corner of the cabin. She finished bandaging Zerelda's arm and rushed over to investigate the prone figure. Archie lay on his side, scarcely making a sound. His body, covered with blood, had been torn open just under his third rib by a bomb fragment, and his intestines gaped from a wound in his side. He looked like a goner to her.

"Poor boy! Poor boy! Lord help you!" she screamed and began crying loudly.

Zerelda, still stunned and half-conscious, cried out, "Archie! Archie! Are you all right? Is the boy all right?"

The servant went over to Zerelda, who was sitting on the bed, and placed her arm around her shoulder. "Miz Samuel . . . I think Archie is dyin'."

"No! No!" Zerelda cried out. "He can't be!"

Prompted by the sound of the explosion and gunfire, a neighbor of the Samuels, a farmer named Chanceller, arrived and offered to go to Kearney to bring a doctor. Dan Askew, who lived on the farm next to the Samuels, arrived about the same time. Two hours later, Dr. James V. Scruggs arrived in a buggy, but it was too late. Jesse and Frank's half-brother, Archie Peyton Samuel, age eight, had died. A large crowd attended the funeral held two days later. Many people in Missouri were angry about the Kearney events and demanded that something be done about the alleged lawlessness of the Pinkertons. Local newspapers screamed, "The Crime of a Century" and "inexcusable and cowardly deeds." In March, an Amnesty Bill was originated in the Missouri legislature proposing amnesty for Jesse and Frank James and Bob, Jim, and Cole Younger, but the bill failed by one vote. Those unfriendly to the bill called it the "Outlaw Amnesty Bill." Those sympathizing with it thought that the two families had been singled out for Yankee vengeance. Nothing was ever learned publicly concerning the fate of Jack Ladd.

April 12, 1875

Dan Askew had just returned home from a trip to Liberty, Missouri, to purchase corn for the new planting. After supper, he walked out the back door of his small frame home into the moonlight carrying the family water pail. He sought to replenish it at the cistern on the back porch. After cranking his bucket full of water, Askew reached into the pail. Drawing a shiny tin cup to his lips, he swallowed the cool, refreshing liquid. Several pistol shots rang out, and slugs tore into his body, one through his head, two into his chest. Askew fell onto the porch with a loud thud and lay in a lifeless heap. His wife and daughter, hearing the shots, ran to the porch and found his bleeding body. They saw three men fleeing from behind a nearby woodpile. Within a week, Frank and Jesse James were in Wichita Falls, Texas, visiting with their sister Susie Parmer and her husband, ex-Missouri guerrilla Allen Parmer.

13

July 7, 1876

Louis Pete Conklin of St. Louis, baggage master on the Missouri Pacific Railroad, finished arranging the bags he had loaded at Sedalia. His train, composed of two day coaches, two Pullman sleepers, a smoker, a baggage-express car, and an additional express car, was headed for St. Louis. Since it was a sultry evening, Conklin had opened the side door of the express car to cool things off, but it was still hot, and he wiped the perspiration from his brow with a handkerchief. Working on his accounts at a small desk nearby was John B. Bushnell, the U.S. Express Company messenger. Finally satisfied with the baggage, Conklin moved a wooden folding chair over to the open door of the car where he could relax in the cooler air.

"Say, John, why don't you take a break, take in some of this cooler night air?" Conklin said, smiling at Bushnell.

"My word, you couldn't buy cool air from an Eskimo tonight," Bushnell replied. "Nope, better keep at these records. I got to be ready when we get to Tipton."

"Aw! Come on, you ain't got that many accounts," Conklin responded.

At the Lamine River several miles from Otterville, Missouri,

Joe Fickell, a watchman, guarded a new bridge being constructed. Fickell sat under a hickory tree overlooking the new bridge. A bright moon soared overhead, and the light sparkled on the river below. It was light enough so that he could see the outline of the stonework done on the bridge supports that day. Occasionally, Fickell scratched himself; the chiggers were beginning to eat him alive, and mosquitoes swarmed and droned around his ears. He swatted at them without effect.

On nights like this, when he had time to think about it, Joe thought his job as watchman didn't pay enough. But then, he reflected, he didn't have to do all that much either. In this case, he just had to lean up against a tree in the middle of nowhere in case some fool hillbilly decided to ride up to the bridge and steal building materials and cement. Still, Joe didn't like the idea of feeding the mosquitoes, curse 'em. Occasionally, during his day shifts, Joe had had to flag down a train when the workmen needed to cross the tracks with wagonloads of material. But during night duty, Fickell usually sat idly smoking his pipe and killing time. He wondered what time it was and reached into his pocket to pull out his watch. He could barely make out what looked like 9:57 in the moonlight. He'd been glad to see the sun go down; it had been a scorcher. But it was still steaming hot. He could feel a light, hot breeze against his face. It must be 95 degrees yet, he reckoned. Fickell heard rustling behind him.

"Get 'em up! Raise your hands!" someone shouted at him.

Fickell twisted around to view the man addressing him. He was perhaps six feet in height and wore a broad-brimmed hat. Though it was dark, Fickell noticed that a bandanna covered the lower part of the man's face. Dark, sparkling eyes and arched eyebrows appeared above the scarf, with a flowing duster covering the rest of the stranger. What Fickell noticed most, though, was the large revolver in the fellow's hand.

"I said get your hands up! On your feet and off your butt!" the stranger shouted. Fickell rose to his feet and raised his arms above his head. The stranger walked around him, patting his clothing, looking for a gun. But no one had thought Fickell needed a gun out here in the sticks.

"Where's your signal lantern? I want it," the gunman demanded. Bob Younger emerged from the shadows and joined Samuel Wells, alias Charlie Pitts, the outlaw confronting Fickell. Younger wore a duster and had his face covered in the same manner as Pitts. Large Colt navies were pointed at the watchman. Since he had left his lantern nearby, Fickell led the armed men to it and handed it to Pitts.

Charlie Pitts knelt next to the lantern, raised its globe, and screwed up the wick. He pulled a match out of his pocket, scratched it on his pants, and ignited the lantern. A red light gleamed as the wick caught. Fickell looked at the two strangers and could better make out their features in the flickering light. The man who had been speaking to him had pitch-black hair, he noticed. A red bandanna over the lower part of his face obscured most of the rest of his looks, but his complexion seemed dark. In the eerie light, he looked like a demon out of hell.

"Come with us, and don't try anything," Pitts said to the watchman. The three men walked north toward the railroad tracks. Pitts walked ahead of the other two men and placed the red lantern in the middle of the tracks. Then he ordered Fickell to drag heavy ties and four-by-fours from the bridge construction onto the tracks for obstructions. It was more work than Fickell had done in weeks.

Aboard Number 8, Conklin continued to relax in front of the open door of the baggage-express car. Suddenly, he felt the train braking. Why was the engineer slowing down? he wondered. Then he heard a loud bang, and fragments of wood rained down on him from the doorframe over his head. Conklin dived for cover; someone was firing at him. Other explosions erupted, and he heard men cursing and yelling.

"All right, you, stay in that car!" he heard someone shout.

"Don't nobody move! We shoot to kill!" roared another man.

"You!" one of the bandits shouted. "Close that window!"

"Get back in that car!" thundered another voice.

The shooting continued sporadically, punctuated by oaths and yelling. Two outlaws, Bill Chadwell—who was using the name William Stiles—and Hobbs Kerry, remained out of sight, tending the horses while their six accomplices robbed the train.

Bill Stanhope, the engineer, had seen the red light ahead and applied his new air brakes, throwing his locomotive into reverse. Even so, the train had screeched slowly to a stop. Its cowcatcher crashed into the debris on the tracks, pushing it ahead of the locomotive. The train finally halted in the middle of a stone cleft that ran through the hill, known locally as "Rocky Cut." Men were firing at the train from all directions. Within seconds, two masked men boarded the locomotive and pointed their big revolvers at the engineer and the fireman, Jake Mead.

"Raise your hands!" a masked outlaw bellowed. "Get down from the engine and do what I say!" The railroad men dutifully scrambled off the locomotive.

In the baggage-express car, John Bushnell peered around the open door of his car as Conklin huddled in the corner. Masked men were running back and forth along the length of the train, firing their pistols and yelling like Indians. It was a robbery all right. Bushnell had the key to the express safe and knew that the bandits would be after it. He ran out the west end of the car, crossed the back platform, and raced down the aisle of the adjoining coach toward the back of the train. He was looking for a place to hide the key to his strongbox. The passengers gaped at him as he rushed by. The noise had terrified them, and Bushnell's wild appearance only excited them further. Some of the men had crawled under their seats, and other passengers were hiding their valuables wherever they could find a place.

"Get out of the way," Bushnell growled at one of the passengers who stumbled into his path. He pushed the man roughly from the aisle and rushed out the end of the car and across the next platform. Shots whizzed by him. He continued running until he reached the rearmost car in the train. "Take off one of your shoes," he screamed to the brakeman when he got there. "I've got to hide the express key." The brakeman, who had pulled out his revolver, looked at Bushnell with uncertainty.

"You heard me! Get rid of that popgun; there are too many of 'em to fight." The brakeman pulled off his shoe, and Bushnell handed him the key to the Adams Express Company safe. The brakeman put the key in the toe of his sock, replaced his shoe, and hid his revolver under one of the seats. Then the two men peered out the back door of the car to watch what was happening.

Cole Younger and Jesse James boarded the baggage-express car, and Jesse held the muzzle of his gun to Conklin's head.

"Hey, where are the keys to these?" Jesse demanded, pointing at the two express safes. "Give them to me—now!"

"I'm only the baggage man," Conklin replied.

"Where is the express messenger?" Jesse asked and shoved the barrel of his gun into Conklin's stomach with a painful jerk.

Conklin winced. "I don't know. Back in the train, I guess."

Frank James, who was conducting operations outside the baggage car, walked by the express car. "What's the matter?" Frank shouted. "Won't that fella give you the key? Shoot him!" Frank was becoming impatient and sought to put pressure on the railroad man to cooperate.

Jesse replied, "He just needs some persuadin', maybe a bullet in his head." He turned to the baggage man. "Take me to the messenger," Jesse ordered, roughly grabbing Conklin by the back of his shirt and shoving the muzzle of his revolver into his back. Conklin moved in the direction of the rear of the train.

As they proceeded through the coaches, a woman screamed and several men cowered beneath their seats. Most of the passengers gaped at the masked outlaw. Finally, Jesse reached the caboose where the two railroad men stood with amazed expressions on their faces.

"Who is the messenger?" Jesse demanded of the baggage man. Conklin pointed to Bushnell.

"All right, partner," Jesse said, aiming his revolver at Bushnell. "I want the keys to the express safes or I'll blow your brains out." Jesse's eyes sparkled with intensity, and he placed the muzzle of his gun against Bushnell's head. Bushnell looked into the outlaw's blinking blue eyes and had no doubt he meant what he said. He turned to the brakeman.

"Give him the key, Ned. He means business." The brakeman stooped down and removed his shoe and sock and handed the key to James.

"Where's the other key?" Jesse demanded. "There are two safes."

"He gave me only one," said the brakeman.

"Uh, that's right," Bushnell blurted out. "There's only one key. The other safe is a special express safe; it's not opened till the train reaches Chicago. I'm tellin' the truth, so help me God!"

"We're goin' back to the express car, the three of us," Jesse answered. "Stay in front of me and move fast."

When they got back to the express car, Jesse found the engineer and fireman under Cole's guard. Frank and the other outlaws were still outside the cars, firing their weapons to keep the passengers inside.

Jesse stuck the key the brakeman had given him into the U.S. Express Company safe and opened it. Then he handed the green bundles of bills to Cole, who plopped them into the gang's signature wheat sack. Meanwhile, Bob Younger—who had overheard that there was no key to the Adams Express safe—had run to the locomotive and grabbed a coal pick to break open the remaining safe. He returned with the tool and handed it to Jesse.

"Here, try this," he said, gasping for breath.

Jesse grabbed the pick, drew it over his head, and with a

broad arc struck the safe a hard blow. The pick made only a small dent in the safe, and the impact made Jesse's hands sting. "More muscle," Cole said reaching for the pick. He took the pick from Jesse, placed the handle in his hamlike hands, and raised it over his head. He rammed the pick down in a hard stroke, and the point stuck in the safe, driving a small hole in it the size of a walnut. Younger struck the safe again and again, until he tore a ragged hole in it the size of a large orange. When he attempted to reach into the safe, though, the hole was too small. Jesse stepped forward and urged Cole aside.

"I'll handle this," he said and reached his smaller hand directly into the safe. "Give me your knife, Bud," he said to Younger. Cole reached into his pocket and handed Jesse a small penknife. Jesse threaded his arm into the hole and cut a long incision in the leather bag holding the currency. Then he pulled out bundles of greenbacks and handed them to his accomplice, who dropped them into the sack. Soon, twenty-five thousand dollars in bills rested there. Crumpled letters were also taken out of the safe and ripped open to reveal any money.

When they had completed the robbery, Cole turned to Conklin: "I need a drink." The messenger pointed to a water pail in the corner of the car.

"Come!" Cole said to Conklin, motioning him toward the water with his pistol. When they reached the large pail, Cole grabbed the dipper hanging from the bucket and filled it with water. "Drink," Cole said to the baggage master. When Conklin had tested the water, Cole took the dipper from him and drank himself. The other outlaws followed suit. It was a hot, humid night, and the outlaws were dressed in sweltering dusters.

In one of the coaches, the Reverend J. S. Holmes preached to the frightened passengers. "My friends!" he began. "We are sinners in the eyes of God! Tonight, we are besieged by Satan's henchmen. Our time is at hand! We must repent! Soon, we may

join our Heavenly Father—all too soon, brothers and sisters!"
"Amen!" several of the passengers cried out.
"Let us lower our heads in prayer." The minister paused for
a moment, then continued. "Oh, Heavenly Father, we seek
thy favor. We are besieged this fearful night. Our lives hang
suspended between heaven and hell. Some of us, *I know*, are
not ready! *No, some are not ready!*"
"Amen! Amen!" passengers cried out.
"As we stand facing Death's summons," the minister continued,
"I say to you, brothers and sisters, those who have not repented,
step forward! Step forward and accept Jesus!
"Judgment is at hand!" Holmes went on, raising his voice to
a higher pitch. "Flee Satan, that Prince of Darkness, and accept
the Lord thy shepherd. Step forward, brothers and sisters. Step
forward. Accept his blessed mercy and avoid the eternal fire!"
The minister looked inquisitively around the car and noticed
one man staring in his direction.
"You! You, with the raised head. Step forward." The man he
had singled out ducked his head and pretended the minister
was referring to someone else. He had been so electrified by the
minister's words that he had raised his head unconsciously to
watch him as he spoke.
"Lucifer, that cloven-footed fiend, must be crushed!" the
minister exclaimed. "Tonight, my brothers and sisters." Then
Holmes looked skyward. "Oh, Father, protect these humble
sinners, I beseech thee, and lead them to thy holy light!
Hallelujah! Hallelujah! God be praised!"
"Amen! Amen!" answered the chorus of excited passengers.
Outside the cars, Charlie Pitts whined to Frank James,
"Hey, let's go back to the cars. I need one of those fancy
watches, a 'super.'"
"No," Frank replied. "We've been here too long. All out!"
The men began walking in the direction where Bill Chadwell
and Hobbs Kerry held the horses. Only Jesse James remained.
He was listening to the voices now rising in song from Reverend

Holmes' car. A blend of voices wafted melodiously across the warm night air.

Though, like the wanderer, the sun gone down,
Darkness be over me, my rest a stone,
Yet in my dreams I'd be, nearer my God, to Thee!
Nearer my God to Thee! Nearer to Thee.

Jesse stood transfixed, unable to move, his mouth forming the words "Nearer to Thee." The music was beautiful to him; he loved the old hymns, and he stood for a moment singing the words. Then he shook himself back to reality and turned toward the express messenger and baggage master, who stood staring out the door of their car at him.

"Say, boys," Jesse yelled to them, "if you see any of Allan Pinkerton's boys, tell 'em to come callin'! We'd like to meet 'em!" Then, laughing, he walked off in the direction of the other outlaws. A few moments later, the two men in the express car heard the muffled thunder of hooves riding off into the night.

August 2, 1876

On July 8, the governor of Missouri, Charles H. Hardin, had offered a three-hundred-dollar reward for the arrest of any of the bandits who robbed the train near Otterville. Meanwhile, Chief of Police James McDonough of St. Louis and noted Cincinnati detective Larry Hazen, assisting McDonough, received word from an informant that a man named Hobbes Kerry of Granby, Missouri, was involved in the Rocky Cut railroad robbery and was flashing stolen gold. They traveled to Granby at railroad company expense and arrested Kerry. The outlaw apparently had drawn attention to himself by brandishing large sums of money in that poor southwest Missouri town.

When detectives took Kerry to Otterville, a farmer identified him as one of the men who had been in the area several days before the robbery. After intensive interrogations, Kerry broke down and confessed to being a participant in the crime and named as his accomplices Bill Chadwell, Charlie Pitts, Clell Miller, Bob Younger, Cole Younger, Frank James, and Jesse James. This incriminating evidence directly linked the Jameses, Youngers, and others with the train robbery.

August 13, 1876

As the sun jutted over the horizon, twelve Pinkerton men pulling one riderless horse spurred their mounts. They had traveled to Missouri by train from Chicago and brought their horses with them. After disembarking in Kansas City, they were now less than a mile from the home of Samuel Ralston, the father-in-law of Frank James. Rumor had it that Frank was hiding there. For the purpose of surprise, they hoped to reach the Ralston farm before dawn.

Soon, the horsemen arrived outside the gate of Ralston's country home and dismounted. One of the men untied the ropes that lashed down the battering ram the detectives carried with them. Once the ram was untied from the horse it was anchored to, four men grabbed it by its handles and walked briskly up to Ralston's front door. The other detectives circled Ralston's house and took up firing positions. At a signal, the four men grabbed the handles of the battering ram and charged into the front door of Ralston's home. The door collapsed in an explosion of wood and jangling hinges, and the detectives hurtled into the parlor.

In the kitchen, Sam Ralston and a visitor had been drinking coffee. Ralston had just eaten his breakfast and was preparing to do his morning chores: milking the cows, slopping the hogs, and throwing a few ears of corn to his steers. The unsuspecting men jumped in amazement at the racket. Within seconds,

Pinkerton agents brandishing guns surrounded them. The detectives grappled with the two men, twisted their arms behind them, and fastened handcuffs to their wrists.

"Identify yourselves!" yelled one of the agents, a short stocky man with black hair and a walrus mustache. "You! Old man!" the stocky man screamed, poking a stubby finger into Ralston's ribs. "Who are you?"

"Why, I'm Sam Ralston," the elderly man replied defiantly. "What do you jackasses mean breakin' into my home?"

"Shut up!" the stocky man replied. "We have a search warrant. Answer my questions and hold your blather. Is this man Frank James?" he said. "I warn you, you must tell me the truth!"

"Of course he ain't. He's my neighbor, Joe Connelley. Now, get out of my house!"

"You!" the interrogator continued, grabbing Ralston's visitor by the arm. "What's your name?"

"Joe Connelley, of course. I live at the next farm. What's it to you?"

"Shut up!" the stocky man replied. "I'll ask the questions; you answer 'em! James," Billy Pinkerton continued, addressing Ralston's visitor, "you thought we'd never catch up with you. Well, you'll be decorating a rope soon!"

"James?" answered Ralston's visitor. "Who do you think I am?"

"Frank James, of course. You're not fooling us with your lies," Pinkerton declared triumphantly.

"Are you balmy? Do any of you characters have badges?" Ralston's visitor asked.

"Badges? We take care of the badges! You're coming with us."

"I can't! I've got chores to do," replied Ralston's visitor.

"We've go a chore for you, all right—swinging at the end of a rope, by heaven! Grab him, boys!" Pinkerton commanded.

Two burly detectives grabbed Ralston's visitor by the arms and dragged him to the riderless horse they had brought with them. The men rode south toward Kansas City, leaving a trail of dust behind them.

When they arrived at the railroad yard, the officers yanked their prisoner from his horse and led him to a waiting car. Once the detectives had the man aboard, the train chugged west into Kansas. The Pinkerton agents now began an intensive interrogation of Ralston's visitor.

"All right, James," one of the officers started, "it's time you talked. You may not know it, but we have photographs of you. Good ones, too! We know you are Frank James. Why do you keep up these foolish denials? It'll go easier on you if you talk."

Ralston's visitor only shrugged and replied bitterly, "You fellas have got to be the biggest bunch of clowns I've ever seen."

At Pomeroy, Kansas, west of Kansas City, the train stopped, and the Pinkerton agents finally allowed Joseph Connelley, a Clay County farmer, to get off the train. He had somehow managed to convince them that he was not the wanted desperado, Frank James. Connelley, now miles away from home, was incensed. Where did they find such lawmen? he asked himself over and over, more befuddled than angry.

August 25, 1876

A man of average size and build wearing a white suit strode back and forth on the St. Louis station platform, impatient for the train to arrive. Few of the other people on the platform paid much attention to him. But a tall young man in a black suit and vest noticed him and stared. His eyes lighted up in recognition, and he walked across the platform and extended his hand.

"Sir, I think I know you. You are well known in these parts. You're Mark Twain if I'm not mistaken."

Twain, somewhat annoyed with the intrusion, extended his hand to the stranger. He assumed that the young man was one of his many admirers, someone who had read one of his books or perhaps had seen his picture in a local newspaper. But something about the young man interested Twain.

"You are correct, sir," Twain replied. "But I'm surprised to be recognized."

"Oh," the young man continued, "you are well known in your field. So am I—in *my* field. You may have heard of me. I am Jesse Woodson James." Jesse smiled impishly and walked back into the crowd on the platform and disappeared.

14

August 4, 1876

Jim Younger examined the rumpled envelope in his hand. On the upper left-hand corner, it read, "Coleman Younger, Harrisonville, Missouri." Jim wondered what his brother wanted. It seemed like whenever Cole wrote, it was always to ask for something. He hadn't heard anything from the family in months, but he'd recently read a short report in the local newspaper about the Otterville robbery. Some time ago, Frank James had asked him if he wanted to participate in that enterprise, but he had told him he wasn't interested. He was just tired of stealing for a living.

Jim unfolded his pocketknife, inserted the blade into the end of the envelope, and opened it.

Dear Brother,
Come quick. Bob's in a pickle. He bought a farm east of father's old place and needs seed money to make it work. Just got him a pretty young wife too. Hate to see him come to grief. Come quick. A big job's buzzing.

Cole

Jim frowned. He thought he'd seen the last of the robbing and running. He'd had it up to his neck with that sort of thing. But if Bob needed him, that was different. Jim placed the letter back into the envelope and stuck it in his front pocket. He'd have to read it again, after chores, study it carefully. But he didn't like the sound of it. So far, his life in California had been to his liking. Working on the La Panza Ranch for Drury James, Jesse and Frank James' prosperous uncle, had made him into a better cowpoke. But Bob's future was important to him too. He'd always been protective of his younger brother, wanted to see things turn out right for Bobby. Already he was leaning toward buying a train ticket home. Back in Missouri, Cole Younger had guessed as much.

August 19, 1876

Frank James relaxed his long, wiry frame and looked out the window of his railroad car at the endless rows of corn spinning by. He pulled gently on his sandy side whiskers. He'd like to have some of that patch, he reflected. It was rich floodplain acreage along the Missouri River, and the golden ears seemed to fairly burst from their sun-bleached shucks. The train seemed to be passing through a million acres of corn, all prime. Frank wondered how much that corn was worth and, well, where the farmers in Iowa banked their money. As he thought about the corn, he twisted the gold ring on his little finger. Then he raised his right hand and stroked his long English nose with his forefinger. Yes, that was a whole lot of corn!

Jesse, sound asleep, sat across the aisle from Frank. His long legs jutted into the walkway. He was oblivious to the continual clacking of the train's wheels as they passed over the rails on the way north. Clell Miller sat next to Jesse and stared impassively out the window. A few seats behind them, Jim Younger pored over the latest issue of the *Kansas City Star*. Still farther back, Bill Chadwell, Charlie Pitts, and Cole and Bob Younger chatted with each other casually. When they boarded the train, they had looked a lot like a small army in their yellow-brown-colored linen dusters. The thin coats, the usual dress for cattle buyers or drovers, were designed to ward off travel dust for riders on the trail. As the gang knew, they also provided good cover for the numerous revolvers they had stuffed in their belts and into holsters around their waists.

Twenty minutes later, the train began to slow down, and its whistle sounded sharply, alerting the people of Council Bluffs of its arrival. As the train puffed its way up to the station platform, the engineer rang the bell, and the people on the platform jostled their way forward to get a better view of the newcomers. The new ticket holders grabbed their bags and moved closer so they could board the St. Paul-Minneapolis Express. Two small children, a boy and a girl, held their mother's hands tightly and gaped at the train in amazement. As it approached them, it looked like an iron monster with a single, huge eye. Then, steam fumed from the train's wheels, and one of the youngsters began crying.

Finally, the gang of people admiring the train parted ranks and allowed the new ticket holders to board. An attractive young woman came down the aisle and sat at the window seat in front of Jesse. When the train had begun braking, the outlaw awakened from his slumber, and he now eyed the new travelers suspiciously. A few moments later, a stout young farmhand with tousled brown hair passed by Jesse, bumping into the outlaw's feet carelessly. The man threw a small bag onto the metal basket overhead and sat down next to the young woman. The woman looked at him in dismay.

"Sir, I'm sorry. That seat is taken," she said politely.

"Haw!" the heavyset young man laughed. "I know it is. I got it."

"But—I mean—I was savin' it for my husband," she replied.

"Hey, they ain't no saved seats on this train," the farmhand answered, smiling broadly through crooked, tobacco-stained teeth.

As the young lady's husband approached, he seemed apprehensive. A short, slightly built man, he appeared intimidated by the young lout.

Jesse watched this little drama interestedly. Then, suddenly, his face reddened. He reached his arm over the seat in front of him and clubbed the young farmhand on his shoulder with his fist. "Hey, pard, can't you hear the lady? Her seat's taken." The farm boy, startled at first, turned around aggressively and looked Jesse straight in the face.

"Say, what's it to you, anyhow?"

Jesse sprang to his feet and seized the farmhand by his collar. With his other hand, he grabbed the back of the young man's bib overalls and whirled him into the aisle. Then, he dragged him thrashing toward the car's exit. When he got to the back platform, Jesse hurled the fellow headlong down the stairs.

"And don't come back, you rowdy!" Jesse called after him. Then he adjusted his clothing and went back to his seat, relatively unruffled.

Clell Miller, lost in thought, had hardly looked up during the dispute. He wondered if there were any pretty little things in Minnesota. It had been awhile, and he was looking for a woman. He'd heard there were plenty of girls up north. He'd find him one, maybe a blonde—that sounded good to him. But, hey, he was open to redheads too, he chuckled to himself. He guessed he'd just look around, measure the market. Clell had been told when they decided on the Minnesota robbery that the gang would spend three days in Minneapolis. That meant whooping it up to him, and he'd been looking forward to the trip for weeks.

It would be something different for the gang, robbing a Northern bank. They had always felt a little self-conscious about robbing Southern people; it was about time they made a little visit to the Northern nabobs. Chadwell had mentioned the bank in Northfield, Minnesota, as a possible target. It was owned by Benjamin "Beast" Butler, old "Silver Spoons," the wartime Yankee governor of New Orleans. He'd heard that the locals in New Orleans had had Beast's picture painted on the bottom of their chamber pots during the war to express their disdain for him. Yes, Clell wouldn't mind sharing some of Beastie's gold. And there was Butler's son-in-law, J. T. Ames, the carpetbag governor of Mississippi during what the Yankees jokingly called "Reconstruction." He had money—lots of it—in the same bank. But to Clell, money was money. He just needed money, that's all. Chadwell had told them that the Mankato Bank was the ripest target in Minnesota, and Frank James said that he intended to examine that institution first.

Like Clell, Jim Younger had barely noticed the fracas between Jesse and the young farmer. Even so, if Jesse had needed any help, he and the rest of the boys would have lent quick assistance. Jim, though, had recognized the young farmhand instantly for what he was, a loud-mouthed, spineless bully.

Jim was reflecting on the planned raid into Minnesota. He was apprehensive about it. Jesse had said that Bill Chadwell knew the area and would be able to guide them in their escape after the robbery. But what if something went wrong? Minnesota was like the dark side of the moon to Jim and the rest of the Missouri boys. What would happen if Chadwell were killed during the robbery? Without him, how would they make their way through the northern country in their escape, find the right roads and bridges, tell one lake from another, grope their way through the endless woods and morasses? The rest of the gang was relying on luck; Jim believed you made your own luck, and sometimes that wasn't easy. Once they pulled off the robbery, if things didn't turn out well, there was no one to turn to for help, no relatives, old friends, or ex-Confederates to hide them or cover for them. They'd be at the mercy of the posses and the Yankees' hirelings. Jim was filled with foreboding. Something about the operation was wrong, he believed. His heart wasn't in it, for one thing. Jim thought he would just prefer to be in California riding the range than hurtling through space on a hunk of greasy iron. As the train chugged north, Jim fell into a deep sleep. The next thing he knew, the conductor was screaming, "St. Paul! St. Paul! Final stop, St. Paul!"

Jim stirred himself and looked around. Jesse and Frank were already in the aisle, reaching for their bags. Jim raised himself to his feet and grabbed for his own bag. As the bandits disembarked the train, they clustered together for a few minutes, deciding their next move. They attracted little attention. Frank suggested that the men divide into small groups and pick different hotels to stay in until they got their bearings. After asking some of the locals on the station platform for information, Cole and Bill Chadwell decided to stay at the Merchant's Hotel at Third and Jackson. That would be the gang's headquarters in St. Paul. The others chose the Nicollet Hotel, a bawdy house outside town. They thought a large group of men would attract less attention there than elsewhere. And besides, that's where the male entertainment was, and no one, the police especially, was likely to ask embarrassing questions of its boarders. They might even share in the place's take, for all the gang knew.

"Hello, man! Here!" Frank James yelled at a buggy driver passing by. The driver yanked on his reins and pulled to a stop. Frank ordered the driver to the Nicollet. Cole Younger called down another driver, and a buggy rushed up to the outlaw's side.

"Merchant's Hotel," Cole cried out to the driver, and he and Chadwell boarded the buggy. When they arrived at the hotel, they walked briskly through the lobby and up to the desk clerk.

"We want a room," Cole said to the clerk. "What have you got?"

The clerk opened his book and looked at his room chart. "Well," he said finally, "we have a room, 2E, upstairs. How would that suit you?"

"Give us a downstairs room, and how much?" Cole countered.

"Three dollars a day for the two of you."

"Is it ready?" Cole challenged.

"Yes," the clerk replied, "but it's money in advance." Cole nodded his head in agreement and reached into his pocket and plunked down a five-dollar gold piece. The manager scooped the coin from the counter and replied with two silver dollars.

"The key, my good man. The key," Cole demanded aggressively.

The clerk reached under the counter and produced an iron key and handed it to him. Then he pushed his register toward Cole. The outlaw grabbed a pen from the counter, dipped it into a nearby inkwell, and with a short flourish, in his finest, bold hand wrote, "J. C. King." Cole extended the pen to Chadwell and he scribbled, "S. T. Cooper."

August 21, 1876

The gamblers at Guy Salisbury's tavern, between Jackson and Roberts Street on East Third Street in St. Paul, had been playing a desultory game of faro with some greenhorns and had become bored. It was no fun diddling these yokels. They longed for a real game of cards and no more penny ante maneuvers. As the gamblers yawned through another round, the door flung open and four members of the James gang, dressed in flowing dusters and broad-brimmed hats, entered the room. The men marched into the tavern with a cocky air, an easily apparent swagger that made the gamblers uneasy. Three of the bandits sauntered up to one of the gaming tables and took places. Cole Younger pulled some gold coins and silver dollars from his pocket and stacked them in front of him.

"Say, King," said Frank James, turning to Cole, "do you suppose these fellas would like to play a man's game of poker?"

"Why don't you ask 'em?" Cole replied.

Frank turned casually toward one of the gamblers across the table from him, and the man nodded in the affirmative. Then Jesse, who sat at the table next to Frank, laughed. "Say, these fellas can't wait to clean our plows, don't you know."

The gamblers all wore a blank expression on their faces, but their eyes glittered with furtive thoughts. Who were these men, and what was their game?

"Say, I'm near hot," Jesse complained. "Got to get outa this coat and stretch my arms." He rose and took off his duster, draping it over the back of his chair. At the same time, he pulled two large six-shooters from his holsters and laid them on the table. While he was at it, he lifted a bowie knife from its sheath and placed it on the table. Frank followed suit.

"Reckon you're right, Howard," Frank said. "All this hardware just gets in the way of a good, *clean* game." Cole drew his guns also, and the three men moved their weapons noisily onto a table close by. The gamblers, despite themselves, gaped at the newcomers in wonder. Without consulting each other, they had already decided to play conservatively.

As the dealer dealt out the first hands, Cole observed his hands shaking.

"My good man," Cole remarked, "your hands are shaking. Is there a draft in here? Is the door open too wide? You know, I think what you need is a good, stiff drink." Saying this, Cole rose and went over to the bar to grab a bottle of whiskey and a glass from the bartender. He returned to the table and poured the dealer a glass filled to the brim.

The gamblers remained nervous and edgy, and after several hours of play, the dealer and his shills had lost $150 between them. As the play progressed and the gamblers' losses grew, they itched to draw from their store of hidden cards, but when they glanced at the stashed weapons on the table nearby, they thought better of the tactic and remained honest.

Several times during the play, the dealer looked sharply into the eyes of the outlaws, attempting to fathom them. Their cold stares unnerved him. The dark-bearded player, Howard, blinked incessantly, and that mannerism made the gamblers uneasy. Despite his easy, laughing way, Howard looked like a keg of dynamite ready to go off. His laughing banter seemed superficial to the gamblers, and they noticed that while he often smiled and laughed, his eyes remained cold and impassive. The gamblers were relieved when the game finally ended and the strangers raked in their earnings and left. The strangers had been hard pickings.

Back at his room that evening at the Nicollet, Clell Miller stared at himself in the mirror. Yes, he was a good-looking chap, all right. In a new, strange town, though, he didn't have much of a chance with the local women. But he wasn't looking for friendships anyhow. He knew what he wanted. As he combed his hair, he decided he'd visit one of Mollie Ellsworth's girls at the hotel. He had seen some of them passing through the lobby, and they had caught his fancy. In fact they'd made his blood fairly flame. He'd noticed their thin waists, cinched in to emphasize their broad, voluptuous hips. He liked their bright rouge and lipstick too. They weren't like the girls back in Kansas City. They were fairer and their eyes were accented with gaudy eyeliner and mascara. As they passed through a room, they left an aroma of cheap but tantalizing perfumes. When he saw them, Clell had had to catch his breath. Something wild stirred in him.

A few minutes later, Clell sauntered into the parlor of the Nicollet House and eased into a high-backed, plush sofa. He looked above him in wonder at the glittering glass chandelier hanging from the ceiling. Some joint, he thought; looked like some poor rascal's idea of a millionaire's mansion. He could hear soft, sentimental music coming from the musicians located in a side room adjacent to the parlor. The last light of day slanted into the parlor through the lush, red drapes that hung from the windows. Despite his experience of such places, it always seemed odd to Clell that brothels often looked like palaces. But he liked this place. Yes, he liked it a lot.

As he reflected on his surroundings, Mollie Ellsworth, the local madam, passed through the room and stopped short, noticing an early customer. A woman in her middle forties, she had her hair pulled tightly into a bun and looked and dressed like a schoolmarm. Her prim, small-rimmed glasses accentuated this false impression.

"Say, big fellow, are you looking for some excitement?" Mollie finally said to Clell.

"What kind of excitement are you offerin'?" Clell drawled back in his low, husky voice, a grin covering his face.

"Well, that depends on what you're looking for. Like to see some of the girls?"

"Sure," Clell answered quickly. "How about a blonde." Without answering, Mollie left the room and in a few minutes returned with a small, shapely girl with long, waist-length, colorless hair. The girl was strikingly attractive, but what really attracted Clell to her was her costume, made of a sheer material that revealed every line, fold, and blush. Clell was impressed and nodded to Mollie. The madam motioned the couple to follow her, and the three walked up a winding staircase. Mollie led the two down a dark corridor. At the end of the hall, she opened the door of a room.

"She's yours, big boy," Mollie said. Clell handed her a bright coin.

Clell walked into the room with the girl and looked around. There was a bed; he'd expected that. And there was a small table next to the bed with a kerosene lamp turned low. It had become dark since he'd entered the parlor downstairs. He went over to the bed and sat down. The girl followed and sat down beside him. Clell looked down at her. She appeared attractive enough, but when he looked her over, she appeared younger than he'd expected. He noticed also that there were dark, unnatural circles under her eyes. None of this failed to make her any less enticing; in fact, her jaded appearance only further attracted him to her.

"Say, how old are you?" he asked the girl.

"Old enough," she replied. "Why?"

"How'd you get into a place like this?"

"Well," she explained, "my daddy died two years ago, and my mama couldn't keep me. So I'm here."

"That's life," Clell consoled her. "You just never know what's goin' to happen next, do you?" Then he laid his hand on the young girl's thigh. As he did so, she reached her arm around his waist.

Clell twisted around to face the girl, grabbed her in his arms, and kissed her hard on the mouth. He hadn't had a woman in some time, and he buried his mouth in hers, relishing the soft, wet touch and ignoring the acrid taste of whiskey and tobacco clinging to her breath. Then Clell stopped for a moment.

"Say, what's your name?" he asked.

"Lovina," the girl replied, "Lovina Petersen." Clell thought maybe she had made up the name.

August 25, 1876

Jesse walked into the Williams Brothers Book Store in Minneapolis and browsed among the shelved books and pamphlets. He was looking for maps. As Jesse probed the shelves, John Williams, the manager of the store, approached him.

"Sir, may I help you?"

"Well, I reckon you can," Jesse replied. "I'm doin' some surveyin' for the railroad south of here, and I'm goin' to need some good maps."

"What counties are you interested in?" inquired Williams.

"You got some maps of Rice, Le Sueur, Watonwan, and Blue Earth Counties?" Jesse asked. He knew that these were counties where the gang would be looking at banks and also were along their expected escape route.

"Follow me, young fellow," Williams prompted, grabbing Jesse gently by the arm. "I think I've got just what you're looking for." He led Jesse to the other side of the store where he kept his county maps.

"Are you going to be in this country long?" Williams questioned Jesse. While he talked, the storekeeper pulled several maps out of a cabinet drawer.

"Well, it all depends," answered Jesse. "If I find good maps, I might not be around long." Williams handed several maps to Jesse. After poring over them, Jesse turned toward the store manager.

"I think these will do. What do I owe you?"

"Brother, they come to eighty-five cents," the storeowner replied. The two men walked over to Williams' cash register, and Jesse handed the manager a silver dollar. Williams banked it and reached into the register. He pulled out a dime and a nickel and placed them in the outlaw's hand.

"Much obliged," Jesse said and walked out the front door of the shop and into the street. The young man seemed a solid enough fellow to Williams, this young man in the flowing duster.

August 26, 1876

Four men in dusters stood at the reception desk of the National Hotel in Red Wing and signed their names. The register read, "J. C. Hortar, Nashville; H. L. West, Nashville; Chas. Wetherby, Indiana; and Ed Everhard, Indiana." Then Frank and Jesse James, Clell Miller, and Jim Younger grabbed their bags and climbed the stairs to their rooms. It was 10:00 A.M., and they wanted to freshen up a bit after their train ride from St. Paul before going out on the town.

Around 12:30 P.M., after taking lunch at the hotel, the men set out in pairs to visit some of the local livery stables. Frank and Jesse walked into A. Seebeck's Livery Stable and hailed the proprietor.

"Sir," Frank addressed the owner. "I am Ben Woodson, and this is my partner, John Howard." Frank reached his right hand toward Seebeck, and the men exchanged firm handshakes.

"Seebeck, here," the livery stable owner introduced himself.

"Say, we're lookin' for good, hard-runnin' horses, don't you know," Frank said. "Have you got any?" Then Frank paused. "We don't want no nags, only your best horses, you understand." Seebeck motioned the two men over to one of the stalls and pointed out a bay mare.

"How about this one?" he asked.

Frank looked the horse over carefully, examined her girth, height, and stifle, her withers and belly. He was interested in a horse with spirit too. This horse didn't impress him. He

stooped and lifted one of the horse's hooves and examined it.
"How old is she?" Frank questioned Seebeck.

"Near as I can tell, three years," Seebeck answered.

Finally, after examining the horse thoroughly, Frank said,
"I'd better try out this pony." Frank thought the horse might be
a charger but was uncertain.

Seebeck opened the stall, placed a bit in the mare's mouth,
and handed the reins to Frank. Then he threw a saddle over
the horse's back and cinched it. Frank mounted the mare and
rode into the street then put the spurs to the horse to test her
meddle. She was a mite slack, Frank thought to himself as he
galloped. After a short ride in the country, he rode back to the
stable and dismounted. Seebeck was waiting for him.

"What do you think of her?" Seebeck asked.

"Don't want her," Frank replied firmly.

"What's wrong with her?" Seebeck questioned, somewhat
crestfallen.

"No spirit! And I doubt her bottom too," Frank answered,
referring to the horse's endurance. "We need strong horses."

"What you fellows looking for, racehorses or something?"
the stable owner replied in irritation.

"What we're lookin' for, you ain't got," Frank answered
curtly. "Good day!" With that pronouncement, Frank and
Jesse walked out of the livery stable and down the boardwalk.

At about the same time, Cole Younger and Charlie Pitts were
in St. Peter looking for horses. They had registered that morning
at the local hotel, the American House, under the names J. C.
King and J. J. Ward of Virginia. Their first day brought them
little luck. Around noon on August 27, however, they bought
a horse from a man named Hodge and later another from a
farmer called French. They bought their gear from Moll and
Sons, completing their purchases.

That afternoon, as Cole returned from breaking in his horse
outside St. Peter, he noticed a little girl, perhaps nine years old,

staring at him from the front yard of her home at the edge of town. He rode up to her.

"Say, little girl, what's your name?"

"I'm Horace Greeley Perry," she replied in a firm voice.

"Well, Miss Perry, what's a little tyke like you doin' with such a grand name?"

"I won't always be so little," the girl replied defiantly. "My mama told me so! Besides, I can ride a horse! And I'm going to grow up to be a newspaperman like my pa."

"Well, little lady, you must pardon me," Cole responded.

"Hey, but will you still be my friend when you're a big, important newspaper woman?"

"Uh-huh," the little girl replied without hesitation.

"Then come up here and show me how you handle a horse," Cole said. He reached his arm down and lifted the little girl up into the saddle in front of him.

"Now, let's see what kind of a horseman, uh . . . horsewoman you are," Cole continued. He handed the reins to the little girl and then poked the horse gently with his heels to force it into a walk. After a short ride, he dropped the little girl off at her home.

Later that afternoon, Bob Younger and Bill Chadwell, who had just arrived from St. Paul, joined Cole and Pitts. Bob and Chadwell had registered at a local hotel as B. T. Cooper and G. H. King. They had spent the last few days in St. Paul after missing the train that carried their fellow outlaws to St. Peter. Soon, they had purchased horses too. All the men at St. Peter were horsed and ready.

The next day, August 28, Cole Younger and Charlie Pitts rode to Madelia and registered at the Flanders House hotel, owned by Thomas Vought. After checking into his room, Cole started a conversation with Vought concerning the country around Madelia.

Cole began, "I'm impressed with the country around here, so many lakes, such wonderful scenery. We're planning on buyin' some cattle soon and drivin' 'em west. You have such a number of lakes in the area, it's hard for a man to find his way through the puddles. I've a herd to drive. How do you suggest I get 'em through the area south of Lake Hanska and north of Wood Lake, I mean on the way to Lamberton? It's a puzzle to a newcomer. Someone said there's a bridge that must be crossed."

"I'm not surprised that you ask, and you are not the first," Vought answered Cole. "If you're going to Lamberton, you go north out of Madelia about five miles, then head due west down the La Salle Road. That's the sure way over the Watonwan River."

"Thank you, my friend, just the information I needed," Cole replied. Younger was looking for the best escape route out of eastern Minnesota, and he'd found it.

Back at Red Wing on the twenty-seventh, the James brothers test rode some horses at J. Anderberg's Livery Stable, down the street from Seebeck's. The two brothers selected one lively sorrel and a dun horse. Meanwhile, at another livery stable in town, Jim Younger and Clell Miller purchased two bays, one with white hind feet and another with white hind legs. Both had white spots on their foreheads.

On August 28, late in the afternoon, the four men at Red Wing bought saddles at E. P. Watson's place. They told him they were cattle drovers. The next morning, the four men rode out of town in a southwesterly direction toward Faribault, in the direction of St. Peter. All of the outlaws had good, fast horses under them. The quality of their horses drew unwanted notice, but the outlaws were willing to pay that price; in a pinch, they wanted the best horseflesh available. By September 1, the entire gang had congregated at St. Peter to begin coordinating their future banking enterprise.

September 2, 1876

Frank James stood under a tin canopy that formed the porch of Johannes Bjorge's Feed Store. The First National Bank of

Mankato was across the street. Jesse stood next to Frank and the brothers puffed on cigarettes, slowly exhaling the smoke in pungent clouds. Then Frank walked across the street and stood in a crowd of men milling around the lot next to the bank. Masons were constructing a new commercial building there. Frank watched one of the bricklayers stick his trowel into the mortar. He shook the trowel, making the mortar adhere to it, then dressed the bottom and ends of the brick with a narrow margin of mortar and, in a blur, placed the brick flush with the line strung from both corners. Then he grabbed another brick. Frank smiled to himself. He was shaping up as a pretty good "sidewalk superintendent." As he looked around him at the pack of loafers and geezers, he reflected that there were too many people hanging around the bank. While they posed no physical threat to a robbery, it occurred to him that they might act as messengers, rallying others to the spot once a robbery took place.

No, Frank didn't like the look of it. Too many people, and the construction would probably be going on for some time. But he was still undecided. He turned from the crowd and walked through the front door of the bank. One of the bank clerks was counting out money for a customer. He looked up as Frank entered then turned back to his business. The cashier at the next window motioned Frank to his window.

"Good mornin', sir," Frank saluted the cashier. "I'd like to change a fifty." Frank reached into the inside pocket of his duster, pulled out his wallet, and removed a green note and handed it to the cashier. Frank was cashing a large note so he could find out where the cashier kept his larger bills. The cashier took the note, held it tightly in both hands, and raised it to the light coming in from the front window. After examining the bill, he laid it down on the counter.

"Looks good," he finally answered. "What sort of change pleases you?"

"Ones, fives, a couple tens—no big bills," Frank replied.

The cashier placed the fifty under the till and counted out

Frank's change on the counter, calling out each bill as he laid it down. When he was through, the cashier looked Frank over. He looked like someone of substance, the clerk thought, maybe a drover or cattle buyer since he wore a duster.

Frank thanked the cashier, spun around, and walked out the front door of the bank. While the banker counted out money for him, Frank had surveyed the bank thoroughly. There were two clerks and a cashier; three teller windows, all low enough and wide enough for easy passage; a single side door; and two rather dusty windows facing the street. That was good and would offer little opportunity to prying eyes. All in all, Frank thought, the place looked ripe for picking. As he crossed the street, he noticed Jesse talking to a stranger and was dismayed. This was no time for friendly chitchat, he thought. As he approached the two men, he heard Jesse erupt.

"I don't know you, don't you hear me?"

"Aw, Jess, what's your game?" the stranger replied.

"Get away from me," Jesse said menacingly. The man looked a little confused and walked down the street shaking his head.

"Who was that fella?" Frank questioned Jesse.

"A fellow from Baltimore that I met when I visited you last year to throw off the law," Jesse answered.

"He recognized you!" Frank exclaimed.

"Yes," Jesse said, "no helpin' it."

"I don't know," Frank pondered aloud. "This place is lookin' worse by the minute. Too many people millin' around, and now this fella; I don't like it."

Jesse remained silent. He had the utmost respect for Frank's judgment, and in this case, he agreed with him. Who knew where Robinson, the fellow he had been talking to, might carry his story.

Frank took a last, wistful look at the bank and turned to Jesse. "Tell the boys we've better plans."

Minutes later, across town at the sheriff's office, Charlie Robinson was remonstrating with one of the local law officers.

"I tell you, it's him, Jesse James. I know him from Baltimore."

"Baltimore?" the sheriff's deputy replied. "Hey, I thought the James gang was from Missouri," and the deputy laughed out loud.

"Not when I knew him," answered Robinson. "And, say, I want a reward when you fellas capture him." The deputy laughed again, uproariously.

"Reward? What sort of liquor do they serve in Maryland? You sure this fella you knew wasn't President Grant or Ruth Hayes? I hear they been out electioneering these days." Robinson recognized that he was getting nowhere with the lawman and walked dejectedly out of the sheriff's office and down the street.

15

September 7, 1876

Three horsemen rumbled across the iron bridge over the Cannon River at Northfield, Minnesota, and passed by the Scriver Block, a group of buildings containing numerous shops, including the First National Bank of Northfield. The town sprawled before the riders, and to their right, several hundred yards away, Carleton College sat atop the only hill in a rolling plain. Behind the three riders, in the distance, rode three more riders, also members of the gang.

Townsman John Archer stood at the corner of Division and Water Streets and eyed the newcomers. What horses! he thought to himself. Flashy. On Water Street, G. E. Bates, a shopkeeper, stood at the entrance of his haberdashery talking to C. C. Waldo, a traveling salesman from Council Bluffs, Iowa. Bates saw the horsemen ride by and remarked about their appearance to Waldo.

"Sir, look at those men and their mounts!" Bates said to the salesman as they looked out the door. Bates was impressed with the spirited horses and the large men mounted on them. But he didn't wholly appreciate the look of the riders. They exhibited a bold swagger, like they might be rough fellows to handle. The storekeeper ceased his reverie and followed Waldo back into the store to examine cloth samples.

The riders continued past him to the railroad depot and dismounted. Cole Younger, astride the lead horse, climbed off his mount and turned to the two men with him.

"Boys, did you see yon café?" he asked, pointing in the direction from which they had come. The men nodded. They had noticed the eating place too. The men tethered their horses and sauntered toward the café, known as Jeft's. Cole entered the restaurant first, followed by Frank and Jesse James. As Cole looked the place over, the proprietor, Tom Jeft, greeted him.

"Morning, men. You gents havin' breakfast?"

"Yes," replied Cole and pointed to a table by the window. "We'd like that place."

"Suit yourselves," replied Jeft and ran to gather some silverware and cotton napkins. In a few moments, the café owner returned.

"What are you going to have, gentlemen?" he asked as he laid the silverware on the table.

"What have you got?" Frank replied.

"You name it, boys: bacon, eggs, ham. Do you like potatoes? Name your medicine."

"Say," Frank responded, "fry me some eggs, over light—four of 'em—with taters on the side. Dice them taters," he added. "And bring coffee."

"I'll take the same," Jesse chimed in. Cole went on to specify his order. After the orders were taken, Jeft walked back to the kitchen, and the bandits settled into their seats. They left their broad-brimmed hats and dusters on.

When Jeft returned from the kitchen, some of the men sitting at the back of the café were arguing about the upcoming election. As he passed, one of them addressed him.

"Say, Jeft," an old fellow in bibbed overalls said, "I bet yah Ruth Hayes is goin' to plow ol' Tilden under in the fall election. They ain't no doubt about it."

"Well, maybe so," Jeft replied, not wanting to debate the subject.

Frank James, a staunch Democrat, listened to the talk and his face reddened.

"Hey, café owner!" he finally shouted. "Are you sayin' the Republicans are goin' to win this election? What sort of bet you talkin'? This man has one thousand dollars that says Tilden is goin' to trounce Hayes' butt!"

All the men in the café looked at Frank, then turned their heads toward Jeft for his reply. Jeft looked serious for a moment and then answered deliberately.

"Well, sir, I was just passin' the time of day, actually. I wouldn't bet the better part of a quarter on all the politicians on this earth. In my estimation, the whole lot of 'em ain't worth my time and money." Frank smiled cynically, seeming mollified by Jeft's reply, and turned back to his friends.

After attacking their lunch, the bandits walked back into the street and examined the town. Frank noticed that the village was busier than he'd expected. He knew that might cause trouble if anything held up the robbery, but he kept his reservations to himself. The men ought to know they were taking risks; bank robberies were rife with possibilities for trouble. No one knew that better than he and the boys. But Northfield was their last option if they wanted to leave Minnesota with a decent haul. They'd staked a lot of money on this northern adventure, so Frank was willing to take more risks than usual. Outside the restaurant, he walked over to Cole.

"Bud, why don't you go over and check out the bank; then we'll talk."

Cole nodded, pulled down his hat brim, and walked across the street to the First National Bank.

Inside the bank, Joseph Heywood, the acting cashier, forty years old, studied his accounts, carefully adding and subtracting the long columns of tedious figures. Heywood was a small, tidy man with clean, shiny nails. His hair was combed back carefully and slicked down lightly with oil. All of this gave him a circumspect air. The regular cashier was away attending the Philadelphia Centennial Exposition, and in the interim, Heywood was in charge. He took the responsibility seriously. Younger entered the bank in his flowing duster, receiving little attention at first. Finally, Heywood looked up from his accounts and stared blankly into Cole's face. A cattleman, Heywood thought to himself, and returned to his figures.

Cole walked up to Heywood's teller window and reached into his pocket. He pulled out a fifty-dollar bill and laid it on the counter.

"Sir, I need some change," Cole said. Heywood, mildly irritated by the newcomer's intrusion into his world of computing, picked up the bill and examined it.

"What sort of change?" he finally answered, directing a quick glance at Younger.

"Small bills," Cole replied, adding, "Your locals are averse to my large greenbacks."

Heywood counted out the bills carefully for Younger— Heywood did everything carefully—and then returned to his calculations. Younger watched to see where Heywood placed the bill, in this case, beneath the main money tray.

Cole tucked the small bills into his wallet and surveyed the bank carefully. Yes, it would do, he thought to himself; it would do very nicely. He turned on his heel and walked slowly out the front door, closing the door behind him, then strode across the street and sidled up to Frank.

"It'll work," he whispered.

"It's a mite busy along the street," Frank replied quietly. "We may have to drive the locals into cover. We will need to get in and out quickly, though—no tarrying." Cole nodded in agreement.

Frank and Cole stood on the corner for a few minutes waiting for Jesse and the other gang members who had already ventured into town, Bill Chadwell, Clell Miller, and Jim Younger. Then the men sauntered back to the railroad station, mounted their horses, and rode out of town. When they were several miles from town, they turned down a small, winding trail through a forest of oaks and pines and rode to their camp. Within an hour, Bob Younger and Charlie Pitts arrived from Millersburg and joined them. The gang was now complete. No one noticed Bob and Charlie's flushed faces when they arrived. They had been drinking from a quart of whiskey all morning, and both men were "three sheets to the wind," as they called it. Frank gathered the men together and spoke.

"Boys, it's time. Cole has looked the bank over. Here's how we do it: Jesse, Bob, and Pitts, you will rob the bank. Cole and Miller will stand guard outside to prevent trouble. Bill, Jim, and I will wait on this side of the bridge into town in case there's a hitch. If the boys in the bank need help, they'll fire their weapons, and the rest of us will ride in to support 'em and get 'em out of town. Remember, we must rob it quick. Then, we will get out on the run. We mustn't dally! There are lots of people in town, and we don't want a pitched fight. Cole, tell 'em how the bank's laid out."

Cole motioned Jesse, Charlie, and Bob over to a piece of exposed earth nearby and brushed a few pine needles and branches aside with his hand. With a stick, he drew a diagram in the dirt showing how the inside of the bank was laid out, where the tellers stood, where the vault, doors, and windows were located. With that information imparted, the men remounted their horses and rode toward town.

Jesse, Bob, and Charlie crossed the Cannon River at 1:55 P.M. and trotted by the commercial Scriver Block. They turned right onto Water Street and hitched their horses near the bank's entrance, near the side delivery door of Lee and Hitchcock's general merchandise store on the corner. They found some crates under a nearby stairway, dragged them to the corner, and sat down on them to while away the time until Cole and Clell Miller arrived. Bob scribbled idly on the side of a nearby hay scale with the stub of a pencil and chatted with Charlie. Still a little drunk, he talked louder than usual.

When the outlaws saw Cole and Clell cross the Cannon River bridge, they rose and walked toward the bank. Charlie strode into the bank with Jesse and Bob close behind. In the excitement of the moment or addled by alcohol, Bob forgot to close the bank door.

The three men walked directly up to the counter and pulled their Colt revolvers. Charlie, acting as the gang's spokesman, barked fiercely, "Throw up your hands! We intend to rob the bank, and if you halloo, we will blow your brains out!"

In front of the outlaws was a high, curving counter that extended around the cashier and clerks' cage. Behind the counter to their right, with his desk against the wall, sat Heywood, the cashier. To their left, where the counter curved, sat the astonished teller, Alonzo E. Bunker, and his gape-mouthed assistant bookkeeper, Frank J. Wilcox.

"Who's the cashier?" Charlie demanded.

When no one answered, the infuriated Pitts pointed his pistol at Bunker: "You're the cashier!" Bunker shook his head. "Then you are cashier!" Charlie continued, waving his revolver angrily at Wilcox.

"No, sir," Wilcox replied, his voice quavering in fear as he answered. The outlaw then stared at Heywood, who sat at a desk next to the cashier's window.

"The cashier's not in," Heywood said before the outlaw had a chance to query him. Heywood was excited but not fearful. During the war, he had been an infantryman in the 127th Illinois Regiment and had fought at Vicksburg. He was known to be cool under fire.

Charlie, affected by the liquor he had been drinking and noting that Heywood sat at the cashier's desk, hurdled through the cashier's window, Jesse and Bob close behind. "You are the cashier! Now open the safe or I'll kill you!"

"It has a time lock," Heywood countered firmly. "It cannot be opened now."

The main bank safe was inside a large vault, the outside door of which had been left open. Heywood now realized that he had carelessly left the door to the inner safe only closed, not locked. His mind raced with wild apprehensions of his possible disgrace.

"Let's see about that safe," Charlie replied and walked through the vault door. Heywood sprang to his feet and attempted to close the door behind the outlaw, but Jesse leaped forward and grabbed Heywood by his shirt and held him. Charlie, wild with anger, walked back through the vault door into the teller's cage. He pulled a large knife from its sheath, grabbed Heywood in a firm headlock, and drew the blade across the cashier's throat, making a small scratch. He hoped to intimidate the cashier into cooperating. Instead, Heywood thrashed wildly, heaving and jerking until he freed himself from Pitts' grip.

"Murder! Murder!" Heywood screamed in a loud voice. Jesse, who had allowed Pitts to take the lead up to this point, struck Heywood on the head with the barrel of his revolver, and the cashier crumpled to the floor, dark blood welling through his neatly combed hair. Charlie grabbed Heywood again by his shirt collar and dragged him into the vault.

"Stop stalling and open the safe or I'll blow your head off!" he screamed wildly. He held his pistol next to Heywood's right ear and pulled the trigger. The gun roared, firing a bullet past the cashier's head and into the bank's wall. Smoke filled the room.

While Charlie was only trying to scare Heywood, Bunker, not able to see exactly what was happening, heard the pistol and thought that Heywood had been shot. Believing he was next, he panicked and dashed wildly through the side door of the bank. Bob, who had been watching him, fired but missed, and the teller ran into the street. As Bunker reached the sidewalk, Younger followed him and fired a second shot. This bullet tore through Bunker's right shoulder and exited under his collarbone. The impact shook him, nearly knocking him to the ground. Energized by fright, Bunker righted himself and fled down the street.

From outside the din of gunshots and yelling could be heard, and Charlie rushed to one of the cashier's trays and scooped up the coins and loose bills, throwing them into the grain sack he carried. Another tray immediately under the first tray contained a considerable amount of money, but Pitts, in his excitement, failed to notice it or misremembered his later instructions from his counterparts. The street outside the bank was ablaze now with gunfire. Within seconds, Cole Younger rode up to the front door of the bank and screamed: "The game is up and we are beaten!" Behind him, the bandits could see a figure prone in the street.

Heeding his warning, Bob and Charlie scrambled through the cashier's window and ran for the door. Jesse stopped for a moment in the window before exiting the cashier's cage. He was incensed at Heywood. The little, contentious rascal had ruined everything. His friends were being killed in the street, and this stubborn little weasel believed he had carried the day. Jesse turned around and fired. The bullet struck the cashier in the head, and he pitched forward onto the floor, dead. His brains and blood were splattered on his desk, and dark blood collected in a pool under his head.

While Jesse, Bob, and Charlie were doing their work, Cole and Clell stirred up a hornet's nest in the street. When the outlaws entered the bank, Bob Younger had forgotten to close the door behind them. Noticing this, Clell walked over and closed it. Cole, meanwhile, stood in the street next to his horse, pretending to cinch his saddle girth. Across the street, a young college student, Henry Wheeler, stood in front of his father's drugstore and watched the two strangers closely. They acted suspiciously, he thought. Wheeler, a stout, muscular young man, was a medical student at Michigan University, and he was known around town as a sportsman. He liked to hunt and kill large animals—elk, deer, and bear—a skill that would be useful to him today, but applied to men.

Yes, there was something peculiar about these fellows, Wheeler thought. They seemed to be dawdling needlessly. Why

RIDING VENGEANCE WITH THE JAMES GANG

did one of them close the door of the bank? What was it to him if it were left open?

About this time, J. S. Allen, who owned a hardware store around the corner, approached the bank. Clell intercepted him. "The bank is closed!" Miller snapped.

"I'll find out for myself," Allen responded and reached for the bank door aggressively. Miller grabbed him by his arm, swung him around, and shoved him away from the door, knocking him onto the sidewalk. Allen rose to his feet quickly. He understood now exactly what was going on, and he ran down the boardwalk screaming, "Murder! Robbers! Get your guns, boys; they're robbing the bank!"

Clell fired at Allen twice but missed. Allen fled around the corner and dashed out of sight. He raced to his hardware store and began handing out guns and ammunition to the men clustered in front of his shop. J. B. Hyde, the Reverend Ross Phillips, James Gregg, and Elias Stacy armed themselves with Allen's shotguns and pistols and filled their pockets with cartridges and shotgun shells filled with buckshot. The men scattered into the shops around Water Street, taking up firing positions.

Wheeler, who at the first shots ran to a nearby store to search for a gun, by this time had found a breech-loading carbine. He primed the weapon with ammunition and raced up the stairway of the Dampier House hotel, directly across from the bank, and ran into Room No. 8, on the second story. He raised one of the windows and steadied his carbine on the sill.

Over at the bridge, the waiting outlaws heard firing and raced up Division Street. They turned right into Water Street, firing their revolvers rapidly. Frank James and Bill Chadwell wheeled their horses in front of the bank, shooting into the windows and doors of the local businesses and screaming at the locals to get off the street.

From the back of his store, G. E. Bates heard loud firing and ran to the front of his store to look out. One of the bandits saw the merchant standing in the window and rode toward him. "Get back in there!" the outlaw cried.

Bates rushed to the back of his store, loaded a shotgun, and returned to the front door. He pointed the gun at one of the bandits circling in front of the store and pulled the trigger. It made a dull click. Bates returned to the back of the store looking for another weapon. He discovered a seven-shooter but no ammunition for it. He ran to the front door, nonetheless, and pointed the empty weapon at one of the horsemen.

"Now, I've got you!" Bates screamed at the outlaw, indulging himself in a foolish bluff. One of the bandits spun around on his horse and fired two shots at Bates. They struck his front window and a shower of glass shards rained onto the haberdasher's floor.

Anselm Manning, the proprietor of Lee and Hitchcock's hardware store adjacent to the bank, ran into the street with a loaded Remington repeating rifle and engaged the bandits. Manning had been a Civil War soldier, and the sounds and sights of a good fight gave him little fear.

The outlaws, meanwhile, passed up and down the street, firing their revolvers, attempting to clear the way for the bandits who would be leaving the bank shortly. As Bill Chadwell rode by, Wheeler's rifle roared, and a bullet tore into the outlaw's heart. Chadwell's horse balked, and the bandit tumbled over its neck in a lifeless tangle, landing in the dust. Without its rider, the horse milled aimlessly in the midst of the chaos.

Manning then walked to the middle of Water Street to make war on Cole Younger. Manning raised his rifle, took aim, and fired. The bullet struck Younger in the thigh, and the outlaw winced and fired back but missed.

"Jump back now, or they'll get you," Bates yelled to the hardware dealer. Manning took Bates' advice and retired around the corner and out of sight. Now, he played a cat and mouse game with the outlaws, firing at them then moving out of sight before they could return fire.

Clell Miller trotted back and forth down the street on his horse, and Elias Stacy found him in his sights. Stacy's shotgun boomed and sprayed the outlaw with deadly buckshot. Miller recoiled but remained seated in his saddle. Seeing him ride past, Manning walked into the street and raised his rifle.

"Take good aim before you fire," Bates shrieked at him. Manning did so, and his bullet hit Miller flush in the chest. The bandit's large body shook, and he slid heavily from his saddle, falling face down on the ground. He lay for a moment on his stomach, then pulled himself slowly up onto his elbows. He held that position for a few seconds then collapsed from shock and loss of blood. Cole rode up to Clell, dismounted, and rushed to his aid.

"How goes it?" Cole cried out. Clell tried to answer but lost consciousness. Cole unfastened Clell's holsters and pistols and buckled them around his own waist. His friend wouldn't need them any more. Cole jumped back onto his horse and continued firing.

What were the men doing in the bank? What were they doing? Cole thought desperately to himself. It was time for them to get out! Cole rode his horse onto the sidewalk and up to the entrance of the bank. He screamed to the outlaws in the bank that the fight was over. Then he rode up the street to clear the way for the getaway. As he proceeded, three men rushed from a saloon and ran across the street in front of him.

"Get back!" Cole screamed at them.

Two of the men turned back, but one of them dashed directly into his path. Cole shot him in the head, and the man fell in the dust, blood pouring from the wound. The man, Nicholas Gustavson, a Swedish immigrant, spoke little English and had understood nothing that Cole had yelled at him.

From his position inside a doorway, J. B. Hyde emerged and fired both barrels of his shotgun at the two outlaws still standing and retreated to reload. The Reverend Phillips stepped into position and fired. James Gregg, inside the door of the drugstore, leaned around the corner of a doorframe and fired two quick revolver blasts. Down the street, in a doorway of the first floor of the Dampier House, Elias Stacy's shotgun thundered again. Dust and gun smoke hovered in clouds as revolvers, rifles, and shotguns boomed sporadically. Frank James hugged the neck of his horse, leaning sharply to one side of his mount to avoid the main fire, an old Indian trick. He returned a rapid fire across the back of his horse, but targets appeared only momentarily then disappeared quickly behind doorways and windows.

The outlaws in the bank finally rushed into the street and mounted their horses. Only Bob Younger failed to seat himself. Bob noticed Manning preparing to fire at him and took up a defensive position behind his horse. Manning fired and Bob's horse grunted and fell in a lifeless heap at the outlaw's feet. Younger ran behind the stairway leading to the second story of Lee and Hitchcock's and took shelter behind some pine boxes. From this vantage point, he fired at Manning, hoping to drive the hardware dealer around the corner or kill him. If the opportunity arose, Bob planned to mount Chadwell's horse, which was still wandering around in the street.

Wheeler, in the meantime, had busted open a powder sack, poured it down the throat of his rifle, and shoved a ball and wadding down the barrel of his carbine. He was ready to fire again. He peeped over the windowsill and watched the fight below between Manning and Bob Younger. Wheeler slid the muzzle of his rifle stealthily over the windowsill and took careful aim at the bandit. He was as cool as if he were shooting an elk, and his excitement and passion were the same. Wheeler took a small breath, expired some air, and squeezed the trigger. The bullet smashed into Bob Younger's right elbow, and the outlaw's arm fell limply to his side. Blood coursed down Bob's shirtsleeve, but he managed to hold onto his pistol long enough to secure it in his left hand. He had no idea where the bullet had come from, but he assumed incorrectly that Manning had fired it.

Bob realized he must abandon his vulnerable position,

and he ran toward Manning, firing with his left hand. The hardware dealer darted around the corner and out of the line of fire. As Bob ran, he saw Bates standing in the window across the street and sent a shot whizzing in his direction. The bullet burst through a plate-glass window of Hananer's Clothing Store and grazed Bates' cheek and the bridge of his nose. A trickle of warm blood ran down the haberdasher's face, and he dashed for cover.

Bob noticed that his comrades were leaving and shouted after them: "Boys! You're not leavin' me; I'm shot!"

Cole, mounted on a bright sorrel and wounded in the thigh, heard his brother's cry, spun his horse around, and galloped up Water Street under heavy fire. Racing to his brother's side, he reached down and pulled him mightily up into the saddle. With Bob seated firmly in front of him, Cole drove his spurs into his horse's flanks and galloped toward the bridge leading out of town. Bullets and buckshot whistled by the two men and stirred up plumes of dust in the street.

By now, most of the bandits were wounded. The bodies of Clell Miller, Bill Chadwell, and the ill-starred Gustavson lay in twisted heaps in the street. As the riders fled town, the bells of Carleton College peeled loudly, summoning the townsmen to the scene. At the same time, the local telegraph operator clicked messages to towns along the railroad north and south of Northfield, alerting them that the outlaws were at large and describing their appearance and that of their horses. On leaving town, the gang had planned to wreck the Milwaukee and St. Paul telegraph station to prevent them from sending out such an alarm. But they were so riddled with bullets that they abandoned that part of their plan. One of America's great manhunts was underway.

After crossing the Cannon River bridge, the gang streaked southwestward toward the town of Dundas. A mile outside Northfield, the men stopped to dress their wounds. All of them were bleeding. Frank James, shot in the thigh, pulled a shirt from his saddlebag, ripped it into long strips, and tied the pieces around his bleeding leg. Blood from a nasty shoulder wound ran down Jim Younger's left arm and dripped from his fingertips. All Jim could do was stuff rags inside his shirt to stanch some of the bleeding. He was suffering shock. Cole, after pulling Bob off their shared horse and leaning him against a tree, took strips of a shirt and wrapped them around his brother's arm to halt the blood flow. Then he rolled some of the same strips around his own bleeding leg and tied the ends in a knot. Once the bandits had dressed their wounds, they remounted their horses and brought them to a gallop, hoping to gain a lead on the posses they knew were gathering.

In Northfield, young Wheeler was organizing a pursuit, but it would take him nearly an hour to assemble the fifty men needed to take up the chase. Meanwhile, the outlaws galloped southwest on their powerful steeds, stirring up a dense cloud of dust. Bob Younger was so weak that his brother had to steady him in the saddle with his right arm while holding onto the reins with his left. The outlaws were exhausted, but they goaded their horses into a fast gait. After leaving Northfield several miles behind, they slowed their pace to a trot to protect their horses. They needed to preserve the animals in case a posse intercepted them along their escape route. The outlaws' course was southwestward, toward Sioux City and Dakota Territory, but that destination was several days and nights away at best. As they passed through Dundas, Charlie Pitts spotted a farmer, Phillip Empey, hauling a load of hoop-poles. Pitts rode up to the man, dismounted, and grabbed the reins of his horse.

"We need your horse!" Pitts shouted at him. When the farmer resisted, Pitts struck him in the face with his fist, knocking him into a ditch. Pitts then drew his bowie knife and cut through the leather straps and bands holding the horse's harness, removing its working gear. Then he shortened the reins. Pitts jumped on his own mount, pulling the captured animal behind him at a trot. A few miles outside Millersburg, the gang met another rider. Jesse rode up to him and motioned him to halt.

"We're after horse thieves and need your saddle," Jesse said sternly.

"Uh," the man answered. "I need this saddle."

"Get off that horse," Jesse demanded, pointing his revolver at the man. The farmer looked at the rough, haggard men, noticed the blood on their boots and clothing, and dismounted. After they saddled the horse Pitts had been leading, Cole helped Bob atop the new mount, and the gang rode away. Bob, barely conscious and slumping in his saddle, clung desperately to the reins. The bandits galloped through Millersburg at 4:00 P.M. A few minutes later, Frank and Jesse rode through town. They had lagged behind the rest, acting as a rear guard.

At 2:45 P.M., the telegraph operator in Faribault received a message about the robbery and passed the news on to his townsmen. An hour and fifteen minutes later, four men from Faribault formed a small posse and rode to Shieldsville, on the Millersburg road and along the outlaws' possible escape route. They believed that a large reward would be offered for the death or capture of the bandits and were eager to take their share. Once they arrived at Shieldsville, they learned that no one had passed through the town. Disgusted, they stopped at the local saloon for a round of drinks while they planned their next move.

Chad Johnson, one of the men from Faribault, stood at the bar. He reached for a celluloid scraper and drew it across the top of his freshly drawn mug of beer, wiping off the excess foam.

"Boys, this is what I need!" he said, taking a long drink and wiping the foam from his mouth with his sleeve. "This will fuel us. It could be the James and Younger boys we're after. In that case, it could be ugly. But that don't matter to me, fellas. There's bound to be a reward for their capture—a big one. That'd come in right handy for me. I don't know about you, but I could use a new horse and tack. But it ticks me off that these are Southern men. If we catch 'em, I say we hang 'em!"

"Ditto!" the fellow next to him said. "Don't you suppose the gang's reputation is just newspaper talk anyhow? You're right; I betcha there's gonna be a big reward for gettin' 'em. Everyone from the governor down wants 'em."

Outside the saloon, as the men from Faribault talked, six riders rode up to the water pump and dismounted. One of them, Cole Younger, began pumping a tank full of water for the horses. As he pumped, the other outlaws led their horses to drink. The men then cupped their hands under the pump to capture a quick drink for themselves.

A curious old man standing in the yard noticed them ride up. He watched them for a few minutes then walked over to make conversation.

"Say, boys," he said, noticing the slaver coming from their horses' mouths, "it looks like you boys been givin' your horses quite a workout."

Cole, who was busy pumping water, ignored him as his brother, still mounted but leaning awkwardly over the neck of his horse, slumped into unconsciousness and slid onto the ground. The old man looked down at Bob's blood-soaked duster with bug eyes.

"Hey, what's wrong with that fella?" he questioned the outlaws.

Jesse walked over to the old man. "Don't worry about him, Grandpappy, we're goin' to hang that cuss! We've been on the trail of horse thieves. He's one of 'em. We aim to get 'em all." As Jesse spoke, Cole helped his brother back onto his horse.

The old man, puzzled by the scene, toyed with his whiskers for a moment and then walked slowly back into the saloon and shuffled over to the bar. He had noticed that all the men at the pump wore the same costumes, voluminous dusters. That seemed odd to him.

"Hey, boys, have you noticed them fellas at the pump?" the old man questioned. "They look rough and tough. You boys know anything about 'em? One of 'em is bleedin'.'"

"What?" Chad Johnson replied, turning away from his beer with a startled expression on his face. "I never noticed anybody ride up." Johnson slid off his bar stool. "I guess we'd better have a look." The four men laid down their beers and headed for the door. As they entered the yard, they recognized the outlaws immediately by their dusters and dashed for their guns, which they had stashed on their horses. Frank James, still saddled, saw them run out of the saloon and intercepted them, pointing his revolver at them.

"Get back in that building, or I'll kill every one of you!" he cried.

The men from Faribault slowly retreated back into the building, grumbling as they went. The outlaws finished watering their horses, remounted, and rode back onto the main road. As they exited the saloon yard, Jesse, riding at the rear, fired a fusillade of bullets into the pump and barrel, riddling the tank with holes. As the outlaws rode away, small spouts of water spurted out of the bullet holes and splashed onto the ground.

When the bandits had ridden out of sight, the men from the saloon dashed outside, mounted their horses, and spurred them to a gallop, taking up the chase. A couple of miles down the road, six other men linked up with them. They had been riding toward Shieldsville and were looking for the outlaws too. Farther down the lane, four more men joined the posse. Now fourteen men raced after the bandits.

At 5:05 P.M., near a ravine four miles west of Shieldsville, the posse caught up with the outlaws and began firing. Because they had only two shotguns and the rest revolvers, the posse closed on the bandits cautiously. Two miles farther down the road, Charlie Pitts' saddle girth broke, and he began to slide off his horse. Recognizing his predicament, the rest of the gang, in a predetermined maneuver, turned their horses around in the middle of the road and formed a loose rank.

"Give 'em a volley, boys," Cole shouted. "Ready, boys . . . Fire! Ready, again . . . Fire!"

The volleys fired by the outlaws forced the pursuing posse to fall back in disarray. As their pursuers regrouped, Cole pulled Pitts up into the saddle with him, and the gang sped away. Within ten minutes, even with Cole and Charlie doubling up on the same horse, the gang began to pull steadily away from the posse. The speed and stamina they counted on in their horses was paying dividends. One hundred men, however, were afield and searching for them in the area.

As they rode for their lives, large droplets of rain began to fall, followed by a torrential downpour. The gang stopped for a few minutes to put on the black oilskin slickers they kept rolled up behind their saddles. They were glad they had purchased the raincoats when they arrived in Minnesota.

Eventually, the outlaws saw a farmhouse in the distance. Uncertain where they were, they decided to query the owner and take him along as a guide and hostage. Turning off the main road, they went down a short, winding trail. Frank and Charlie dismounted and went to the front door of the house. Frank pounded loudly on the door with his fist. Moments later, a farmer named Sager answered the rapping.

"What do you fellows want?" Sager challenged, opening the door cautiously.

"We are a posse after horse thieves," Frank answered. "We need one of your mounts."

"By whose authority are you asking for it?" replied Sager sharply, leaving his door only partly open.

Frank lunged forward, throwing the full weight of his shoulder against Sager's door and knocking the farmer to the ground. Frank pulled his revolver from under his raincoat: "Here's our authority. Now take us to your barn, and make it snappy."

"You'll have to wait until I get my coat," Sager replied, a little more compliant.

"Forget your coat," Frank answered angrily. "Come now!"

After commandeering Sager's horse, Frank forced the farmer to guide them to Waterville, which the outlaws knew lay somewhere ahead, near what the locals called the "Big

Woods." If the posses chasing them became too hot on their heels, Frank planned to take shelter in the woods. As they rode toward Waterville, Charlie Pitts' horse, the one taken from Sager, suddenly balked and refused to move. Pitts spurred the horse sharply, but it only became more obstinate.

"Get off," Jesse said to Pitts. After Charlie dismounted, Jesse walked over to the horse, took it by its tail and bridle, and attempted to wheel it in circles, trying to distract it. Nothing worked; the horse refused to move, and the outlaws were forced to abandon it. Charlie and Cole doubled up again. Meanwhile, Bob Younger's wound throbbed painfully, and he became nauseated. The gang stopped for a minute while he vomited. Jim Younger was also in agony. But the outlaws were tough men, used to adversity, and they took their suffering in stride. The gang soon arrived at a fork in the road.

"Which is the way to Cordova and which Waterville?" Frank demanded of Sager.

"That's the way to Cordova," Sager said, pointing north. "Waterville's the other way."

After receiving the information, Frank ordered Sager to return home, telling him not to look back on fear of death. As Sager rode away, however, he peered out the corner of his eye long enough to assure himself that the bandits were trotting in the direction of Cordova. Minutes later, deceiving their guide, the gang doubled back and proceeded toward Waterville. Reaching the edge of that town, the bandits turned south along a rough trail and rode for several miles.

When they happened upon a deserted house in the middle of a wood, it was nearly dark. They decided to put up there for the night. The rain continued to pour down in sheets as the bandits tied up their horses, carried their gear into the house, and unrolled several of their blankets for their seriously injured men to lie on. Then Charlie and Cole walked behind the house to look for a pump and source of water. They had enough water for drinking purposes but not enough to clean their wounds before rebandaging them.

"Come here a minute, Charlie," Cole said. When Pitts walked over to him, Cole pulled his companion's bowie knife from its sheath and limped over to a slender fir tree. With a few strokes, he hacked off a slender branch, rounding off one end to form an improvised cane. After looking around the backyard of the farmhouse, the two men finally found a small well and pump. When it failed to respond to Charlie's pumping, Cole poured water from his canteen down the pump's mouth to prime it. Pitts pumped again vigorously, and within seconds, a stream of fresh water gushed onto the ground. Both men smiled grimly and filled their canteens.

After finishing this little chore, they walked back to the house, pulled out their bags of tobacco, and rolled themselves cigarettes. Not having smoked since early morning, the two men lit up and stood in the doorway of the farmhouse, puffing heavily on their cigarettes as they watched the rain pour down.

"Well, Younger, what do you think?" Charlie asked, turning to Cole.

"Pitts," Cole answered, "I think we have just experienced the longest day of our lives."

16

September 8, 1876

A map of Minnesota lay on the desk of Capt. John Brisette, chief detective of the St. Paul police force. He looked for Northfield on the map, and his finger traced the road leading southwest through Dundas, Millersburg, Shieldsville, and Waterville. According to information he had received, the bandits had ridden through the first three towns and were headed in the general direction of Waterville and Mankato. Perhaps they were fleeing toward Sioux Falls and intended to head south from there, he pondered. But he wasn't ready to jump to any grand conclusions. Brisette looked up from his map.

"Jimmy," Brisette said, speaking to patrolman James McFerrin, seated at a desk nearby, "I'm leaving you here while we head south. Get me some good maps of the southern counties, and bring them to me at Waterville. The men and I will arrive there by train shortly. The telegraph operator at Shieldsville says the bandits passed through that town headed for Waterville. We'll catch their scent and take up the chase. We've got big game to bag."

"Right, boss," McFerrin answered, rising from his chair. "I'll get what I can. But I'd rather leave with the rest of you boys."

"You'll be in for the kill, Jimmy. I promise you. Wait, before you go," Brisette added, "we've got to send a telegram to the governor. I'll compose it; I want you to send it. I'm asking for reinforcements. I want Pillsbury's authority to hire twenty war veterans, good shots, men with nerve. I want Henry and Remington rifles too, lots of firepower."

Across town, on the other side of the Mississippi River, James Hoy, chief detective of the Minneapolis police force, mounted his horse. Hoy was a stout Irishman with close-cropped brown hair and fists like hams. Standing next to him, still dismounted, was Minneapolis mayor John T. Ames, the son of a major shareholder in the Northfield Bank. Ames jumped astride his mount, and his spirited horse stamped its hooves nervously on the moist ground. Soon, fifteen horsemen clustered around the two men. Rain had been pouring down since dawn, and the men's black slickers gleamed.

"All right, men," Hoy said in a thick Irish brogue as he turned to his troop, "all of ye fall into a column of fours!"

A few minutes later, Hoy cried, "Giddup!" and spurred his horse to a position at the head of the formation. The policemen, their blue pants and brown boots showing from underneath glistening raincoats, rode through the town four abreast in an orderly column. Their Remington and Henry rifles and shotguns bristled from their saddle sheaths, and a crowd gaped at them from the boardwalks. They had never seen so many policemen in a single troop. Some of the throng had lined the street since daylight hoping to witness the early moments of what they believed would be a great manhunt. From the size of the crowd, it was evident that everyone in town knew about the Northfield robbery, and nearly everyone believed that the notorious James-Younger gang had committed it.

When the policemen got to the local train station, they loaded their saddles, equipment, and rifles on a freight car and jumped aboard the passenger cars of the St. Paul and Winona line for the trip south. When they reached Northfield, authorities there would provide them with fresh mounts.

South of Waterville, Frank James sat on a blanket, leaning against the parlor wall of the deserted house where the outlaws had stayed the night. The sun, hidden by thick clouds, dimly lit the room, and a driving rain beat on the shingled roof overhead. Frank had risen early. He always rose early, prompted by some internal clock. He noticed that his stomach was rumbling. He and the men hadn't eaten since noon the day before, he realized, and he was hungry, curse it. They'd have to find some food, he reckoned. Frank worried that the lawmen would be searching for them, and the deserted house where they stayed was a virtual beacon.

Frank reflected on their predicament. Yesterday had been one of the worst experiences of his life. He was astonished at how things had gone so badly. He had noticed after the raid that some of the men had been drinking. But that wasn't the only reason for their failure. The boys had just taken too long in the bank. He had urged them to be quick. When someone had shouted an early alarm, it had aroused the townsmen, and they had put up a good fight. It was just bad luck, that's all. Their luck had played out, and they were in a fix. They'd just have to muddle their way out of it.

What was needed now was a cool head. They had wounded men unable to fend for themselves. That complicated matters. He reckoned the woods were teeming with pursuers, and the wounded men were millstones around their necks. The gang usually split up when they were pursued, making themselves hard to find, difficult to engage. With men flying in every direction and doing unexpected things, posses were thrown into dithers. They usually forced posses to separate into smaller squads in order to follow their various trails. Of course, if they faced a posse, six men were better than one. But if they were going to survive, they must eventually separate. And if they stayed in this house much longer, their lives would be in jeopardy. They needed to move on in a jiffy.

Frank had not wanted to rouse the men early because he

knew they were exhausted from their wounds and exertions. But he knew the rain would impede his pursuers too, slowing them down. He was familiar with posses. It would take them awhile to sip their coffees, dawdle over their breakfasts, boast to their wives about how brave they were, and stash a flask of whiskey in their saddlebags for nerve.

After thinking it over, Frank was convinced that the outlaws' best chance was to flee into the Big Woods north of Waterville, camp there long enough for their wounded to recover a mite, and then make a run for it. Yep, Frank thought, that's what they ought to do. But, first, they needed some grub.

Jesse sat nearby and was carried away by his own thoughts. He wondered for a moment what Zee was doing—and Jesse Junior, his year-old son. They were a world away, seemingly irrelevant at the moment, something he shouldn't be thinking about even. His mind quickly turned to his own plight. They were in a pickle, all right. But the gang had been in fixes before. They'd either thought their way or fought their way out of them. He didn't expect the current situation to be any different. Still, he hoped there weren't that many boys in blue out looking for them. They'd lost Miller and Chadwell, so the gang was short on bite. Still, he believed there wasn't a policeman or sheriff on earth who could bring him in alive. And if they got him dead, he'd take plenty of them with him!

Jim Younger had tossed and turned all night. He'd gotten only a few cat winks of sleep because the pain from his wound had roused him continually from his slumber. And with daylight, he had awakened to a continuous, throbbing pain. He removed the wadding from his wound and leaned over to examine the hole in his shoulder. It looked worse than he'd expected, red, even in the faint light, as if it were becoming infected. Maybe this was his last hurrah, he thought. He reached for the small pint of whiskey that lay next to him and pulled out its cork. Turning the bottle sideways, he held his thumb over the opening and dribbled whiskey on the wound and the area around it. As much as they had disliked to, they had had to use good whiskey to treat their wounds.

He looked around him in the gray light. Charlie Pitts was sound asleep in one corner, his blanket pulled tightly around him. Brother Bob, to the right of Pitts, appeared to be awake. Bob was probably in as much as or more pain than he was, and he pitied him for it. He noticed that it was cooler this morning, and he hoped it would warm up.

As Jim awkwardly rebandaged his shoulder with strips of cloth, he listened to the downpour pounding on the roof. Once they left the house, the rain would drench them all to the bone. Jim stopped wrestling with the bandage; he'd have to have someone help him tie it up.

Jim wondered how he had allowed himself to participate in this insane venture. He'd been apprehensive about the robbery from the start. They had traveled halfway across the country to a strange state to pull off a robbery they could have committed at home, where they would have had an easy getaway. Now, they'd botched the operation good and were smack-dab in the middle of endless woods, marshes, and swamps—and all shot to flinders, to boot. Jim worried, for the first time, if any of them would escape. He considered what sort of reaction the robbery had had on the Minnesotans. The posse at Shieldsville had jumped on them immediately. That was ominous. How many other posses were out there searching for them? Jim knew if they were captured that they would be lynched. That didn't frighten him. First, they had to catch them.

Cole Younger rose to his feet and hobbled over to Charlie Pitts.

"Hey, Pitts, you goin' to sleep all day?" he said.

"I'm thinkin' on it," Pitts answered and rolled over to face Younger.

"Say, Charlie, I got a question for yah. Did you ever eat a carp?" Cole hoped to start a little morning repartee to enliven things.

"Yeh," Charlie replied, rubbing his eyes. "It was just awful."

"No! No, my friend; they're delicious!" Cole replied. "How did you cook it?"

"I fried it," Charlie answered.

"No, no. You don't fry carp," Cole admonished him.

"Well, how *do* you cook them?" Charlie asked. "I've heard lots of ways. They always taste the same, terrible."

"That's 'cause people don't know how to cook 'em. I tell you, it's simple. What you do is just get some ordinary clay and mix it into stiff dough. Then, you mold the mud around the carp, form it into a regular jacket. Do you get it, Charlie? Do you get it? Next, you build a fire and place the fish in the middle of it and cook it for twenty minutes in the coals." Cole stopped talking.

"Then what do you do?" asked Charlie, his curiosity aroused.

"That's easy," answered Cole. "You take the clay out of the fire, break it open, throw away the fish, and eat the mud!"

Charlie smiled wryly for a moment and then looked up at Cole soberly: "Partner, I could eat a raw carp right now. And that clay don't sound so bad neither."

Cole, chuckling to himself, limped over to Frank.

"Mornin', Buck. What d'you think?"

Frank looked up at Cole with a serious expression on his face. "Well, Bud, we are in a tight spot, ain't we. I'd hoped we'd be miles from here by now, but the injuries, the hot pursuit—I hadn't counted on it. We'll just have to struggle our way through, that's all, figure a way out of this. I think we should head for the Big Woods north of town. The roads are sure to be filled with police and posses; the woods will give us some cover until we get our bearings and our feet under us. It will give the boys a chance to rest."

As the rain continued to pour down, the gang moved north along the trail toward the Waterville road. Charlie Pitts, riding scout, looked to his left and noticed a faint trail of smoke rising from the woods.

"Hey, boys! Look yonder," he called to the men behind him.

"You're right, Pitts," answered Jesse. "Let's have a look. I can almost smell food."

Ahead of them, the outlaws noticed a small path leading in the direction of the smoke, and they turned off the main trail. They entered a small wood where they traveled through oak and ash trees. Finally, they reached a glade and were greeted by the wailing of hounds. Around a neck of woods, a small cabin was nestled, and the men rode up to it and dismounted. Jesse unbuttoned his raincoat to allow himself easy access to his revolvers. He walked up to the door of the cabin and rapped on it loudly. Moments later, a middle-aged woman with brown hair tinged with gray opened the door. She wore a white apron, and her hair was gathered in a tight bun.

"Mornin', fellas," the woman said. "What's your business?"

"Howdy, ma'am," Jesse replied. "I hope you'll pardon us. I'm John Howard, and these men are my posse. We've been out all night after some danged mule thieves. Have you seen any strangers leadin' a couple of black mules?"

"No, can't say as I have," the woman replied.

"Well, those thieves have managed to give us the slip, dang 'em," continued Jesse, "but we are hot on their trail. We've been ridin' all night and are tuckered out and hungry, ma'am. Would you mind fixin' us a breakfast? We have money."

"Why sure," the woman answered. "I'm Mrs. George James, by the way. My husband is off doing some chores, but he'll be back soon. Sorry to say I haven't much food to spare. I have some milk and bread, though, that I could give you boys. I've precious little meat at the moment."

"Ma'am, we'd be happy to settle for a light meal this mornin'," Jesse replied. "Boys," he said, raising his voice and turning to the rest of the outlaws, "Mrs. James here is goin' to offer us her hospitality." The bandits dismounted, took off their wide-brimmed hats, and shook the rainwater from their coats. They walked into the cabin, their spurs jingling.

Mrs. James ran for a pitcher of milk and laid it on the kitchen table. Then, she dashed into the pantry and picked up two loaves of dark bread. Reaching into a cabinet, she pulled out a knife and cut the bread into thick slices. Leaving the room again, she returned shortly with a plate of fresh butter. The outlaws' eyes bulged in anticipation.

"Some of you men can take a seat while I get some glasses," she said, "but I don't have enough chairs for all of you."

"Ma'am, that's all right. Don't you fret yourself about that," Jesse answered. "We've got to get on the road promptly. We'll finish our food and soon be gone." As he spoke, Jesse gobbled some bread and washed it down with fresh milk. It tasted wonderful to him. The rest of the outlaws also devoured their bread and milk eagerly.

"Say, ma'am, we suspect those mule thieves will cross the Cannon River. Do you know of any fords nearby?" Jesse asked in hope of learning more information about the nearby country.

"Friend," Mrs. James replied, "there's a ford just north of here."

"How does a fella get there?"

"Well—that is, if I were you—I'd head north, cross the Waterville road about five miles from here, then continue until I reached the first trail leading westward. I'd turn left there and stay on the same trail for a mile or two. You'll come to a fine ford. If those thieves are in this neck of the woods, that's likely where they crossed the river."

"Much obliged, ma'am," Jesse replied. After a few minutes, the outlaws finished their meal and prepared to leave. Jesse was the last to go.

"Ma'am," he said, turning to Mrs. James, "you sure are a fine lady to help us out. Here's somethin' for your trouble." Jesse reached into his pocket purse and handed her three shiny dollars.

"Glad to help you boys," Mrs. James replied and closed the door quietly behind the men. She wondered who these men were and if they were telling her the truth.

Shortly after the outlaws left, George James returned home. His wife told him about the visitors and said that they had asked about the ford.

"Mary, you have been feeding outlaws!" he cried out. "Those

are the very fellas the lawmen have been looking for in the
Big Woods this morning. They robbed the bank at Northfield
yesterday and killed some people."

"But they looked like such fine gentlemen."

"Yeh, fine gentlemen! They'd shoot a fella fer a dime," James
replied. "I'm riding over to the Waterville road and warn the
law. A bunch of them was over there when I left."

James ran from the house, mounted his horse, and galloped
back to the Waterville road. By this time, the road was crawling
with lawmen, most of them entering and exiting the Big Woods.
James linked up immediately with Capt. John Rodgers' posse
and told the captain about the outlaws and where he thought
they were headed.

"Get on your horses, boys," Rodgers ordered his men.

Within seconds, Rodgers and his posse, accompanied by
James, raced toward the Cannon River ford, using a different
route than that Mrs. James had given the outlaws. James knew
the country well and showed Rodgers a shortcut to the ford that
would allow them, hopefully, to get there before the outlaws
and set up an ambush.

When the men reached the Cannon River, James led the posse
southward along the east bank of the stream in the direction of
the ford. When they neared the crossing, Rodgers dismounted
and ordered some of his men to cross the stream and set up an
ambush on the opposite bank of the ford. Meanwhile, Rodgers,
James, and another posse member walked around a crook in
the river. As they strode around the bend, George James did a
double take: the bandits were approaching the river directly in
front of him. They had gotten to the ford first.

"There they are, Rodgers!" James exclaimed. "We've got 'em!"

James raised his .10-gauge, single-barreled shotgun to his
shoulder and fired. As the sound of James' shotgun reverberated
down the river, Rodgers and his posse fired their weapons also,
but their shots strayed.

As he approached the river, Jesse heard gunfire and saw spray rising in the river in front of him from the impact of bullets. "It's too hot, boys, too hot! Let's get out of here!" he shouted to the other outlaws. The bandits spurred their horses and raced along the floodplain and out of sight. As they sprinted along the bank of the river, Jesse noticed another crossing site, not as good as the first, but fordable. The outlaws dismounted, grabbed their horses by their halters, and pulled them into the swirling river. The river was over its banks, and the muddy current surged around horses and men. As they reached deeper water, the outlaws let go of the halters and grabbed their horses' manes. Striving against the fast current, the horses made an arcing course across the stream, dragging their riders along. When they reached the opposite bank, the horses dug their hooves into the soft mud and scrambled onto solid ground, dragging the outlaws out of the river with them. The outlaws remounted their horses and spurred them westward into a tangle of woods.

Once in the trees, the bandits slowed their horses to a fast walk, steering them through a maze of branches. They looked for a route where they could advance more rapidly. Behind them, screams from the pursuing posse could be heard. The outlaws turned their horses northward, in the opposite direction of the shouting, and drove deeper into the woods.

"Head into the swamp and erase our trail," Jesse directed. Once in the swamp, however, the horses bogged down, and the men had to search for an easier passage.

Sheriff Ara Barton's dismounted posse spread out in a long, winding rank that extended across a portion of the Big Woods, a forest rank with hard maple, basswood, poplar, ash, and a smattering of pine. It was 10:00 A.M., and the men trudged manfully westward across soggy ground. The rain ran down the men's slickers and drenched their pants legs and boots. Occasionally, they stepped into marshy ground and sank deep into the mud. When they reached solid ground, their feet made squishing noises inside their wet boots. Thirty minutes later, John Andersen, a member of the posse, noticed that he had lost contact with the men on his left and right.

"Bart! You out there?" he shouted to the fellow who had been walking to his left. Andersen heard only gun volleys in the distance. The outlaws must be in the area, he realized, and his blood ran fast. He'd been pretty bold earlier, when he was with the rest of the posse, but now that he was alone, he grew nervous. What if he ran into the outlaws? Where were the rest of the men? He began walking faster, becoming more apprehensive with each step.

"Phillips!" he called out. Still no one replied.

Ahead of him, Andersen heard a sound and pulled back the hammer on his .12-gauge shotgun.

"Bart? Is that you?" he screamed, but there was no reply.

Andersen now began walking obliquely to his right, hoping to catch sight of a posse member in that direction. Minutes later, he heard a rustling and pointed his gun in the direction of the sound. A deer loped noisily across his path.

Andersen gave a sigh of relief. He must keep his nerve, he thought. Tramping farther to his right, he saw something moving in the green branches. Startled, he cocked his gun and pointed it in the direction of the disturbance. His finger tightened instinctively on the trigger and his gun roared.

"Who's shooting at me?" came back an outraged voice from the woods. A posse member burst through the trees, his face flushed with anger.

"Someone shot at me," he screamed. "Was it you? Was it you, Andersen? I heard shot passing through the branches."

Andersen regained his composure.

"Who? Me?" Andersen replied. "Nope, d'you think I'm nuts? I heard it too. I don't know where it came from. I been hearin' shots all over. What's goin' on?"

"Well, the shot sounded close," the posse member replied, still angry and suspicious.

The men moved apart again and continued trekking westward. As he walked, Andersen broke open his shotgun, removed the spent shell, shoved another into its place, and closed the gun with a muffled click.

The thunder of hoofbeats filled the air, and twenty-five horsemen raced from the woods onto the open prairie. The tails of the horses were suspended in a streamlined arc as they galloped through the short brush into a wood beyond. When the riders neared the trees, they pulled back on their reins and entered the woods at a trot, weaving their way, snakelike, through the elms and ashes. The riders wore red strips of cloth around their right arms to identify themselves as members of a common posse.

Sheriff Davis's Faribault posse rolled down the muddy road to Waterville in four wagons, each pulled by four workhorses. When the wagons reached the Big Woods, Davis's lead driver pulled back on the reins and turned his percherons right, and his wagon moved forward slowly, forming deep ruts. The other wagons followed.

Ten posse members sat in the back of each wagon, steadying their rifles and shotguns against the wagon walls. The rain dripped steadily down their raincoats, onto their pants, and into their boots. Inside their waterproof coats, their clothes were wet from their sweating bodies. As the wagons passed north into the woods, the posse saw wagons, buggies, and horses parked indiscriminately along the way. Farther down the road, they entered an open vista in the woods and saw armed men plodding in the distance. Finally, Davis's wagons reached an area of the woods where no ruts or tracks marked the road.

Davis jumped down from his wagon and motioned the following wagons forward. The drivers of the three trailing wagons moved up until they were directly behind Davis's own. The sheriff then walked back to the middle wagon and spoke to the men loudly.

"All right, boys," he began. "This is going to be a pretty disorganized affair. No one's had a chance to coordinate it. We're just going to pick out a stretch of woods and scour it. We've been told that none of the outlaws has passed through Elysian, so they're likely in these woods.

"I want each captain to make a list of his men and keep track of them. Let's have no stragglers. We'll be letting you out along the road at one-hundred-foot intervals. Try to keep that distance between you. When we've all unloaded, I'll fire my pistol. Then I want you all to start walkin' west; that's to your left. Don't lose sight of the men on your flanks; keep in contact with them. We'll be stretched out for more'n half a mile. When we've walked about two miles straight west, I'll fire my pistol twice. Then, I want everyone to proceed to the middle of the line and we'll regroup. Do you understand?" Everyone remained silent.

"I want you to control your fire," Davis continued. "If you see strangers, order them to lay down their guns and advance to be recognized. Don't fire on your own men!"

With these instructions, the lead wagon moved up the road and stopped, periodically letting off its men. When the first wagon was emptied, it pulled over to the side of the road, and the second wagon began letting off men. Within fifteen minutes, Davis fired his pistol, and forty men plodded westward through the Big Woods searching for the outlaws.

Around one o'clock, as the outlaws continued in a northwesterly direction, they came to a river bloated by rainfall. It appeared unpassable, so they rode along the stream looking for a bridge. Suddenly, Pitts, who was acting as a scout in their front, rode back within view of the outlaws and raised his arm, indicating for them to stop. He motioned with his index finger for one of the outlaws to come forward.

Frank James trotted up to Pitts and sidled up to his mount. "What's up, Charlie?" he whispered.

"Men ahead," Pitts answered.

"How many?"

"Eight or ten, I reckon. There's a bridge up there, and they're guardin' it."

Frank thought for a moment. "Let's ride up to 'em, pretend we're a posse, and see if we can relieve 'em," he said.

Pitts grinned. "Good idea, Buck!"

Frank rode back to the other bandits. "Boys," he said, "there's a bridge ahead with a band of men guardin' it. We'll make contact with them, play like we're a posse, and see if we can replace 'em as guards."

"Let me talk to 'em," Jesse pleaded.

"All right," Frank said. "If they pull anything, we're behind you and we'll drill 'em. Ready, boys?" he asked, turning to the rest of the outlaws. The men nodded and urged their horses forward. When they reached Pitts, they slowed, allowing Jesse to advance a dozen yards to their front.

As Jesse approached the bridge guards, he waved to them. "Halloo, boys!" he shouted.

One of the guards waved back, and Jesse rode up to the bridge. The rest of the outlaws trailed Jesse some fifty feet to his rear.

"Howdy!" Jesse greeted the guards cheerfully. "I'm John Howard and these are my boys," he said, pointing to the men behind him. "Whose posse are you?" he asked the lawmen.

"We're Harrison's men," a middle-aged farmer replied. "Who you fellas with?"

"We're freelancers," Jesse replied. "If it's all right with you, I'll call my men over," he added.

"Sure, sure," said the farmer, who was the spokesman for the guards at the bridge. Jesse motioned to the other bandits, and they approached the posse at a walk and dismounted. In case of trouble, the solid ground made a much better firing platform.

"How you boys doing?" the farmer said to the new arrivals, putting his pistol back in his holster as he spoke. "Caught any of them ornery bandits?" he asked, chuckling heartily.

"Yep," Frank replied, "I shot a furry one back a piece, a long-eared, mean-lookin' critter, looked an awful lot like my son's rabbit though. How about you fellas? Caught sight of any of 'em?"

"Nope. Ain't seen nobody nor nothing," remarked the farmer, talking rapidly. Frank noted that despite the man's good spirits, his pupils were dilated and he looked a bit excited.

"Say," Jesse continued, "you boys been workin' hard, and you've got yourselves all wet and muddy and such. Why don't you let us boys spell you a while, watch the bridge for a piece, while you dry out?"

"I don't think Harrison would like it," the farmer replied. "We promised him we'd stick to this place like glue till he sent us relief. But thanks for the offer."

"Well, that's downright disgustin'," Jesse answered. "We were lookin' forward to bein' of use to you boys. Are there any more bridges ahead that need watchin'? We sure would like to be helpful, don't you know."

"Nah. They're all watched—all of 'em. Why don't you boys ask Sheriff Barton to schedule you for a shift?"

"Where is he?"

"Oh, he's up north a piece. At least that's where he was the last I saw him."

"How far north?" Jesse questioned, trying to draw more information out of the man.

"Oh, I suspect about a half-mile, at his headquarters along the river," the farmer answered.

"Good," Jesse said. "We'll try to link up with him. Much obliged to you fellas."

Jesse motioned to the other outlaws, and they remounted their horses and pushed northward along the river. Then, when they were out of sight of the bridge, they moved east to avoid contact with Barton's posse. As they proceeded east, the sound of loud voices and occasional firing reached them across the woods. Posses seemed to be everywhere. After traveling a short distance, the bandits turned north again, riding through a marsh to avoid contact with the lawmen.

By late afternoon, using their compasses and maps, they calculated they were somewhere in the northwest part of the Big Woods. When they came upon a small clearing at the top of a hill, they decided to make camp for the night. The rain had stopped. After tethering his horse, Pitts drew his bowie knife and hacked down three small trees an inch or more in diameter, making them into seven-foot-long poles. Jesse, Frank, and Cole helped him. With the poles, the thickest ends of which were pointed, the men made a rough shelter, driving them into the soggy ground and forming a teepee-like structure. They tied the poles at the top with strong twine from Pitts' saddlebag. Then they cut several slender branches and curved them around the middle of the shelter, using them for lateral supports. Finally, they covered the structure with blankets, leaving one end of the shelter open. This improvised tent would give them some protection from the wind and rain.

Next, they tended to their horses, searching for anything green in the woods—bushes, weeds, leaves—to feed them. The pickings were slim. Finally, the men clustered together to talk over their situation.

"Well, boys, I think we ought to start a fire. It's gonna be wet and cold tonight," Cole said, beginning the discussion.

"I don't think that's a good idea," disagreed his brother Jim. "Someone might see it. We're on a hilltop."

"So what if they see it," Pitts chimed in loudly. "There's bound to be other fires in the woods tonight. No one's goin' to notice ours. The posses are goin' to need to keep warm, just like we are, and they'll be usin' fire for their suppers."

To resolve the argument, Pitts offered to climb a tree to see if there were signs of fires. The others agreed and Charlie clambered up a nearby tree and looked out over the vast forest. The clouds had lifted for the moment, and the view was splendid. In fact, from the top of the tree, Pitts could see a mile or more. As he viewed the countryside in the waning light, he counted the signs—faint wisps of whitish-gray smoke—from at least eight or ten fires in the distance. After a few minutes, he descended the tree.

"Boys," he said, as he reached the ground, "there's at least ten fires out there."

"That means that most of 'em must have gone home or into town for the night," Frank responded. "Those fires are likely camps from road and bridge guards."

"None of 'em are close," Pitts added.

Without discussing the matter further, the men returned to their tent and searched for logs and branches. Within minutes, they had created a roaring fire. Soon, it became dark.

In other parts of the woods, nearly sixty men clustered around bonfires. They were from the posses of Sheriff Dill of Winona County, Davis of Faribault, Finch of Blue Earth, Barton of Rice, and Deputy Sheriff Harrison of Ramsey. Some of Brisette's and Hoy's men were also present in small numbers, as well as men from Owatonna and Eagle Lake. Even a few Pinkerton agents had stopped their roaming and made camp. But Frank had been right; most of the men were road and bridge guards. More than three hundred men had gone home or into Waterville for the night. Most of them would return the next day, joined by another six hundred from all over southern Minnesota. Meanwhile, the rain began falling in a torrent, and the drops sizzled on the many fires.

That day the following news bulletin appeared in the *Minneapolis-St. Paul Pioneer Press:*

A reward of $1,500 will be paid by the state for the capture, dead or alive, of the men who committed the raid, and afterwards escaped, on the bank of Northfield on Sept. 7, 1876, or a proportionate amount for any one of them captured.

J. S. Pillsbury
Governor

17

September 9, 1876

Bob Younger woke to a sharp pain in his right elbow. In his sleep, he had rolled over on his arm, and the pain had awakened him instantly. Instinctively, he tried to close the fingers of his right hand but could flex them only a little. During the night, he had worn his raincoat under his blanket for extra warmth and to shed the cold rain that dripped continuously on him through the top of the shelter. The raincoat had caused him to sweat freely, and now he was as thoroughly doused as if he had been standing naked in the rain. But at least his raincoat had kept him warm, and the shelter had kept the bulk of the cold rain out and warded off the wind. Bob wondered if the rain would ever stop.

As it grew lighter, the men began to twist and turn. Frank threw off his blanket and sat up to roll a cigarette. He filled the tent with a swirling cloud of fragrant smoke.

During a lull in the storm, the men went out to their horses and arranged their gear. The sky was overcast but the clouds were dark, and more rain seemed likely. Before leaving their campsite, the outlaws conducted a parley inside their tent to discuss their plans for the day.

"I think we should mount up and break through their lines," Pitts suggested.

"Have you looked at our horses, Charlie?" Frank replied.

"There's no 'dash' in 'em. They're exhausted. All that mirin' around in the swamps and sloughs has finished 'em. And with all our hard ridin', our saddles have ground sores into their backs. Besides that, the horses are too easy to recognize."

"Buck's right," Cole broke in. "The horses are finished, and we're surrounded. Too many of 'em are after us. We must abandon the mounts, flee on foot, and steer away from the roads. We can get new horses later, and they'll be harder to recognize and track." The others generally agreed with Frank and Cole.

"Our best chance is to head into Waterville on foot," Frank continued, "abandon our horses there for good, and fetch some grub. Then we'll head southwest on foot until we find fresh horses and runnin' room. Cole's right; we must travel unbeaten paths. The wounded will slow us down if we make it a race with our pursuers. The law likes to operate on solid turf, in broad daylight. If we stay off the roads, move at night mostly—travel through the swamps even, when we have to—we'll make it a decent chase." When Frank stopped talking, the rest of the outlaws nodded their heads in agreement.

Within minutes, the outlaws were riding south through the woods toward Waterville. Pitts rode point to detect the presence of lawmen. The rest trotted several hundred yards behind him, hidden from view for the most part by trees. Occasionally, Pitts halted to let the men catch up.

At one point, Pitts stopped and waited for the rest of the men. When they rode into view, he signaled, raising his arm and waving it back and forth. The outlaws rode forward and surrounded him.

"There's a cabin ahead," he said, "and smoke's comin' from it. There's a couple horses in the corral. What's our move?"

"We'll ride in and take the horses," Frank answered. The other men agreed.

Amid the howling of hounds, the outlaws rode to the dooryard of the cabin and dismounted. Frank, in the lead, strode up to the house and pounded on the front door. A farmer named Ludwig

Roseneau opened the door and peered out. He was aware that outlaws were afoot in the Big Woods and was apprehensive. "What do you fellas want?" Roseneau greeted them suspiciously. The men outside his door were big, tough-looking fellows with grim expressions on their faces. "Howdy! I'm Sheriff Davis of Rice County," Frank answered. "We're searchin' for outlaws. Some of our horses have foundered. We must have yours." "I can't spare them," Roseneau said.

Frank yanked out his six-shooter from underneath his unbuttoned raincoat and leveled it at Roseneau. "We'll have 'em! Step out of that house!"

Roseneau, shocked at the sight of a pistol pointed at his chest, walked into the front yard. Behind him stood his son, Wilhelm, sixteen years old, and another young farmhand. The boys had been cowering behind Roseneau, out of view. Now they followed Roseneau into the yard while large drops of rain spotted their clothes.

"Come with us," Frank demanded, leading the three toward the nearby corral. "Fetch those horses for me, boys, and make it snappy," he said loudly to the two youngsters.

Running to the gate, Wilhelm raised the wire hoop holding the gate shut and swung the gate open. The boys grabbed the two horses inside by their halters and led them over to the outlaws. Jim and Bob Younger, it was decided, would ride the new mounts. The outlaws quickly saddled the horses and fitted them with bridles then turned their two exhausted horses loose.

"All right," Frank said to Wilhelm, the larger of the two boys, "you're comin' with me. Get up here," he ordered, pointing to his saddle. "You're my guide."

"No! Wilhelm can't go with you! I need him!" Roseneau cried out, distraught that the outlaws were taking his son.

"Shut up!" Frank said to Roseneau threateningly. "Get up here, boy." Frank reached down and pulled Wilhelm up into the saddle. "The boy will be okay."

"Giddup!" Frank kicked his horse, and the outlaws wended their way up the path to the main trail.

"Do many people travel this way?" Frank asked the boy as they reached the road.

"No," Wilhelm answered, "hardly anybody. They mostly use the main trail to the west. It's the closest way to town."

"Good," Frank replied. "Now, I want you to lead us to the Waterville road."

After the men had ridden several miles through heavy woods, the boy told Frank that the road to Waterville was just over the next hill. Frank sent Pitts ahead to confirm it. When Charlie signaled back to the rest that the road was ahead, Frank ordered Wilhelm home.

"Much obliged to you, brother," Frank said to the boy. "Now, get home. And don't tarry! If we see you again, we'll shoot you."

After watching the boy walk north and out of sight, the outlaws continued to the top of the hill and dismounted. They walked to the edge of the woods and stared down on the Waterville road. Below, several wagons loaded with armed men were proceeding toward the town. The men appeared to be posses, parts of posses, and freelancers. After waiting a few minutes for the road to clear, the outlaws spurred their horses to a trot—that was as fast as they could move—and crossed the road into the forest beyond.

Once in the woods south of the road, they rode some three hundred yards, dismounted, and set up a temporary camp to shelter themselves from the rain. It was raining in earnest again. Clustered in their tent, they made their final plans.

Frank said in a low tone, "This place is crawlin' with cops and posses. We'll tether our horses for good and go on foot into Waterville, stayin' out of view of the main road until we get into town. Then we'll find some food. Once we get our bellies filled, we'll head southwest, takin' our bridles and gear with us. Our saddles will have to stay here. They're too heavy to lug.

"If we run into lawmen in town," Frank went on, "we'll

pretend to be a posse. If that don't satisfy 'em, we'll shoot our way out as a last resort."

The gang stacked their saddles next to a tree and tethered the horses. They hated to leave their mounts tied, but it was necessary. If they turned them loose, their appearance would alert the posses to their location, and there would be hell to pay. Before breaking camp, the men rebandanged their wounds.

Fifteen minutes after leaving camp, the outlaws entered Waterville from the east, charging into the first house they encountered, which they found unlocked. Pistols drawn, they confronted the owner, a man named Kohn, as he was seated at breakfast.

"Good mornin', friend," Jesse said to Kohn in a hard voice. "We've come for breakfast. Get up and bring us some grub— whatever you've got, the best you've got—and be quick about it. We're losin' patience."

The sight of the strangers and their many guns astonished Kohn. He quickly guessed who they were and rose to his feet and scurried to find some ham and eggs to cook on his wood stove. He'd heard that outlaws were afoot in the woods, and incredibly they now surrounded him. To speed his cooking, Kohn opened up a second chamber in the stove and threw in some kindling to start a fire in it. While he was cooking, Cole and Charlie looked through a cupboard for food to take with them.

"Where's your pantry and smokehouse?" Cole demanded.

"The smokehouse is outside the back door," Kohn answered. "The pantry is through that door," he said, pointing to a side door leading from the kitchen. Kohn had decided to cooperate with the outlaws, hoping to come out of the experience with his life. He knew that the Northfield outlaws were killers.

Cole went out the back door and returned in a few minutes with a chunk of ham under his arm. "We've hit the jackpot, boys," Cole called out to the others as he entered the room. He found a cloth bag and dropped the ham into it. Then he went into the pantry and dropped some potatoes into the same sack.

Returning to the kitchen, he began searching for matches. Once he found them, he wrapped them in a piece of oilcloth with his other matches and stuffed the lot into his pocket. Finally, he walked into an adjoining bedroom and snatched some shirts from a chest to use for bandages.

Meanwhile, Kohn cooked the men a steaming meal of scrambled eggs and bacon. When the meal was prepared, he carried the food to the table in two iron skillets, dishing the food onto the outlaws' plates. The gang gobbled their meals. When they were finished, Frank approached Kohn.

"We are much obliged to you, my friend. We may return your hospitality some day. But when we leave this house, I want you to stay put. I'm leaving a guard in yonder trees to ensure that you do. If you want to stay alive, be sure that you stay where you are." Kohn wondered if Frank was lying, but he decided to do just what he was told.

The outlaws tramped out of Kohn's house on a northward course. By this time, the town was filled with armed men, afoot and on horseback. Ignoring the lawmen, and indistinguishable from them, the outlaws strolled through town without incident, exiting through the north end of town into the woods.

As Sheriff Martin Moe and his posse rode down the lane toward Norseland, Minnesota, they noticed a rider approaching them. Moe threw up his arms and called for the rider to halt. The rider stopped in the middle of the road.

"Identify yourself!" cried the sheriff when he came abreast of the man.

"What do you mean 'identify' myself?" the rider declared.

"You heard me! I'm Sheriff Moe of Sibley County. We're looking for bandits. Who are you?"

"How do I know you're a posse?" the man replied, becoming angry at what he considered the impertinence of total strangers. Then the rider became somewhat intimidated and relented. "Well, if you must know, I'm E. B. Tull from Damel in

Meeker County. Have you got any more infernal questions?"

"Get off that horse," Moe answered, drawing his revolver. "You're under arrest!"

"What for?" Tull asked indignantly. Moe turned to one of his men. "Get the handcuffs, Jim."

Tull dismounted and two of the posse members twisted his arms behind his back then fastened heavy steel shackles onto his wrists.

"All right," Moe continued, now facing Tull. "Tell us again who you are—and don't give us any more of your smart lip."

"I told you who I am," Tull replied. "Can't you fellows hear?"

Moe, enraged by Tull's behavior, struck him in the mouth with the back of his hand, and a dark trickle of blood ran over Tull's lips.

"Let's hear it again. Who are you? What's your full name?" Moe repeated.

"I'm E. B. Tull; Ezekiel is my first name. I teach school in Damel. What's the meaning of this beating?"

"Shut your mouth," replied Moe, "or I'll knock your teeth down your throat! How long have you taught at Damel?"

"I've taught in Damel for fifteen years! Everybody in town knows me. Everybody!"

"Why did you hesitate about telling us your name? Are you sure your real name isn't James?"

"What're you talking about?" Tull replied angrily.

"That's it, boys!" Moe said, noting Tull's abrasive demeanor. "He's going into the cooler. This boy will be singing for us yet."

The James-Younger gang had been crippling along for eight miles with several unmounted posses following closely behind them. None had gotten near enough to see them or fire at them yet, but they had identified the outlaws' tracks and now dogged their trail. In order to elude the posses, the gang moved deeper into a slough, believing that would make it harder for their pursuers to track them. In this way, they also avoided the mounted posses swarming the area, who could quickly outrun them in the open country. The going was tough and it was raining lightly. As Jim struggled through the mucky, water-soaked slough, he tripped over a log and plunged headlong into the water and mud.

"Ow!" he cried out as he fell, twisting to avoid falling onto his wounded shoulder. He reached into the oozy mud with his right hand and raised himself on one knee. He pulled himself upright and attempted to pull one of his feet from the muck. Instead, his foot popped out of the boot. Jim placed his foot back in his boot, swiveled it into place, and pulled hard. This time, the boot popped loose. Then he pulled his other boot free and quickened his pace to catch up with the others.

Finally, the men halted to rest. Pitts, however, strode several hundred yards to the south edge of the swamp to check on their pursuers, as he could hear voices coming from that direction. At the edge of the swamp, Pitts peered between the trees. His dark brown eyes were riveted on a group of twenty men riding directly south of his location. He could see their blue pants legs extending from underneath their raincoats. They were obviously police, and they were advancing at a trot through tall prairie grass in a clear section of the timber. Pitts slogged back to the rest of the outlaws and reported what he had seen. In response, the gang moved deeper yet into the swamp.

By 3:00 P.M., they had staggered their way onto an island in the slough, and they moved into its wooded interior and set up camp. In a short while, they had built a tent like the night before. After looking at their maps, they determined that they were somewhere in the vicinity of Elysian, close to German Lake.

Soon, rain fell again in a violent downpour. Around 4:00 P.M., the men clustered together under their tent for supper. Pitts drew his bowie knife from its sheath and cut off chunks of ham for the men to eat. Then he opened up the sack of potatoes and sliced them into small chunks for each man. The outlaws ate the potatoes raw, peelings and all, and felt lucky to do so. They feared that setting a fire would reveal their position.

Over a thousand lawmen and searchers had been in the field that day, but as the rain intensified, most of them returned to their homes or to lodgings in the nearby town of Elysian. That included Detectives Brisette and Hoy and most of the sheriffs.

As Frank gnawed on a piece of ham, he began cynically contemplating his pursuers. Yes, he said to himself, he'd wager that while he and the rest of the outlaws were in the woods exposed to a raging storm, the sheriffs and detectives—every jack one of them—were at home drinking whiskey by now. That's exactly where he wanted them, he thought. If the rain stopped, it would offer him and the boys an opportunity to break through the ring of lawmen encircling them. They must make a dash for it; it was their only chance. But it was getting dark and it would be difficult, maybe impossible, to flee in the pitch-black; the clouds must thin. Maybe there was a moon above those clouds. He hoped there was.

John Brisette, chief detective of the Minneapolis Police Department, and Sheriff Dill and his posse from Winona huddled with their men on the main street of Elysian and discussed their next move. They had been struggling down the roads and byways around the town all day looking for the outlaws. Their horses were exhausted, and as nightfall approached, the posses had gone into Elysian to give the animals and men a rest. It was a good opportunity to warm their throats with a few shots of their favorite "medicine." As they talked over their situation, Judson Jones, the leader of a small volunteer posse, intruded into Brisette's exclusive circle.

"Say, Brisette," Jones said, walking up to the detective and interrupting his discussion. "I'm Judson Jones, head of the Le Sueur posse. I've got something I want to talk over with you."

"You'll have to wait until we're through with our present business," Brisette answered curtly.

"There's no time for that," objected Jones. "I've got some important information about the outlaws."

"All right, let's have it," replied the reluctant Brisette, more than a little irritated by the intrusion from this upstart. "Make it quick. Dill and I have important matters to discuss."

"It's this," Jones said. "I've been talking to the locals. They say there's an island out in the slough north of here that's a hangout for crooks and thieves. They say that's where the outlaws are likely to be. I'm convinced they're right."

"What makes you so sure they are there?" Brisette countered brusquely. "They could be anywhere in these wild woods."

"You mean you're not going to check the island?" Jones replied, irritated by Brisette's response. "Then I'll go there myself with some of my men."

"You'll do nothing of the sort!" Brisette said heatedly. "We don't want the woods filled with amateurs and lunatics shooting at anything that moves. If anyone goes to the island, it'll be Dill and me. And I don't know as we intend to. But I want you to stay away from that island. We don't want people running into our line of fire."

"That's telling him, John," Sheriff Dill broke in. "We've got enough problems without unauthorized, roving bands. We'll decide how this hunt will be conducted, Jones." Jones stalked off angrily and told his men that they would have to forget about the island.

Meanwhile, back at Northfield, the bodies of Jim Chadwell and Clell Miller had been misidentified. Miller was identified as Chadwell and Chadwell as Charlie Pitts. This identification, made by the noted Cincinnati detective Larry Hazen, held up for two weeks. Nobody had taken the time, however, to tell Pitts of his recent demise; he might have argued that they had stretched the truth a bit.

When the rain continued in earnest, Brisette and Hoy jumped aboard the 4:00 P.M. train and rattled off to St. Paul and Minneapolis. Brisette was soon back in his comfortable home in St. Paul, garbed in his favorite robe, and standing by the fire, toasting his backside. His wife had made him a toddy, and he sipped on it luxuriously.

"Ah, Mary, this hits the spot!"

"I'm so glad you were able to get back tonight, my dear," his wife said soothingly. "It's horrid out. But don't you think the outlaws may get away?" she asked.

"There is no way, simply no way," Brisette replied. "We have 'em corralled in the woods, men all around 'em. We have 'em locked in a trap. Tomorrow morning, I will return to Elysian and finish 'em."

What Brisette did not know was that most of his men had turned in for the night also, at the town of Elysian, and only a few guards remained in the woods on the remote chance that the outlaws were on the move.

"I'm so proud of you, my dear," Brisette's wife said, inflating her breasts to the ultimate dimension allowed by her tight corset.

Across the river in Minneapolis, Detective and Mrs. Hoy were having a similar conversation, the only difference being that her husband had a tall glass of clear Bourbon in his paw. Frank James knew his enemies well.

Around 9:00 P.M., Frank realized that the rain was not letting up. He eased out from under the tent where the outlaws lay and rose to his feet and looked at the sky. While it was dark and rainy, there was enough light to see, if only barely. That indicated that the clouds were thinning and the moon was likely rising above them. Thirty minutes later, Frank looked outside the tent again and craned his neck skyward. The rain still pelted down but not as severely as before. And, yes, it was getting lighter, all right. It was getting a lot lighter, he thought. Above the clouds, there must be a moon. A cynical grin spread over Frank's face, and he returned to the tent.

"Boys," he said, waking the napping men, "this is our chance! The rain is letting up, and it's gettin' light enough to move. The lawmen have us surrounded, but I'm guessing there are few of them at their posts. It's miserable out, and they think we will sit tight. Yes, it's right for us. It's our chance, boys. We *must* move on! What do you say?"

His speech was met at first with silence in the tent and a few deep groans. The idea was disagreeable to all of them. Then the men began shuffling nervously. Finally, Jesse broke the silence.

"Buck is right. We must move. They have us corralled, but they won't be expectin' us to move now, so it's the perfect time!"

Cole turned toward his brothers, "Jim, Bobby, can you fellas make it?"

Both men answered yes without hesitation. Neither of them felt like moving, of course, but they knew that it was absolutely necessary if the gang were to escape. To stay where they were was to ensure a noose for all their necks. The men all rose and prepared their gear.

Soon the outlaws were pawing their way through the woods in the rain and darkness. As they moved through the brush, branches slapped their faces and tore at their arms and legs. They squinted to avoid the effects of this pummeling and groped their way westward, off the island, and through a flooded marsh. They made their way onto soggy but solid ground again, where they picked up the pace. Several times, they were forced to stop to allow Bob and Jim, who were the most severely wounded, to rest. Frank and Cole used homemade canes to steady themselves. The going was rough for all of them, but the men hobbled along the best they could.

Occasionally, the outlaws stopped to look at their compasses, a difficult task. At these times, one of the outlaws held a compass in one hand, shielding it from the rain with his other. A second outlaw illuminated the compass dial with a match, attempting to shield the flame from the wind. In this way, the gang set their course for Marysburg, six miles to the west. That town, they believed, was outside the cordon the lawmen had placed around them at Elysian. They knew, however, that once the posses learned of their breakout, they would move quickly to corral them again. Before that could happen, the outlaws hoped to find a refuge, an abandoned house or some place to hide. As they passed through the woods, they saw fires in the distance and occasionally heard the loud voices of the guards left by the posses.

At dawn on September 10, the rain stopped, and the sky grew light. Soon, they came across a church. After looking at their map, they concluded it was the one at Marysburg. They moved farther north, where they entered a dense stand of hard maple, basswood, and white and red elm. They desperately needed a place to hide. Continuing through the woods for some distance, they came upon a small stream and entered it to destroy their trail. For the next quarter-mile, they walked in the cold, wet streambed. Finally, Frank, who led the procession, raised his hand.

"Okay, boys. Here's where we turn. Leave as little sign of our passing as possible. We'll head into the woods for several hundred yards and make camp."

When the men left the stream, Jesse, who had been walking at the rear of the procession as a guard, followed and then walked backwards for a hundred feet, erasing the outlaws' tracks with the sole of his boot as best he could. Then he caught up with the rest of the men. Because of Jesse's excellent marksmanship, he usually acted as the rear guard when the outlaws were on the march. For that reason, the posses were already aware of his peculiar footprint, small in size with a square toe and narrow, high-heel print.

"Let's make our camp here," Frank said as they reached a small clearing. "We'll push on to Mankato later tonight."

September 11, 1876

Buuuuuuuck! Buuuuuuuck! Buuuuuuuck! Jim Younger slid his hands underneath a squawking hen and grabbed her legs.

He reached for the hen's neck with his other hand and silenced her. Turning around in the moonlight, he exited the hencoop as quickly as his legs would carry him. Behind him, he could hear the farmer's dogs wailing in the distance. The farmer might check to see what the racket was, so Jim ran into the woods with his prize. After several hundred yards, he slowed his gait to a walk. He reached down and cut off the chicken's head with his pocketknife and let it bleed. He felt miserable. He never thought the day would come when he would be raiding henhouses. He thought that was about as low as you could go. But it was necessary, he knew.

Jim looked around him and attempted to get his bearings. The moon was full, so it was relatively easy for him to find his way. It was a long trek back to camp, but at least he had gotten some food for the boys. It had made him feel useless depending on the others for food the last few days. He wanted to be responsible for his own survival. For that reason, he had been the first to volunteer for tonight's raid. The gang was staying in an abandoned house on the Kron farm near Mankato and had eluded the police so far. But sooner or later, Jim reckoned, the police and the posses would learn of the house and surround them. The only reason the gang hadn't pushed on was to allow him and Bob a chance to regain their strength. Jim felt bad about that. But Frank and Cole were hobbling around too; they were all in poor condition.

Unknown to Jim, earlier that day, four wagonloads of picked men and scouts from St. Paul, led by Chief of Police James King, had traveled to Mankato from Northfield with needlenose guns, fine European weapons. Sheriff Dill and three men from Winona County and Detective Brisette and his squad of eight were also on the road from Janesville, headed for Marysburg. In addition, Minneapolis chief of police Munger, Chief Detective Hoy, and Officers West, Hankinson, and Shepherd—with Henry repeating rifles and three hundred rounds of ammunition—were in the Marysburg area. A multitude of uncounted sheriffs and their men, as well as volunteers from the surrounding towns, were also in the field.

The next afternoon, September 12, the outlaws were still in their abandoned house ten miles northeast of Mankato. After eating lunch, they gathered to discuss their situation. The James boys thought it was time for the gang to split up. Most of the outlaws, with the exception of Jim and Bob, were now in passable physical condition. If the gang hoped to escape the area, some of them needed to make a run for it, break through the police lines, and flee southwest toward Sioux City and Dakota Territory. Once some of them broke through the lines, it would take the pressure off the rest, who could either hole up to recuperate or flee along a different route.

Frank started the discussion: "Boys, it's time we separate. We're surrounded. Sooner or later, the posses will catch up to us if we don't move on. We've been lucky so far, but it will happen; they'll be on us, and it will be impossible for us to fight 'em off. If we split up, we will give them something to think about. It has hardly occurred to them that we might become six targets instead of one.

"We need to split up into at least two units. Jesse and I have decided to attempt an escape. When we make our dash, it'll take the heat off the rest of you. You will have to decide how you want to travel, but Jesse and I will go together. We'll take one more man, if one wants to come. What do you say?"

"Yes, I've been thinkin' the same," Cole began. "My concern has been for Jim and Bob. But they're better. We don't want to hold the rest of you back. We'll go together and either run or hole up somewhere. If Pitts wants to go with us, that's fine too. That's up to him. What do you say, Charlie?" Cole asked, turning toward Pitts. Charlie yanked on his mustache nervously. He liked the Youngers.

"I'll go with the Youngers," Pitts replied. Cole looked relieved; he could use Charlie's help.

"Tomorrow night," Frank explained, "we'll cross the Blue Earth River using one of the bridges—whichever is least guarded. I understand there's a covered bridge over the river and a railroad one nearby. If we have to, we'll shoot our way across. What do you say, boys? Once across the bridge, we'll separate and go our own ways."

"Agreed," Cole answered. "What time do we move?"

"We'll start after midnight," Frank replied, "when they least expect us to be on the move. After we cross the bridge, an absolute hell will break loose! They'll be confused and runnin' in every direction like chickens with their heads cut off. That'll give us a chance to break out."

"Tomorrow morning, we'll head for Mankato and find a place to hole up for the day. Then, when it's dark, we'll make our move."

September 13, 1876

In the early-morning light, the gang pulled up stakes and headed southwest toward Mankato. It was raining hard again. As they walked through a pasture beyond the Kron farm, they crossed the path of a cowherd named Jeff Dunning who was tending cattle. Once they saw Dunning, it was too late to conceal themselves, so they approached him. Dunning was a farmhand for a farmer named Shaubut, who lived near the Kron farm.

"Ho! Good man!" Cole Younger hailed the herder.

"Good morning," Dunning replied as Cole and the other outlaws walked up to him. Dunning noticed that the men wore blankets under their raincoats, which he thought odd. And they had bridles, with sets of spurs tied to them, strung over their shoulders; also odd, he thought. He looked the men over carefully with that rustic nosiness born of a solitary life; he didn't like what he saw. He also noticed sizable bulges protruding from their raincoats at about waist height. They looked like rough customers to him.

"Say, good fellow," Cole said, making easy conversation with

the farmhand, "what brings you out so early in the rain?"
"Just tendin' my cows," Dunning answered blankly.
"Mighty fine cattle, too," Cole replied. He looked Dunning
over carefully, examining his face for any signs of suspicion.
The farmhand looking at him was a picture of raging curiosity.
Cole knew they would have to take him in tow.
"I suppose you know who we are?" Cole said coyly to the
cowherd.
"I reckon I do," Dunning answered foolishly.
"Who?" Cole countered.
"Maybe some of them Missouri boys," Dunning replied dryly.
"No, we come from a lot farther away than that," Younger
lied, drawing his Colt revolver and shoving it into Dunning's
chest. "You appear to be a bright fellow, though, just as I had
supposed. Charlie, make a harness for this man with your
bridle straps. He's lookin' for cows, but first he must show us
the way to Mankato." Pitts took one strand of a set of reins and
looped it through Dunning's belt, making a sort of rough leash.
"What's your name, cowherd?" Cole asked Dunning.
"Uh, Jefferson," the man said.
"No last name?"
"It's Dunning. What's yours?"
"Jansen," Younger claimed, keeping a straight face. "Jim
Jansen. And these men are my brothers."
Cole took out a small notebook and put Dunning's full name
in it. "Well, Jeff, my good man, we are going to keep you on a
short leash while you show us the way to Mankato. For now, I
want you to walk across yon road. Walk slowly; we'll be directly
behind you."
Dunning walked across the Wardlaw Ravine road at the head
of his leash. As he moved, the bandits, one at a time, stepped
into his tracks so that only one man's footprints appeared after
they had passed.
The men walked for several miles out of view of the road.
Finally, they stopped for a few minutes and tied Dunning to a

tree. In hushed tones, they talked to one another concerning his fate. The Jameses thought that if Dunning were released, he would run immediately to the police. For that reason, they thought he should be killed. The Youngers, however, thought Dunning should be spared. Pitts suggested an alternative, that Dunning be left tied to a tree, but the Youngers thought that he might die if no one found him soon. All agreed that Dunning was now impeding their movement, and they decided to let him go.

"All right, Dunning," Cole finally said, walking back to the cowherd and unfastening the bridle straps girding his body. "We've decided to let you go, but we have your name. If you should be so foolish as to run to the police, we will be certain to search you out and kill you. Do you understand that?"

"I reckon I do," Dunning replied with a sober face.

"So, shoo! Good morning to you!" Younger said to him.

As Dunning walked away, Jesse followed him with his eyes: "I still think we should shoot that man. Dead men tell no tales." Dunning was too obtuse to even shudder at this remark.

Before turning Dunning loose, Younger had taken his matches; they would need them. After leaving the outlaws, Dunning immediately ran back to his employer, Shaubut, and within an hour, Shaubut was galloping for Mankato to carry the news of the outlaws to the posses staked out in the town.

The result was predictable: mayhem broke loose. The streets of Mankato soon teemed with citizens, posses, onlookers, newspapermen, children, old coots, and the village crank, all seeking information. Meanwhile, the telegraph wires chattered to Minneapolis and St. Paul. Thirty more stands of arms were on their way by the next train. At the same time, Brisette and Hoy, the detective chiefs, rallied their men and entered the woods, this time on foot. Hoy set out with Munger, Mayor Ames of Minneapolis, and Officers Hankinson, Shepherd, West, and Tinsley. The posses led by Sheriffs Dill of Winona County, Davis of Faribault, Finch of Blue Earth, Barton of Rice, and Deputy

Sheriff Harrison of Ramsey were also in the field in force. Men clambered through the hills and ravines around Mankato like colonies of ants. This time, the lawmen were better organized. Gen. George Pope of Mankato—cool-headed, experienced, with the confidence of former army commands—had assumed overall command of the pursuit and set up headquarters at the Clifton House hotel in Mankato. Out of this headquarters sped messengers to the various posses and police instructing them where to set up their picket lines and informing them of replacement schedules. The ten square miles of country swarmed with lawmen and pickets. Mayor Wiswell of Mankato provided the men with supplies and teams of horses. The chase had now become a well-orchestrated hunt.

During the day, two men calling themselves John Schaffer and George Krunz were arrested. Schaffer and Krunz told the arresting officers that they were poor grasshopper farmers who had been ruined recently in Dakota Territory. Dubbed "suspicious looking" and "mysterious" by authorities, they were chained and carried to the Mankato jail. Within hours, several other men were arrested, one of whom claimed to be the advance agent for a Dr. Menoway.

Meanwhile, at 8:00 A.M., just outside Mankato, the James-Younger gang had settled down to an excellent breakfast at the home of Graf Stolzburg. Within an hour, they began searching for a foolproof hideout.

18

September 14, 1876

The gang crept through the dark woods cresting the hill overlooking the Blue Earth River. As they stumbled over branches, they made snapping and rustling noises, but the lawmen stationed in the area seemed unaware of their passage. Several hundred yards to the south, the dark silhouette of a covered bridge loomed. A railroad trestle lay a hundred yards farther upstream, beyond the outlaws' vision but known to them.

"There she is," Frank whispered to the other men. "We must check her out."

Charlie Pitts leaned over and scooped up several small rocks. "Let me do it," he said. "The rest of you stay here."

Within a few minutes, Pitts had positioned himself on the bluff overlooking the bridge. Reaching into his pocket, he drew out a small stone and hurled it at the bridge some one hundred or so feet away. A muffled thud sounded. A number of seconds later, a dark figure emerged from the shadows, walked over to the bridge, and looked up at its roof. Satisfied that he had heard nothing more than a creak in the wooden structure, he retired into the darkness. Pitts made his way back to the outlaws.

"It's guarded," he whispered.

The gang trudged along the bluff until they reached the road leading to the covered bridge. They crossed the road quickly and proceeded to the second bridge.

"I'll test this one too," Pitts said in a low voice.

Creeping closer, he raised his arm and flung several small stones. This time, he missed the bridge, and the rocks fell into some nearby bushes, making a faint noise. No one emerged to check on it, so Pitts cupped his hands and made the muffled cry of a bird, signaling his comrades forward. Soon, they gathered around him.

"No one showed," Pitts said.

Frank replied in a whisper, "Let's be watchful. They may just be hiding. If anyone fires," he said, turning to the other clustered men, "make it hot for 'em and keep movin'."

The outlaws scrambled down onto the railroad right of way and stumbled along the rails leading to the bridge. It was raining lightly. When they got to the bridge, Frank turned to the others. "Careful, it's slippery," he whispered.

Leading the way but encumbered by his wound, Frank groped along the bridge supports, struggling to keep his balance. The others, carrying their bridles over their shoulders, followed. Beneath the bridge, hidden from sight, two men and a boy looked up fearfully at the shadowy figures. They had heard the earlier rustling in the bushes and chosen to remain silent. Finally, the boy turned to the other guards.

"Ain't we going to shoot?" he whispered.

Neither of the older men answered. The guards watched as the six outlaws groped and teetered their way across the bridge and disappeared into the darkness. The older men had wanted no gunplay. After all, they had wives and children at home to think about. They had volunteered to serve as bridge guards on a rainy, miserable night, hoping to see a good show. They'd seen it but hadn't wanted to be a part of it.

"I'm going for help," the young boy said disgustedly and headed over the bluff to the other bridge. Once he reached the bridge guards there, he told them that the outlaws had passed through, and one of the guards left to spread the general alarm. As Frank had expected, pandemonium broke loose. Within fifteen minutes, General Pope had roused his men at the Mankato hotel. Leaping out of their beds, they yanked on their clothes and raced into the woods surrounding the town. The citizens were also awakened from their sleep. But it was a dark and rainy night, and the search for the outlaws proved futile.

During the night, the James brothers and the Youngers separated. By sunup, the Youngers, accompanied by Charlie Pitts, had walked ten miles in a southwesterly direction and were approaching Minneopa Falls, where they made camp. Pitts, who was in the best condition of the four men, went foraging. He returned shortly with a young turkey and three pullets taken from the roost of a minister who lived nearby. Pitts flung the birds down next to the small fire the men had kindled and leaned against a tree to rest.

"Well, I got some," he said to the other men proudly. Jim and Bob beamed at the sight of the birds and began plucking them roughly as Cole stirred the fire to generate more heat. Once the chickens were plucked, they were tossed into the flames, and the tongues of fire cleaned them thoroughly. There was no time to create a spit and roast the birds. Cole threw a few ears of corn into the fire, shucks and all; he had gathered them during their night's walk. While the men were concerned about the smoke the fire made, they were starving and determined to eat at all costs.

Nearby, the posse of Mike Hoy and Mayor Ames was tracking the outlaws, pursuing the gang through the night on foot.

"Look, smoke!" Hoy exclaimed, noting the faint wisps of smoke rising from the trees directly ahead. The lawmen quickened their steps.

"It's them," Ames said to Hoy, and they scrambled through the woods excitedly.

"Yes!" Hoy answered, turning toward the other officers.

"Unlock your safeties, boys! Careful with your fire; other lawmen are in the area."

Pitts and the Youngers heard the noise of scrambling feet and muffled voices in the woods adjacent to their camp. Snatching their gear, the outlaws hurtled headlong into the brush. Stumbling through the darkness, they rushed southward and away from the lawmen's voices. Behind them, they heard the booming Hoy: "Keep to the right, boys!"

Moments later, Hoy shouted again, "To the left, men!" Every time Cole heard Hoy call out, he steered the outlaws in the opposite direction.

Finally, the outlaws were headed directly west and slowed their pace to a fast walk. After covering about a mile, they slowed the pace again and slanted to the southwest. For the time being, they had eluded the police. Meanwhile, the posse was more interested in examining the outlaws' campground and the remains of their meal than in catching them.

A mile north of the Youngers and two miles west, Frank and Jesse James walked through a dense wood. They were moving in the same general direction as the Youngers. Around 11:00 A.M., they entered a wild area scarred with deep ravines. They came upon a small stream and entered it for several hundred yards to erase their tracks. Then, turning right, the brothers moved into the woods along a ravine, leaving as few signs of their passing as possible. Continuing along the ravine for several hundred yards, they reached a small clearing and stopped.

"This should do," Jesse said, turning to Frank.

"Yes, let's camp here till nightfall," Frank replied. "There's too many of 'em after us to continue in daylight."

The brothers threw down their bridles and set up a temporary camp. Soon they were fast asleep.

After dark, they roused themselves and set off over the top of the hill, emerging once more onto level ground. The moon was bright, and they continued their course due west, striding at a slow gait to preserve their energy. When they found a rough trail, they trekked down it for more than a mile. They had chosen to stay off the main roads, believing that was where the bulk of the lawmen would be found. The trail they followed was little more than a primitive path, but it finally intersected with a more established road, which went generally westward.

Traveling along this lane, they came upon a cleared section of land. Inside the fence to the left of the road, barely distinguishable, were cattle munching on the rank grass. Ahead, they saw the dim silhouette of a house, and beyond that a corral and barn. It was past midnight and the house was dark. The farmer and his family were probably asleep, Frank assumed. As they approached the farmhouse, a chorus of yelping hounds sang out. The brothers quickly skirted the house and headed directly for the corral and barn. If the noise woke the farmer, he would think his animals were baying at stray dogs or a bitch in heat, Frank reckoned. As they bypassed the house, the brothers walked by a small garden. Jesse leaped over the rail enclosing it and snapped off several ears of green corn, stuffing them into the pockets of his raincoat. Neither man had eaten recently, so the food was an important find.

The brothers headed for the corral and looked through the fence. Their eyes lit up. At the other end of the paddock was a black gelding. Only one horse, Frank thought, in disappointment. If there had only been another! Then, despite his desperate condition, he remembered Shakespeare's words in *Richard III:* "A horse! My kingdom for a horse!" Frank smiled. That's what he liked about the man: he talked about life.

When they had taken the corn moments earlier, they had thought only of eating it. Now it would be useful in capturing the horse. Jesse walked over to the fence and extended an ear of corn toward the animal, at the same time talking softly, soothingly, monotonously, attempting to calm it. The horse turned toward the brothers, pricked up his ears, and stared at them intently. Then the horse took several steps toward them and stopped. Jesse pulled the shucks from the corn and split the ear in two, throwing one of the halves on the ground in front of the horse. The horse looked at the corn for a moment, approached it, then gnawed on it with his large teeth. Taking the ear into his mouth, the horse ate it. Then he looked at the brothers expectantly.

Jesse continued to talk to the horse and reached the other piece of corn over the fence. As the horse walked toward the brothers, Frank stepped backwards slowly, out of the way; this was Jesse's show. With the ear extended from his left hand, Jesse reached into his right pocket and pulled out a short length of rope and unraveled it, letting one end drop to the ground. When the horse reached for the corn, Jesse let him nibble on it. He pulled his left arm slowly backward, forcing the horse to move closer—then stretch his head and neck over the fence—as he nibbled. With the horse's neck arching over the fence, Jesse reached his right arm stealthily over the horse's mane and dropped the rope around the animal's neck. He reached under the horse's chin with his right hand and grabbed both ends of the rope and tightened it slowly. He had him a horse! Jesse led the horse slowly along the fence toward a nearby gate.

"Buck," Jesse said to his brother quietly, "open the gate, and I'll bring this critter out where we can work on him properly." Frank walked slowly over to the gate and opened it, and Jesse led the horse out of the corral. While Jesse held the horse, Frank installed its bit and bridle. With this done, Frank led the horse over to the corral fence and Jesse scaled it and mounted. Jesse reached down and pulled his brother up behind him.

Well, Frank thought as they rode off, they might only be riding bareback, and they were double mounted, it was true, but they would make a run for it now, get as far away from the pickets and guards as they could, head for the open prairie. They'd find another horse later.

"Okay, brother," Frank said, "let's see what this nag will do."

Jesse jabbed the horse with his heels, and the brothers trotted away from the farm in a westerly direction.

Gen. George Pope, in the meantime, had established a twelve-mile arc of pickets along the roads and bridges to the north and south of Lake Crystal to snare the James gang when it rode through. The James brothers were riding toward Luma Lake, south of Lake Crystal and thirteen miles west of Mankato, and heading right into Pope's trap. The road they were traveling on was a dirt track that led to the western Minnesota prairie. While most of the pickets who manned the bridges and roads around Lake Crystal were members of organized posses or the Minneapolis and St. Paul police, the remote bridge the Jameses were headed for was guarded by a group of young boys placed there for the night. They carried crude, single-shot rifles and shotguns, hoping against all logic to stop the experienced gunmen if they chanced to ride their way.

Because there were so many roads and trails blazed through the area, the leading lawman thought only a small chance existed that the bridge guarded by the young boys would be the outlaws' route. The boys themselves were cavalier about their roles, and once it began raining, all but one of them found a dry place under some nearby trees to pass the night. The rain was coming down in earnest now, and only Richard Roberts, a boy with a more hopeful imagination than the rest, thought it possible that the robbers might pass their way, and he stuck stubbornly to his post.

About 1:00 A.M., the rain eased and Roberts heard an odd noise coming from the east—a sort of sucking, smacking sound. He didn't recognize it, but it was the sound of horses' hooves engaging and disengaging the muddy road. Soon, the noise became louder and a horse, double-mounted, came around a curve in the road and approached Roberts.

"Who's there?" challenged Roberts as the dark figures approached him.

"Giddup!" shouted one of the riders and the horse spun around in the middle of the road.

Roberts raised his rifle and pulled the trigger, his dreams of adventure a reality. His gun boomed, and the horse in front of Roberts bolted, throwing its two riders to the ground. Jesse and Frank James, thrown from the back of their horse and astonished by the rapidity of what was happening, pulled themselves to their feet and ran for the nearby woods. Roberts fumbled for another cartridge. By the time he had his rifle loaded again, everything was silent and the outlaws were out of sight. Roberts walked over to where the men had fallen and picked up a large felt hat. A hole pierced its crown; he hadn't missed the bandits by much, he exulted.

The James brothers scrambled south through the woods for some time and then slowed down and walked westward. By 3:00 A.M., they had traveled four miles, passed through a cornfield owned by a farmer named Rooney, and entered a pasture owned by a man named Seymour. They saw a corral and large barn owned by George Rockwood, a local farmer, and made a beeline toward it. They peered through the corral's fence and rejoiced. The best looking team of grays they'd seen in ages—magnificent horses—were at the far end of the corral. All the brothers lacked were bridles.

The James boys entered the barn adjacent to the corral, and Frank reached into his pocket and pulled out a match to light. The brothers made their way to the tack room and after lighting several matches, they discovered some bridles. Returning to the corral with two of the bridles in hand, the brothers played the same trick they had used earlier on the black horse. The dominant gray responded first to their lure, followed minutes later by the other gray, which was already becoming chummy. Through extremely good fortune, they soon were mounted on one of the county's finest teams.

Setting a course for Lamberton, Minnesota, fifty-five miles to the west, they brought their horses to a steady trot, covering as much ground as possible and placing as many miles as they could between themselves and the posses. Once they reached the country beyond Lake Crystal, the brothers followed the main road west, quickly outstripping their pursuers. That was Frank's strategy, to move unsparingly, at a relentless pace, onto the prairie. The lawmen likely would judge the outlaws' progress modestly. But the James boys were creating their own break-neck standard, one that astonished and befuddled their pursuers and gave the outlaws a big head start. When the lawmen finally received telegraph word of the outlaws' whereabouts from people who had seen them pass, they were forced to carry their posses by rail to locations where they thought the outlaws might be. At these drop-off points, the lawmen would have to rent or buy fresh horses, all the time guessing when, where, or more importantly, if the Jameses would show or if they had already passed through that area. The James brothers doubted the posses were well enough led to catch them in this way, to pursue two men over this vast, nearly trackless prairie. In the meantime, the Youngers had virtually disappeared as far as the posses were concerned.

At sundown, Frank and Jesse rode up to a house five miles south of Lamberton, a stop on the Winona-St. Peter Railroad. They had traveled an amazing fifty-five miles that day. Frank, barely able to walk because of their rigorous, saddleless ride, knocked at the door of a German farmer.

"Vat you boyss vant?" the old German greeted them when he answered the door.

"We'd like a place to stay tonight," Frank replied. Frank hated Germans; he'd hated them since the war, but he would play nice with this German if it meant a bed and a meal.

"Vell, come in. I find place for you. Vat's de madder vid you boyss? Why you cripplin' 'round so?" He was also puzzled at why they were wearing raincoats, as it wasn't raining, but he kept the question to himself.

"We rolled our wagon over just east of here," Jesse replied as he entered the German's parlor. "We got roughed up."

"Vere you boyss headin'?" the German asked.

"Lamberton, come tomorrow," Jesse replied. "How're the roads that way?"

"Oh, dey okay, I guess. You got good horses, boyss. Dey get you dere."

"Yeh," Jesse answered. "Old Bob and Betty are good nags, all right."

"How are the roads past Lamberton?"

"Vell, it's been vile since I been dat vay. Dey vass good den," the German answered.

Before the brothers turned in for the night, they bought some grain and grain bags, rope, and a small quantity of hay from the German. They quickly jury-rigged functional equivalents of saddles using bags of straw, and pieces of rope were employed for girths and stirrups. The bags of hay, they hoped, would protect their sore butts from the pounding punishment caused by the jostling of their horses over the rough prairie. After long hours riding bareback, the brothers could scarcely stand or sit down. Even after rigging their horses with hay saddles in this way, whenever they would dismount the next day, to drink or to relieve themselves, they would be in excruciating pain.

After leading the James brothers to a spare bedroom, the German looked for an old sheet to use for bandages. Frank had told him that he had injured himself in the accident, but as the farmer helped bandage up the leg, he noticed that the wound looked like an old one. It also looked remarkably like the injury caused by a bullet. The German kept this idle reflection to himself. What was it to him? Their wounds cared for, the brothers fell instantly to sleep.

At sunup the next morning, September 16, Frank and Jesse mounted their grays and rode west. They had crossed a number of rivers and streams, left the woods, and were now on the open prairie. Several times that day, they stopped at clear streams and dismounted to drink. Stooping down, they cupped their hands full of water and raised the cool liquid to their mouths to swallow. When they got up, they could barely straighten their stiff, aching backs. Jesse helped Frank mount his horse by knitting his hands to form a stirrup; Frank helped his brother in turn. Frank's wound made it hard for him to get around, and as they grew weaker, the brothers were forced to mount their horses by scaling fences and sliding into their saddles.

Around 2:00 P.M., the brothers had ridden twenty-five miles and were five miles south of Lake Shetek, near the Des Moines River. So far, no one had blocked their path, and they had seen no lawmen, but they were convinced they were close behind. The brothers were hungry, so they stopped near a river crossing at a farm owned by a man named Swan. When they knocked at the door of the farmhouse, the farmer's wife answered the door as her husband was away on business.

"Good afternoon, gentlemen," she greeted them.

"Afternoon, ma'am," Jesse replied. "We've just had a wagon accident on the prairie, got ourselves banged up a bit and lost our wagon. We're headed toward Pipestone and we're nearly starved. We'd sure appreciate it if you'd provide us with somethin' to eat. We've money to pay for it."

"Why, come in, men. Take off your coats," she said. "Have you fellows been traveling through a shower?" she continued, noting the raincoats they wore to conceal their guns.

"Nope, ma'am," Jesse answered. "We lost most of our clothes with our wrecked wagon, and the sun's been beatin' down on us so blamed fierce that we're usin' these coats for protection.

"But, ma'am," Jesse continued, "you don't need to trouble yourself with hostin' us. We've got an important meetin' in Pipestone. If you'd just bring the food out to us and hand it up to us on our horses, that'd do plumb fine." Knowing they might need to ride away quickly, Jesse and Frank wanted to stay on their horses to keep a close lookout for posses. And it was very painful for them to mount and dismount.

After several minutes, Mrs. Swan brought a pitcher of milk, some glasses, and some buttered bread. The James brothers sought to control their enthusiasm over the food; they were literally starving. As they reached for the glasses of milk, their eyes noticeably bulged in anticipation.

"Ma'am," Jesse said. "Would you happen to have any cooked meat on hand?"

"Sir, I'm sorry, but I haven't started dinner yet," she replied.

Within ten minutes, the outlaws were on their way again, this time at a fast walk, the only gait left in their exhausted horses. The brothers were headed toward Worthington, twenty-eight miles to the south.

While Jesse and Frank made their way across the prairie, the detectives and various posses were in hot pursuit. After learning of the outlaws' breakout at Luna Lake, they had organized their forces for the chase. On the night of September 15, Det. Mike Hoy and his party debarked from a train at Lamberton and set up camp at Three Lakes, thirteen miles south of the town and eight miles south of the homestead where the Jameses were putting up for the night. Sheriff Barton and his men were about three miles south of Hoy. The next day, Saturday, September 16, at 10:00 A.M., Sheriff Dill and his posse left a train at Lake Shetek and proceeded west of the lake ten miles. When they left the train, they were on the same course as the James, but now they were going in the wrong direction. Other posses were responding to false reports that the outlaws had been sighted near various southern Minnesota villages. The lawmen were searching for needles in a haystack.

The James boys continued south from Swan's place and reached the last house on the frontier at 4:00 P.M. By nightfall they had come upon a road ten miles west of Worthington. They turned right and headed for Luverne, a town not far from Dakota Territory. Along the way they passed the home of Charles Drury. Drury's yard was filled with hitched horses, so they rode by without stopping.

That night, Sheriff Town of Worthington received word of the outlaws' presence. Drury had reported seeing two men fitting the description of the outlaws passing his home. Town organized a thirty-man posse the next morning, but he was a number of hours and miles behind the outlaws. Meanwhile, in the early-morning hours, an express train from Worthington steamed into Luverne, warning the townsmen there of the outlaws' expected arrival.

At midnight, Detective Brisette and his men arrived in Worthington and embarked on horseback for Luverne, directly on the outlaws' trail but six hours behind. When he failed to encounter them on the way to Luverne, he promptly jumped on a train and headed back to St. Paul where he was met by a warm bed and other amenities.

At 10:30 A.M. on Sunday morning, September 17, the Jameses approached the Rolfe farmstead on the Rock River, eight miles northeast of Luverne. By this time, to protect their horses from complete exhaustion, they had dismounted, using their horses only to carry their gear. The outlaws were desperately in need of fresh horses, and their pace had dropped to less than two miles an hour.

When the brothers reached the Rolfe farm, they knocked at the farmer's front door. Rolfe's wife answered, Mr. Rolfe having gone to town to buy some supplies. Mrs. Rolfe was surprised at the beaten and miserable men at her doorstep.

"Good morning, gents," she said to the men.

"Mornin', ma'am," Jesse replied. "Could we bother you for breakfast?"

Mrs. Rolfe looked the men over carefully. Aside from their rough appearance, they looked decent enough, she thought, just down in the tooth. She noticed that the toes of the men's boots were red from walking through the grasslands, and one man, the one with a black beard, had on fancy boots with high, narrow heels and square toes. They could be the boots of a dandy or gambler, she reflected. Their horses, two grays, looked like they had had the life run out of them, and the exhausted animals stood in the yard, their heads drooping. She bet they needed water too. It was a bizarre sight, the bedraggled men, worn-out horses, and the rope stirrups and hay saddles. "You men look in mighty rough shape," Mrs. Rolfe said. "What have you been doing? You look sick."

"Well, ma'am," Jesse answered, "we wrecked our buggy a few miles back, and my partner here busted two of his ribs. As for myself, my rheumatism is hurtin' right smart," Jesse said as a way of explaining the two men's lack of mobility. "Is there a telegraph office in Luverne where I can wire my wife about our situation?" Jesse asked.

"Why, sure," Mrs. Rolfe replied. Jesse and Frank nodded at the answer, trying not to show disappointment. The brothers knew that if there was a telegraph office at Luverne, the law likely knew the direction they were heading. For that reason, they resolved to avoid the town.

As the James brothers walked into her house, Mrs. Rolfe wondered if they were telling her the truth. Both of the men, though young, shuffled like old gandies.

"Would you like some tea?" Mrs. Rolfe asked them.

"No, ma'am," Jesse answered. "But we'd sure like to have some milk and bread if you've got any." He knew that was about all these poor farmers could spare.

The outlaws sat down at the Rolfes' table and slumped in their chairs. "You sure you men aren't sick?" Mrs. Rolfe said. "I'll go for a doctor if you like." She set a pitcher of milk down on the table.

"We're okay," Jesse assured her, "just a little weak from our accident."

Mrs. Rolfe noticed that one of them, the one with the sandy mustache and stubble beard who hadn't spoken at all, weaved from side to side as if he were going to fall out of his chair any moment. She was concerned about the condition of the men.

After Jesse and Frank had eaten, they left the house and returned to their horses. They led them to a watering tank and allowed them to drink. Then they pulled the horses over to a fence and slid painfully onto their backs. They set off at a slow walk in a westerly direction. The horses seemed finished, Mrs. Rolfe thought, as she watched the men ride off at a snail's pace.

The outlaws eventually passed through an area of high pinnacles and ravines where they dismounted again and led their horses to protect their strength. Near nightfall, they remounted the animals and approached the house of a man named Nelson. As they neared the home, they found its owner sitting on a fence, smoking his pipe.

"Howdy," Frank said. "How's it goin', my friend?"

Nelson, a garrulous fellow, began a long-winded account concerning the condition of his crops, the weather, the state of the union, and the general nature of his asthma. As he did so, he interspersed his palaver by puffing on a pipe, sucking on it, and twiddling the instrument as if it were a child's toy. He confirmed Frank's belief about pipe smokers: if a fella smokes a pipe, you might just as well forget him. Finally, Frank interrupted Nelson's endless monologue.

"Hey, grandpa, are you goin' to sit on that fence all night?"

"Well," Nelson replied, "I guess not. I ought to check up on the missus. No telling what that old girl's up to. When I talked to her some while ago, she was just a fussin' and a rearin' and comportin' herself—you know what I mean—and a carryin' on. I don't know about that old lady!" Nelson reluctantly turned over his pipe and meticulously dropped the ashes onto the ground, it seemed to Frank almost a grain at a time. Nelson returned with slow steps to his house, a disappointed expression on his face. No sooner had his door closed than the James brothers rushed for his barn and corral. Soon they had two black horses ready to ride. Before riding away, Jesse walked over to his old gray horse and patted it.

"Well, Bob, I'm gonna have to leave you. You're a mighty fine horse. Take it easy, partner." Jesse gently rubbed the horse's neck. "Take care of ol' Betty, you hear," he said in reference to Frank's gray. Jesse walked over to a fence and mounted his new horse, and the brothers rode away. Before they had made it very far, though, they noticed that their horses were acting strangely, wandering erratically from the roadway. Finally, the brothers painfully dismounted and looked their horses over carefully. Almost instinctively, Frank waved his hand in front of one of his horse's eyes and then the other. The movement made no impression on the animal.

"Outrageous!" he yelled. "This horse is as blind as a bat—in both eyes, too!"

Jesse turned to his horse and tried the same experiment. His horse was blind in one eye. The brothers were in little better shape than they had been with their old horses. But at least they were in a heavily wooded area now, and if a posse overtook them, it would be simpler to elude them. It was a thieves' paradise, in fact. Even so, they couldn't afford to tarry there for long; they had to move beyond these woods and onto the prairie again. The only reason they had avoided the law thus far is that they'd never let the grass grow under them. Their constant motion had prevented the lawmen from fixing their position long enough to isolate and attack them in force. The brothers had suffered from hunger, exposure, and the excruciating pain of riding nonstop for over 150 miles, but they refused to give up, and they plodded onward. The newspapers referred to them as "the Flying Two," but they hadn't been doing much flying lately.

The next morning, September 18, the brothers realized that for the first time since they had left Luna Lake, a posse was trailing them. After they crossed into Dakota Territory, Frank noticed that the posse failed to gain on them. Led by Sheriff John Rice, the posse was simply following them, like vultures, waiting for them to stop or drop. Apparently the posse feared making contact with the outlaws and was waiting for reinforcements. When the Jameses intersected the road heading south to Sioux Falls, Dakota Territory, they turned left onto it. Soon they ran into a young boy riding on a pony. They stopped him and asked him about the road farther south. Then Jesse, who was increasingly irritated by their pursuers, made a request of him.

"Boy, would you do me a favor? Some men are following us about a mile back. Do you see that dust back there? Well, that's them. I want you to give 'em an invitation for me. Tell 'em to hurry up. Tell 'em I can't wait much longer for 'em." Then he scribbled an obscene note and handed it to the boy to pass on to the posse. The message must have made the pursuers think better of their course of action because they eventually let the brothers slip away.

"Well, I couldn't be more disgusted with the way this manhunt has been conducted," Judson Jones complained to a friend seated next to him on the smoker of the Winona-St. Paul line on its September 18 morning run to St. Paul and Minneapolis. Jones, who had suspected earlier, and rightly, that the outlaws were on an island near Elysian, had participated in the manhunt for the outlaws from the start and he and his friend were part of the Le Sueur, Minnesota, posse.

"It sure hasn't gone well, has it?" his friend replied. "And I don't know why either. The robbers seem to have gotten away clean."

"It needn't have been that way," Jones continued in a gruff, sarcastic tone. "The posses should have followed the outlaws closely, nipped at their heels, instead of traipsing around the country on railroad cars, led by a bunch of lazy detectives like that worthless Hoy, with whiskey flasks bulging from their vest pockets. The only way to catch these outlaws is to go after them like hounds, take up their scent, and pursue them relentlessly. We have lost their trail now, and it's our own fault. We have simply not kept the heat on those boys."

Seated at the other end of the smoker was Chief of Detectives Mike Hoy. He was chatting with a crony of his, a newspaper reporter. When he heard his name mentioned, his ears pricked and he stopped talking. Now he followed Jones' every word. Hoy's face reddened and his hands quivered with rage.

"There's not a doubt about it," Jones continued loudly, still talking to his friend. "Had it not been for that dead-head drunk

Hoy and that sluggard Brisette, we would have had those men in irons by now."

At this last statement, Hoy jumped to his feet and rushed back to Jones' position in the car. "I'm a dead-head drunk, ye say? Is that what ye called me?" he said in his thick Irish brogue, facing Jones menacingly. "Is that what ye called me? Was it? Was it?"

"What I meant to say, if you want to know," Jones answered, remaining calm and determined, "is that the James boys have thoroughly out-generaled you, Hoy, and that goes for Brisette too—from beginning to end, first, last, and absolutely. Am I clear?"

Hoy, white with rage, struck Jones in the face, breaking his cheekbone with the force of his huge fist. For good measure, he struck Jones twice more in the head and face with both fists. Jones slumped into his seat unconscious, bleeding from his nose and mouth. Hoy walked back to his seat and took his place next to one of Minneapolis's favorite newspaper columnists. The reporter had been fawning on Hoy all morning to get the latest information concerning the pursuit of the outlaws. He later reported about the incident in the *Minneapolis-St. Paul Pioneer Press*, noting that Judson Jones was given a "deserved whipping."

Shortly after eluding the posse on September 18, the James brothers discarded their black horses and seized two more grays. They were now within five miles of Sioux Falls. When they saw a stagecoach approaching them from the south, they reined in their horses and stopped in the middle of the road. As the coach drew closer, Jesse flagged it down.

"Howdy!" he hailed the driver. "Wonderful mornin' we're havin'. How are the roads ahead?"

"Well, they're pretty good," the driver replied. "Most of the muddy places are dried up. In fact, there's a pretty fair stretch of road all the way to Sioux Falls." As the driver talked, the outlaws surveyed his horses. They appeared to have been on the road some time and were as tired as their own. After wishing the driver a good day, the outlaws continued southward. The driver hadn't asked them about their hay saddles. That had surprised Jesse a little. Drivers were ordinarily a nosy sort, and he knew for certain that the driver had noticed their condition.

On Tuesday, September 19, the outlaws rode through East Orange, Iowa, and on Wednesday, they stopped for breakfast in Le Mars, Iowa. Keeping up a brisk pace, by 4:00 P.M. they had reached a point within eight miles of Sioux City. When they arrived near James Station, a stop on the Illinois Central Railroad, they saw a man in the road ahead of them. He was driving a buggy pulled by two fine horses. The man beckoned to the brothers. He was Dr. Mosher, on his way to see a rural patient, but he'd gotten lost and needed directions.

As the brothers rode up to him, Frank remarked to Jesse, "Watch him closely. He looks like a detective to me." Frank had come to this conclusion because of the quality of Mosher's clothes, unusually fine for a traveler. The brothers drew their pistols.

"You are the man we want!" Frank said to Mosher.

"What? What do you mean?" Mosher answered, confused by Frank's speech and astonished at the pistols pointed at him.

"You are a detective," Frank said.

"No! I'm just a country doctor trying to find one of his patients. I'm lost. I've been looking for the Garretson farm for more'n an hour. Can either of you help me?"

"Yes," Jesse said, chiming in, "he looks like a detective, all right. He's dressed too smart for someone travelin'."

"Would I be a detective with all these medical tools?" responded the uneasy Mosher, opening his small bag and showing them his stethoscope and medicines.

Frank decided now that he had pegged him incorrectly. From his speech and general demeanor, he appeared to be just what he said he was, a country doctor. He was too civilized and mannerly to be a detective, Frank concluded. The brothers searched Mosher and his belongings carefully, nonetheless, and discovered that, yes, he was a doctor all right.

"Well, sir," Frank said, "you have come just in time to help us. We are goin' to trade you horses. Ours are finished, and we need fresh ones. Pull your buggy over into yon woods. I want your clothes too." When the two men had exchanged clothes, Frank, who was happy to see that he and the doctor wore about the same size, walked up to Mosher. "I was in an accident up the road, partner. I want you to re-dress my bandages."

As Mosher was working on Frank's leg, the doctor looked down at the pants Frank had given him to wear and noticed the smooth round hole that had caused the wound. It was surely a bullet hole. He didn't know who these rough men were, but they sure weren't Methodist ministers!

When he had finished bandaging Frank's right leg, the outlaws ordered Mosher back onto his buggy, and the three men rode south toward Sioux City. After several miles, the outlaws let Mosher out by the roadside.

"Walk north and don't turn around if you want to stay alive," Frank ordered.

After leaving Mosher, the brothers rode his buggy all the way through Sioux City. They saw no signs of lawmen but refused to stay long enough to look for any. They felt safer on the open road.

By this time, it was becoming dark, so the brothers stopped along the banks of the Missouri River to rest their horses and their own weary bodies. They had run into the river just south of Sioux Falls, and the sight of its familiar waters made the brothers feel like they were almost home. Before they got off the buggy, they sat for a few minutes just looking at the river. The setting moon sparkled on its surface. In the twilight, Jesse saw an eagle flying down the river, probably headed for its roost, he thought. Within moments, the darkness on the horizon had engulfed the bird.

Frank edged the buggy closer to the riverbank and reined in the horses. Crawling down painfully from the buggy, he tethered the horses to a small tree. The brothers walked to a spot overlooking the river and sat down, leaning against a tree and stretching out their legs to relax. The two men, nearly dead of exhaustion, watched the current as it flowed powerfully southward. Soon the moon went down, and the glittering surface of the river and the blue sky disappeared. All that was left was the black flowing current and a slate-gray sky that turned darker by the moment.

Frank fumbled with his papers and rolled a cigarette in the darkness. He raised the cigarette to his lips and took a long drag. With the cigarette dangling from his mouth, he folded his fingers in a position almost of prayer as he gazed out on the river. He marveled at the river's power and dark beauty. He and Jesse were lucky to be looking at that old river again, he thought. It had been bleak for a while. If the law had been luckier, the two of them would have been dead by now. But they'd outrun the law and outthought them to boot. Frank smiled in grim satisfaction.

In the faint light, he looked down and saw that his hands were covered with mosquitoes. He brushed them aside, but the mosquitoes merely swarmed back onto his hand in a cloud. He reckoned the little beasts were all over his face and neck too. Well, suck on, little fellows, he said to them silently, there's plenty more blood where that came from. He'd escaped plenty of bloodsuckers lately; these little ones weren't worth a hoot and a holler. Now only a few local sheriffs and their toadies were still in the picture. Frank believed that he and Jesse could manage them. But he was tired of the running and fighting. It seemed like he'd been fighting and running since he was a boy. First it had been the soldiers; now it was policemen. He figured they were all the same, part and parcel, hired henchmen and stooges of the brokers, bankers, and politicians. He reckoned that he and Jesse would just keep contesting with them until they ran out of juice.

Jesse sat next to his brother and looked out over the river.

In his state of mind, the river seemed to mirror something in his spirit. A darkness like death settled over him. He seemed rudderless, low enough to cry, if he'd had it in him. All the things that had been happening to him for the last three weeks, maybe during his whole life, seemed to be coming down on him like an immense weight. He turned his eyes toward heaven.

"Dear God," he whispered, "thanks for savin' our lives." Moments later, he lapsed into sleep.

Frank continued to smoke his cigarette. He wondered what had become of the Youngers and Pitts. They were good men. He hoped that he and Jesse's run for it had helped them, taken the heat off them. But they were on their own hook. He and Jesse would lay low for a while. Sooner or later, a bank or train would drop its guard, and they would find another good haul. They'd just had a bad run of luck, that's all, just a bad run of luck.

A few minutes later, Frank grabbed the stick he used for a cane and righted himself.

"All right, Jess, wake up!" he said to his brother. "Let's go and look for a better place to camp. These skeeters will carry us away if we stay here." Jesse opened his eyes, raised himself to his feet, and the two brothers walked slowly, side by side, to their buggy.

19

September 21, 1876

The Youngers and Charlie Pitts had been laying low for a week in the country around Madelia. Believing that the law had dropped their guard, the outlaws started out at sunrise, in broad daylight, in a westerly direction, traveling along precisely the same prairie route that the James brothers had followed a week earlier in their perilous escape. But the area around Madelia was well populated, and the Youngers would not go unnoticed.

Around 7:00 A.M., the outlaws approached the Ole Suborn farm near the town of Linden in Brown County, about seven miles north of Madelia. Suborn's son, Oscar, saw them milling about in the nearby woods and thought their behavior unusual. They were abroad too early for travelers, and they didn't look like hunters. Oscar observed, moreover, that one of them brandished a large revolver, and another appeared to be injured. Oscar was convinced that they were the Missouri outlaws who were still unaccounted for. Oscar told his father about the mysterious men loitering in the woods, but his father scoffed at the idea. They could be anybody, the father reasoned, travelers, hunters—anyone—so he sent Oscar out on his normal morning chores. The boy was a bit too imaginative, the father believed. But being a normal, inquisitive farmer, Ole wondered who the men were.

While the boy attended to his chores and Ole milked the family cows, two of the men went to Suborn's house and asked his wife if she had some milk and bread to sell. Thirty minutes later, two more appeared and purchased more milk and bread. When Ole returned from milking the cows and heard from his wife about the visits, he began to view the men more suspiciously. Finally, when Oscar had completed his chores, Ole let the boy go into Madelia to warn officials of the suspected outlaws' presence.

Within minutes, Oscar had saddled and mounted the family nag and raced toward Madelia. Near town, which was several miles away from his home across open, rolling prairie, his horse stumbled in a hole, and Oscar flew through the air and landed in the mud. The young man, shook but unhurt, scrambled to his feet, remounted his horse, and set off again for Madelia.

Arriving in town, he went to the Flanders House, a hotel owned by Col. Thomas L. Vought, a family friend to whom Oscar's father had told him to report. After being admitted to the hotel, Oscar hurriedly told the colonel about the strangers. Sheriff James Glispin, who was visiting with Vought at the time, listened to the boy, and when Oscar had finished his account began questioning him.

"Did any of the men appear to be wounded?" Glispin asked.

"Well, one of them had his arm in a sling," Oscar answered.

"Was there any blood on his clothes?" the sheriff continued, further exploring the possibility that the boy had made contact with the escaped outlaws.

"I didn't see any," Oscar replied. "But, uh, I remember one of the men limped," he added.

Glispin became excited. He was confident that the boy had discovered the missing outlaws. Within fifteen minutes, the sheriff had enlisted Colonel Vought; Capt. W. D. Murphy, a Civil War veteran and justice of the peace; James Severson, a local clerk; and Dr. Overhott, a local doctor, to accompany him in pursuit of the outlaws. The men armed themselves and mounted their horses. Before leaving Madelia, Glispin, a young brown-haired man of average height and Irish descent, alerted the rest of his townsmen concerning the outlaws, telling them to arm themselves as quickly as possible and ride west in his support. In the meantime, he would fix the outlaws' position and dog them until he had assembled enough men to apprehend them.

After traveling west of Madelia for two and a half miles, Glispin's posse halted a rider.

"Have you seen any strangers on the road?" Glispin asked the rider.

"Well, a few miles back, I passed four men walking in the same direction as you're heading," the man answered.

"What did they look like?" the sheriff questioned.

"Didn't notice," the man replied. "They were big men, I know."

"How far ahead are they?"

"About four miles, I'd say."

"When you get to Madelia," the sheriff requested of the man, "tell the posse gathering there to head up the north branch of the Watonwan River. Tell them I'm hot on the outlaws' trail. Tell 'em to come quickly."

The sheriff ordered the posse to a trot, and they charged across the soggy prairie. Within an hour and six miles west of Madelia, Glispin saw the outlaws in the distance, near the right-hand outlet of Hanska Lake. When the outlaws spied Glispin, they turned south toward Hanska Slough, a shallow swamp, where they believed the lawmen and their horses could not follow. Glispin rode to within gunshot range of the outlaws and shouted, "Halt!"

The outlaws ignored him and ran toward the slough. Glispin and a member of his posse drew their pistols and rode to within a hundred yards of the fleeing men. When Cole Younger saw them approaching, he turned around and yelled at the lawmen: "What do you want?"

"Throw up your hands and surrender," the sheriff screamed.

"Come on; we won't hurt you," Younger taunted. Glispin

knew it was a trap, and he and the other posse members fired a volley at the outlaws. One of the bullets splintered the sapling Cole was using to steady himself, and the outlaw fell forward into the slough. Quickly rising to his feet, he turned toward the other members of his band. "Let's give 'em fire, boys!" he yelled. They spun around and fired a volley at the posse.

Glispin's horse was nicked by one of the bullets, and the mount of a Norwegian accompanying the sheriff fell to the ground dead. Glispin and the rest of his posse dismounted and crouched until the outlaws stopped firing; moments later, they remounted their horses and took up the chase again. They charged the outlaws until bullets whizzed dangerously by them, when they again retreated out of range. As the posse backed off, the outlaws retreated farther into Hanska Slough.

As the posse held itself out of range, four poorly armed farmers joined Glispin, and the sheriff divided his force. He sent Captain Murphy and the farmers around the west end of Hanska Slough while he and the rest of the men circled the slough from the east. In this way, the sheriff hoped to channel to his advantage the direction the bandits fled. By the time Glispin's men had circled the slough and taken up the chase again, however, the outlaws had traveled south to within three-quarters of a mile of the Watonwan River. The outlaws were seeking cover in the brush that lined the riverbank.

As the outlaws neared the river, they passed through a narrow band of woods and saw a house owned by a farmer named Andrew Anderson. Near the house, two teams of horses were hitched, just the number of mounts the outlaws needed for an escape, and they rushed for them.

Several miles back, Horace Thompson, the president of the First National Bank of St. Paul, and his son, on a hunting expedition with four female friends, had identified the outlaws and pursued them from a distance. It was their wagons that were parked in Anderson's yard. The Thompson party had followed the outlaws out of curiosity and in the hope of aiding in their capture. Now, they were in the thick of the dangerous pursuit.

Mrs. Anderson, who had been hanging the wash, saw the outlaws running toward her house. She noticed, too, that the hills to the north were swarming with horsemen, teams of wagons, and men on foot, all trekking southward in the general direction of the Anderson farmstead. Mrs. Anderson ran to her back porch and waved a large handkerchief, hoping to attract the posse's attention and help. The women accompanying the Thompsons also waved their handkerchiefs and screamed, but their shouts were out of earshot of the posse. Mrs. Anderson ran from her porch to warn her husband, who was working in a nearby field.

When the two Thompsons saw the outlaws moving toward them four abreast, they cracked open their shotguns, removed the shells filled with birdshot from their chambers, and replaced them with large goose shot. Then they took up a position (perhaps foolishly) facing the outlaws. When the outlaws saw the Thompsons reloading their guns, however, they believed the hunters were loading rifles and were part of the posse pursuing them. Armed with only revolvers, the Youngers and Pitts cautiously retreated out of range and toward the river.

When they reached a bend in the Watonwan River, the outlaws waded into the turbulent water, swollen from recent rains and numbingly frigid, and swam awkwardly across, holding their revolvers over their heads to keep them dry. Once across, the outlaws, drenched in muddy water, ran into a thicket of head-high plum and willow trees. Within minutes, some 150 armed citizens, some well armed, converged on the area from across the rolling plain. As the Younger brothers and Pitts hid in the brush discussing their plight, some of their pursuers crossed the Watonwan River to the east and west of them. Meanwhile, 50 citizens mounted a considerable bluff just south of the outlaws and took up a position overlooking the bend in the river where the men were concealed. Pursuers now streamed east and west along the south bank of the river in the direction of the plum thicket, closing in on them. On the north bank of the river, just across from the outlaws, men took up firing positions, completing the encirclement. Soon the men on the north bank of the river began firing random shots across the water and into the plum and willow trees where the outlaws were hiding. It was 2:00 P.M. The outlaws continued to take refuge in the brush, hoping to hold off the posse of citizens until nightfall, when they planned to break through their cordon and escape.

Captain Murphy, a former military man, guessed the outlaws' intention and suggested to Glispin that they seek volunteers to go in after them. He offered his services as a former army officer to lead the group. Recognizing the veteran's expertise, Glispin agreed and transferred the leadership of the charge to the older man, leaving himself second in command. However, the sheriff retained the authority for obtaining volunteers from the large group of men surrounding the outlaws.

"All right, men, gather around me!" he shouted to those assembled on the south side of the river. "The bandits are in the brush, and we mean to capture or kill them. Captain Murphy has agreed to lead a small squad in a charge. I will be with him also. Who will go with us as deputies? I need brave men, well-armed men—good shots."

A long silence met Glispin, and then, one by one, a small squad of courageous men separated themselves from the crowd and walked toward the sheriff. They were Colonel Vought, George Bradford, Charles Pomeroy, James Severson, and Benjamin Rice. Another man volunteering to fight walked several steps toward Glispin then wavered and returned to the citizen volunteers.

Murphy now assumed command and formed the men into a skirmish line facing the river directly to their north. The volunteers stood south and east of the brushy, five-acre tract where the outlaws were hiding. Murphy positioned his men in a rank at fifteen-foot intervals.

When the men had formed, Murphy shouted, "Now forward,

men!" and the volunteers advanced toward the river. Vought, Bradford, and Pomeroy were armed with double-barreled shotguns, Murphy with a Colt revolver, and Glispin, Rice, and Severson with rifles.

When they neared the river, Murphy ordered the men on his left flank to halt while he wheeled the right flank of his small posse around into a position perpendicular to the river. Now, with the posse facing due west, he was ready to sweep through the five-acre stand of brush where the outlaws were hiding.

"Forward, men!" Murphy shouted again. Glispin was positioned nearest to the river, with Murphy and the rest of the men to his immediate left in a long line that snaked through the woods.

Hidden in the trees, the Younger brothers and Pitts checked their revolvers and spun the cylinders to ensure that they were in working condition.

"Charlie," Cole said, turning to Pitts, "if you want to surrender, go ahead. This is where Cole Younger dies!"

Pitts was silent for a moment, then replied bluntly, "I reckon I can die as well as you, Younger." Then Pitts walked ahead of the rest of the men and acted in his usual role as the advance guard.

Soon the posse moved within sight of the outlaws and began shooting. Glispin caught a glimpse of one of the men and dropped to one knee and squeezed the trigger. When Glispin kneeled, Murphy, walking next to him, thought the sheriff had been shot and opened up a hot fire in the direction of the outlaws, quickly exhausting his ammunition. Aware of Murphy's plight, Glispin strode over to him and handed him a spare revolver. The men now advanced together, firing as they walked. As the volunteers pushed their way through the brush, the outlaws retreated inadvertently toward the river, but when they reached the water, they found themselves the object of gunshots from the other bank. Reversing their direction, they were forced to move back toward the oncoming posse.

At this point, Glispin realized that his small posse was getting low on ammunition and screamed to the larger group of men well behind him: "Come forward, men! We need ammunition and help!" The mob gathered on the outskirts of the brush remained motionless. None of the assembled men even turned to look at one another in embarrassment.

As the volunteers advanced farther into the brush, Charlie Pitts jumped to his feet and aimed at Glispin, who was fifty feet to his front, but missed. Glispin, without thinking, fired a shot from his carbine at the outlaw, and the bullet struck home. The wounded Pitts ran in a diagonal direction away from his attackers, but the volunteers continued shooting. Pitts, hit in the heart, arm, and hip, fell dead.

Firing their revolvers rapidly, Jim, Cole, and Bob Younger rose from the brush in an explosion of gunfire and billowing gun smoke. The posse continued its rain of bullets, and within minutes, Cole and Jim were knocked to the ground and lay bleeding from a number of wounds. Bob continued blazing away with his revolver, but finally he ran out of ammunition. Throwing his revolver down, he signaled with his uninjured arm that he was finished.

"I give up! The rest of the boys are shot to pieces!" he yelled.

Shot to pieces they were. Cole had been hit in the eye and suffered seven other wounds. Bob, other than his injured arm from the Northfield raid, was shot in the lung. Jim's jaw was shattered by a rifle bullet, and he had three additional wounds, besides the serious chest wound he had gotten earlier in Northfield, which was far from healed.

Among the posse members, George Bradford received a minor wound to his wrist. A briarwood pipe Captain Murphy carried in his vest pocket saved his life by absorbing much of the impact of the bullet that struck him in the chest. The pipe had shattered under the force of a .44-caliber slug, but Murphy received only a painful bruise.

"Keep your guns on him while I disarm him," Murphy ordered the others and advanced to take Bob Younger's revolver. Now that the firing had stopped, some of the citizens who had watched the fight began chanting, "Shoot them! Kill them!"

Glispin shouted at the men angrily, "If anyone harms these men, I will shoot *them!*" This threat quieted the crowd's lynching impulse. They had only been avid to attack the outlaws after they had been captured.

Bob was ushered to a waiting wagon. Two of the posse members grabbed Jim Younger under the arms and loaded him aboard. Barely conscious, Jim leaned over the edge of the wagon and spit out several teeth, fragments of bone, and other bloody matter gagging him. A woman in the crowd rushed to the edge of the wagon and handed him a handkerchief to stanch the blood running from his mouth. Then she jumped back into the crowd. Cole Younger was also carried to the wagon and loaded on board. He was conscious but bleeding from a variety of serious wounds. When Colonel Vought saw Cole being placed in the wagon, he walked over to examine him. Cole looked up at Vought and smiled weakly.

"Why, it's my old innkeeper, is it not?" Cole said in a weak voice, recognizing the owner of the hotel where he had stayed one night while he and Charlie Pitts had reconnoitered the area around Madelia.

"Ah! Mr. King!" Vought replied with an amazed expression on his face. "I recognize you now. You were one of the linen-dustered gentry that once stayed with me. I must say I'm surprised to see you here. Now I understand why you asked me so many questions about our bridges and lakes."

Pitts' body was soon loaded onto the same wagon as the wounded Youngers, and the outlaws were taken to Madelia, the Watonwan County seat. As they entered the town, the nearly dead Cole Younger raised himself to a sitting position in the wagon and doffed his hat to the throng of onlookers who lined the town's main street. Some clapped their hands. What? Cole thought to himself. Am I dreaming? They are cheering us? I thought they would be lynching us. The crowd shoved and jostled, straining to get a look at the outlaws. What Cole failed to fathom was that the crowd viewed the outlaws as some kind of celebrities, matinee idols, maybe. The search and capture of the outlaws had excited the curiosity of the local people thoroughly.

When the deputies who accompanied the wagon reached the back of the Flanders House hotel, they found a great mob assembled. The horsemen dismounted, tied up their mounts, and pushed aside the crowd so the outlaws could be taken into the hotel.

"Get back! Get back!" screamed Sheriff Ara Barton, leading the way.

"Madam! Get that child out of the way!"

"Stand back, you!" he yelled at another onlooker.

The sheriff's deputies carried the prisoners inside the hotel and laid them down on the kitchen floor. Then the deputies returned to the wagon and picked up the bloody body of Charlie Pitts.

The town doctors by now had been summoned and attended to the outlaws' wounds. Dr. Overhott, who was also one of the posse members, unbuttoned Jim Younger's blood-drenched shirt and removed it. Because Jim was considered the most severely injured outlaw, he received the first treatment.

"Get me some clean water and rags!" Overhott shouted at one of the deputies in the kitchen. "And take off the other men's clothing," the doctor added, motioning to the idle deputies milling about.

One of the deputies pulled off Cole Younger's boots and stripped his feet of the rags wrapped around them. His socks had long since disintegrated, and he had replaced them with fragments of underclothing. After undressing the outlaw, the deputy threw his bloodstained clothing in a gory heap.

Once he was brought water, Overhott began cleaning Jim's worst wound, the one to his jaw. The doctor wiped away the dark blood flowing from the outlaw's mouth and pushed wadding inside to stop the stream of blood. Then he pulled out a small poker-like instrument from his bag, a tool he used to cauterize wounds. He handed it to one of the deputies.

"Heat this up in the fire," he said. "Get it hot, plenty hot!" The doctor knew that the blood flowing from Jim's mouth had to be stanched or the outlaw was finished. While he waited for the deputy to return with the poker, Overhott wiped away more blood from Jim's arms and shoulders, rinsing his rags repeatedly in a bowl of water.

Meanwhile, Dr. Cooley, another attending physician, cleaned Bob and Cole Younger's wounds. When Cooley put burning iodine on Cole's wounds, the outlaw did not even flinch. These are tough men all right, Cooley thought to himself. The doctor placed a bandage over Cole's eye, but he left the rifle ball imbedded near the eye alone. The slug was dangerously close to the outlaw's optic nerve, he had noted.

When the deputy returned with the hot poker, he positioned the handle so that Overhott could get hold of it. Grasping the tool in his right hand, the doctor opened Jim's mouth and applied the instrument to the bleeding tissue. The flesh sizzled and a foul-smelling steam issued forth. Once he had done the best he could with Jim's wounds, Overhott began working on the other men. It didn't cross his mind until later that the men he was bandaging were the very ones he earlier had been trying to shoot full of holes as a member of the posse.

Once the outlaws were cleaned up and bandaged, Overhott ordered them put in bed: Jim and Cole, the two most seriously wounded, in one bed, Bob in a bed in a nearby room. It would be a painful and restless night for the men. A heavy guard was placed around the hotel, more in an effort to keep possible lynchers out of the jail than to keep the prisoners in, for the outlaws were in no condition to escape. In fact, Jim and Cole were not expected to live through the night.

Charlie Pitts' body was stripped—a compass, a wallet with

five dollars in it, and a map of Minnesota were found in his clothing—and laid on the floor with a sheet thrown over it. Later, the sheet was rolled back on one corner so that visitors, who soon appeared, could see the chest wound that had killed him. All night, people filed by the hotel, peering in the windows to view the outlaw's body.

The next day, when regular citizens were allowed to enter the hotel and pass by the body, by this time in a casket, one of the local ladies placed flowers on Pitts' chest. Another young lady strewed wild daisies at his feet. Some of the newspapermen later came to the conclusion that this behavior was inappropriate, even obscene; however, when the flowers were placed, the event was reported matter of factly. But the news concerning the outlaws soon became more carefully edited and orchestrated—and negative.

On the morning of September 22, an immense crowd gathered around the Flanders House hotel hoping for a chance to see the prisoners. Only a few reporters, early in the morning, were allowed inside to talk to them. A police guard stood outside the hotel and in its hallways to fend off other would-be visitors.

Around 9:00 A.M., Bryce Higgins, a reporter for the *Minneapolis-St. Paul Pioneer Press*, was led into the hotel by a sheriff's deputy and taken to the bedroom where Cole and Jim Younger lay. When he entered the Youngers' room, Higgins saw two weak and wounded men lying side by side in the same bed.

"Good morning, sir," Higgins greeted Cole. "I am Higgins of the *Pioneer Press*. I'd like to talk to you."

"Good day," Cole answered the reporter in a friendly tone.

Jim, in a nearly lifeless stupor, remained silent.

"Would you mind answering a few questions for me?" Higgins began. "Our readers are anxious to learn about you."

"Speak on," Cole answered.

"Well, to begin with, have you any views that you would

especially like to pass on to the people of this area? They know you are arrested for robbery and murder."

"As spokesman for the family," Cole answered promptly, "I would like to express our thanks to the citizens of Madelia. They have treated us with wonderful kindness, and we are grateful for it. When we were brought in as prisoners, we fully expected to be lynched. But the Lord has spared us, and for that, we are thankful."

"Everyone believes you to be the Younger brothers. Is that true?"

"Yes," Cole answered. "We are they. I am Cole Younger, and this is my brother Jim beside me. Our other brother, we are told, is with us but in another room."

"How are you feeling?" the reporter continued. "You appear to be much under the weather."

"Yes, we have been through a lot," Cole replied. At this instant, Dr. Overhott entered the room.

"Sir, I will have to ask you to leave!" the doctor said to the reporter, much irritated. "These men are in a very weak condition, and I will not be responsible for their condition if you stay an instant longer."

"Please excuse me," Higgins answered. "But would it be possible for me to talk to the other prisoner? The people of this community are interested in these men and have a right to know about them."

"Yes, you may talk to the other prisoner for a few minutes," Overhott relented. "The other prisoner is in better condition than these men. But make your questions short."

Overhott led Higgins down a hallway and into Bob Younger's room. Bob was reading the local newspaper. Higgins walked up to the outlaw and extended his hand. Because his right hand was disabled, Bob returned an awkward left-handed handshake.

"Good morning," Higgins greeted Bob.

"Howdy," Younger replied.

"I have just been talking to your brother Cole. I am a reporter for one of the local newspapers. I'd like to ask you some questions. Our readers are much interested in finding out about you boys." As he spoke, Higgins noted that Bob's leg was shackled to the brass bed he was lying in.

"Shoot," Bob said.

"First, how did you happen to come to this country to rob banks?" While he was speaking, Higgins reached into his pocket and pulled out a cigar, lit it, and handed it to Bob without even asking him if he smoked.

"It was a fool trick, that's what it was," Bob replied, taking the cigar from Higgins and taking a long draw on it. He blew out a large cloud of pungent, not particularly pleasant-smelling, smoke.

"Do you understand what trouble you have caused and what the results are likely to be?" the reporter asked.

"Yes, I do. But we are rough boys," Bob continued, "used to rough work. We will abide by the consequences, whatever they may be."

"How did you get into this sort of life?"

"We tried a desperate game and lost. That's all. Circumstances sometimes make men what they are. In my case, if it had not been for the past war, I might have been something. But as it is, I am what I am."

"You went through a lot in your attempt to escape from the posses. What was it like?"

"I'd never experienced anything like it before," the outlaw answered, rolling his eyes.

"Who were the men that got away?" Higgins went on, attempting to get an admission that the James brothers were involved in the robbery and murders.

"We are not at liberty to say," Bob replied firmly.

"By the by," the reporter added, "are you aware that we have sold fourteen thousand copies of the *Pioneer Press,* all telling of your deeds?"

"No," Bob smiled, "but I'm glad somebody is makin' some money. I'm out five hundred dollars myself."

Higgins later described Bob in his column as a "fine looking specimen of manhood who speaks in a low, gentle tone, using the best language, no oaths or slang." In fact, Bob Younger was more attractive than many of the stage celebrities of the time, and some of the friendlier reporters began referring to him as the "Knight of the Bush." Later, other newspapermen took offense at this flattering portrait of the outlaw and sought to paint the brothers in darker hues.

Down the hall from the reporter, Sheriff Ara Barton checked on Jim and Cole's condition. As he entered the room, Cole met the sheriff with a friendly hello.

"I presume you are the sheriff?" Cole asked, reaching out his hand.

"Yes, I am," Barton answered, returning the handshake.

"You will get a reward, without doubt," Cole began, "but I want to ask a favor of you."

"What is it?" Barton replied.

"It is this. If any of them cowardly detectives come here, don't let them in to see us. I don't want to see them nor have to talk with them!"

"We'll see about that when the men arrive," Barton replied, not committing himself.

After the reporter left, a succession of visitors, hundreds of people from every walk of life, passed through the halls of the hotel to see the outlaws. Some of them returned to the makeshift jail for second and third looks. Some of the ladies brought the outlaws lemons, candy, and nuts. Men offered them cigars and tobacco. Through all this, Jim Younger continued to stare blankly at the ceiling of his room. On the occasions when he awakened for a few minutes, the jailer tried to get him to drink some soup or gruel, for he had no use of his upper jaw to eat solid food.

While Jim was asleep, Sheriff Barton had him examined for a scar on his thigh from the wound left by Deputy Sheriff Daniels at the Monegaw shootout. Barton had been told that the scar was a good way to verify the outlaw's identity. None of the lawmen were sure if the wounded man was Jim Younger or not, and even though they found such a scar during their examination, the lawmen still remained unconvinced. A lawman from Missouri had sent them a wire earlier telling them that from his knowledge of the gang and the description of Jim, the captured outlaw was the infamous Cal Carter, a desperado from Texas. This rumor began to take on a life of its own, even though Cole and Bob steadfastly insisted that their captured comrade was none other than their brother Jim. The lawmen and reporters were certain the outlaws were lying. As one reporter said, "They are as artful liars as they are reckless murderers." To set the matter to rest, Barton sent for Chief of Police James McDonough of St. Louis. The chief was scheduled to leave St. Louis at 8:00 P.M. that evening on the Kansas City & Northern Railroad to provide a final verification of the outlaw's identity. On the way, he would pick up two of his trusted scouts at Moberly, Missouri. These men were familiar with the James-Younger gang too and had been pursuing them for years.

While the hundreds of visitors passed by his room, Cole comported himself with great ease. When an old lady stopped in his doorway, the outlaw looked up at her. "I hope you will pray for me," he said.

"I will! I will!" she promised.

"My dear mother must be sad to hear of our plight," Cole continued. "Her boys have been the unmaking of her, and after she worked so hard to make us into good Christians. Please pray for her, dear lady. She is more deserving of the Lord's comfort than are we." Then Cole and the old lady broke down and cried together. The reporters watching the scene were beside themselves with indignation, believing that Cole was playing on the emotions of these simple people. One of the reporters described Cole as "a swaggering foul-mouthed bully then—disarmed penitent now." Another reporter said he was a "fine-looking well-informed man" who displayed a "remarkable intelligence." Every reporter had his own slant on the outlaws.

During the afternoon, Cole whispered to himself, but within

hearing of one of the reporters in the room, "I don't believe it! I don't believe it!"

"What don't you believe?" asked the reporter, avid for a story.

Cole answered, "Byron says, 'death is the end of all suffering—the beginning of the great day of nothingness,' but I don't believe it."

That day, Sheriff Barton received orders from Minnesota governor Pillsbury, who was attending the Centennial Exposition at Philadelphia, Pennsylvania, for the Youngers to be imprisoned in the Rice County Jail at Faribault. Barton would have to transport the outlaws by rail to that town.

September 23, 1876

Inside a large casket surrounded by crushed pieces of translucent white ice lay the stiff body of Charlie Pitts. A luminous fog rose wispily over his corpse. At sunrise deputies had carried his remains to the Madelia railroad depot, and it now rested in one of the freight cars ready for departure to St. Paul, where he was to be embalmed. The lawmen wanted his body to remain intact long enough for someone to identify him positively and allow for the collection of reward monies. None of the Youngers would say who the dead outlaw was, nor would they admit that the escaped outlaws were the James boys. The reporters had been describing Pitts in the newspapers as looking like a "polished gentleman" or a "human hyena" and "conscienceless enemy of society," depending on the writer's particular fancy or perspective.

After sunup, the Younger brothers were carried by wagon to the train. Word had spread of their departure, and people lined the streets of Madelia in great numbers, straining to see the outlaws as they rode by. Mothers pointed at the wagon so that their children might remember they had seen the outlaws, a great event, apparently, for the townspeople. On reaching the depot, the bandits were loaded aboard a passenger train bound for Mankato. As they left town, both sides of the track were lined with people hoping to catch a last glimpse of the bandits. As the train passed through the various towns, people lined the tracks and swarmed onto railroad platforms, jostling each other roughly, their faces aglow with morbid curiosity. Finally, the train pulled slowly into Mankato, where the criminals would be transferred onto a train to Owatonna, the next leg on their trip to the Rice County Jail. The people on the station platform pushed and elbowed each other, stretching their necks to get a look at the outlaws as they descended from their car.

The outlaws stopped at Mankato for breakfast, after which they were loaded onto a carriage and whisked off to another railroad station in town, where they were to be transferred. Young men and boys ran beside the carriage, peeking impishly into the windows at them. When the men reached the station house, it was jammed with people, and a path had to be made so that the bandits could board the train. Once the Youngers were inside the railroad car, some of the citizens attempted to force their way in and were turned back roughly by the police.

Conductor Mersen helped Cole as he limped to his seat.

"Were you expectin' us?" Cole inquired.

"Yes, sir, we were," Mersen answered.

Cole and Jim were placed on a bed made between two seats. Jim, still weak but conscious, reached over and pulled up the blind to let in more light. A number of men and women, their noses pushed grotesquely against the glass, peered at him through the window. Jim looked at them coolly, as if they were flyspecks. He wondered who these people were and what they were doing gawking at him. In a nearby seat Bob toyed with his mustache and read the latest issue of the *Mankato Review*. Outside the car, Sheriff Barton talked to a newspaper reporter.

"Sheriff," the reporter said in his usual self-important tone, "our readers want to know why you're not taking the outlaws through St. Paul so that the citizens there can get a good look at them. You are taking them straight to Faribault. How do you justify that?"

"Sir," Barton replied, "I'm not a showman. My duty is to take these men to Rice County by the shortest and quickest route. Their crime was committed here. The people of St. Paul are your concern."

When the bandits got to Owatonna, a new crowd met them. Someone seemed to be telegraphing word ahead of their arrival times, and at all of their stops the people surged into the streets, pushing and crowding each other for a look at them. Apprehensive about their reception at Faribault, an even larger town, the sheriff placed the outlaws on the caboose of a freight train and forbade the telegraph operator to transmit messages ahead reporting their arrival. Barton feared a panic. Unfortunately, he was too late, as crowds already were forming at the two stations in Faribault. But no one knew when the outlaws would arrive or on which train, so the sheriff had a small advantage in his quest for secrecy.

Barton sent false telegrams to key people in Faribault, telling them that the outlaws would not arrive that day. But the crowds were cynical and formed anyway. People had been swarming in the streets since as early as 11:30 A.M., and the levee was filled with people of every age, sex, and condition. On Jackson Street, someone started the rumor that the outlaws were to arrive at the upper train landing, and people ran there in a throng. Then, when the train came, the engine swept by the upper landing and pulled into the Jackson Street landing below. The outlaws quickly were loaded on an omnibus to be carried to the jail. Nearly the entire population of Faribault and the surrounding area followed them, walking, running, and on horseback. Despite all these interruptions, within thirty minutes, the outlaws were incarcerated in the Faribault jail. It was midnight.

Several hours later, Charlie Pitts' body, which had been left on the train, arrived at St. Paul and was placed in a side room in the rear wing of the state house. Photographer C. A.

Zimmerman took Pitts' body out of the casket, placed it on a table, and propped it upright. While one of his helpers held Pitts in position, Zimmerman photographed the body for interested lawmen. Later, sightseers began arriving, many of them young women interested in catching a glimpse of the now-famous (or infamous) outlaw.

Two young women walked through the halls of the state house searching for the room where Pitts' body was held. When they saw an officer standing by an open door at the end of a dark hallway, they asked him about Pitts. "Where's the body?" one of the young ladies asked in a quiet voice, assuming the man would immediately know who they were seeking. The officer pointed toward the open door next to him, and the women entered. A gaslight hung from the ceiling above Pitts' casket and lit the interior of the room eerily. The ladies walked slowly up to the casket and looked in. Pitts' face, discolored and ghastly white, contrasted starkly with his coal-black hair and rank black mustache in the unsure light. The ice around his body seemed to glow, and the women stared at him for a long time, seemingly transfixed by his appearance. Finally, they tore themselves away from the corpse. But some time later, they returned for another look. Dozens of people soon wandered into the room, gathering around the casket to observe a member of the infamous James-Younger gang.

The next day, a reporter in the *Pioneer Press* wrote that Dr. J. H. Murphy had "pounced upon him [Pitts] with his scalpel, and instead of showering lilacs or camellias or rhododendrons or chrysanthemums or daffodownddillies upon this red-handed villain, the doctor sliced him open and dissected him and disemboweled him." Pitts' bones would be carefully cleaned to be used as a specimen for one of the local doctors' offices. Fellow outlaw Bill Chadwell's skeleton had received the same treatment and had already been claimed by doctor-to-be Henry Wheeler, the hero of the Northfield raid, to be used as a trophy and specimen for his own office once he received his doctor's degree.

20

September 24, 1876

The Youngers were imprisoned in the Rice County Jail with a strong guard stationed outside the building and two guards within. In addition, fifty men had been selected as an emergency force in case the outlaws' friends tried to rescue them or the prisoners attempted an escape. The special guards, armed with Springfield rifles, were kept in an engine house near the prison. A wire, attached to a bell, was extended from the jail to the engine house and could be jerked by the jailers to warn the guards of trouble.

The jail was a stone building with a large frame house attached to it for the sheriff's quarters. The prison proper was thirty feet by twenty feet and was composed of four grated cells placed against two walls. The cages were of flat iron gratings instead of bars. The cells, seven feet by three and a half feet in size, were just big enough to get a bed inside. Bob Younger, who was six feet, two inches tall, slept with his feet propped up against the iron grating. Outside the cells was a railing of one-inch iron piping that separated the prisoners from the visitors' walkway. During the day, the jail keepers placed Cole Younger's bed outside the barred-off area so that he could meet visitors or questioning lawmen. A great pressure had been put on Barton to make the prisoners accessible, and the sheriff, for political reasons, complied. Cole was so badly wounded that he was not considered a threat to escape.

Around 5:00 A.M., doctors began arriving to look at the brothers' injuries. A Dr. Dennison examined their wounds and cleaned them, focusing especially on Jim Younger's jaw, from which the doctor extracted a number of bone splinters and small fragments of bullet. Two surgeons, Rose and Wood, extracted several bullets and buckshot that had been overlooked earlier or deliberately passed over. The doctors agreed among themselves to leave several of the more deeply imbedded slugs where they lay, especially the one near Cole's optical nerve and the one that had broken Jim's jaw and lodged near his brain; the risk of removing the bullets was considered excessive. When the doctors had finished their surgery, the outlaws' wounds were rebandaged, and they were returned to their beds.

Within minutes of the doctors' departure, citizens from all over southern and central Minnesota began trooping through the jail to view the prisoners. Outside the prison, a line of people waiting to see them extended for more than two city blocks.

"You boys are an awful long way from home," one of the visitors remarked to Cole as he passed by his bed.

"You're right," replied Younger weakly. "I'm afraid we selected the wrong place to take our vacations."

"Yeh," replied the wag, "but I suspect you boys won't be with us that much longer."

"We shall see," replied Cole, understanding instantly the man's cryptic remark suggesting that he and his brothers would be hung soon. Cole had decided to humor the locals, not wanting to prompt any late-night necktie parties by vigilantes.

A woman passing by Cole looked at him soulfully. "Are you being given adequate care, my son?" she asked in a compassionate voice.

"Madam, we are," Cole replied. "And I thank you sincerely for your interest. We are far from home, and your concern is deeply appreciated."

"We are glad to give it," the woman continued. "May the good Lord bless you and have mercy on you."

"And you, also. Thank you for your kindness," Cole replied, turning on the charm for which he was well known.

"Dear man, have you repented?" the woman asked.

"Yes, madam, I have."

"Good! Did you know that there are men who say you should be hanged? I'm against it, you know."

"Good for you," Cole replied. "Was it not Matthew who said, 'Blessed are the merciful, for they shall find mercy'? Those who would have us die should be directed to James 2:13. There he tells us, 'For he shall have judgment without mercy that hath shewed no mercy.'"

"Amen, brother! I believe it," said the woman. Later, a reporter sarcastically called Cole "a bible-reading martyr."

As Cole dutifully made conversation with the locals, at the local fairgrounds the men called the "Brave Seven"—the men who had apprehended the Youngers at Madelia—were introduced to the crowd. As each man's name was called out, he stepped forward to loud applause, punctuated by cheers, whistles, and screamed expressions of adulation. A master of ceremonies announced that the men would get $240 each for their heroism. The boy, Oscar Suborn, who had alerted the locals to the Youngers' presence near Madelia, would receive $56.25, quite a sum for a young boy. But none of this information was true. The governor of Minnesota had not yet even formed a commission to decide how the money was to be divided, and the announcement was made to embellish the occasion.

Meanwhile, at St. Paul, Chief of Police James McDonough of the St. Louis Police Department, his officers Russell and Palmer, and C. B. Hunn of the United States Express Company examined the body of Charlie Pitts. They had learned that his real name was Samuel Wells. As they looked over the body, they identified Pitts by his thick, short feet, dark black hair, height, weight, and scars.

An hour later, McDonough and his party joined a large group of dignitaries from St. Paul and Minneapolis for the trip to Faribault to question the prisoners. Among the people traveling with McDonough were Mayor Maxfield of St. Paul and Chief of Police King of Minneapolis; Dr. Murphy; Col. J. L. Merriam and his two sons, William and John L. (no one wanted to miss the show!); Superintendent Lincoln of the Sioux City Railroad; Col. Girart Hewitt; Detective R. C. Munger; John Ames of Northfield; and Johnston and Yates of Madelia. At Mendota, another forty people from Minneapolis joined the party. The entourage included many of the fine ladies of the Twin Cities. When this crowd reached Faribault, an intense scramble ensued to acquire the proper transportation to take them to the county jail. The more resourceful rode in horse-drawn taxis; others traveled by their own power.

When they arrived at the jail, at the corner of two streets, just below the courthouse, the visitors found it surrounded by several hundred people frantically attempting to get inside to see the prisoners. Some were visiting the jail for the second or third time. Many of the people were complaining because they were now barred from entering the building. But the sheriff had, as he put it, "bigger fish to fry"; his important visitors from the twin cities had arrived, and he was now the center of attention. Barton's deputies pushed back the crowd to make way for the dignitaries.

McDonough led the main party into the jail. The rest of the visitors straggled behind him. The chief of police strode up to Cole Younger, who was seated on his bed and reading the morning newspaper. Cole had a bible placed handily and visibly on a nearby table. Since Cole had been chosen spokesman for the Younger brothers, it was he whom the visitor addressed.

"Hallo, Cole, how are you?" McDonough said to the outlaw. Chief King of the Minneapolis police and the wealthy John Ames of Northfield stood directly behind McDonough.

"Good morning, McDonough," Cole replied as he slowly

looked up from his paper. McDonough had thought that Cole would be surprised when the detective recognized him on sight, for the detective had only recently obtained a rare photograph of the outlaw. Now it was the detective who blinked in amazement. Younger knew who *he* was.

"You know me?" McDonough replied, trying to make his tone sound casual.

"Yes, I once watched you in a St. Louis train station when I was passing through. I am surprised that you failed to recognize me at the time."

"I did not have a picture of you then. I do now," the detective replied, chuckling.

"I noticed," Younger answered knowingly.

"Did they tell you that we have the James boys?" McDonough went on.

"No," replied the outlaw coldly. "I'm surprised our captors would not mention such an important capture."

"Yes, we got them," McDonough continued, lying and waiting for some sort of response or betraying sign in Cole's face. But the outlaw remained impassive.

Finally Cole responded. "How do you know that it is the James boys you have?" he queried the detective coyly.

"The wounded one confessed," the detective said.

"The big one?" Cole replied slyly.

"Yes," McDonough answered, hesitating at first.

"Good boy to the last!" Cole said. From this point on, all of Cole's replies were couched in the terms "big one" or "little one," until McDonough tired of the game. Of course, McDonough had no idea which of the Jameses was the "big one" or the "little one." In fact, the brothers were virtually the same size, Frank only a little taller than Jesse. McDonough had no idea what either of the brothers looked like in any precise way.

"Tell me, good fellow, who was the dead one?" McDonough said, referring to Pitts.

"We refuse to say," Cole answered.

"Then tell me, again, who were the men who got away?"

"We have agreed not to tell that either," Cole replied stiffly.

"Who is that fellow?" McDonough continued, pointing in Jim's direction. Jim lay in his bed staring impassively at the ceiling while another prisoner fanned him.

"He is my brother Jim," Cole said.

"Oh?" McDonough responded incredulously. "We are told that he is Cal Carter, the Texas desperado."

"I believe I know my own brother."

"We'll see about that. But it would be better for you if you admitted who he is now."

"He's a Younger and our brother," Cole said adamantly. "If you will bet your ignorant friends one thousand dollars that he is, we will back you and prove it, if we have to bring his mother here."

"Is that arm wound all you've got?" asked McDonough turning to Bob Younger, who lay in a nearby cell. He had found himself at a dead end in his discussion with Cole concerning Cal Carter.

"No, I've got 'em all around me," Bob replied and turned back to his newspaper.

King, who had been silent up to this point, stepped forward and handed Cole a picture. "Look at this picture. Do you know this man? We know him as Wells. You know him, don't you?"

"There are a great many Wells in the world, I suppose," Cole said evasively. "Possibly, this is one of them."

"Tell me, what part did you play in the robbery at Northfield?"

"I choose not to say," Cole answered.

"We know you rode the white-faced horse, and we believe you killed a man named Gustavson."

"There was no intention to kill anyone."

"You lie!" John Ames said, pushing past McDonough and King and confronting Younger heatedly. "You did your best to kill Mr. Manning!"

"No, not at all. We fired first only to frighten him."

"Again, you lie. There were bullet holes everywhere," Ames insisted.

"I have never killed a man in cold blood in my life!" Cole said heatedly.

"Why, you have killed a hundred men, and one was this Swede on the streets of Northfield!" Ames said, his face flushed with anger.

"The killing was an act of impulse. There was no intention to kill anyone," Cole answered angrily. "But I lack the patience to talk with you. I may be dying at this instant."

"That's doubtful. You look healthy enough to me," Ames replied.

"Sir, I may die, and if I do, I trust I am prepared for a better world than you."

"You hypocrite," Ames replied testily. "A sweet life you have lived to prepare for a better world."

"Go away and let me rest!" Cole exploded.

At this last remark, the visitors began retiring from the jail. Mayor Maxfield, who stood nearby, tried to get Ames and the rest to return so that the questioning might proceed but was unsuccessful.

"No! Don't call them back! They are illiterate!" Cole ranted at Maxfield. "They do not appreciate the sublime life I have led!"

After the dignitaries from the Twin Cities retired from the jail, the jailer opened the prison again, and hundreds of people formed into a line to enter. During their stay in the Rice County Jail, the Youngers were host to over five thousand visitors. Pitts, back in St. Paul, was the silent host to another two thousand.

As McDonough walked outside the jail with Ames, he turned to King. "Yes, without a doubt, the badly injured one is Cal Carter." The two men looked knowingly into each other's eyes.

Later the same day, Cole asked Sheriff Barton to telegraph his uncle, Dr. Twyman of Jackson County, Missouri, to tell him that the Younger brothers were in the jail at Faribault. Later, Twyman informed Henrietta Younger, the Younger brothers' sister, of their plight. She was heartbroken. She was very attached to them, and

Jim had been her main support for years and was paying for her expenses at a seminary in Lexington, Missouri.

"All right, men, wake up! I've got some unpleasant news for you," Sheriff Barton said, rousing the prisoners before sunrise two days after their arrival at the Faribault jail.

The Youngers rolled over in their beds and looked up at the sheriff with bleary eyes. The sheriff and his deputies stood in front of their cells with shackles in their hands. The deputies strode up to Cole's cell first, turned the heavy iron key in the lock, and creakily opened the heavy iron door. Without being asked, Cole rose painfully to a sitting position and extended his feet toward one of the deputies, allowing him to slide the manacles around his ankles and lock them. A chain extended from one manacle to the other. It would be an encumbrance, all right, Cole thought, but he would have to live with it. Then the deputies locked Cole's cell and went to the other brothers and performed the same exercise.

"Now, I know this isn't pleasant for you boys, but I have no choice," Barton said. "Our visitors were quite upset the other day that you were not in chains. They are important men, so I must keep 'em off my back. The newspaper fellows have been complaining for weeks about the same thing, but they don't count. They are just houseflies in the order of things.

"Well, now that you fellas are up, you might as well have your breakfast. I've got a fella coming with some food in a few minutes.

"Incidentally," the sheriff went on, "the local newspaper took a poll yesterday as to whether you boys should be hung or sent to jail."

"What was their conclusion?" Cole asked wryly.

"Seventy-one were for hanging, six said no."

"What a pity for them. The seventy-one are not the twelve that will decide it," Cole replied.

That afternoon, the Youngers were visited by George P. Wilson, the attorney general of Minnesota, who read them a warrant charging them with robbery and murder. Cole, as the family spokesman, waived the hearing and arraignment, feeling that it was only a formality anyway. In the meantime, the Youngers acquired three Minnesota lawyers for their defense: Thomas Rutledge, G. W. Batcheldor, and Thomas S. Buckham. The prosecutors, they learned, would be George N. Baxter, attorney of Rice County, and their current guest, Minnesota attorney general George Wilson. The brothers had already planned to plead guilty if they were charged with murder to avoid the death sentence a jury likely would impose.

Later that afternoon, the Younger brothers were visited by their sister, Henrietta, nineteen years old and affectionately called "Retta," and their aunt, Mrs. Fannie C. Twyman, a tall, straight, circumspect woman of forty-five, both from Missouri. Before Retta was brought into the jail, Jim was sequestered in a special room by the lawmen. Retta had been deliberately scheduled to meet with Jim first so that Barton could witness her reaction to meeting her supposed brother. If there was no reaction, he could be sure his prisoner was the infamous Cal Carter.

When they arrived, Sheriff Barton led Retta and Mrs. Twyman to the open door of the room where Jim was kept. When Retta saw Jim through the door, she ran to him and threw her arms around him.

"Jim! Jim!" she said. "This is so bad! If it hadn't been for Cole and Bob, you wouldn't be here. They enticed you into this, didn't they? Oh, my dear brother! Oh, what shall I do? There is no one to care for me now that you are gone." She began crying and tears ran down her cheeks. Jim tried to console her, but all that came out was undecipherable mumbling. His mouth was still horribly swollen and his tongue numb. He held Retta in his arms and tried to comfort her. Both of them knew that a woman without a guardian, husband, or family support in the nineteenth century was in desperate straits.

When Retta was taken to see Cole and Bob, she embraced them and shook their hands but was noticeably cooler. Before

she left, Cole gave Retta an inscribed religious book that he
had obtained since he arrived in jail. He told her when they
parted that she should go back to school. He didn't suggest
how she should pay for her studies. The newspapermen who
watched the proceedings reported all of this and more in
the next day's St. Paul and Minneapolis newspapers. Retta
was described as nineteen to twenty years old, a little below
average in height, with a slight figure, light brown hair,
fair complexion, and a rather prepossessing personality.
Mrs. Twyman was depicted as having a "kindly face and
determined spirit."

"There! There! Don't you see him?" screamed Bob. "He's
going to shoot! See! Look out!"

"Wake up, Bobby. Wake up," Cole said, reaching through the
iron grating of his brother's cell to shake him. Bob looked up,
wild-eyed and bewildered. Then he realized he'd been having
a nightmare and rolled over in his bed and tried to return to
sleep. But it was not easy; the lights in their cell glowed twenty-
four hours a day. Aroused by the noise, the guard rose from his
chair and looked into Bob's cell, somewhat confused. Then he
shuffled back to his chair, sat down, and was soon asleep again.

November 17, 1876

The witnesses in the Younger case were questioned by 11:00
A.M., and at 12:30 P.M., the grand jury entered the courtroom of the
Rice County Courthouse and seated themselves. Levi Nutting,
the jury foreman, presented four bills against the prisoners, and
it was decided that they would be arraigned that afternoon.

At 3:45 P.M., the Youngers were taken from the jail and lined
up in the street outside. Cole was placed in the middle, with
Bob on his right and Jim to his left. Sheriff Barton, his deputies,
and the chief of police formed directly in front of and behind
the prisoners. The Youngers were linked together with handcuffs

and wore leg shackles. A squad of men armed with needlenose rifles was placed immediately in front of and behind Barton and the other lawmen. Once the procession was formed, Barton yelled, "Forward," and the outlaws, hampered by their shackles, stumbled and shuffled toward the courthouse three hundred feet away. Fifteen hundred people lined the street, filled the sidewalks, and spilled into the intersections, all straining to catch a glimpse of the prisoners as they walked by.

The Youngers were marched to the back of the courthouse and ushered into the building through a rear door. Once inside, they were directed to seats reserved for them at the front of the courtroom, near the judge's bench. In seats adjacent to their own, Mrs. Fannie Twyman and Retta Younger were seated. The women smiled wanly as the brothers took their seats. When they were seated, Mrs. Twyman reached over and took Jim's black felt hat and placed it on her lap. Although the temperature was not especially hot, Mrs. Twyman fanned herself nervously. Retta, who was dressed in black and wore a cloak trimmed in fur, sat next to Mrs. Twyman. Under her veil, her face expressed profound sadness.

The Younger brothers were shaved and dressed in neat dark trousers and white shirts, with gold studs at their necks. The courtroom was packed, and a number of people stood in the aisles. Some of the people in the hall who had never seen the outlaws before became excited when they entered the courtroom and stood on their seats to get a better look at them.

Sheriff Ara Barton, irritated by the proceedings, rose to his feet. "Everyone will be seated!" he said in a high-pitched voice.

Then the prosecuting attorney, George Baxter, got up and cleared his throat. "The state calls for the arraignment of Thomas Coleman Younger, James Younger, and Robert Younger for indictment number one, found against them on the seventeenth instant for the murder of Joseph Lee Heywood."

The Youngers' lawyer, Thomas Rutledge, stood up and replied, "The prisoners are in court and are prepared to plead."

Baxter turned toward Rutledge, "I suppose the irons should be removed." A long consultation then arose between the Youngers' lawyers and the prosecutor. This concluded with several deputies unlocking the brothers' shackles and removing them.

"Call the prisoners," an officer of the court finally announced.

"I call for the arraignment of Thomas Coleman Younger," Baxter said.

Cole stepped forward and faced the judge.

"You are called to plead to indictment number one," Judge Samuel Lord said. "Do you understand which one that is? For the murder of Heywood."

"Yes, I plead guilty," Cole replied firmly. He could hear the people in the courtroom gasp although his plea was not unexpected.

Following this, Lord pronounced the other indictments against Cole and received the same replies: yes, he was guilty; yes, he was guilty. Then the judge ordered the rest of the Youngers to the front of the courtroom and got the same pleas.

Baxter rose to his feet. "I shall move for the impaneling of a jury to ascertain the degree of guilt of the prisoners. And as I understand the counsel for the defense desires to argue the motion, I shall ask that it be postponed until the afternoon." All of this was a mere formality because a study had already been made of the statute, and it had been found that as long as the Youngers pleaded guilty to all charges, their penalties were to be mandatory life sentences.

When the Youngers returned to the courtroom later that day, they found it still chock full of observers. This time, however, several people jeered at them as they entered.

When the prisoners were again seated, their second attorney, G. W. Batcheldor, rose to his feet. "The prisoners are ready to receive their sentences if the state is prepared," he said in measured tones.

"The state is ready," Baxter replied.

The Younger brothers rose to their feet and walked before the judge's bench.

"Have you anything to say, any reason why sentence should not be pronounced?" Judge Lord asked the prisoners.

"No," the brothers said, more or less in unison.

"Not one of you?" asked the judge.

"Nothing," one of them replied.

"It becomes my duty, then," the judge went on, "to pass sentence upon you. I have no aid or comfort for you. While the law leaves you life, all its pleasures, all its hopes, all its joys are gone out from you, and all that is left is the empty shell. I sentence you, Thomas Coleman Younger, to be confined in the state prison at hard labor to the end of your natural life. And you, James Younger . . . " The judge went on to condemn all of the brothers to a life of imprisonment in the Stillwater, Minnesota, penitentiary." Retta and Mrs. Twyman burst into tears and threw their arms around each other. The Younger brothers were shackled, handcuffed, and taken from the courtroom. When they were out of sight, their lawyers comforted Retta and Mrs. Twyman, who continued to sob loudly. The two women would continue to stay at the home of Sheriff Barton until the Younger brothers were transported to the state prison.

November 20, 1876

At 10:00 A.M., the Youngers were transported to the railroad station and loaded aboard a train bound for St. Paul. Cole and Bob were shackled together and sat on one seat, while across from them, Jim sat chained to Phineas Barton, the sheriff's son. Retta Younger and Mrs. Twyman were seated in the next set of seats in front of them. Across the aisle from the prisoners, several newspapermen eyed the prisoners eagerly, watching their faces, hands, and gestures for any signs that might inspire a brilliant story. When several of the reporters sought to interview Retta, she refused to speak to them, not liking what she referred to as their "impertinent and unfeeling questions."

In the next day's newspapers, the reporters heaped scorn on the convicted robbers and killers. One of the reporters said of the Youngers: "So the romance is knocked out of all of this murderous business. We have three vulgar and brutal ruffians, every one of whom richly deserves a gibbet!" The reporter went on to describe Cole's "impudent and malignant stare" and said that he didn't look at all like "a gentleman of leisure, who had traveled over the world, and having seen all that is worthy of seeing is glad to retire to private life." Rather, he saw in Cole's "sinister visage a good picture of an Italian bandit, or a buccaneer of the Spanish Main, or a Parisian thug, who can be hired for a dollar and a half to murder any man, woman, or child. That's the kind of devil Cole Younger is when he's examined through common-sense spectacles."

The same reporter complained that the Youngers were "Northfield pets," the same "cutpurses, cut-throats, and tigers" who had been "flattered and pampered for weeks at Faribault, where they received their visitors with a benignity and a patronage that was something royal in its style." But, in reality, the reporter maintained, they were "simply three low, cunning, desperate rascals whose long career of robbery and murder has stamped their character upon their vicious and repulsive countenances." Whereas an earlier reporter had said of Jim that he had "a quiet, inoffensive look that one little expects to find," the above reporter said that Jim "glared at his captors with a combination of impudence and audacity that was not pleasant to see."

When Barton and his prisoners reached St. Paul, they were met by two dozen dignitaries, many of whom had not taken the earlier trek to Faribault and now took advantage of their last opportunity to see the infamous Younger brothers. Barton introduced the brothers to these people and then transferred his prisoners to the train bound for Stillwater. When the Youngers reached that town, they were transferred onto a wagon and taken to the penitentiary.

November 22, 1876

Cole had been in the Stillwater prison for only two days, but he thought it was hell, all right. The day before, the three "fresh fish," as the brothers were called by the jailers and other inmates, had been taken to the prison barber. He had sheared their locks like they were so many sheep. Now they were convicts #899, #900, and #901, and they donned well-worn, second-grade prisoner outfits: loose-fitting dungarees decorated with black and gray checks. A checkered cap with a visor thrown in for good measure completed their outfits. In addition, they had been measured by the "Berlin system," which meant that their heads, trunks, fingers, ears, feet, and arms were now identified to the satisfaction of the Minnesota penitentiary system for permanent identification purposes. They had been given personal cells, five feet by seven feet in size, with iron floors, a bible, a mirror, a spoon, two cups, two towels, a comb, soap, a water jar, and a bed and linens. What more could you ask for? Cole thought to himself. A lot! he answered bitterly. But Cole had been in the regular Confederate army in the war, and he had decided that this was a whole lot like it. He intended to submit to prison obedience in the same spirit that he had earlier adapted to the Southern army. In short, he was determined to survive. Cole also learned that he would be allowed to see his brothers only a single time each month and only for a few minutes. Furthermore, he was not to speak to them at any other time, or to anyone else for that matter, unless the work he was engaged in during his daily chores required it. No, this was not a men's club; that was clear. What is more, the Youngers had learned early on that the jail was infested with bedbugs, and the prisoners all crawled with them.

Someone rang a gong and Cole moved slowly in the direction of the dining room. There was no hurry, he thought; he was going nowhere, really. As he entered the room, he searched for Jim and Bob, but they were hard to pick out. Everyone looked the same, like characters on an artist's canvas, all black and gray and wearing the same garb, so many thugs, an unsympathetic person might have suggested. Then, out of the corner of his eye, he saw Bob seated across the room. They had been forbidden to eat together, so Cole found a wooden bench nearby and sat down.

He looked straight ahead and held himself erect, his arms folded, as he had been ordered. It was strictly forbidden to gaze around the room. He began signaling for his meal. He held up his right hand, and a guard promptly walked over to him and laid down a slice of bread on his plate. Then Cole held up his cup and another guard approached him and filled it with water. He raised the cup to his lips and drank slowly. A few moments later, he raised his fork and yet another guard brought him a pan filled with coarse chunks of almost inedible beef. The guard placed a portion of the meat on Cole's plate then looked steadily into his eyes. Cole nodded, indicating that he had enough; he realized that he must eat everything put on his plate. Finally, Cole raised his knife over his head, and someone brought him potatoes, completing his serving. He had learned all the special rules and signals to be executed by prisoners in the cafeteria.

After finishing his meal, Cole laid down his knife, fork, and spoon on the right side of his plate, as the rules prescribed, and folded his arms. Minutes later, another gong sounded, and the prisoners rose to their feet, their hands to their sides, and formed a ragged line. Another gong sounded and a guard cried, "Forward!" The prisoners walked out of the cafeteria in lock step, each with an outstretched arm on the shoulder of the man in front of him, all with their eyes to the front, but moving nowhere, actually.

Epilogue

With the Younger brothers imprisoned at Stillwater, Minnesota, lawmen began to focus directly on the James brothers and anyone associated with them. In October 1876, Chief of Police James McDonough of St. Louis sent Sgt. Morgan Boland and a group of police officers to scout Kansas City and the area around it for signs of the remaining outlaws, who were thought to have been wounded in Minnesota. McDonough relied on his own officers for investigations, distrusting the local Missouri police and fearing interference by local Missourians. After receiving reports from Boland, McDonough believed the James brothers were back in their home county, their presence indicated by the pickets the officer's men identified along the roads around the Samuels' family farm. A posse led by Sheriff John S. Groom, on November 22, 1876, surrounded the James home near Kearney, and someone at the farm fired a gun into the air then fled into the woods. McDonough believed this was clear evidence that Frank and Jesse James were back in their old haunts.

Lawmen were still hampered by the amazing lack of photos of either of the James brothers. All they knew, from the wildly varying descriptions available of the brothers' appearances, is that they were both tall and one had sandy whiskers. In fact, the James brothers were able to openly circulate throughout society without fear of recognition by police or nearly anyone else.

From 1876 to 1879, the James brothers were accused of

robbing banks and stages in a variety of places, but none of these charges was substantiated reliably. The *Tribunal* of Liberty, Missouri, branded one of these stories about the James brothers "Humbug big!" For three years after the Northfield debacle, the James brothers remained relatively inactive, signs the Northfield disaster had taxed them, maybe even shocked them with a dose of reality. However, the brothers, or at least Jesse, returned to banditry on the evening of October 8, 1879, in the robbery of the Chicago & Alton Railroad at Glendale in Jackson County, about fifteen miles east of Kansas City. The tiny town, in usual James fashion, was commandeered, and the station agent was ordered to put up a red flag. When he refused, one of the bandits shoved a revolver into his mouth, and he "weakened," according to a *Kansas City Times* reporter. Rocks were also piled on the tracks to ensure that the train stopped. When the train arrived at 8:00 P.M., random shots were fired to force the passengers to take cover, and the express car was boarded. The messenger, William Grimes, attempted to escape with the money from the safe, but he was captured and knocked unconscious by the butt of one of the robbers' revolvers. About six thousand dollars was obtained in the robbery.

In November 1879, George Shepherd, a former member of the James gang who had been convicted and imprisoned in a Kentucky penitentiary for the Russellville, Kentucky, robbery on March 20, 1868, concocted an elaborate hoax concerning the supposed death of Jesse James. A Marshal James Ligget had asked Shepherd to participate in a scheme to capture the outlaw. Shepherd's role was to infiltrate the gang and, at the appropriate moment, allow Ligget and his men to arrest Jesse James. Rather than pursue this dangerous assignment, Shepherd later told Ligget that he was unable to lure Jesse into a trap and that a situation had developed during which he was forced to kill the outlaw. This story was bandied about in the press for some time, with some newsmen subscribing to it while others called the story "cold-blooded lying." Although Shepherd's story was false, other ex-guerrilla associates of Jesse James who participated in Shepherd's ruse confirmed his account for lawmen.

On July 15, 1881, the James gang struck again with the robbery of the Chicago, Rock Island & Pacific Railroad. The train left Kansas City at 6:00 P.M., and when it arrived at Cameron and later Winston, Missouri, in Daviess County, five to seven outlaws boarded it. When the conductor, William Westfall, began collecting fares in the smoking car, a tall man with a black beard and wearing a duster pointed a pistol at him, ordered him to raise his hands, then shot him in the back. As Westfall fell, the man in the duster fired a second shot, and the conductor tumbled out the back door of the car and rolled off the side of the train dead. It was a deliberate murder. Within seconds, the outlaws unleashed a volley of bullets that sprayed the inside of the car, killing Frank McMillan, a stonemason returning home after working on a nearby railroad bridge. The reason for Westfall's murder was obvious. On January 26, 1875, he had been the conductor of the train carrying Pinkerton agents to the Samuels' farm. The agents had attacked the home, letting loose a bomb that had killed the Jameses' younger half-brother. After the killing of the conductor, the outlaws robbed the express car and forced the train to stop at a predetermined place. They rode away on horses that had been provided by other members of the gang. Eyewitness accounts later placed Jesse James in the area of the robbery

The *Chicago Times* now called Missouri "the Outlaw's Paradise." Missouri newspapers responded by accusing the Chicago newspapers of attempting to blacken the fair reputations of Kansas City and St. Louis in order to enhance the fortunes of Chicago businesses.

The political response to this latest robbery was an urgent meeting called by Missouri governor Thomas T. Crittenden with officials of railroad and express companies operating in the state. These men met in St. Louis on July 26, 1881; the outcome was an announced reward for the arrest and conviction of the James brothers. The reward was $5,000 each, or some $150,000 in today's money, for the apprehension of both brothers. The reward for the arrest and conviction of the outlaws' accomplices was $5,000, with a total sum for the capture of all the men, in today's money, of over a quarter of a million dollars. Crittenden was courting traitors among the James gang's members and supporters.

By this time, political events were leading to the downfall of the James gang. The Republicans in Missouri were using the gang as an issue to attack the Democratic Party and its politicians, who were blamed for the failure of lawmen in the state to arrest the outlaws. The Republicans, in addition, claimed that the robberies were bad for Missouri businesses, that their activities were deterring immigration to the state, discouraging capital investment, and preventing the growth of new industries. Another development that should have created a chilling response in the James boys and other gang members was the election of William H. Wallace as the new prosecuting attorney of Jackson County, Missouri, the county just south of the James farm and centered by Kansas City. Wallace had made it the cornerstone of his campaign that he would arrest and prosecute the James gang. Republicans and some Democrats supported Wallace, but his political strength was weaker in the country districts.

None of this flurry of activity deterred the James gang, and less than two months after the train robbery at Winston, the gang struck again, this time back at Blue Cut, near Glendale, in the same area where they had robbed a train in 1879. This time, on September 7, 1881, the gang used a red lantern to flag down a Chicago & Alton train. Engineer Jack "Chappy" or "Choppey" Foote and his crew were stopped by a black-bearded bandit and his accomplices. Henry rifles were fired in the air to intimidate the passengers. This technique, except for the choice of Henry rifles, was a standard James gang tactic. The outlaws also piled stones on the railroad tracks. After two of the outlaws entered the express car, they struck the messenger, H. A. Fox, with the butts of their pistols, knocking him unconscious. As usual in James holdups, the almost one hundred passengers were robbed of valuables.

Unusual in this latest robbery was the admission by the man with the black beard that he was, indeed, Jesse James, and, shockingly and brazenly, he wore no mask, also a strange departure from normal James procedure. After threatening engineer Foote, the man in the black beard offered him money, saying, "You are a brave man, and I am stuck on you. Here is two dollars for you to drink the health of Jesse James with tomorrow morning." This is the first time any member of the James gang admitted who he was during a robbery, a strange incongruity suggesting that Jesse was either not involved in the robbery or he was slipping psychologically. After handing Foote two silver dollars, Jesse, or a man purporting to be him, offered to have his men help Foote remove the stones obstructing the tracks. Foote said that was unnecessary, and as he left, James said, "All right, pard, good night."

The James gang—Frank James, some have said, participated in the robbery also—and their newly recruited accomplices were blamed for the robbery. The fact that the gang's newer members had no ties to the Civil War was increasingly eroding sympathy for the outlaws in Missouri. Even so, the gang still had many fervent supporters.

The seeds for their destruction, however, had been sown. A James gang accomplice in the Glendale robbery of 1879, Tucker Bassham had been arrested and indicted for that robbery in 1880. After pleading guilty, he was sentenced to ten years in the Missouri State Penitentiary. William Ryan, a.k.a. Tom Hill, whom Bassham had implicated in that first Glendale robbery, was captured in Tennessee and returned to Missouri for trial. Prosecuting attorney William Wallace convinced Governor Crittenden to pardon Bassham in return for his testimony against Ryan and any other information he shared with the law.

Ryan's trial was to be conducted in the area around Crackerneck, an old Missouri guerrilla stronghold near Glendale. The location increased apprehension about the safety of the witnesses, jury, judges, and Wallace himself. Governor Crittenden, aware of the situation, sent a considerable supply of weapons and ammunition for the use of Jackson County lawmen. In his testimony, Bassham implicated Bill Ryan, Ed Miller (brother of Clell), Dick Liddil, Wood Hite (a cousin of Jesse), and Jesse James in the 1879 Glendale robbery. Armed with this evidence, Wallace obtained Ryan's conviction, and he was sentenced to twenty-five years in the penitentiary. Subsequently, Bassham received death threats, his home in Crackerneck was burned, and he was forced to flee the area permanently.

From this point on, the campaign against lawlessness in Missouri was waged more successfully. In February 1882, Clarence Hite, Wood Hite's brother and a cousin of Jesse, was arrested and brought to Missouri to stand trial for the train robbery at Winston. Hite eventually refused trial and pled guilty, causing many to wonder if he had revealed more information about the gang to law officers in exchange for favors. In late March 1882, Dick Liddil surrendered, fearful, some say, that Jesse suspected him of having provided authorities with further evidence against the gang. Liddil also was aware of the disappearance of another outlaw, Ed Miller, whom Liddil believed Jesse had murdered to quiet him. Liddil's fears were further magnified by the fact that he and Bob Ford had shot and killed Wood Hite recently in a fight over the affections of a woman named Martha Bolton. For these reasons, Liddil turned over state's evidence on the gang, surrendering himself to Sheriff James H. Timberlake of Clay County. It was the information Liddil provided to the police that prompted Clarence Hite to plead guilty.

Shortly thereafter, on April 3, 1882, the newspaper headlines reported the death of Jesse Woodson James in St. Joseph, Missouri. Since November 1881, Jesse had been living in that town with his wife, son, and daughter under the assumed name of Thomas Howard. During the other recent robberies, he had been living in Kansas City, Missouri, under the name J. T. Jackson. With Jesse's death, the police released the news that he had been planning to rob the Platte City bank with Bob and Charles Ford as his accomplices.

Before Jesse's death, the two Ford brothers, operating as spies and perhaps assassins for Kansas City police commissioner Henry H. Craig, Clay County sheriff Timberlake, and Governor Crittenden, were living in the James home and sharing the family's hospitality. On Monday morning, April 3, the three outlaws were in the Jameses' living room. Jesse laid down his six-shooters on a bed, stood on a chair, and straightened and dusted a picture. That was just what Bob Ford had been waiting for, and he drew his revolver and shot Jesse in the back of his head, killing him.

When questioned by the St. Joseph police, Zee James, Jesse's wife, claimed the body was that of Thomas Howard. The Ford brothers, meanwhile, fled the house and wired Crittenden, Timberlake, and Craig to inform them of Jesse's death and claim the reward money. When Jesse's mother arrived, her grief and that of Jesse's wife convinced nearly everyone that the body was that of the infamous outlaw. Crittenden, Timberlake, and Craig rushed to the scene along with a number of other people who knew Jesse. Former friends and enemies of James testified that the body was his, including Sheriff Timberlake; William Clay, a farmer who was acquainted with Jesse; ex-Missouri guerrillas Harrison Trow and James Wilkerson; and Mattie Collins, Dick Liddil's mistress, who had no reason to misidentify the man. Moreover, the body had all the necessary scars in the right places and a missing finger, sufficient to identify it as that of Jesse James.

Bob and Charles Ford were indicted for murder in the first degree, pled guilty, and were sentenced on April 17 to death by hanging. Crittenden, Craig, and Timberlake, meanwhile, admitted that they knew the Fords were associating with Jesse in order to betray him to the police; indeed, it was done with their complicity and agreement. But they denied being direct accomplices to the killing. Bob Ford agreed with their interpretation of events. Once Crittenden received notice by telegraph of the Fords' death sentence, he immediately sent unconditional pardons for them to law officers in St. Joseph. No one knows how much the Ford brothers received of the twenty-thousand-dollar reward money (some three hundred thousand dollars in today's money) offered for the capture of Jesse James.

The sensation aroused by the assassination reverberated throughout the nation, and in Missouri, Governor Crittenden experienced a huge backlash of ill will for his role in James' death. Many Americans believed the killing was reprehensible. A writer for the *New York Illustrated Times* thought otherwise, screaming in his column, "Claude Duval, Robin Hood, and Brennan-on-the-moor were effeminate sun flowered aesthetes compared with the Jameses and their sworn confederates." Eulogies and excoriating diatribes concerning Jesse James filled newspaper editorials all over the country.

A week after the slaying, the owner of the house where Jesse and his family lived in St. Joseph charged an admission fee of ten cents for people to view the property. Much of it had been defaced already, almost destroyed by relic hunters who carried away even small splinters of wood from the place as souvenirs.

After Jesse's death, there was a widespread belief that Frank James would avenge his brother, and word of sightings reached newspapers from such disparate places as Texas, St. Louis, New York, and Kansas. John Newman Edwards, the newspaperman who had worked at St. Louis, Sedalia, and Kansas City newspapers on the Jameses' behalf, was trying feverishly to find some way to save Frank from the fate visited on his brother. On August 1, 1882, Edwards wrote to him saying, "Do not make a move until you hear from me again. I have been to the Governor himself, and things are working. Lie quiet and make no stir." Edwards is said to have composed a long letter on Frank's behalf asking for amnesty, to be sent to Governor Crittenden, with Frank signing it and mailing it from St. Louis on September 30, 1882. In response, Crittenden revealed that the Missouri constitution barred him from granting a pardon for crimes before a conviction had been received. He said that once the court acted, and if it should find James guilty, he would then decide his course of action. Unless Crittenden and Edwards had privately settled on a deal, that statement could have given little hope to Frank James.

Nonetheless, on November 4, a train from St. Louis arrived in Jefferson City with John Edwards and Frank James. They registered at the McCarty House under the names "Jno. Edwards, Sedalia," and "B. F. Winfry, Marshall, Missouri." The two men took a leisurely walk around the town, returning later to their hotel rooms. At five o'clock that afternoon, Crittenden, his staff, and several other government officials assembled in the governor's office attended by newsmen. A writer present said Crittenden, who was desperate to recoup his political fortunes and thus willing to appear more sympathetic toward the former guerrilla, was so effervescent that he acted like a child ready to open a Christmas present. After the governor showed those present the letter he had received from Frank James, the group discussed its contents. Then the door opened and James and Edwards appeared and walked up to the governor. Edwards said, "Governor Crittenden, I want to introduce to you to my friend Frank James." The men exchanged pleasantries, then Frank, extending his revolvers in front of him, said, "Governor Crittenden, I want to hand over to you that which no living man except myself has been permitted to touch since 1861, and to say that I am your prisoner." It was theater at its best.

Crittenden ordered Finis C. Farr, his secretary, to place Frank under the custody of the Jackson County sheriff in Independence. Frank and John Edwards then returned to their hotel room until arrangements were made to carry the outlaw to his destination. Meanwhile, several hundred people, including Governer Crittenden and his wife, visited the

McCarty House to give Frank and Edwards their regards. The following day, James, Edwards, and another reporter, Frank O'Neill of the *St. Louis Republican*, left for Independence by train. Along the railroad route, people thronged to catch a glimpse of the train carrying Frank James to jail, almost as if he were the president of the United States traveling to the White House to be inaugurated. Hundreds of people met the train at Independence, where Frank's wife, young son, and mother were waiting for him. Frank and his family stayed the rest of the day at a hotel in Independence, but that evening, he ventured over to the jail and checked in, so to speak. He would not be allowed bail because of the charge pending against him for the killing of Pinkerton agent John Whicher.

Soon observers began noting that prosecuting Frank James would not be as simple a matter as originally supposed. The climate in Missouri to try a former Confederate patriot was not encouraging. The James brothers had been members of a guerrilla force led by William Clarke Quantrill, one of whose purposes had been to protect pro-Southern Missourians' property and lives during the war, when most of Missouri's fighting-age men were in the South fighting for the Confederacy. The situation had left western Missourians vulnerable to the terrorizing Jayhawker brigade of Gen. James Lane from Kansas, marauding Red Legs, and overzealous Missouri Union militias. Many people believed that the trial could easily end up in a hung jury or one for acquittal. Besides that, Frank James, aided by John Newman Edwards, assembled a formidable defense team, including former Missouri lieutenant governor Charles P. Johnson, former congressman John P. Phillips, William M. Rush, C. T. Garner, John M. Glover, Joshua W. Alexander, and James H. Slover. Phillips, moreover, was a commissioner of the Supreme Court of Missouri. The prosecution had also assembled an army of notable counsel, including William H. Wallace and William D. Hamilton, the prosecuting attorney of Daviess County. In addition, four lawyers from Gallatin, John Shanklin, Marcus

A. Low, Henry C. McDougall, and Joshua F. Hicklin, had been recruited. To accommodate the ticketed crowds, the court was held in the Gallatin opera house. Judge Charles H. S. Goodman would hear the case. Out of one hundred possible jurors, the final twelve consisted of Democrats, members of Frank James' political party, who also were young, wealthy farmers. This was a dark omen for the prosecution.

Once the testimony began, the defense and the prosecution countered each other effectively, producing a clear draw. While Frank James' alibi was flimsy, the testimony that he had killed Frank McMillan during the 1881 Winston train robbery was weak and relied solely on the word of Dick Liddil, a convicted horse thief, traitor to the James gang, and alleged murderer, a situation that in those days didn't sit well with most jurors. At one point, Gen. Jo Shelby was called onto the stand, and the presence of this grand hero of the Missouri Confederacy galvanized the ex-Confederates in the jury and in the audience, even though he was highly inebriated—no, just plain drunk. The next day, he testified again, but in a sober state this time, and he excoriated William Wallace for a variety of faults and solidified the support of ex-Confederates for Frank James. Shelby repeatedly asked the court if he could shake hands with Frank but was denied the pleasure. Ultimately, after three and a half hours of deliberation, the jury acquitted James of the charges, and a huge roar of applause filled the opera house.

A howl of displeasure, however, arose in many of the nation's newspapers after Frank's successful defense. Despite the acquittal, many people sympathetic to James continued to object to the testimony of a paid-off, convicted felon like Liddil, considering such men unreliable witnesses. They also considered Liddil traitorous to his companions, thus an unsavory character. In the eyes of much of the public, Wallace and his supporters clearly were sore losers, as many members of the prosecution continued to rail about the trial's defense attorney, Congressman John P. Phillips, the apparent star of the trial. Newspapers and public figures also attacked Gen. Jo Shelby for supporting James. Shelby fired back: "I am aware how the press of the country is yelping. Let them yelp. It only nerves me to stand the closer by an ex-Confederate who is in trouble."

After Frank's acquittal at Gallatin, an attempt was made to charge him with the robbery at Blue Cut, but because the testimony against him, again, would be from Liddil, the case was considered weak. It was thrown out when Governor Crittenden refused to pardon Liddil to erase his felony conviction. The charge against Frank for the murder of John Whicher was also dropped when it was found too difficult to prove him guilty. James, nonetheless, was immediately charged with the robbery of the paymaster at Muscle Shoals, Alabama, on March 11, 1881, a federal crime, which thwarted Missouri prosecutors' attempts to indict him for other Missouri crimes and preempted lawmen in Minnesota, who sought to charge him as well. Now the federal courts had jurisdiction in the case, so Frank was remanded to Huntsville, Alabama, to stand trial. He was arraigned in a federal court on the Alabama charge on April 17, 1884. Yet again, the prosecution relied on Dick Liddil, and Frank countered by producing a witness, Jonas Taylor, a Tennessee blacksmith, who had shod his horse at the time of the Muscle Shoals robbery. In Taylor's record book was written the name B. J. Woodson, Frank's alias. Frank was acquitted. Back in Missouri, the men who had been seeking to imprison or hang Frank James, William Wallace and Gov. Thomas Crittenden, found their political careers at an end, destroyed by their unpopular cause.

After many years of effort, the attempt to obtain pardons for the Youngers bore some fruit. Warren C. Bronaugh, a Confederate veteran and farmer from Henry County, Missouri, in 1882 began a campaign for the release of the Youngers. He said he owed his life to Cole Younger for his warning of an imminent attack on Bronaugh by a large Union force during the Civil War. To support his effort, Bronaugh assembled an array of prominent Missourians, including lawyers, U.S. senators, and a former Minnesota governor. West Virginia senator Stephen B. Elkins, a Republican, who had been a Union soldier during the Civil war, also worked for Cole Younger's release. Younger had saved Elkins' life when he was a captured spy during the war, vulnerable to almost certain execution. On July 10, 1901, James and Cole Younger were freed from prison on a conditional parole: they could not leave Minnesota. Bob Younger had died earlier, in 1889, of tuberculosis. Jim, in a state of depression over a failed romance, committed suicide in 1903. The next year, Cole was given a full pardon and returned to Missouri.

Frank James and Cole Younger were free men. They remained relatively active the rest of their lives, Frank working as a racetrack starter at country fairs and other races; a shoe salesman in Nevada, Missouri; a clerk at the Mittenthal Clothing Store in Dallas, Texas; a horse handler in Paris, Texas; a doorman at Ed Butler's Standard Theatre in St. Louis; and a timer at the fairgrounds in the same city. Cole and Frank, in 1903, traveled together with the James-Younger Wild West Show, but in deference to stipulations included in his pardon, Frank could not perform. The public, in general, still considered both men to be victims of the circumstances of their earlier lives as Missouri guerrillas and the violent state of affairs in western Missouri during and after the Civil War. After 1901, Frank lived mostly at his old family farm at Kearney, dying there on February 18, 1915. Cole, after pursuing a successful career as a lecturer on what he had learned in his life—crime does not pay—lived only one year longer than Frank, dying at Lee's Summit, Missouri, on March 21, 1916, concluding a famous outlaw era.

Zerelda Samuel, the James brothers' mother, supported herself with her farm and, in part, by charging twenty-five cents admission to the many people who wished to visit the grave of Jesse James. Until 1902, Jesse's body reposed in the corner of the Samuels' yard under a coffee bean tree. At that time, the body was moved to the town cemetery in Kearney. For many years, people from all over the United States regularly sent Zerelda flower seeds to plant on her son's grave, enough to plant the entire farm in flowers if she chose, her husband, Reuben, once remarked. Zerelda died on February 10, 1911, while returning home from visiting Frank in Oklahoma. Afterward, Frank and his wife, Annie Ralston James, lived on the Samuels' farm near Kearney with their son, Bob. Annie passed away on July 6, 1944, over a generation after her husband died.

Zerelda Mimms James, Jesse's wife and the mother of their two children, Jesse Edwards James and Mary Susan James, died in Harlem, just north of Kansas City, in 1900. Ironically, perhaps, Jesse Edwards James, the son of the outlaw, became a practicing attorney in Kansas City and California.

While all the participants in the James legend passed away long ago, people still visit the James farm today, arriving from every corner of the earth. The story of the gang continues to thrill audiences. The legend and reality of the James-Younger gang lives on.

Author's Note

As a historian, I began writing this novel about the James-Younger gang with some trepidation. So many people consider novels to be just made-up stories, fantasies. Most historical novels in the past have been obvious fabrications, the authors of which used real characters but falsified the events of their lives considerably and imparted personalities to their characters that were not even remotely close to those they had in real life. But a growing trend by readers today is to demand that historical novelists stick close to the facts. I believe that is the right tack, and I have pursued it in this book.

The problem, of course, is more difficult than it sounds. When you read an orthodox history about a famous man or woman, especially one from the past, little is known in precise detail about how they thought, what they said at important junctures in their lives, and exactly what they did and when and how they did it. When you are dealing with outlaws, as I do in this novel, even less is known about the subjects of your book, who, in the case of the members of the James-Younger gang, remained largely hidden for over twenty years of their lives while they operated as guerrillas then notorious outlaws. For understandable reasons, the Youngers, the Jameses, and their accomplices used aliases and attempted to blend undetected into society. Only when they committed crimes did they make recognizable public appearances, and then they nearly always

364

wore masks and denied later that they were involved. Thus, for a considerable length of time, few lawmen or ordinary persons knew what the leaders of the James gang looked like, with the exception of their friends and a handful of enemies, until all were captured. Only then did photos of the James brothers appear, and even then but few of the Youngers were known.

A lot has been written about the James and Younger brothers over time. Much of it was false or distorted because accurate information about them was lacking or because the writers wished to sensationalize their lives or twist its importance. Writers also allowed their personal politics to affect their descriptions, and they either demonized the gang or glorified it, neither interpretation of the gang being accurate. Through the years, however, serious writers have accumulated enough information about the gang to allow writers today to sort out the James-Younger legend and determine a fairly reliable, but still far from perfect, account of their lives.

Before writing this book, I researched the James and Younger families for several years, fascinated by their story, which took place in my family's home area, near where my mother's side of the family lived. My grandfather George Quell, in fact, lived on a farm just north of Cameron, Missouri, in a house not more than two hundred yards from the train tracks that carried the James gang during their train robbery near Winston, Missouri. Both my grandfather and my great-grandfather Joseph Quell lived on a farm seven miles southwest of Cameron, at Keystone, at the time of the robbery—also along the tracks of the Chicago, Rock Island & Pacific Railroad, where the James gang rode by as passengers around 7:00 P.M. on the evening of July 15, 1881.

In expression of my interest in the gang, I wrote two historical articles on the James gang for *Wild West* magazine. I was also interested in the Border War, which the Younger families and James families participated in, and wrote articles on the subject in the London journal *History Today* as well as in *Journal of the West*. I also wrote a comprehensive history of the Border

War in 2005 titled *Civil War on the Missouri-Kansas Border* for Pelican Publishing Company. So I am particularly well acquainted with the context in which the James and Youngers lived their lives, as well as that of the other gang members. From my research, I am also familiar with how Missourians spoke in years gone by.

I have steeped myself in most of the books about the gang, the most scholarly and accurate one being that of Dr. William A. Settle, Jr., in *Jesse James Was His Name: or, Fact and Fiction Concerning the Careers of the Notorious James Brothers of Missouri* (University of Missouri Press, 1966). Other significant writers who have expanded research recently on the subject are Marley Brant and Ted Yeatman. But for a comprehensive understanding of the subject, I also acquainted myself with many of the books that created the legend of the James-Younger gang, such as those by James W. Buel, Robertus Love, Homer Croy, John Newman Edwards, Frank Triplett, Emerson Hough, and others. I also read the more credible books of Paul Wellman, James D. Horan, Augustus C. Appler, H. H. Crittenden, and Carl Breihan, an old acquaintance of mine. All of the above, including the many articles on the subject that I have read, provided me with a thorough understanding of what has been said about the outlaws and their families over the years and gave me a mental grasp of the information that has circulated about the gang for over a century. The scholarly books, however, have been the main underpinnings for the facts I have used in this book.

I also read voluminous accounts in newspapers contemporary with the operations of the James-Younger gang. For instance, my descriptions of the gang's movements after the Northfield raid, the Youngers' capture and the James brothers' escape, and the trial of the Youngers were garnered from newspaper accounts obtained on microfilm reels from the *Saint Paul Pioneer Press* and *Minneapolis Tribune* over a four-month period contemporary with the events. The most reliable newspaper accounts, I discovered, were almost invariably those filed by newspaper reporters closest to the scene of the action. The Kansas City and St. Louis newspapers had only a little additional valid information and considerable misinformation.

Ultimately, however, I had to assemble a vast amount of disparate information on the subject and use it in the novel in the best way I could. In such a book, no matter how much information you have assembled, the facts will be sketchy at the most personal level: the daily activities of the subjects of your novel, their specific conversations, precise movements, and personal thoughts and beliefs. Ultimately, as in all realistic novels, the author must, to a large degree, using all of the facts at his disposal, imagine the personalities of his characters, their speech patterns and words, and reconstruct their actions into a careful and plausible scenario driven by the author's vision of what occurred. That vision is the product of the author's depth of knowledge, intuition, and judgment about his subject. With facts and imagination under proper control, the author creates his tale, like a sculptor molding his clay carefully into its final product. And the end result is what the reader experiences. Hopefully the story is satisfying for you and provides you with a tale of the James gang that is not only accurate, but also transcends the ordinary limitations of cold history.

DATE DUE